The Vanished Priestess

Forge Books by Meredith Blevins

The Hummingbird Wizard
The Vanished Priestess

The Vanished Priestess

An Annie Szabo Mystery

Meredith Blevins

FORGE®

A Tom Doherty Associates Book
New York

THE VANISHED PRIESTESS: AN ANNIE SZABO MYSTERY

Copyright © 2004 by Meredith Blevins

This book is printed on acid-free paper.

Title art by Jonathan Bennett

A Forge Book
Published by Tom Doherty Associates, LLC
175 Fifth Avenue
New York, NY 10010

www.tor.com

Forge® is a registered trademark of Tom Doherty Associates, LLC.

ISBN 0-765-30780-4

EAN 978-0765-30780-4

First Edition: October 2004

Printed in the United States of America

0   9   8   7   6   5   4   3   2   1

To women and men creating new lives:
willing to risk and fly, to trust and fail, to laugh at the
clock, and live in bold colors.

〰

And most especially to Win Blevins, my magnificent
dancing bear, rocking me in the secret world of dreams.
My eternal partner.

The Vanished Priestess

One

The circus is good for you. It is the only spectacle I know that
while you watch, it gives the quality of a truly happy dream . . .
—Ernest Hemingway

. . . except for the trapeze. Call me crazy, but in my world a
dream where gravity doesn't exist is called a nightmare.
—Madame Mina to Annie

*C*ircus is an old slice of America that still rocks my imagination.
It blurs lines, it tickles my toes, it is outrageous.

Contortionists and glass-eaters, elastic and skeleton men, Orien-
talists riding elephants, drag-queen clowns and bareback riders,
aerialists and flyers, women with tattoos of Tom Mix, Babe Ruth,
and several US presidents wrapped around their thighs. I flipped
through more old sepia photographs: two Martians, three Aztecs,
and one man named *Zip What is it?*

I was up to my ears in notes about this collective spirit. I'd been
hired to write a six-article series for *Jumbo Times,* and, thanks to my
neighbor Margo, I had enough material to write six books.

I sat at my kitchen table sorting through old articles and circus
route books. I noticed a faint hum, and the hum grew stronger,
keeping time with a rhythmic beep. Blood pounded against my
eardrums, maybe a first winter cold. Then the floor buzzed beneath
my feet.

No cold had ever given me a buzz.

I opened my door and stepped outside. What I'd heard was the
repeated warning beep of a large truck in reverse, and what I'd felt
was the redwoods rattling my yard. A beefy guy wearing low-slung
jeans and a Raiders' sweatshirt was motioning his partner to steer
left, then right, with a series of frantic arm gestures. They maneu-
vered a white trailer backward between my trees. They'd decided

the trailer should rest on my ancient basketball court, the only semi-level spot on ten acres.

I had not ordered a new trailer.

I waved my arms and hooted. I couldn't get their attention. What I got was Madame Mina.

She roared in, crouched behind the wheel of her limo. She careened around the truck, slammed on her brakes, stuck her head out the window, and whistled between her fingers. Mina not only got the truck drivers' attention, she set a line of dogs barking all the way up the canyon.

Madame Mina was my dead husband's mother, a Gypsy fortuneteller, the inheritance he'd left me. I was in my twenties when my husband died, which meant I'd had Mina far longer than I'd had Stevan. When I married him, I did not know I was gaining a temporary husband and a permanent mother-in-law.

Mina told the guys the trailer's direction was wrong, that a front door *must* face east.

I told the drivers to take a break and pointed them to the Golden Bear Deli. Mina asked them to bring her back a pastrami on rye, hold the mayo.

They bounced away in their pickup over stumps and river rocks, a WIDE LOAD flag attached to their right side-view mirror. The flag hit one of the trees and bent at a ninety-degree angle. When the last of their dust followed them down the road, I turned to Mina.

"This trailer doesn't need to face east," I said. "RV World is south, due south."

"Return it?" She put her hand over her heart. "You want me to curl up under a bush like some old bag lady?"

No, I didn't want her to curl up under a bush like some old bag lady. It was cold outside. Summer . . . That might be a different story. "Mina, a trailer just landed in my yard. Could we talk about why?"

I motioned her toward the house. She ignored me.

"It's too white," she said, considering her purchase, rubbing her chin. "You think lavender, or go straight for purple?"

"Purple. Mina, what's going on?"

"Mr. Chen sold his building in Chinatown and my rent went

sky-high. He says we're too old for San Francisco. I say we just outgrew it."

"You still have the Mystic Cafe."

"Don't remind me. When the city decided to buy my place on Haight Street, they never said when they'd open their fancy wallet. Impact reports, council meetings . . . Mystic Cafe is kaput."

"We can make it feel like home until the city pays you. We'll forget the cafe, buy new furniture, your old clients will visit."

We? Desperation was breathing hard down my neck.

"Nah, I don't have the heart for it," she said. "Besides, I let a homeless girl, plus her boyfriend and ten million cats, move in until the wrecking ball comes."

Mina wore a scarlet shawl, cut velvet, and she tossed it over her shoulder. She studied the fuzzy redwood bark and looked at her feet. She coughed into her hand, muffling her words.

"A place to live is not the whole entire story," she said.

"Why doesn't that surprise me?"

"Those crazy Badras are still mad because I yelled at their daughter. It was a funeral! I was in a bad mood," said Mina. "They've put spells on me left and right, they swiped my two favorite cars and left them at the wharf—birds now use them for bathrooms. Even the Gypsy court is on my back." She lowered her voice. "I need a place to lay low."

It was a good story, but I didn't buy it.

"Lay low because of the Badras? And miss all those opportunities for revenge?"

"I'm too tired for revenge."

"Mina, revenge is one of your basic food groups."

"I really hate that you understand me. Can you just accept this is important?" she said. "I've humiliated myself by planting myself right in your front yard."

"Yes, you have."

"And it's not like I'm a rock or a tree."

No, something far less flexible. I'd awakened around dawn that morning, that's the one good thing about winter, dawn occurs at a decent hour. My cool house was made close by a fire and a strong cup of coffee. I'd watched roses bloom across the eastern sky, and

I'd almost heard the pale clouds roll over and blush. I savor quiet times. They don't come often, and they sure don't last long.

"You know," I said, "that Capri, your suddenly sober daughter, is now working at Margo's Cirk?"

"I may have heard something like that. Capri doesn't tell me every inch of her life."

HAH! I heard the tone, and I understood exactly why a forty-by-eight-foot piece of livable lawn furniture was now in center court. It was time to drop the truth bomb and stand back.

I pointed to the rickety gate straddling my property line. "Margo's place, all 425 acres of it, is just through that gate and over the hill, and Capri's teaching there, and she's not speaking to you, and that's why you're here."

Mina turned red, she stamped her right foot, and she exploded.

"How am I supposed to spy on my daughter from San Francisco—it's sixty miles away! She hangs up when she hears my voice, letters I write come back unopened. Capri has made prying into her life impossible."

"Capri's drying out. She needs to disconnect."

"She's mixed up in the head," Mina said. "I don't want to wreck her recovery, but how could seeing your own mother make you want to get drunk?"

"You know where her buttons are."

"Of course I do. I installed them."

"You push them."

"I do that?"

"Yes. Could we talk about this in the house?"

I heard a whoosh and a snap, looked to the top of my hill, and saw a giraffe's head towering over an old barn on the edge of Margo's property, the edge of our joint property. The giraffe chomped a poplar branch, chewing with all the peace of an elongated Buddha. It lifted its head, gazed in our direction.

The first time I'd seen a giraffe above my tree line was twelve, fifteen years ago. I'd chalked it up to an evening of cheap red wine. But no, the next morning it was still there, a genuine giraffe. Then a couple of elephants, next some albino goats. Up went a Big Top and a row of bunkhouses made nearly invisible by a stand of century-old California oaks. I called the county, and I asked them what was going on. Margo Spanger had procured a wildlife license. I'd heard of Margo, who hadn't, but I'd never met her. As long as I was living next to a zoo, I figured I might as well get a story out of it. I phoned her, we talked. We felt like long-lost pals catching up.

A decade after Peter Max and Andy Warhol had gone flat and stale, just around the time Cristo was making fabric waves, Margo dropped full-blown onto the art scene. She'd transcended radical, she'd left hip in the dust. Her art made people angry, it made them think, sometimes it made them cry. She safaried with the governor, sailed with a senator, and stroked the press. They quoted her off-hand remarks as if they were spontaneous. They weren't.

With exquisite timing, just as a huge exhibit of her paintings depicting women as mythological beasts and warriors opened, Margo came out of the closet. This was before people knew their friends and family *had* closets.

Then she took to the hills, literally. Margo bought several chunks of land west of my small chunk. The press lost interest in her activities about the same time she lost interest in the press. After I interviewed Margo about her zoo, I concluded that she'd used her fame and money to produce an original art form. She created one of the first new American circuses, a one-ring phantasm of primal performances. Her new art supplies were flesh and bones, skin and fur, foam and fabric.

She was a good neighbor, and the only problem animals had been a pair of humans, a married couple. One of their fights ended in the near death of the wife, the husband was jailed. Margo experimented with circus arts, mostly trapeze skills, to teach the woman self-confidence. It worked, then it worked for other women. A quiet little van began shuttling women from San Francisco's Mission District to spend a weekend at the circus with Margo.

Her art took on larger proportions. She fashioned new lives on armatures of raw nerves and courage, but it took money. The proceeds from ticket sales to her very chic Cirk paid for trapeze rigs, weekend shuttles, teachers, and insurance.

A branch crashed to the ground. One giraffe nuzzled another's neck, an invitation to enjoy the feast. White background noise filled the air. Mina was still talking, and I'd lost track of her thoughts. That can be dangerous.

I said, "Sorry, I didn't catch that."

"I'll enjoy seeing those animals out my window. They have good faces."

I wrapped up tight in my sweater and got Mina moving toward the house. I brewed fresh coffee and warmed my hands above the woodstove. Mina stood by the stove warming her bottom.

"Margo's Christmas show ought to open pretty soon," she said. "You think Capri's going to be in it?"

"She's teaching trapeze, not performing—the performers are practically kids."

"Capri wanted to fly for an audience again. I think."

Margo kicked off each season with a show that was Nutcracker gone Barnum. Most folks who could afford $250 per seat never knew how much good their money was up to—the activities funded by Cirk were kept secret.

"I can't push Capri's buttons from the audience," Mina said. "I just want to get a look at her. Want to see Cirk with me?"

"I already have plans to go."

"Can I tag along?"

"Can I talk you out of it?"

"No."

"Okay," I said. "You can come."

I was clear about her Capri situation, I even understood it, but we still had the trailer to straighten out. I'd give it one last shot.

"Are you sure about this move? Your clients need you."

Mina pointed in the direction of the prefabricated rectangle with windows and two doors cut out of the siding. My old basketball hoop hung suspended above the trailer's fake chimney. Santa could slam-dunk his goodies without having to leave his sleigh.

"Don't worry, loyal clients will find me anywhere," she said, "new ones, too. My family needs me more than San Francisco does."

That trailer bugged me, and I didn't think purple would make me feel any better about it.

"I don't want you here for a few months," I said, "then leaving that thing behind when a new man or the highway calls."

"I don't ever," she said, "want to live in a house without axles again. When I go, it goes."

I supposed it wouldn't take long for her to curse me to nine levels of hell or for Capri to give her the slip. I sealed my resignation with a question. "What about the water and the toilet?"

"I've got a friend who lives under tremendous stress, a plumber." Mina shook her head, sympathizing with his solid waste and PVC dilemmas. "He's hooking the trailer up for several healing sessions," she said. "Then, no problem, I'll move in."

Moving in. "Mina, that plumber better get here fast."

"No kidding. My first client's coming this afternoon, and we can't do *that* forever. The atmosphere in your house isn't right."

"Margo's coming over for lunch . . ." I said.

"Don't worry, I'm sure she'll be gone by the time Mrs. Liu arrives."

And thus it came to be that Madame Mina, my personal circus, moved in on me.

Two

*M*argo sipped her bourbon, the ice jinking the sides of her tumbler. We were working our way down a fifth of Jack Daniel's. I don't remember what I'd fixed for lunch, but we both enjoyed it.

She placed her drink on a stack of photocopied papers. She removed the glass when she noticed the bubbled, ink-smeared ring. Margo smoothed the top page with her right hand. She handed me a route book and she shoved a few photos at me.

"Get a load of these two," she said, the Jack Daniel's stretching her Southern drawl like a hot wad of chewing gum. "The bride and groom of the year."

I looked at the yellowing picture of a woman large enough to play nose tackle. Next to her stood a tiny gray man any third-grader could use to wipe up the playground.

"Stop it," I said, giving Margo a playful push. I almost fell out of my chair. No more pushing, and no more Jack.

"I'm not kidding," she said. "Hannah Battersby and Jonathan."

"Were they in love?"

"God, no. The wedding was produced and directed by their boss. See this?"

A normal-sized man held Hannah's elbow. She was wearing a wedding gown, and he sported a healthy shiner.

"Let me guess. A jealous lover who got on Jonathan's bad side."

"The wedding cost the boss a black eye, courtesy of Hannah, but he was determined to make it happen."

Margo poured herself a slim line of bourbon and looked at the sky while I riffled through the pages of a 140-year-old route book detailing the guests and gifts.

"Why insist on the marriage?"

"Good press. Marrying two freaks gave the public an opportunity to think about sex." Margo lowered her voice until she sounded like a soap opera queen. *"How would six hundred-pound Hannah and seventy-pound Jonathan, Barnum & Bailey's 'Living Skeleton', perform on their wedding night? Would poor Jonathan* survive *their wedding night without being squished to death by his giantess wife?"*

"I guess even the Bible opens with a sex scene gone wrong, complete with snake and duped male."

"Yep," she said, "sex has been a primary marketing tool since Eden."

Margo lifted the bottle of bourbon and studied it. "You want to split the last corner?"

I said she could finish it off. She did.

She told me about her newest Cirk production, and it sounded spectacular. As always, two tickets, second row, were waiting at the box office for me. We talked about our art and the ways it had changed, the ways we'd changed. We laughed about how hard we'd tried to collect adult attributes, and how much fun it was tossing that heavy baggage out the window.

Margo said, "Only one thing I know for sure anymore, and that's my place in the universe. I find beauty wherever it is and translate that discovery into joy."

"Maybe art's a sacred evolution . . ."

"Where bliss appears in flash moments, sticks out its tongue, and falls over laughing."

I looked at the empty bottle of bourbon and wished we were starting all over.

We chatted about nothing, about everything—her animals, my worries, our hopes, the stage lighting, Lili's physical health, Lili's mental health, the costumes she'd designed. Nothing new on the

Lili front—Lili was paranoid and jealous and creative and was, for some reason, the light in Margo's eyes. The booze caught up with Margo, and she rambled on about their trips to Sorrento, the citrus-scented air. I indulged her walk down memory lane.

I eased more papers in front of her, eased her into the now. Margo flipped through original and copied newspaper clippings.

"I don't know how you're going to narrow this down into six tidy articles," she said.

"That's *my* place in the universe, and I'm good."

I'd found one photo of ten people standing in a straggly line. They were tall and hairy, they carried frilly fans and parasols.

"This is a strange assortment of people," I said.

"Drag queens." She flipped three photos in front of me as if they were from a deck of playing cards. "Slats Beeson, a wire-walker for Barnum and Bailey. He slipped in and out of sexual personas as easily as you slip into a new nightie. Lots of gay guys clowned."

"I had no idea."

"There was a vibrant drag culture at the turn of the century. Scientists of the day called them 'third sexers.' "

I couldn't believe this, and I never knew when Margo was pulling my leg. After all, this was the woman who had recently slipped a whoopee cushion under my seat at a fund-raiser attended by the terminally rich.

"Are you leveling with me?"

"The cooch show," she said. "Men paid for having sex with other men in sideshow tents."

I was running that little corner of history through the squirrel cage called my brain. *Jumbo Times* would never go for it. It would take research, but some publication would bite.

"You don't have to write about it," Margo said. "I'm supplying you with the truth, it's up to you if it stays buried."

"Sometimes you spook me out."

"Sometimes I spook me out, too."

The sun slipped behind a cloud. Gray light covered the table like dingy linen, and the dim light muted our mood. Margo stood, holding on to the edge of the table. She gathered her wobbly dignity. Arms wide, theatrically, she told me to keep the route book, plus any others she had. Forever if I wanted, she'd had them too long and was lightening a life filled with many possessions. More theatrics. When the Jack wore off, she'd forget the grand gesture.

Then she leaned across the table, balancing on the edge, nailing me with her eyes, deep and strange and wise.

"Annie, do you ever think about the big stuff?"

"Not if I can help it."

"You know what I ask myself every day?" The bourbon on her breath blew my skin warm, but her words were a chill. "How much is my life worth? How much will I risk to stay alive?"

"Margo, maybe you should sit down."

"Ignore me," she said, smiling, shaking her head. "I'm drunk."

Margo laid a sloppy good-bye kiss on my cheek. She wandered up the hill, fumbled with the latch on our mutual gate, and disappeared.

A clap of thunder. I gathered Margo's collection of books and papers. Soon the rain would come.

Three

Mina crinked my wrist in her direction and looked at my
watch.

"There's a wall clock above the oven. With large numbers."

"It's a nice one, too," Mina said. "How was lunch with Margo?"

"Fine. Odd at the end . . ."

"Details later. I've got to get prepared," she said. "Mrs. Liu's due
any minute." She bustled between the teakettle and several small
packs of herbs.

The name sounded familiar. "Do I know her?"

"Sure you do, an old customer from Chinatown. She thinks her
husband's fooling around. Again. I tuned in, she's right, but it's not
with the woman she thinks. It's some big red-headed woman. Mrs.
Liu's going to go nuts. I've got to manage this delicately," Mina
said. "I tell people, 'If you don't want to hear the truth, don't ask
me.' They ask anyway, and things start flying. You might want to be
out of the house when she gets here."

I considered the things I didn't want flying across my living
room.

"Mrs. Liu's not chasing me out of my own house."

"Okay. Lots of times they don't pay after they've heard bad
news, but I've got her MasterCard number on file. She breaks anything, we'll put it on her card."

Having Mrs. Liu's credit information didn't calm my fears about
breakage and general destruction. I stashed my grandmother's tea

set, and a few other items of sentimental value, in my bedroom. No reason for innocent antiques to be sacrificed on the altar of marital truth.

Mina buzzed around the living room, and rearranged a couple of chairs. I sat at my kitchen table. I organized my research: social history, nineteenth-century circus, modern circuses. I had a separate stack of freak material, including an account of a freak revolt. I could sell this stuff to *The National Eye*.

I banged out three sentences, another three, then a couple of good paragraphs. The roll was on. A typewriter's a percussion instrument when you work it right. Lost in the music, I almost didn't notice the giant, cherry red SUV pulling up in front of my house. A Chinese woman teetered out of the cab.

Mrs. Liu.

I recognized her from a few brief encounters in San Francisco. One involved my own personal nudity. I could have sworn she'd shrunk several inches since then. This barely seemed possible considering she was, maybe, five feet zero in high heels.

Mrs. Liu didn't bother knocking on my door, she walked right in. This was Mina's new place of business. My house was now open to anyone with a problem and cash or credit. I waved Mrs. Liu into the living room, and she skirted the table where I sat surrounded by my debris.

Mrs. Liu closed the door between the living room and the kitchen. I got up and opened it. As long as the woman was in my house, I was allowed to eavesdrop.

She tossed her purse on the couch and plunked down. She leaned back and kicked off her heels.

"This time I have decided to kill my husband for good."

Whoa! Straight to the point.

"He was fooling around with Old Lady Wong again," Liu said. "He even moved in with her. Now he's started up with someone new. Old Lady Wong and me, we both want him dead. Wong's paying for half this visit. Wong is a snake, but at least she's fair."

Mina nodded her head like an expensive shrink and waited for Mrs. Liu to change her mind or give her more information. Mrs. Liu obliged.

"What I want," Mrs. Liu said, "is to get rid of Mr. Liu permanently, collect his life insurance, and take a trip to Hawaii."

Mrs. Liu was going to recover from committing murder by lying under a palm frond laced with warm tropical breezes three thousand miles away from her husband's dead body.

I leaned into the living room to measure Mina's reaction. She was busy sizing up Mrs. Liu and her intent. Madame Mina held the little woman's hands, closed her eyes, and rocked back and forth. Mina stood up and felt the glands in Mrs. Liu's neck, massaging oil down either side and stopping at her collarbone. Mrs. Liu sat perfectly still and let herself be poked and stroked.

Mina opened her eyes slowly as if coming out of a trance.

"All these things you tell me," Mina said, "who wouldn't be mad enough to kill someone fifty times over? But somewhere out there is your soul mate. What good is it going to do if, just as you're about to find each other, you get tossed in the slammer?"

"There's another man for me?"

"You bet. But what happens? You're rotting in a cell, one husband is dead, the future husband is dying of a broken heart, and you're wearing a black-and-white-striped outfit that is very unflattering." Mina rested her chin on the palm of her hand. "You're too small to carry off a large pattern and look beautiful. We've got to think this through."

So far, so good. No flying objects. Mrs. Liu sat looking at the ceiling, biting her lower lip, deep in thought.

Mina said, "Do you ever dream of a man you don't know, but you feel like you miss him anyway?"

"All the time."

"Exactly as I thought. I'll give you a potion to hurry your true love along before you do something dumb. Have you got a pen?" Mina asked. "Take this down: Eat one apple, no more, every day. I'll give you ginger and ginseng tea. Drink it twice daily. If you can find hemp, take it—I've lost my source. Before bed, drink two strong cups of yohimbe. Light a purple candle and imagine your lover holding you. Feel the peace. All anger to your husband will be gone."

Mina pulled a pouch from a brocade satchel next to her chair.

"Slip this vervain to Mr. Liu, it decreases lust. This we'll do to protect the women of the world."

Mrs. Liu tucked the pouch into the pocket of her red blazer.

"As a practical matter, take your husband's belongings and throw them out your bedroom window into the street. Your neighbors will know you have the upper hand in this matter, and your dignity will match your peace."

It sounded as if Mina and Mrs. Liu were almost done tidying up Mrs. Liu's life. I put my circus article and typewriter aside. The writing roll was long gone. I pulled out a box of Christmas cards. This year I would mail them before February. Into each card I slipped a picture of my family and barnyard pets. I wrote a note and addressed the cards by hand. I wished each and every person a wonderful new year, including people I hadn't seen for twenty years. Right then I loved them all. I poured myself a glass of wine and licked an envelope.

I imagined a big party, sort of a giant reunion in the sky, everyone laughing, everyone feeling good toward each other. Old lover's faults were forgotten and forgiven, betrayals were dismissed. Old friends and lovers forgave me, and a lot of good music danced between my ears. I was having a great old interior time until the kitchen door shot open.

I blasted straight into the present.

Abra flew in.

A fiery red welt shaped like a handprint stamped my youngest daughter's cheek. The base of Abra's neck was a circular blush of fingerprints. Her son's legs straddled her hips, and he sucked his fingers. Joey's eyes were huge and round. He did not make one sound. His fear was a silent scream that filled my chest and squeezed my heart from the inside out.

Four

Mina and Mrs. Liu jumped off the couch and ran into the kitchen. I wanted to howl, but I was frozen in a white world without words. I stood and put my arms around Abra and the baby.

My beautiful daughter. Her face was streaked with tears, makeup ran in charcoal rivers. Tears collected in the red welt, others passed by on their way to her neck, where they'd meet with more disaster. She patted me like I was the one who needed fixing.

"Rory's under a lot of pressure," she said without prompting. "He's not really like this."

Mina and Mrs. Liu approached Abra, shoulder to shoulder.

"I've also suffered this," Mrs. Liu said. "You leave now, while you're young. He doesn't deserve so fine a person."

Mina didn't collect any money from Mrs. Liu, who hugged Mina good-bye. The small woman climbed into her SUV.

Mina held the baby and rocked him. She tickled him, she cooed, she tried to ease him out of his silence. I ached for the sound of Joey screaming his head off. The three of us sat together, Abra worrying the edge of her sweater into fuzzy threads.

I placed a cup of tea in front of her. I jammed my breath down my throat, the only way I could control my voice. I laid my hand on top of hers.

"Abra, what the hell is going on?"

The wall clock ticked down time, filling the room with heavy dread.

"I'm hoping," Mina said, "that we're sitting here all quiet because your husband's dead body is covered with tire tracks, and none of us have to worry about seeing his face again."

I ignored Mina. I agreed with her, but I ignored her.

"I grabbed Joey and my purse," Abra said, "and came here."

"Men who treat their wives bad don't forget they have them for very long," Mina said. "He'll be here soon."

"He probably thinks I'm at the mall."

"Life goes down the toilet, and you shop?"

Abra set her jaw. "No."

I was scared and horrified, plus guilty for not spotting the trouble—this couldn't have been the first time my daughter had been abused.

I reached across the table, held her, and told her she was safe. Her muscles relaxed. She fell into me like water pouring over . . .

The door flew off its hinges, and it hung by one long piece of splintered pine. A boot smashed through the middle panel. Rory ripped the door off the last bit of battered lumber, flinging the door into our yard.

He shoved his face into Abra's and grabbed her wrist. Soon there would be a bracelet of bruises to match the necklace of them around her neck.

"You stupid bitch," he growled. "I told you not to get your mother involved in our lives."

My focus was fine-tuned and ultraclear. I walked to my bedroom. Returning to the kitchen, I aimed my shotgun at eye level, Rory's eye level.

"You know what this is?"

"I'm not an idiot," he said. "Would you put that down?"

"Let go of my daughter's wrist."

"This is my wife."

"You've lost the right to be her husband."

Mina slipped into the living room with Joey. He'd fallen into a stupor against her chest, which pumped protection.

There we were face to gun, gun to face, and he sneered at me. Sneered.

He said, "You don't have it in you."

"Don't push me. You broke into my home, my daughter looks like a train wreck. Justifiable homicide, and it would stick."

He ignored me, and he kissed Abra's hand. "Come home, Baby."

That was too much. The muzzle pressed into his cheek just below his eye. "If you come here again, you're a dead man."

Reality slapped Rory upside the head. His face turned white, and he let go of Abra. Freed of Rory's grip, Abra moved next to Mina.

Mina spit at Rory. "Men who hit women are the worst kind of cowards, there's even a special hell for them. With any luck, you'll learn about it firsthand. Soon."

Rory regained his color, and he rolled his eyes in a circle. He tried to imagine how he'd gotten involved with this gun-toting, curse-spewing, interfering Gypsy family. We tried to imagine how we'd let a financial consultant into our family. He turned on his boot-cut Lucchese heel and walked out the hole that used to have a door in the middle.

I watched him climb the hill, watched him walk to his car. He stopped and squinted in our direction for maybe three seconds. I trained my gun on him. He drove off just as the trailer deliverymen returned with Mina's pastrami sandwich. Help had arrived, but we didn't need it.

Mina took care of the drivers. She informed them we'd reached an agreement, and the trailer was staying. They roared off before we could change our minds.

My hands were sweating, but I jacked the shells out of my gun, methodically replaced them in a box, and put the gun back in its locked case.

With Rory dispatched, Mina looked into Abra and held her eyes. "Joey's asleep on the couch. It's hard for a two-year-old to watch his mother get hit. Now. You never answered your mother . . . What the hell has been going on in your house?"

It was the first time I'd ever heard Mina swear.

When my brain started working, when my voice was once again familiar to my own ears, I phoned Lawless. And I called him from my bedroom so that Mina and Abra couldn't talk me out of it.

Five

Detective August Lawless was a thin man, a tall man. He was leathery and brown, brushed with a pale blue that softened his edges. If he wore cologne, it would be faint and old-fashioned. Bay Rum. Lawless smoked too much. He felt like a walk between odd-angled Monterey pines in a Sunday fog. Quiet. Smart. No snazzy fireworks.

We'd met during a murder investigation he'd worked on for SFPD. I was too close to the victim, so his death stood always in our shadow. My emotions had been knife-edged, and sometimes that knife spun and nicked me, sometimes it cut Lawless raw. We hadn't trusted each other and had every reason not to. After the catastrophe was cleaned up, we found in the rubble of that time a fledgling friendship. Trust snuck up on us.

After a full career in SFPD Homicide, Lawless retired. He and his wife moved to the Russian River, just north, about forty-five minutes from my home. Retirement didn't work—he drove his wife nuts, he drove himself nuts. How many times can you alphabetize someone's cleaning products and spices? Lawless became a PI. His wife Ruth supported his decision to leave her home alone.

I knew Abra wouldn't want to share the details of her life with a stranger or the police. But this had to be reported, and she had to be protected. I thought Lawless would have a better chance providing what she and Joey needed than the police would. And I wanted a non-family member to tell her Rory's behavior might be common, but it wasn't normal.

Eyes open or closed, Abra had chosen her mate. But Joey didn't have a choice—he'd have to ride out their relationship. He was barely finished being a baby, and I wanted him safe. My daughter could offer him no guarantees.

Lawless said he'd get cleaned up and come over. I had about an hour to prepare Abra and Mina for his arrival.

He said, "I'll tell Abra you've asked me to be her bodyguard until Rory calms down. If she wants more, that's up to her."

"She'll be angry that I got you involved."

"She has to deal with this, and you'll have to deal with her. Don't back down."

He was right. Abra couldn't put this at my door, even my ex-door, and expect me to pretend the situation didn't exist.

Mina and Abra were talking in the living room when I entered.

"Rory gets upset when Joey crawls around his office and messes around with his papers," Abra said, "but it's hard to keep an eye on Joey every minute."

Mina whapped herself on the forehead with the palm of her hand.

"Let me get this straight," she said to Abra. "You own a house with enough room for three families plus their best friends. You have four fancy cars, most of them aren't American, and one boat you never use. But that man cannot afford an office away from home?"

"He likes working at home, no rush-hour traffic . . . you know."

Mina looked at me and shook her head. She said, "Why do you think the universe lets so many crazy people have money? It only makes them worse."

Low moaning mixed with the wind rising off the ocean whirled its way between the trees. The ghastly sound rolled through the windows and under the cracks.

Mina's eyes grew large, she lifted her head, and was perfectly still—she looked like a hunting dog.

"Your trees have been taken over by spirits. Maybe moving my trailer here wasn't such a hot idea."

We stayed close to each other and walked into the new night. It was only 5:00 P.M., but it felt as if several days had been crammed into half of one.

We followed the sound to its source. A digitized choir of New Age angels had holed up inside a battery-powered teak music box. The box sat in the crotch of an apple tree, the gnarled branches sounding as if they were experiencing ecstasy or being tortured. I pulled down the box, pushed the sound pin to the *off* position. You could almost hear the tree sigh its relief. Rory had crammed a note to Abra under the lid. I handed it to her, and she stuffed it in her pocket.

We looked up in time to see Rory's shadow skitter up the hill, and we heard the rattling of trash cans as he crashed into them and pulled himself out of the ripe mess. I hoped a week's worth of coffee grounds and banana peels were plastered across his suede jacket.

"How long do you think he's been skulking around out here?" Mina said. "With those sneaky German cars, it's hard to tell when someone's coming or going."

Beneath her bruises, Abra paled. She ran into the house.

"That man's a kook," Mina whispered, maybe to me, maybe to the world. "Who needs him?"

Rory had almost reached his car. He'd stopped twice to brush himself off, and once he tripped over a tree stump.

Mina dug into her skirt pocket, pulled out her car keys, and hustled to her limo. "See you later," she said. No word of explanation.

She whizzed past me and stuck her head out the window without slowing down. "Getting pizza."

She slammed the pedal to the metal and turned her steering wheel sharp as she crested the hill. His car door was wide open, and he was about to climb inside. Mina almost had him. My gun was the least of his worries—he didn't have one clue about Mina and her wild dance with large American cars.

Abra, out of breath, appeared next to me. "Joey's fine."

I put my arm around her shoulder. "I know."

Rory sped off, his car weaving at top speed. Mina's limo was no match for his quiet blaze of expensive wheels. She gave up, cranked her car into reverse, cut a curve, barreled back toward the house, and stopped in front of us with a bump and lurch.

"Change your mind about pizza?" I said to Mina.

"Pizza? Oh yeah. I figured, why waste my gas. Let's have it delivered."

"You almost hit my husband with your ridiculous car!" Abra said.

"Oh. Pardon me! An accident is not the worst way to go, it's already got the word *accident* built right into its name. Let's go inside and call for pizza. All this stress has given me an appetite."

Abra phoned for pizza, Mina rummaged through my refrigerator. They moved around each other without speaking a word. Rory had smothered our family with his angry blanket. I was afraid Abra'd run home and thank him for rescuing her from her loony family.

It's not like she was entirely wrong about the family. The next time Mina caught sight of Rory, she might not miss him. She'd expect me to help her ditch the body and, in my present mood, I probably would. Abra was trapped between the life she hadn't chosen and the one she had. Neither was working for her.

As long as things weren't going well, and since he'd be arriving any minute, it seemed like a good time to bring up Lawless.

"Could we forget about food for one minute?" I said. "Abra, we need to call the police, and you need to file a report."

"Forget it." She put down the piece of toast she'd been buttering for several minutes. "That would send Rory right over the edge."

"No cops," Mina said to me. "He's already over the edge, but we're in one piece"—she looked at Abra's face—"pretty much. And I have never called the police for one thing in my entire life that I can remember, and believe me, that's something I would remember. We can handle this ourselves."

"How about calling Lawless?" I said.

"Who?"

"Lawless. My old sort-of buddy from SFPD."

"I thought he'd retired," Mina said.

"He just got his PI license."

"Police is still the police."

"We could hire him for a temporary bodyguard. I don't want this house, or Abra, torn apart hinge by nail."

Mina looked at the empty space letting in moths—it didn't

matter how much wood I tossed on the stove, it was still chilly inside.

"I guess a big guy carrying a gun might settle Rory down," Mina said, "and we can always fire Lawless if it doesn't work out."

Abra pulled out some long-lost spunk. "Would you both stop talking about me as if I'm invisible? It's my life, and I don't want any cops." She slowed down. "Well, maybe a bodyguard, but just for the next few days. I don't have much in my checkbook."

"We're three grown women for God sakes," Mina said. "We can figure out how to pay for one man."

Joey toddled out of my bedroom with sleep in his eyes, a sweet smile for his mom, his arms raised. Abra ran her fingers through his hair. Tiny ringlets of red-blond curls hugged his head.

She held him tight, held him until he squirmed and wanted down. She said to me, "Call Lawless. Now."

"You're sure?"

I wanted the decision to be hers. Well, I wanted her to think the decision was hers.

"Joey needs me to get real before something like this"—she ran her hand across her face—"happens to him."

I faced her full-on. "You're very brave."

"Right." Her voice wore a sarcastic edge, like she couldn't handle hearing one good thing about herself.

"I'm going to feed Joey some Cheerios," Abra said, "and give him a quick bath. Okay if I put him in your bed?"

"This is still your home, too."

"Maybe he'll be asleep before Lawless gets here. By the way," she said to me, "you are the only person who'd know an ex-cop named Lawless."

Now she sounded familiar. Abra hoisted Joey to her hip and carried him down the hall.

"I like that man's name," Mina said. "It has character." She craned her neck, checking to make sure Abra was out of earshot. "Unless that boy's asleep in three minutes, he'll be awake when Lawless arrives."

I opened my mouth to protest.

She put up her hand. "Don't waste your breath. I know he's already on his way, and it's not because of any mystic hanky-panky."

"We've got to protect Abra from her legally wedded maniac."

"I agree. And since Lawless isn't exactly the police anymore, and since I don't see any choice other than getting rid of Rory ourselves, I'll even act nice with him."

"Thanks."

"You're welcome," she said. "My clothes and a few other important things like two cats are still in the limo. You get the cats, and I'll find something to sleep in. I'm too tired to talk with an ex-cop."

I took another look down the hall, and I whispered to Mina, "Part of me is sorry you missed Rory up by the mailbox."

"You're a good mother, of course you're sorry," she said, "but listen. He was right in front of me, and I bungled it. You think I'm getting soft, that maybe I missed hitting him on purpose?"

"Not a chance."

"Thank God. Get those cats, and I'll find a nightgown."

Six

*O*utside, the earth was cold, slightly damp. Spongy-sharp redwood needles pricked my feet and squished between my toes.
I wore thick calluses from a barefoot life. Moonlight spilled down
my shoulders, and my shadow walked three steps ahead of me. It
was a very particular Valley of the Moon full moon—perfectly large,
deep yellow, and round—as if a casaba had made love with a planet
and this was their child.

More than once I've asked the moon to take my feelings, shake
them, and roll them on the gaming table of life. I've asked her to
wrap my naked body in cool white sheets of passion present and passion past. After so many years and all that intimacy, her beauty still
knocks me out.

Beauty and disaster walk the same roads, I know that. I know it,
but I don't understand it. Why was Rory allowed this same lunar
miracle? I try to believe we need both dark and light in people
to maintain balance, to do the eternal hokey pokey. That works for
my head, not for my heart.

I found the cat carrier and opened its door. Two blobs, one orange, the other gray, exploded in a grenade of fur and claws into
the night. One ran up a tree, I didn't see the other. Cats. Mina
could find them tomorrow.

I stood beneath the moon a little longer, soft and safe. In that reflected light, the sun's harsh spirit dissolves to silver silk. The moon
beds us, she fills our dreaming nights with immense possibility. The

moon, giant mother, keeper of secrets, the one who says secrets aren't really necessary, that every truth is hers and she's big enough to hold them all.

Somewhere along the line I must have screwed up my own mothering job royally. Maybe if I'd been more serene, more accepting, easier with others, myself.

Lawless pulled into my driveway, his old Suburban packed with jumbled shapes. While he'd been alphabetizing his wife's life, he'd apparently ignored his own world. He parked, thrashed around in the back of his truck, tossed junk left and right. He pulled out a dark roll, stuck it under his arm, and found a toolbox.

I searched for a witty hello, but Lawless cut me off. He put his arm around my waist and walked me to the house. We stopped three feet in front of the doorway. He frowned at it. Lawless walked back to his Chevy, got out his camera, and a sudden flash illuminated every dark edge of the battered hole. Lawless walked across my yard and took two pictures of my door lying flat on its back. My feet were getting cold.

We walked inside the kitchen, I poured him a cup of coffee, and he went to work with the roll of visquine and duct tape. I started to protest. He told me to shut up, and I did. He took one long sip of coffee, set the mug on the counter. His utility knife slashed until the plastic fit the empty space perfectly.

I started to thank him, and he cut me off again. I sipped my coffee, he picked up the phone and made a call to Pete of Pete's Hardware. Lawless asked Pete to send over a new door tomorrow, solid core, and to send some kid who knew how to install it. He asked that it be billed to his account.

Mina ambled in and waved a careless hello to Lawless. She was wearing the XXL T-shirt I wear to paint and clean. It had been hanging on a hook near the dryer.

"This is pretty colorful," she said. Mina studied my walls, peered into the living room, and touched the trim around the doors, again surveying the T-shirt she wore.

"At least it's clean and it fits," I said.

"Who's complaining? It's just that I've never been dressed like a wall before."

She turned in a circle as if she were standing in front of a mirror at Macy's deciding whether to blow two hundred bucks on a dress.

Then she noticed our new visquine door. "It's nice to have a man around." She nodded in approval. "You fixed it good as new."

"Not quite."

"Good enough for now, but"—she turned to me and shook her head like I was three miles behind a lost cause—"look at this T-shirt! No wonder you've got trouble keeping a man."

She pointed to the band on Lawless's finger. "How long have you been married?" she asked him.

"Almost forty years, got my wife the same year I got that Suburban out front."

"Some advice from an old woman? A wife is not a Chevrolet— don't ever let her hear you talk about your car and her in the same breath."

"Good advice."

"No kidding. Listen, that's a long marriage, especially for a cop. You like your wife?"

"I love her."

"But do you like her?"

"She's my best friend."

"Does she wear things like this ratty drop cloth with sleeves to bed?"

I waited for the blush to start at the top of Lawless's forehead and head south. It didn't happen. He'd seen too much to be embarrassed by the nuts and bolts of life.

He looked up at her with a twinkle. "My wife sleeps naked. We both do."

"I knew it. This is what makes a good marriage," Mina said. "Both sleep naked, or the wife wears a sexy nightgown. People make the simplest things in life, like having a good marriage, such a big complicated deal."

She waved good night, but was stopped by a second thought. "And don't think," she said, turning to me, "that I'm going to sleep in my new trailer tonight with that kook on the loose."

"I don't want you out there with that kook on the loose," I said to her.

"I'll tell Abra she's got company. Then I'm lying down with the baby."

Good night, Mina. Good night moon, good night little boy sleeping under the moon . . .

Lawless scrunched his brow. If I read him right, it was scrunched in dread. During the years he'd dealt with this scenario, he'd worn the anonymity provided by his SFPD badge. Preparing to talk with a young woman about spousal abuse after you've been chatting with her grandma about nighties—this was new territory.

Abra walked into the kitchen, wiping her hands on the back of her jeans. She sat down with us, acknowledging Lawless with a quick nod. Then she fell into a round of silent jaw-clenching.

"What's that look on your face?" I turned the volume knob on my voice up a few notches. "Abra, you asked me to call him."

She matched my volume and raised me one. "You must have called before I asked you to."

Lawless studied Abra's face, also her neck and wrists. She caught him watching her out of the corner of her eye.

She pointed to her face. "I know what I look like," she said. "You don't have to stare."

Mumbled grousing moved toward us, grew louder, and formed words.

"Hey, what's all this about? A man comes to fix our door, and you don't act decent with him?" Mina shook her head in Abra's direction, patting her shoulder. "I'm sure you'll apologize later. Listen, I only walked into the middle of all this yelling because you need this."

Mina pulled a green pouch from around her neck and motioned for Abra to bend her head. "Mandrake root, for protection. Don't take it off."

"I still have the root you gave me when I went on my first date. Somewhere."

"That wasn't with this husband, was it?"

"No, I was kind of away from the family when I started going with Rory."

"Figures. Wear this even in the shower. It's a plant, it doesn't mind getting wet."

Mina rested her hands on Abra's shoulders. "And don't get mad with your mother," she said. "I'm the one who called Lawless."

"You did not."

"Sure I did. You want to know why?" She kissed Abra's forehead. "I knew it'd be good for me."

Abra tried a tiny smile. "What are you talking about?"

"Here I am, an old woman. I'm trying to be brave, but I'm on the move, and I don't have a man. I just inherited a bunch of dough that I'm not going to get until lawyers and the city nibble it to bits. I try not to think about that money, I try not to want it. Maybe I'll give it away. This spins around my head until I'm dizzy. My only daughter isn't talking to me, so I follow her to the middle of nowhere—you know I'm not crazy about trees, I like cities, the move here is a last resort—and I don't even know if your mother's going to be nice and let me stay. It's not like she's the easiest person to get along with, but I certainly don't have to tell *you* about your mother."

"Abra," Mina said, "with just one rotten husband you've made my life simple. Now I have just one thing to worry about. You."

"Nobody wake me or Joey up. I haven't fallen asleep with a baby for a long time. Maybe I'll slip sweet dreams inside his head."

Seven

Abra asked Lawless if they could start over. She thanked him for coming over and for fixing the door.

"You women have a funny idea of *fix*. You need a handyman around here."

Abra shivered. I didn't know if it was from the cold or from her life.

"Let's sit in the living room," she said to him. "I don't know what we're supposed to say to each other, but I kind of want to get it over with."

We arranged ourselves on the furniture. Actually, I tried to blend in with the furniture or fade into the paneling. Blending wasn't working for me, and I couldn't get comfortable enough to fade. I should have stayed in the other room. Abra caught me fidgeting.

"Mom, I didn't tell you what was going on because I didn't want to keep being the family screwup. This marriage was bigger than bad grades, bigger than totaling two cars before I'd turned seventeen, it was bigger than getting married without telling the family."

"That one I completely understood. You are not a screwup."

She tucked her feet under her bottom, pulled her sleeves down over her wrists. "Anyway, what could you have done? Told me to leave him? I wouldn't have."

"You ladies mind if I smoke?" Lawless asked. His voice was a warm, nubby tweed.

Lawless could have smoked an entire pack and finished it off with two fat Cuban cigars for all I cared. He was our oasis of sanity, and an oasis deserves to have whatever it wants. He smoked, Abra joined him. What the hell, I bummed one of his cigarettes, too. My head whirled, my mouth tasted like a burned burrito. I stubbed out the cigarette.

Lawless took a puff and rolled the smoke around in his mouth as if it were fine French wine instead of a rasty Pall Mall.

"Abra," he said, "unless you're a dog or a psychopath, life's full of regrets about the past and worries about the future. We have to let go of that—we hold on to who we are and remember why we're here."

She said, "I think it's too late."

"Too late?"

"Most of the time I don't remember who I am, not really."

I shot out of my seat, stunned. "What do you mean?"

Lawless shot me a *Shut Up!* look. Abra glanced in my direction, gave me, almost, an identical look. I sat down.

"I mean," Abra said, looking at Lawless, not at me, "that I go to the grocery store, and I can't remember if it's me who loves dark chocolate or if it's Rory. But if I get it wrong, he pouts, he screams, my stomach turns into a knot. I feel swallowed up. I don't know how this happened."

Her voice trailed off, more sleeve-pulling. She looked tiny and vulnerable trying to rub her cold hands warm, blue veins showing through pale skin. I was filled with wormy hate, and I wanted her husband to feel pain.

"Why have you stayed?" I said. "You're smart, you're gorgeous . . . Should I go in the other room? I can't shut up."

They both said no at the same time.

"But please let me talk with Abra," Lawless said. "Raise your hand if you feel an outburst coming on. Warn us."

Abra smiled. Normally that comment would have gotten Lawless a quick comeback, but he was right. I needed to get out of the middle, this was Abra's life we were talking about. Or in my case, not talking about.

I'd lost her dad before she was born, I was drunk from the day he died until she was several months old. Maybe I'd made her feel unwanted, unneeded before she'd taken her first breath. Then she found someone who needed her, needed her in a sick way, but needed her just the same.

Lawless motioned to Abra's face and neck. "I'd like to take a photo of your injury."

I cringed and waited for her response.

"I don't think this face needs to be recorded."

"It should be," he said.

Her voice went to steel. "I thought you weren't a policeman."

He blew a puff of smoke toward the ceiling and studied his cigarette. He gave her time.

"Okay, no pictures, not now," he said. "You're tired. I understand."

I sat silent, wondering how such an incredibly stubborn young woman had been run over by a cretin in shiny shoes, but I stuffed a sock in my thoughts and behaved myself. I turned my head, perusing the bookshelf behind me as if I were looking for something to fill a blank mind. The books on that shelf were old. They were musty and crinkly, some pages were glued together with bug carcasses of the sort that eat yellowed paper. I found a Kurt Vonnegut paperback, *Welcome to the Monkey House.* The futuristic life he'd built was not nearly as weird as it had turned out standing in the middle of it thirty years later.

I opened the book and tried to read. Print was a lot smaller back then. A flash went off, another one. Apparently he'd talked Abra into being photographed. Good.

The men in Abra's life were off-center. One nutty uncle, my brother, was holed up in the desert fasting and visioning, meditating and eating peyote. I loved Jack, but I couldn't understand why it was taking him so long to figure out who he was. He was not all that complicated. Abra's Gypsy side of the family was weighed heavily in favor of women—the men died off left and right. No wonder she'd picked Rory. She didn't know any better.

Lawless leaned forward in the big recliner, he spread a large hand on either knee. He hadn't pushed her, and he had her confidence. His voice bent low, slow, and easy. "Joey saw your husband hit you?" he asked her.

"Yes." Her voice fell, her eyes fell. She wore shame like an antique yellowed gown. It was too heavy for her to bear.

Lawless's voice continued, a warm hand massaging the back of her neck. "Don't be embarrassed. Millions of kids are in the same boat every year. And you're not the one who should feel ashamed."

Abra considered Lawless, then she looked away from him. She said, "This whole thing started with Joey."

"This isn't because of your boy."

"The first time Rory lost it, I was three months pregnant. He didn't want him, Joey was a surprise."

I remembered when she phoned me, told me about the baby to come. I whooped, I laughed, I called friends, I told neighbors for days. It never occurred to me that her husband hadn't felt the same way. This whole thing was driving me nuts.

"You're lucky—your son is healthy. I know that because if Rory had touched her grandson"—he hooked his thumb in my direction—"she'd be at the police station right now tearing down the walls. Surprised? I know how your mother can take over."

He looked at me, held up his hand like a traffic cop. "And don't deny it."

I turned a yellowing page, tried to slow my breathing. Lawless tapped his cigarette pack on the heel of his hand, pulled one out, and lit up. Abra joined him, small hands trembling. She blew smoke to the walls, tried to find her voice, and when she spoke it wavered.

"Last week," she said, "I went to the grocery store alone, I left Joey with his dad." Her voice was a thin strand of words. "When I walked into the house with the groceries, I heard Joey crying. He was locked in the closet. I can't leave him alone with Rory."

"Abra, it's time to leave."

"I'm afraid if I leave, he'll take Joey. I can't lose him."

The muscles in my neck tightened up, the beginning of an earth-moving headache crept along the edge of my scalp. I willed this to be a nightmare. I squeezed my eyes shut, ran one hand across my forehead, and massaged my own shoulders. I unsqueezed my eyes and there stood Mina. Maybe this *was* a nightmare.

"How long have you been eavesdropping?" I said.

"This is my family—eavesdropping isn't possible—it's just paying attention to a slice of my own life. I'm waiting for the right moment to sneak by and grab a couple of diapers and clean sheets. Joey wet through the ones he's wearing, and we're floating in there."

She tromped through the room, found an armload of sheets and diapers, and tromped back through again. We heard her chatting with Joey and flapping sheets. A few minutes passed, no more domestic sounds. She stood, again, in the corner of the living room, her arms around Joey, one hand clutching a diaper.

"I was thinking," Mina said. "What if I find the rat and get rid of him? I'm an old lady, I can take the heat."

Lawless didn't make a move.

"You're not going to arrest me for making death threats?"

"I'm not a cop anymore."

"And you," I said to Mina, "don't look all that threatening wandering around in my T-shirt, carrying a wet diaper and a two-year-old."

"This is the one part about getting old I really hate," she said. "We're going back to bed."

Abra watched Mina disappear with her son. Abra's face wore the puffy-wet evidence of a broken and frightened heart. She looked out the window and into her options.

"Lawless," she said, her voice barely audible, "how do I know that it's the right time to leave? Maybe after he calms down . . ."

"There will always be something to stop you from leaving. A birthday, a holiday. Truth is, *any*time is the right time because there *is* no perfect time," he said. "This means that now is the perfect time."

I saw the Abra I'd loved when she was little. Of the three girls, she was my baby, the sensitive one, the one I worried about. She was designed for a world with a lot less bumps than this one.

She said, "What do I do now? My life isn't great, but it's mine."

"First step—where will Rory look for you?"

"Here."

"Then we'd better get you out."

Her eyes leapt into his, pupils dialating black panic.

"Tonight?"

"You've got a nutty grandmother, a mom ready to rip anyone

limb from limb who gets close to you, and one retired cop with a few tricks up his sleeve. Tonight you're okay."

Lawless cupped her knee with his hand. She lurched back, a startled response. He pretended he hadn't noticed.

"You're right," he said, "it's not going to be easy—losing your life, making a new one—but you have to do it, and I'm going to tell you why."

He leaned back in the recliner and shut his eyes. I closed the cover of *Welcome to the Monkey House*. The room was quiet in the way only an expectant room can be.

"I have a daughter, she married a man I didn't like," Lawless said, his voice a monotone. He'd covered this territory many times. "Start over. I hated him from day one. He rubbed me raw like a bad chemical reaction. I didn't keep my feelings to myself, and it drove my daughter away. We saw each other on holidays, she had one great kid, then another—but there was always this strain between us."

While Abra was loosening up with Lawless, maybe even trusting him a little, I hadn't noticed he was loosening up, too.

"It'd been six months since we'd seen her," he said, "and one day she blows in the house looking like you do now.

"Stupid idiot that I was, I hit the fan, went off about the guy, and next morning she's gone.

"Couple of months later I get a call from her, she's in San Diego and asks can I get her home, now, and I do. When I see her at the airport, I want to cry. She's got a black eye, a swollen cheek. One little kid is holding each of her hands, they're eating ice cream bars, and they're running to me like it's a regular visit with grandpa.

"We don't say a word in the car. The kids chatter away, we stop at McDonald's and get them Happy Meals. I'm mad at my daughter, she should have listened to me but didn't. Truth is, I'm mad at myself, I'm scared to death, and I'm taking it out on her.

"We get home, her mom fusses around, but it's me my daughter's talking to, me she's telling about the trips to the emergency room. I'm a cop, I know the story, but this is different. This isn't *any* woman, it's my daughter.

"My wife's the one keeping us together. She leaves the room to put the kids to bed, and I run it all down again . . . *How did you let that man hurt you, over and over?* And . . . *If that man laid one hand on those kids he's as good as dead.* Blah, blah, blah."

Lawless brushed his hand in front of his face, maybe trying to wipe away the scene replaying inside his head. He opened his eyes and sat up.

"So, there's my daughter. I'm not providing her safety or calm, not giving her one single thing she needs. Just more news about how she messed up. She really needs this, right?"

His voice stopped. He scratched some crud off the armrest. He released one breath and inhaled another that sucked the air right out of the room.

"That night she sneaks out," he said, "and gets a flight back to San Diego. She shoots her husband. Just flat-out kills him.

"My daughter didn't give her lawyer much help, I believe she wanted credit for killing him. There were no records of abuse on file. All those trips to the emergency room—she'd always said that she had an accident, told them she was clumsy.

"Here's how it played out—my daughter was sentenced for killing a man who hurt her, repeatedly, and maybe hurt those grandbabies of mine. She was sent to jail for killing a man who deserved killing. My daughter served ten years, a reduced sentence with time off for good behavior.

"Ten years. My wife and I got the kids, and my daughter missed their ballet lessons, Girl Scout cookies, D's in algebra, the first prom. She missed their lives."

Abra was white; I probably was, too. The room was filled with the story of several lives gone horribly wrong. It was obvious why he wanted to take care of us and why he didn't give two hoots about the cost of one lousy door. Lawless was done being a cop. He was a man who'd lived our situation, and he wanted to spare us the same pain. I hoped he could.

"How's your daughter doing now?" I asked.

He climbed up out of the ooze, almost shook himself as if my voice had woken him and whirled him into my living room.

"Now? Okay. Works as a bookkeeper for a company here in town. But killing that man . . . It killed part of her, too. The shrink says she has post-traumatic stress syndrome. I think of her as a veteran, one who deserves a medal—she survived. So did the kids."

Abra stood and gave Lawless the smallest kiss on his forehead. He held on to her hand and squeezed. "You'll be okay, too."

The longer the day, the tinier Abra became. She walked down the hall to bed, didn't look back.

Lawless stretched in the recliner. I stoked the stove and covered Lawless with a warm quilt. He laid one hand on top of the cover, then the other. That other hand held a .38, a police special. I'd said I wanted to kill Rory. Looking at the man, and the weapon, who could do it was a sharp reality check.

"Lawless, you're a good man."

"I could have done better."

"Don't go there. Right now you're family, and we're counting on you."

"How'd I qualify as family?"

"You're sinking into my lumpy recliner. You're covered with a ratty quilt clutching a gun waiting to see if a lunatic you've never met is going to barge into this house. And you're family," I said, "because you've had it rough and you made it. This family is packed tight with survivors."

He closed his eyes, his mouth slackened. I waited a moment, I shook him gently.

"You going to hear someone if they break through the plastic door?"

"I'm just resting. It's a stakeout rest."

"Okay."

"I really am awake," he said. His lips barely moved when he spoke, his eyes were closed. "Get some sleep, tomorrow we go to Margo's."

"Margo's?"

Oh, brother. Life was a circus, and he was taking us there to buy cotton candy and gape at the high-wire acts. I bent over, peered into his face. If this wasn't sleep, it was a pretty good imitation.

"Get out of here and let me do my job, will you?"

"Okay!" I jumped back, my body running the heart-pump marathon.

His eyes were slammed shut, but Lawless grinned and waved one hand at me—the hand without a gun.

He was skewed enough to be a member of our clan, no doubt about that.

I followed Abra to bed and we curled ourselves around Joey and Mina. Four generations holding on tight until the world stopped spinning, and one honorary family member stuffed in a Barcalounger prepared to make one man's world stop.

Eight

*D*awn came up hard and cold. It clung to the leaves, it covered the hills with ice gray. It sprayed cars with moist white freeze. The delft blue sky was fit for a Scandinavian goddess—high white streaks caressed her edges and slithered to the end of her galaxy. All along the hills, crumpled inside the mossy folds, swirls of smoke drifted from the chimneys of small houses to meet the early sky.

Each home was filled with people getting ready to meet this day. Putting on their makeup, making love, eating Cap'n Crunch, searching for socks that matched, missing someone. All living in the center of their own myths and truths and brilliance.

Grass flattened on the hills beneath frost and wet, a thin green soon to become vibrant winter grass. No thick ocean fog, just a mist that formed from the earth and sky's tangled temperatures.

We'd made it through the night without an intruder.

"You want me to stay with Margo?" Abra asked Lawless. "I haven't talked with her for years. I'd feel really weird going to her place."

"Does she know about Margo?" Lawless asked, arching his eyebrows.

Sounded like a movie title. *About Margo*. I thought I knew everything about Margo: tons of dough, an arty circus, and trapeze weekends for inner-city women—a life that was completely eccentric, completely hers. Wait. Lili. He thought the relationship might make Abra uncomfortable. No, Abra didn't know, and she wouldn't care.

"Abra," I said, "Margo has a girlfriend who would scare the be-jeebers out of any tattooed skinhead skateboarding down South Santa Rosa Avenue."

"Lili Öoberlund. She's not so bad after you get used to her," Lawless said.

"Right. For a short Nazi Lili is just swell."

"Would you forget about Lili! Margo's your neighbor, your friend. I assumed you knew what she does."

This didn't sound good. I envisioned a coven of New Age women dancing in a circle every time the moon moved one inch.

He said, "Margo uses that fancy circus to make money, money for women like Abra."

"I know that, but Abra needs more than one weekend of confidence-boosting."

"Who said anything about one weekend?"

Lawless leaned back and balanced on the two back legs of my kitchen chair, enjoying my ignorance. He laced his fingers behind his head and waited for me to register surprise.

"You have this need," I said, "to drop a verbal anvil in my lap in order to get my attention. You have it, and stop that teenage-boy thing with the chair. You're going to kill yourself."

He sat up straight, all four of the chair legs planted firmly on the floor. "Okay, it's about Margo's bunkhouses."

Bunkhouses? I hoped I was clear out of the ballpark about Lili resembling a Nazi in any way.

"I can see those buildings from my roof," I said. "They house her performers."

"Wrong. Only two are for performers, the other buildings house battered women, and not for one weekend, it's for as long as they need. You don't know what Margo does, what she *really* does, and you live next door. The place is safe—Abra's husband wouldn't know about Margo's place, few husbands do, even while their wives are residents. If a spouse finds the place, we take care of them."

We'd left Nazis and covens in the dust and were headed straight to Sicily, do not pass go.

"You take care of them? What did you do? Quit SFPD and join the Mafia?"

"We simply make sure there's no return trip to Margo's. Some people have to be convinced a little more enthusiastically than others. It's one of the perks about being off the government payroll."

"I thought the perk was going fishing."

"Sure. But not being official anymore, I have the freedom to lean a little harder on people as well as fish."

Lawless was now able to engage in thug activities using the training and connections he'd acquired while on the public payroll.

"That sounds worse than it is," Lawless said. "Maybe I wanted to know if it was possible to shock you."

"I don't care if guys like Rory get thugged once in a while," I said. "It's probably not legal, but it's justice."

"That's how I see it."

Abra sat at the table playing solitaire with a deck of tarot cards. Something one of the Szabo clan taught her—she'd been shuffling those cards around since she was a kid.

I said, "Houses full of inner-city women and kids living right over the hill . . ."

"They're not all inner-city women. A silly generalization and racist to boot," he said, putting me in my place. "There are regular white women, even irregular white women like Abra, who need a safe place to build a new life."

Abra didn't stop shuffling the cards, but her surprise was obvious. One solid night of sleep, and she looked fuller, less trapped. Maybe soon her lungs would expand and she'd be able to breathe again.

Lawless looked at her cards, laid the seven of cups below the eight of swords.

"You surprised about the women?" he said to Abra.

"Surprised you and Margo are friends."

"No mystery there. I wish she'd been available for my daughter."

"Yes, but Margo and her pals love to rock the establishment's boat—they smoke pot, drink wine, and wrap Bohemian Grove in cellophane," Abra said. "Usually she and the police aren't on the same side."

"I don't give a damn about Margo's politics," Lawless said, his skin turning a faint shade of red. "Frankly, there's been more than one of those Grove blowhards I'd like to wrap in cellophane myself."

Last year three ex-presidents visited the Grove and cozied up to the permanent power machine, the tycoons. They all awoke to find their cabin encased in a Saran Wrap cocoon, thanks to Margo and crew. It happened every year, at least some variation of it did. I believed the power elite enjoyed it as much as the unempowered elite.

"We've taken hundreds of women to Margo, by *we* I mean the police. I hate to admit it," he said, "but she's saved more than one cop's wife. The county helps keep her place under wraps by letting zoning variances, ordinances, and permits slip through the cracks. A few of the same elite she annoys offer her protection. I wish there were ten of her—that woman is out there saving lives."

"Lawless, calm down," I said. "I knew Margo helped a few women when they were in a jam. I just didn't know it was her focus. I figured that was Cirk."

"Helping those women eats every dime Cirk earns and more. She spends her own money, but that resource isn't a bottomless well. Not one word of this gets out, understand?"

"No problem."

Lawless snorted. "I shouldn't have said anything that I didn't want an inquiring world to know. You earn your living by being a world-class gossip."

I briefly ran through the ways I could make his life a living hell and stopped myself mid-thought—he was rescuing my kid. But my exasperation level was definitely on the rise. "You really are starting to feel like family," I said to him.

Mina walked into the kitchen, wearing a long purple skirt and a pale pink blouse. She stroked Abra's hair and said, "You are at a fork in the road."

Abra stopped shuffling the cards and looked up into her grandmother's face. What I saw surprised me. A connection so strong—love, large and real—palpable.

"Life's a disaster? Big deal," Mina said to her. "Disaster or success wait around every corner. Getting stuck in the flypaper of fear, that's when life turns sour. When you move on, life becomes sweet again."

"I *am* stuck. I feel like I've forgotten how to move on my own."

"Impossible. Gypsies do not forget how to move. We've just got to pry you out of this one sticky situation," she said, "you'll put on a few pounds, there'll be pink in your cheeks instead of purple— Annie get that look off your face, you and I and Lawless know her cheeks are purple, and if the UPS man comes by, he'll know it, too—pretending does no good."

"So true," Lawless said solemnly. He and Mina could clean up three small dictatorships before lunch and install new governments by dinnertime.

"Mina," I said, noticing the outfit, noticing the glow, "you weren't in bed this morning when I woke up. What have you been up to?"

"I have laid curses on that slimy scum Rory from here to the end of time, and first light helps curses stick. You may think I'm not a threat, but at dawn, completely naked, I am magnificent."

I wondered how many nude early-morning curses had occurred on the streets of San Francisco over the years. I was sure several had been aimed at me.

"Problem is, Rory's type has a strange protection," Mina said. "They really don't know they're crazy, not one part of them knows, and that's a problem."

Mina watched the tarot cards fall, and she watched Abra pick them up.

"Have you noticed," Abra said to her, "the Priestess reversed keeps turning up."

"The Priestess is a woman older than you. She has physical, spiritual, or mental power over the elements. Usually a woman alone." Mina stroked her chin. One gray hair, about half an inch long, sproinged from her chin just to the left of center. "In this group it could be almost anyone. Annie, me, Capri, someone over at that crazy circus getting ready for tonight's performance. The trapeze is very dangerous." She sighed. "I wish I could send a warning."

"Pretty hard to warn someone when you don't know who they are," I said.

"Believe me, this loophole has plugged up the works more than once."

We heard all about an old lover—when Mina had squeezed him in between the husbands and the kids I didn't know—but he was a trapeze artist, a flyer. He was dark and gorgeous, of course he was, then he was dead. The catcher let go of him, there were no spotters, no one to keep him on the apron.

"The man was beautiful. If Alfredo had been squashed by a herd of elephants," Mina said, "he would have done it so gracefully a crowd would have broken out in applause."

She finished her story with, ". . . And the more I think about it, the more I don't want my granddaughter going to that place."

I said, "I went there and lived, did the trapeze weekend—I even conquered my fear of heights."

"Phooey. You did not. You just fly with your fear. And we're not talking about you." She surveyed me as if I were a horse, and she were considering whether to place a bet on me. "Then again, maybe we are. You're alone, you have the power of words."

This had to stop. I hate being in the default position of resident sane person. It sucks the juice right out of me.

I turned Abra toward me, held her shoulders, and said, "Honey, let's not get distracted by . . . whatever it is your grandmother's talking about. Tonight you'll be safe at Margo's. You'll feel lonely. You'll feel scared and excited. You will be free for the first time in a long time. No danger."

"Your mother's right," Mina said. "Keep your eyes open for danger every minute."

"I didn't say that."

"I've got a big stake in this beautiful daughter." She caressed Abra's cheek. "She looks just like me."

Lawless let out a single loud whoop that would circle the valley and still be around to join the pop of champagne corks on New Year's Eve.

Mina said, "What?"

"Nothing, just a catch in my throat."

"Better watch that blood pressure. Sometimes a convulsion is the first sign."

"I'll be careful."

Mina nodded. "This gene pool," she said, placing her hand on her chest, "is not all about glamour. Abra probably got her lousy taste in men from me, too."

While Mina was gazing into her past, Abra leaned over and whispered to me. "The truth. Do you think I look like Grandma?"

"Maybe like Grandma used to look. Just watch your weight."

"You think I don't know what you're saying just because you whisper? I'm old," Mina said, "I am not deaf."

I waited for another convulsion from Lawless, but in the middle of this family back-and-forth, Lawless had disappeared.

"Where's Lawless?" I said to Mina.

"How would I know? I'm supposed to keep an eye on the guy who's supposed to be keeping an eye on us?"

At that moment Lawless and Margo walked through my undoor together.

She gave Abra a hug, a holding, and a haven. My petite daughter was encircled by Margo, all six feet of her.

"Get your son ready," Margo said. "We're going to get you settled in."

"I don't want to go."

"When it comes down to it, no one ever does."

"I want to stay with my family."

"Your husband knows that. Abra," she said, "lose a ten-year-old playing outside in the yard, you've got a chance of seeing him again. Lose your two-year-old, and Joey'd be a grown man before you'd find him."

Margo laid her hand on top of Abra's. "Look, life's a circus, I learned that early. It's supposed to make you gasp with awe, surprise you, thrill you, prick your sensibilities. It's not supposed to scare you, and you don't need to marry the freak show. If you *did* marry the glass-eater, you're allowed to take a walk."

"When are you going to visit?" Abra asked me.

"We're going to Cirk's opening tonight, we'll come early to see you."

Margo bit her lower lip.

"Is that a problem?" I said.

"Keep a low profile, and pay attention," she said. "Men with money hire detectives to tail family members. Men without money snoop for themselves."

"Margo, I don't understand how someone can say they love you"—Abra put her hands in a circle around her neck—"and do this."

"Zero impulse control. They literally can't walk out the door and take a breather," Margo said, no emotion attached, a statement of fact. "They were abused as kids, and I'm sorry about that, but it's someone else's worry, not mine. And don't think," she said, "that I have anything against men. I've helped abused men, too. The pattern's the same regardless of gender.

"Physical wounds heal, but the emotional ones keep you in check. He acts charming, you jump through hoops trying to please him. Something sets him off, and the whole thing starts again. There's a pattern and a rhythm, it's no more complicated than a waltz.

"You walk on eggshells, you have no money of your own. You want to believe he'll change. You feel beaten down, you can't imagine that you have ONE skill anyone would pay you for. You're trapped, you're sure of it.

"You're protecting your child, you're trying to keep the peace, it's an impossible situation. You're living on the edge of a volcano, you walk across it on a tightrope, and you keep smiling. Except when you're alone."

Abra said nothing.

Margo leaned closer. "Here's what else I know. A woman can leave, get strong, and start over. That's what we're going to do."

Margo held both of Abra's hands and would not let her go. Margo would be her temporary reality, her piece of the planet, a solid place to stand.

"This is that quiet time just before the storm hits, I can smell it." Margo turned to Lawless. "Let's go."

Abra took Joey's car seat outside, strapping it into Margo's car.

Joey and Mina sat on the kitchen floor. Joey poured cat food from one bowl into the water bowl, then he splashed. Mina sang him a song in Rom. It sounded like a nursery school song, but it was probably a chant of protection. I hoped so.

Abra walked back into the house with Lawless. Margo picked Joey up. He played with her hoop earrings, she nibbled his hand in return. Lawless said he'd follow them in his car, said they'd take a circuitous route, ten miles out to the ocean and back over the hills on winding roads. Plenty of curves to lose someone, and plenty of space to notice being followed.

"And if we're tailed, I hope it's not by a PI," Lawless said, "I hope it's Rory. There's nothing I'd like better than to meet up with that guy."

Mina patted his chest. "Cop or no cop, this is a man I could fall in love with."

"He's taken," I said.

"I really am taken," Lawless stuttered.

"Relax. It was just my way of saying thanks."

"You can take me anytime," Margo said to Mina. "I think you're terrific."

"God help me. Now I've not only got men falling in love with me, I got women falling in love with me, too. The older I get the less I understand."

"Don't worry." Margo put her arm around Mina's shoulder. "I'd really need to know you better before I'd fall in love. I'm not *that* easy. Besides, my girlfriend's very possessive."

Had someone tried to beat Margo down and failed? I don't know why people worry about the homogenization of humans in this twenty-first polypropylene century. You could build malls from here to Mars, cram it with people carrying identical credit cards, and not one person would have the same story. Margo had learned lots of my stories over the years. There were, obviously, a few stories of her own she'd kept to herself.

"Margo, can Abra meet us in your office before the performance tonight?" I asked.

"Bring her some personal items, family pictures, makeup, anything that'll remind her she's loved. The small space she'll have is temporary, but it's hers. We'll decide if it's safe for her to leave the women's bunkhouse to meet you in the office tonight. First few days are when the husband's most likely to make a move."

Mina kissed Abra good-bye, saying she had a few errands to run—too many good-byes in Mina's life. She zipped off alone, trying to drive faster than her feelings.

So. Abra, Joey, Margo, and Lawless piled into two cars. I stood watching. I pulled my hands out of my pockets, wrapped my arms around my waist, and held on. Abra waved to me through the window. It was a small wave coupled with a small smile. I waved back to her down a long corridor that telescoped out like a bad drug. Abra rode over the hill and around the bend with Margo. Lawless followed close behind.

I sat at my desk pretending I could work. No good. I understood individual words, but I didn't understand what they meant when I strung them together. Freak and Katso, the smart cats who'd hidden from Joey, reappeared and rubbed my ankles furry warm.

I was empty and aching, full of hope and fear. Abra was going to be okay. She was going to be okay. The worst was over. I'd tell myself that until I believed it.

Nine

Failing gives us the chance to start over, but sometimes failing is dangerous. That's why every one of us needs a safety net.

—Margo Spanger to Abra

A set of safety lines is held by a trainer and connected to a safety belt that allows a flyer to work on tricks without the risk of a bad fall to the net. It is a playground, a field of dreams, a place of adventure and it starts with ordinary pipes and cable and nylon. And a good safety net.

—*Learning to Fly,* Sam Keen

*W*hen Jack London moved from Oakland to the Valley of the Moon, a splendid crescent just a stone's throw from the town of Sonoma, he knew what he was doing. Mr. London sucked up life with all the passion of a naked man eating a bushel of mangoes with his bare hands. Treks through Alaska, sailings to the South Seas, wild writing, firebrand socialism, journalistic fervor, a spitfire wife and partner—all these doings seem almost ordinary compared to him becoming a farmer. But that's what he did.

London tossed his enthusiasm into a new arena—he lived in a cottage, grew fruit trees, rode horses, and built a phantasmagorical party house worth millions. It burned down as the furniture was being moved in. That he chose the Valley of the Moon to create another chapter in his mythic adventure is no surprise to anyone who's been there. The ruins of his charred home, Wolf House, wear the greatest beauty and deepest sadness on the night of a full moon, the light filtering through monolithic lava rocks.

This duality of exuberance and despair manifests a depth of magic no circus can touch and few places on earth can match. London understood magic, he knew beauty, and this is where he chose to live. Margo Spanger—who wrestled with beauty, enormous energy, magic, and hard truths—had also chosen this place, just a few miles from London's land, to build her new world.

Just off Moon Mountain Road an asphalt driveway dribbled into a parking lot. This belonged to the circus—we'd left plenty of time to visit Abra before the performance. We drove a few hundred yards beyond the asphalt and turned right onto an unmarked dirt road made bumpy with river rocks. The road led to Margo's office. A smaller road, private and gated, easy to miss, launched off to the left and stopped in front of Lili and Margo's home.

One-hundred-year-old California oaks dotted Margo's property. The apple trees were bare now, so were her cherry and peach trees. A trickle of a creek ran through her property—such a small, peaceful sound—an owl overhead, the rush of wings. Bats had already made their dusk swing through the hills, but Mina carried an umbrella to fend them off. Just in case.

"I don't understand why people want to live places where there are bats. Cities were invented for a good reason."

"London has bats."

"You don't see me living there, either," she said. "Too many haunted houses."

Mina wore a scarf around her head. I don't usually give bats a second thought, but I took one look above to check for flying rodent activity. Why do women worry about bats getting trapped in their hair? I wasn't going to ask Mina. She'd tell me exactly why, then I'd have to hear about some client of hers who'd endured an entire family of bats reproducing in her hair until the woman's head disappeared. Here was Mina, an incredible source for *The Eye,* a woman who was sometimes the bane of my existence, and I had never pumped her for stories. A gross oversight. When life resembled normal, I'd get out my tape recorder and ask Mina to unload. I'd need two or three days with nothing else scheduled and a stockpile of blank tapes.

Mina swung her umbrella above us. The air was bat-free.

We walked up the steps to Margo's office. It was a pioneer home, built in the late 1800s. Wisteria vines, now woody and hollow, hugged the railing. In April, there'd be large purple flowers, lush and glorious, winding their way around the porch.

Margo and Lili began in this cottage, then built themselves a simple ranch-style home, more windows than wood, when the circus and its paperwork spilled into their private lives. After what I'd just learned about Margo's true vocation, I'd also say they built the house to distance themselves from endangered women and angry husbands.

I knocked on the door, the Nazi answered, she told us to come in. "And hurry up about it. Don't let cold air follow behind you," Lili said.

I took off my coat, and Mina worked her way out of layered wool scarves.

Lili sat behind her desk, it was older than the cottage. Her hair was blond and spiky, she was somewhat younger than Margo. Two earrings pierced her eyebrow. It was an improvement. Last time I'd seen her, she'd been wearing an ordinary safety pin as if it was holding up a slip instead of an eyelid.

She folded her hands in front of her. "He was here already. You know that?"

"He who?"

"Abra cannot meet you here," Lili said, "because he's been in this office. She can't be anywhere other than where she is, and that you may not know."

"Lili, this isn't jail. I came to see my daughter," I said. "What's going on?"

"The man with red hair your daughter has found herself married to? He's one of the unfortunate men who have discovered us."

I collapsed on a ladderback chair. I let the circus route book I was returning fall to the floor.

"How?"

"I don't know. He was alone, no private investigator."

"But you got rid of him, right?"

"Not me. Margo's the dragon, she held him for Lawless. But then we lost him."

"You lost Lawless or Rory?"

Lili frowned at me as if I'd just received a D on a basic English exam.

"We lost Rory. Lawless, or someone else, will find him again, but for now he's on the loose. So, you understand, it's not possible for you to see your daughter."

"Sure it is. I just walk out this door and see her."

She shook her head at my stupidity. "We go to her, and he may follow us. If she walks over here, and he's on the property, he may spot her. We wait until Lawless tells us the man's under control. This is the rule."

I looked at Mina. She'd stopped disrobing mid-scarf. She was pulling her coat back on and rewrapping herself.

"I keep it cold in here," Lili said, "it saves money. But you're an old woman. I'm happy to turn up the heat for you."

"No, no, I was just thinking, I could use a little fresh air. Hot flashes, understand what I'm saying?"

Lili looked puzzled, but she did understand what Mina was saying.

"I'll be back when my body temperature hits normal."

"Why layers of coats and scarves when you have the sweats on you?" Lili asked.

"Being a foreigner and everything, you might not know this, but if you're sweating and you go out into the cold, you could come down with pneumonia and drop dead in two days. I'm going through menopause, but I don't want to die about it. That's why all the clothes."

Mina opened the door and closed it quietly behind her. Menopause? I was pretty sure Mina had driven over that mountain years ago and could barely see it in her rearview mirror.

Lili stood and crossed the room. She picked up the route book I'd dropped.

"Margo lent you this?"

"Actually she said I could keep it along with the rest of her books, but it belongs here."

"Strange."

"To give a writer books?"

"It's just that they're very valuable, and she's picky about her belongings. I'm merely surprised."

Lili stroked the cover of the old route book as if she were petting a Persian cat. I almost expected the book to start purring.

"This is from the late 1800s. Very few are in private hands," Lili said. There was some amount of reverence attached to her spiel. "Each railroad circus kept a route book, a very careful diary of every performance in every town. The size of the audience, numbers of whites, blacks, Chinese in attendance . . . It's also a portrait of the circus performers—births, deaths, fights, marriages, accidents. We even learn the storm patterns, weather, thievery, and circus animals gone mad.

"Elephants—a strange and sad story—the first exotic animals in this country. They were sent from Bengal to New York in 1796. The animals were exhibited in barnyards and stables. Obscene.

"Elephant lynchings, shootings, all of it terrible. The animals with the biggest hearts, the ones who wore the biggest smiles, had the hardest time in captivity. They're large and beautiful, but they're frail. They become crazed when they're angry."

"Sounds kind of like Margo."

That wasn't meant to be a joke, it did sound like Margo. At least Lili's description of elephants sounded like Margo. I've never had a personal relationship with a pachyderm, so I'd have to take Lili's word about their behavior.

Lili gave the cover one last stroke, returned the route book to a bookshelf between two framed circus posters. She looked up at the poster nearest the door. She stood back and crossed her arms. She was doing a pretty good impression of a docent, I knew she was going to start again—I could feel it coming—and I wasn't interested. I wished I had escaped with Mina. We'd be very early, but we could sit inside the theater and wait for the show, we could stand in line waiting to get inside the theater. We could be snooping around looking for my daughter. I was beginning to feel the same way I had this morning—that I'd lost Abra again. Mina was probably just outside the door, flapping her arms to keep warm, knowing exactly what she'd missed and waiting for me to get smart and flee.

"You like this poster?" Lili said, directing me toward it with her ice-blue eyes.

How can you like a poster of Siamese twins joined at the head marrying a set of regular twins, fairly regular, except that they were midgets? How could you not? It was stranger than modern art, it was almost perverse, it was kind of cool, and I wouldn't want it hanging in my house. Well, maybe the bathroom.

"I see," she said, "that you're fascinated with the colors. Of course you are."

The colors? I was looking at two sets of mutant twins about to say "I do." I didn't even notice the colors.

"These lithographs—the circus was the first business to use a printing process that produced such astonishing colors. This one poster is very special. A bill poster plastered 5,000 of these in every town before the circus arrived, but in 1898 Barnum and Bailey plastered 27,100 sheets of these posters in New York City! Very few remain."

"The subject matter's pretty striking."

"The circus has always played with our ideas about what is animal, what is human, how they connect. When they do connect, your average citizen goes crazy—it disgusts them, yet they love it."

"Fascinating," I said. "Lili, I missed my daughter, I don't want to miss Cirk. Bye."

I certainly was going to see my daughter, I didn't know how, but I was, and I didn't care if I missed the performance while I looked for her, or if I found Rory by mistake.

"You'll see your daughter," she said, "later. Come back to the office after the show. I'm sure we'll have taken care of the husband by then."

Lili looked at her watch. "But may I have you one more minute?" I must have looked startled, I sure felt startled.

She laughed, small white teeth. "I don't intend to bite you."

Now I was scared.

"Look, I've got to find Mina," I said. "She's an old lady wandering around outside, freezing her behind off. I wouldn't put it past Rory to grab Mina and take off with her just to throw a scare into us."

Lili laughed again. There was nothing resembling joy in her laughter. It was more like a sound effect. "I have no doubt that Mina's sitting in your car with the heater on, the windows rolled up, and the door locked. I also have no doubt that she can take care of herself in any situation. That includes Rory."

"Okay, but make the minute fast."

"I was sorry about your mother's death last year."

"Me too." How did my mother get into this?

"La Rue brought out Margo's rebellious nature. For that I loved your mother. Even at the end, La Rue could still give Margo a run for her money."

"You saw my mother at the hospital?"

I considered this aberrant neo-nut visiting my sick mother, and it gave me the creeps.

For a few people like Margo, and there are only a few people like Margo, love had come in every conceivable package, and a few that were inconceivable. Until Lili came along, I'd considered Margo to be omni-sexual. The train of Margo's desire had slammed on its brakes right in front of Lili's little schnitzel stand, and that, it seemed, was that. Being Margo's friend meant putting up with Lili.

Maybe Lili was collecting her English, but her quiet felt more like dramatic effect—she was pulling out her silence.

Lili had been trained young, East Germany, no surprise, as a contortionist. Somewhere she and Margo had hooked up, I didn't know the details. Margo encouraged her to take up the trapeze and forget the contortionist routine. It was beginning to compress Lili's rib cage, did some damage to her lungs, and a few miscellaneous organs. One East German doctor pronounced her sterile. I didn't consider her gene pool a great loss to the ocean of humanity. And Lili as a mother? Whew! The kid would have finished their homework, I'll say that much. I sat there thinking how odd it was barely to know someone and be privy to the secrets of their internal organs. Anyway, the trapeze didn't work out, she preferred work as a clown and a costume designer. Go figure.

"Lili, I'm glad you saw my mother. I'm sure she appreciated your visits."

She gazed at that freak poster again. I had things to do, and Lili was not one of them.

"Your mother was smart, Margo liked that. She brought your mother Scotch and See's candy. Once when your mother's pain was very bad, Margo smuggled in a joint."

"We all did that."

"I don't smoke it, I don't like the loss of control. But your mother was very grateful. They smoked and drank in the chapel of the nursing home."

"No one got arrested, and my mother's far beyond anyone's jurisdiction now. I've really got to run."

"The nurses knew I'm sure, but they didn't say anything."

No kidding. Who'd reprimand Lili? It'd be *adios,* so long, twenty years in a gulag.

"I don't think your mother liked me," she said.

Where the hell were we going with this? She wanted something from me, that was clear, but I was a mother myself, and just then I needed to make sure my kid was okay.

"Lili, my mom pretty much liked everyone. It was almost annoying."

"She told my lover, right in front of me, that if she fixed herself up, she could get any man she wanted. Told Margo she would be a knockout."

Leave it to my mother. "Sorry, Lili."

"People rarely talk about me as if I'm not there, but I respected her for expressing her feelings. Margo explained to your mother that she did not want a male animal, La Rue accepted that, and they had another toke. I didn't believe Margo, but it was not the appropriate time to discuss it."

Now I knew where we were going. Did I know something about Margo's love life that Lili didn't know but suspected? Lili had me to herself, and she was looking for information. I didn't have any, and I didn't care about the women's love life. I had enough trouble figuring out my own, and it was fairly standard.

I told Lili she was barking up the wrong tree and stood up to retrieve my coat and scarf. A photo above the coatrack caught my eye. It was a family of trapeze artists, flying without a net, above a beach empty of all but pelicans. The photo appeared to be taken when cameras were still new.

"They're beautiful, aren't they?" Lili whispered.

I hadn't even heard her move, but there she was, just to the right of my shoulder. The woman was a cat.

"More than that," I said, "they've let go of gravity."

Lili held my lilac wool scarf. I started pulling on my coat, she helped me with my sleeves. "They are mystical, the flyers, almost like creatures who came here by mistake," Lili said. "Sometimes I think, *When the flyers discover they've landed on the wrong planet, they'll be out of here faster than the speed of light.*"

She held me by the shoulders and turned me around. She wrapped my scarf around my neck.

"I love Margo very much," Lili said.

"I know."

"I want that to be clear."

"I understand."

"I'm not invited to the intimate lunches at your home, the glasses of wine. She offers you priceless circus items that no one else is allowed to touch . . . She cares about you."

"She doesn't care about me that way."

"You know Margo. She's very impulsive."

"You can count on me to show enough restraint for both of us."

"Good. Margo and I, when we were first together, she suggested we try being with another woman, you know, three together. I thought it might satisfy her wanderlust. It destroyed me, I put my foot down, told her not to ask for that again. Ever. Margo was frightened, she thought I might leave her. I love her, but I would have left."

"Lili, Margo is no problem."

The door of the little pioneer cottage burst open, Mina and Margo walked in together, a sling of cold air following on their heels.

"Of course I'm a problem," Margo said. "I hope to be a problem the rest of my life."

Lili said, "I told Annie we were sorry about her mother."

"We loved La Rue," Margo said. She walked straight up to me and tried to plant a kiss full on my lips, I turned my head so it caught me on the cheek. Boy, she really enjoyed yanking Lili's chain. And, when I turned my head, there was Lili. I was caught between the devil and Margo's deep blue eyes.

Mina to the rescue.

"Hey, Annie, this place feels close again—that change-of-life thing—we better get out of here and vamoose to the show. I hope that theater's not too hot, I may pass out." She pulled a used Kleenex from her pocket and dabbed her forehead. "We'll come back after the show, Margo said it'd be all clear to see Abra by then."

"And you definitely don't want to miss tonight's opening," Margo added. "I'm doing a trapeze number, no big deal, just one quick somersault, then off the net."

Lili furrowed her brow. "You shouldn't do that. You're too tall for a flyer, we've discussed this—you're flexible, but you're not young. One fall off the apron . . ."

"I'll fly whenever I want. That's one part of my life you can't touch."

Lili retreated into stretchy silence. The two made a wordless not-in-front-of-the-neighbors truce.

"Fine. You'll be beautiful as always," Lili said to her, and to us she said, "Please do come after the performance. In the meantime, no snooping. Too risky."

"The last thing we want is more trouble," I said.

Mina grabbed my hand, and we scooted past Margo.

When I turned back to say good-bye, Lili and Margo were in each other's arms acting cozy. This punch, dodge, and duck was probably a standard pattern. I hoped that Lawless, or someone else who wasn't busy being in love, was on the lookout for Rory.

We walked outside, into the night, and neither one of those women knew, or cared, that we'd left.

Ten

"D̲id it ever occur to you," Mina said, "to listen to those women and forget about looking for Abra?"

"Not for one minute."

"Me either. Boy, those two! I don't understand being all excited over someone who's just like you. You might as well climb into bed with yourself. The excitement is in the difference."

"Mina, the fact that they're both women and sleep together is the least complicated part of their relationship."

It was beyond dark and then some. The thick growth of redwoods and oak branches gave the moonlight only the barest patch to peek through. Abra was somewhere around here, and we'd find her. This was not a lockup facility, and if we decided, as a family, this wasn't right for her, she was gone. They'd already let Rory slip by them once, and she'd been there less than twelve hours. I didn't see how we could do much worse. We'd drive her to New Mexico if that's what she wanted, we could plant her in the desert with my brother Jack. His off-the-grid insanity, long lost in the exact epicenter of nowhere, had been waiting for a target. Maybe Rory would provide it.

"Just stay to the right of those trees and don't step in the creek," Mina said. "I did that my first time through, and my feet are still blue. That water's freezing."

"Did you find Abra?"

"Yeah, now I've just got to retrace my footsteps, but how you do that in total darkness surrounded by bats I do not know," she said.

"I can't believe you found her."

"You kept Lili busy for a long time. I hope to God not too busy, and if you were, don't tell me about it, I'm sure you would have been doing it for your daughter."

"We weren't busy."

"You're a grown woman, you don't have to explain anything to me. Anyway, I found Abra's bunkhouse using the grandmother thing. I might have to pull it out again."

"Grandmother thing."

"You'll develop it. I could hear the air blow like a bellows magnified a thousand times between her fourth and fifth ribs. Left side."

"Knock it off."

She shrugged. "Okay, okay, I got lucky," she said. "I tripped over something, probably a stupid tree stump, and almost landed right on her front steps. After that it was just a matter of brushing myself off and peeking inside. There she was, I could hardly believe it."

I was about to ask her a question, such as was she sure she hadn't been followed, and what about bringing Abra her stuff, but Mina put her finger to her lips and shushed me.

"I didn't say anything," I hissed through my teeth.

"You were thinking too loud."

"Mina, we should have brought the quilts and pictures."

"I already brought one load. I stashed a bag outside the door with Joey's stuffed monkey so you'd have something to give them."

We walked around the bunkhouse, made sure there was no sign of Rory, no sign of anyone. I stood on my toes and peeked inside. The room was filled with women sitting on each other's beds, kids playing in a corner, piles of beat-up toys, a VCR running a Disney movie. There was Joey sitting on a cot, and there was Abra sitting on the same cot talking to someone, a man it looked like from behind, although his hair was pretty long, and she was laughing as if she didn't have one care in the world.

I knocked and opened the door at the same time. She didn't so much as turn her head when we walked in.

Joey ran to me, smiling at his monkey. I lifted him up. He put his head on my shoulder, released a giant sigh. He raised his head, thumped his chest, and looked at me earnestly. "My big," he said.

"Yes, you are." I nuzzled his neck, he smelled good, he seemed happy.

So did his mother. She was twirling her hair around one finger, acting flirty, not at all like she'd want to hide out at my brother's or anywhere else. The object of her attention was Angel Verona.

Angel was a trapeze catcher. In an attempt to conquer my fear of heights, Margo talked me into joining a weekend group of at-risk women. I felt as if I'd been at risk most of my adult life. I didn't have the slightest clue what that meant until I met those women. They were teetering on the edge of finances, addictions, abuse, family disasters, and they were determined to build healthy lives. My solid little world was an embarrassment.

After I finished the class—my fear of heights still intact—I'd return whenever I had the chance. I loved flying, and the love was stronger than the fear. My body's built right for it—compact, good upper body strength. My heart's built right for it—a love of total abandon.

Angel was the perfect catcher, and one thing led to another. Translation: We had a mild fling that started out great, slid downhill to okay, degenerated to awkward, and then it was over—pretty much. He was too young for me in more ways than years.

There was one moment in our relationship, if you could call it that, that's a photo tacked to the interior wall of my brain. When you're the catcher you sit there, and it doesn't appear as if you're doing anything. In reality, the catcher does everything—at least that's how it feels to the flyer—you're trusting this person with your entire being. Once, lying around on a Monday morning when he wasn't working, and I should have been, I asked him if he ever minded not being the center of attention. He had a glint in his eye that was a little too merry. He said, "If I wanted attention, I'd drop the flyer."

That glint in his eye put a different spin on our nonrelationship relationship. When I'd climb up Margo's hill to fly, I used someone else for a catcher. That didn't mean Angel stopped wandering down the hill to my place every now and then, and it didn't mean I turned him away when he did. The guy was handsome and available—sometimes you don't need much more than that. There's no point in wasting good material, but our dates to meet in thin air were a thing of the past.

Seeing my daughter giddy with him, I understood—he was a giddy-making sort of guy—but the timing was off. She was sporting a fresh black-and-blue tattoo her husband had left no more than twenty-four hours earlier. Her son was sitting on her cot.

"Stop staring at them," Mina said. "She's trying to feel normal. You know how long it's been since she could talk with a good-looking man and not worry about getting into trouble?"

Of course I knew. Since she'd gotten married. But this was not the guy to flirt with if she wanted to avoid trouble.

Abra turned toward me, her cheeks a blush beneath the bruise. "Oh! Hi!" she said. "This is Angel. He works here."

Angel and I behaved as if we'd never laid eyes on each other. He was smooth. So was I.

"A teacher," he said.

I looked at my watch. "A little late for lessons," I said.

"We had an incident. I'm keeping an eye on her until the problem's taken care of."

"Rory broke into the office," Abra said. Her flirty curtain had been raised and was replaced with worry. The bones grew hollow in her face, her skin a few shades lighter. I preferred seeing her flirty. We shouldn't have come. Forget the trapeze lessons, Angel was rebuilding her confidence just by sitting with her.

"I heard. You okay?"

"He can't get to me here. Good thing, because he must be in a total rage by now. Mom, I'm worried about you. Rory could follow you to your car, follow you back home, even be waiting for you at home. He could be anywhere."

"Abra, let's not demonize him. We do that, and he wins. I can take care of myself, and I will if I have to. We concentrate on you." I looked at Angel. "And it doesn't look like there's anything to worry about."

There were fifteen women in the room, with beds for a few more. Each one wore miles of trouble on her face, and no one was bringing them quilts or perfume or pictures or makeup. I should have thought about that. Mina started to bring out the bag I'd packed, and she had the same thought. She put it down, scooted it under the bed with her foot.

"We brought Joey his monkey," I said.

Abra was as happy to see the dirty, stuffed toy as Joey was. "Thanks. Joey'd have a hard time tonight without him."

"No, he's a baby with an easy mind," Angel said, "and sleep comes easy when your mind is still." He patted Abra's leg.

Brother. I remembered sleeping with Angel. Sleep wasn't easy, and it had nothing to do with my mind.

Mina stood up straight and sudden. I honestly thought she was mid-stroke. She stuck her right arm out, stiff, like a mom trying to keep her kids from splattering against the windshield when she slams on the brakes in an intersection. I was alarmed.

"What? What?" I didn't expect an answer, just a quick ride in an ambulance.

She bent one arm. She didn't speak. She put one finger to her lips. Even Angel went still and lost some charm.

She exhaled. "It's okay. You can all breathe now," she said.

Even if they drive you up the wall, you've got to admire a person who can give or withhold permission to breathe.

Mina rummaged through her bag. "Abra, I need some of your private attention." She pulled me over to stand with Abra. "You come, too. I wasn't leaving you out of your daughter's life."

She turned to Angel. "Sorry, but this is between us. Maybe you won't listen for a few minutes."

"No problem," he said. "I've got bedtime stories to tell about flying and God and grace and elephants."

"God and elephants? He has an odd mind," Abra said. "I forgot how familiar an odd mind is."

"Never mind that. Was he waiting in here for you?" Mina asked.

"Rory?"

"No, Angel."

"Yes. Margo brought me in, he was here, they talked, and she left."

"I'm giving you two things," Mina said, "and no arguing. The first is for unwanted love. It's a stick with symbols on it, keep it in your pocket. I don't trust Angel. He likes women too much, and he looks at you like it's been a long time since he had a good meal."

She put her hand over Abra's mouth.

"I said no arguing. Now to the heart of the problem. Let's not pretend all the big handsome men in the world will take care of us. You got a picture of Rory with you?"

She did. It was a family picture taken in a studio. Mina tore off corners until just the likeness of Rory remained, except for the slight angle of his jaw that was torn off with Abra's hair.

Mina held it up, she was satisfied. "This doesn't need to be perfect. Maybe tearing off his jaw will shut him up."

Mina cocked her head in my direction and did not crack a smile. "Annie, this is serious. None of your monkey business."

"Did I say anything?"

"I'm heading you off at the pass."

"Abra," she said, "mandrake root is for your garden-variety crazies. Leave it on, it can't hurt, but here's what we've got—a husband who'd like to kill you."

"He's got a temper, but he's not a killer."

"He doesn't know he wants to kill you, but he does. He'd also like to kill me, your mother, and Margo for interfering. I'm not sure Lawless is safe, either. The husband is filled with rage, more than anyone I've seen, and that's saying a lot. When I tune in, I see a dragon spitting fire, his scales shaking and bristling with anger. I look away fast. It's too much for me.

"We have to turn his energy in another direction. If this works, we're handing him a one-way ticket out of our lives. This ritual will work on one condition—you must absolutely promise that you will not come back with him in another life."

Abra didn't know what to say. There was nothing *to* say when Mina went in this direction. It was like experiencing a force of nature. You believe in earthquakes, but not until you experience them do you BELIEVE in earthquakes. Not until you see Mina in action do you believe she's for real.

"Promise!"

"I promise," Abra said, her eyes dark as a midnight pond. No doubt why an odd mind would seem familiar.

The bunkhouse women and Angel were drawn to our corner of the room like iron filings to a magnet. Soon they'd be lining up for help. Mina might fix every spouse under one big blanket of curses. Who was I to understand the workings of a natural wonder?

Mina slipped Rory's picture under a tall, thick candle. It was white. She lit the candle and instructed the women gathered around not to touch it, not to blow it out, just to let it burn out on its own. She said with any luck it would burn all the way to the bottom. She warned Angel not to interfere because of dumb fire hazards or regulations. It was on a metal plate, it was safe, it would stay on the bedside table. Angel didn't argue with her.

Mina cupped her hands around the flame and bent her head toward its heat. She raised her head, wafting the smoke into fuzzy whirlpools with her open palm. The sweet scent of lemon drifted upon the air. She spoke to the flame.

"Everything you and Abra had between you is gone, it's wiped as clean as a slate on the first day of school. YOU UNDERSTAND, RORY? IT'S OVER!

"Now we'll concentrate together, you ladies join in, the more the better." Almost every woman closed her eyes while Mina spoke. Angel did, too.

"Whatever you have coming to you, Rory, may the universe give it to you. We say this with open hearts. All good things you deserve will come. All bad things will come, too. The universe will give you what you've put into it. Your circle will be complete."

A few women rocked back and forth.

"We now imagine this person and wish him what he deserves, no more, no less."

All was quiet.

She clapped her hands. "Okay. That's it. This isn't a spell, there's no push to it, it's just asking the universe to look in his direction and speed up the clock. Sometimes it works really fast, BOOM he'll get hit by a train or fall off a cliff—not like I want to give the universe ideas—but sometimes the circle takes years to complete. Time is like an old elastic band around your underwear. Sometimes we've got to be patient until we can afford a new pair."

Women asked Mina to bring them candles, she said she would,

but no bad-thought hanky-panky was allowed. They dispersed, Angel sat on a cot, tucking in a kid. Margo was going to love her bunkhouse in the woods filled with burning candles. I hoped my daughter wouldn't get kicked out.

"One more thing," Mina said to Abra. "I feel the husband isn't far off. Maybe your mother and I will take another look around for him."

"Were we looking for him?" I said.

"What did you think?"

"I guess it crossed my mind, but I didn't really want to find him."

"How did you live so long while being such a big coward?"

"Who do you think has longer life spans, cowards or heroes? And I am not a coward, I'm careful."

"Sure you are," she said. "Abra, keep your eye on the dark angel. He wants you—you're beautiful—so that's normal. But there's something going on with him I don't understand. And what I don't understand, I don't trust."

"For God sakes," I said to Mina, "she's supposed to feel safe. You've just told her she's being protected by someone who can't be trusted."

Mina gave me the stink-eye, but when she turned to Abra she was all sweetness and light.

"We've got to run," Mina said. "I want to see the show, and now I know you're okay. Wait a minute . . . Not to change the subject, but to change the subject, have you seen your aunt?"

"My aunt?"

"Capri. How many aunts do you have?"

"I didn't know she'd be here. Who's abusing her?"

"Capri has abused herself more than any lover could—some people have a real knack for that. She's teaching trapeze, or she's performing in Cirk."

"I haven't seen her, but I wouldn't—I was told to stay inside."

I hated this. My daughter was the victim, but she was the person in jail.

"You won't be here forever," Mina said, "and you're not like Capri, you can get away from the person who's been mistreating you. For her it's harder. She's got to live with her abuser, which means she's got to learn to live with herself."

Enough. It was time to let Abra get settled in.

"Hey, Angel!" I called to him across the room. He turned his charm in my direction. It was dim, but I noticed it.

He ruffled a little boy's head. "Story time is over," Angel said.

"We're leaving, you're back on guard duty."

I held Joey, Angel reached for him. I couldn't let him go.

Joey was chewing an old deck of cards he'd found. I looked into him, looked for signs of latent rage that might emerge as an adult. I held him tight again, willing him to be kind. I saw nothing but joy and happiness from chewing the playing cards into mushy bits. We'd saved him soon enough. Still, I couldn't let go.

"Forget about it, Mom," Abra told me. "Joey can't be at your place."

She was right, of course she was. Joey kissed me on the lips. I handed him to his mom.

I walked out, and I didn't look back. I didn't say anything to Mina, walking three steps behind me. If I began talking, my words would plug up. I might really start crying, and it wouldn't be just runny stuff playing around the corners of my eyes. A few steps, a few more steps. My breathing became regular. Fresh air. My heart quieted. A few more steps, and Mina jabbed me with her elbow. I almost went into the creek up to the middle of my new black boots.

"I'll snap out of it. You don't need to dunk me in ice water."

"What was he like?"

"Who?"

"Angel. You've got a real thing about playing with the dark side, don't you? You hang out with Gypsy men, with young Italian guys who have nice behinds . . . You choose men with more cut edges than a crystal bowl."

"Who told you about us?"

"When I see two people pretending not to see each other so hard that their eyeballs practically pop out of their heads from the pressure? What can I say—I notice it."

"He was fine. Let's get to Cirk, we probably missed the opening, but we saw Abra, and she seems okay."

"He was fine? This is how you describe a bargain skirt or a breakfast cereal, not a man."

"Drop it."

"You have a very hard time expressing your emotions. You need to work on that."

Mina must have popped back into the afternoon talk-show viewing audience.

We picked our way back to the office, dodging shapes we were sure had evil intent, only to find they were ferns or bushes. Mina tumbled once more into the creek up to her ankles, but we were in a good mood.

"Abra will get through this," I said.

"I know, but the middle part is going to be hard."

"The middle part is called life, and it is hard," I said, "so we do fun things like go to a circus and for a little while we pretend everything's okay."

"Yeah, I know," Mina said. "It's taken a long time, but I've become a champ at pretending. Sometimes I even forget I'm pretending."

One dim light glowed from the ceiling of Margo's office, turning the room a pale orange. The light floated outside and touched the branches with color. We climbed into my car.

"We have tickets in the second row," I said, "waiting for us at the box office."

"Very nice! And I'm not pretending."

I blew a kiss in the direction of Margo's little pioneer cottage.

"What's that for?" Mina said.

"A safe place for my family. And a thank-you for helping those other women."

Mina made the same smooching gesture.

"That's for good seats. I could never afford this show."

Eleven

"The big top was a powerful fine sight; I never seen anything so lovely . . . the men looking ever so tall and airy and straight . . . and every lady's rose-leafy dress flapping soft and silky around her hips, and she looking like the most loveliest parasol."

—*Huckleberry Finn,* Mark Twain

"Are those the men or the women? You can't tell the difference, even in the places where you really ought to be able to tell the difference."

—Madame Mina to Annie during Cirk

*T*hree blue creatures possessed the stage. They looked as if they'd been mined from the center of the earth—there was a tingling uranium punch to them. The theater was filled with pale light, diffused, an undersea glow that bubbled to an eerie luminescence. Deep black floated above the light, a triumph of weight over weightlessness.

The creatures held thick bungee cords between their teeth. They jumped on the floor, a single thud of soft soles hitting hard wood. Their bounce and the elastic cords carried them high into the black above. One minute, two, they dropped into the foam-green spotlight and stopped ten feet short of the stage. They spun, they wrapped their legs around a twisted maypole. They opened their mouths and let go of the cords, they laid their backs against the pole, they stared at us upside down. Then, as one, they smiled.

Their faces were not fairy, and they weren't clown—they hinted at a form of mutated human life, one spawned on Mercury or Venus, some planet close to home, but not quite here.

Four hundred people in the audience, and there was barely a sound. An occasional cough or an exhaled breath that was sent to a secret place where there was no beauty, and nothing that was grotesque. To a place where judgment and time were on vacation.

When Capri returned from Mexico and proclaimed herself dried out, she was itchy to get back into circus arts. Apparently, she was tired of teaching—she wanted to perform. Well, here we were and there she was. Somewhere.

I looked at Mina, we sent each other a shrug. She hadn't spotted her daughter; neither had I. Mina closed her eyes and hummed softly. Her eyes flew open, and she pointed to the dangling outer space being on the far right. Capri.

I whispered to Mina. "How did you find her?"

"I hummed to her insides, and her insides hummed back. It's kind of like that beeper on your key ring that helps you find your car at the mall. You've got to implant the humming instinct when they're young, or it doesn't work. Do it really young, like I did, and they've got no choice but to answer back."

"This is like that grandmother thing, the air between the fourth and fifth ribs, isn't it?" I said. "You are one piece of work."

"Jeez, no. This one's for real."

Whatever. Capri looked healthy, as healthy as a blue upside-down creature can look. Her body was supple and lithe, it moved in ways mine couldn't imagine.

"She's terrific," I whispered to Mina.

"No kidding!" Mina tapped the shoulder of the man in front of us. He turned around.

She said to him, "See the one upside down with the best legs? That's my daughter."

The man hissed at us to be quiet. Actually hissed. I figured him for a kindergarten teacher. The sound came naturally. "If you two do not be quiet," he said, "I will have you expelled from this theater. Immediately."

He turned, straightened his self-righteous back, and tried to relax. He might as well give that one up. Relaxation wasn't going to happen for him during this incarnation.

Mina waggled her fingers above his head and mouthed some words. She smiled a tiny smile, a smile of anticipation. I was going to enjoy the performance and ignore Mina. Also ignore the rude man in front of us. He'd almost managed to yank me back into ordinary life. I sort of kicked the back of his seat by mistake when I crossed my legs. He scooched around in his seat and released a heavy sigh of long-suffering patience. I went inside myself, closed my eyes, and opened them.

Nothing.

It was being blind in the worst possible way. No shadows, no hint of gray, overwhelming raven black in every direction. Fear rose in my chest and tightened the muscles around my heart. It was beating as fast as a bird's wings flapping against the bars of its cage. Then, sudden purple filled the auditorium, every corner. Purple sat in our laps, it rubbed our shoulders. It faded to pale pink, from peach to vermilion, to brick red. Then, swinging itself back up the bar, it became purple again. My grip on the armrest loosened. I relaxed, soft with a full-spectrum prism washing my head, my hands, my hair.

A voice filled the theater, electronically tweaked and layered, pulsing with sound effects, Margo's voice. It wrapped around and around itself like a heavy vine.

I am escaping, I am letting go of the earth, no thing binds me to this place. This stage . . . Look into it and use this place, these creatures, as your mirror. See the reflection of your ancient soul. I dreamed of sailing before I ever saw a boat, I dreamed of color before I saw paint, I dreamed of flying before I ever saw a bird. Dream your dream and sit inside it.

Other than the sound of goose bumps running up my arms and down my legs, there was silence. Then Margo's words, warbling again, soft and smushed to a deep hum, running up the aisle to the back of the theater and vanishing.

A chorus of voices rose by the east wall, shocking, pure, and primitive. Ancient mothers calling their children home. The walls and the ceiling climbed with color and movement. Creatures of all sizes, ants to alligators to the beginning brine of life, crawled the buttes and bluffs of light. It was a procession of evolution. Even Mina was quieted by the awesome display.

In the middle of this dreamscape four human lizards on the west wall danced an obscene ballet that defied gravity, a mating of the surreal, a promise of more beasts to come. I was aware of watching something intensely private, a moment from another time—maybe ten thousand years from now, ten thousand years ago. I shifted my vision from the wall to the stage. Four garish acrobats wearing flesh-colored bodysuits bounded across the stage.

I could swear the audience breathed as one organism. We had stopped being an audience and had become part of the performance that no longer felt like performance. Our breath brought life to these creatures and sustained them. These creatures would die and be born again, birthed by the single breath of a different human chorus every night.

We'd missed Margo's opening, I was sorry about that. Margo might have been six feet tall, too tall for a flyer, but her flexibility and agility made it work. Her intense desire helped her defy physics. In her youth she'd been blond and built like a fantasy. Time had reconstructed her as a priestess, something larger, more raw than life. This show was truly the mirror of her imagination.

I leaned forward to find my boot, lost beneath the man's seat in front of me. I saw Margo seated in the front row. She was frowning, a frown more like bottled rage than displeasure. It was aimed at someone to her left. Woman or man, I couldn't see.

Mina leaned in close to me. "Uh-oh. See that look on Margo's face? She's one of the few women scarier than me, and she doesn't need props like herbs or spells."

I followed Margo's line of vision, but it scooted off into the murky mush of offstage lighting. Then Margo was up, out of her seat, and gone. Mina was right. I didn't envy the person on the receiving end of Margo's anger.

When the houselights came up, not one creature remained. All had returned to a mythic hole in the ground. The man in front of us stood, he turned to face us. He didn't have anything to say, he just wanted to bestow a dirty look upon us, one that would put us in our place. We also stood, and Mina smiled at him. He ignored her. She motioned for me to stay put while he squeezed out of his row. He tripped on his own feet and fell into the aisle. Mina slipped into her coat.

I offered to help him up. He refused.

Mina chuckled until we were halfway up the aisle.

"You've got to love those real serious types," she said. "They're the easiest people to lay low-level bad luck on."

We waded through the crowd, poured into the parking lot, found the car, and inched our way through the traffic trickling out onto the highway. Most cars were turning left, back toward town, we were heading the other way, to Margo's office. I didn't need to see Abra again, but if she was waiting, I didn't want to let her down.

Easing our way to the front of the crowd, we turned right. We rolled to a stop in front of Margo's office. Shouting from inside rattled the walls. Three voices, maybe two.

I looked at Mina. "You want to walk in on that?"

"I've had enough yelling in my own life without walking into someone else's noise."

I agreed. Abra probably wasn't in there—not in the middle of that minor war—I decided to write a note and tack it on the front door under the message clip.

I fumbled in my purse and found a paper and pen. Mina bent over and told me to use her back as a desk. I dropped my pen, found it in the dark, and started to write a note that Abra would probably never see.

Things were heating up in there. The anger bounced out the windows, playing a medley of old standards. A few of the ones I could make out were: "You're a liar, and a cheat!," "Why do you always have to drag that up and throw it in my face!," and "Oh, go to Hell!"

Forget the note. I snapped my purse closed, Mina straightened up. The door burst open, and Angel ran out. His eyes were red and swollen; he ran past us, didn't even seem to notice we were standing there.

Mina whispered, "What do you think *that* was about?"

One more oldie but goodie flew out the window. "You know what? Just forget the whole damned thing!" Silence.

I said, "Only money and jealousy are that loud."

"Has to be money with those two."

I thought about Lili's slippery concern regarding Margo's possible interest in a man, and I thought about her pumping me for information to confirm her suspicions.

"I don't think money's a problem for them."

"Why would two women fight about a good-looking guy?" Mina said. "Hey, did that sound as stupid to you as it did to me?"

"At least."

"You want to go inside now that the yelling's stopped?" Mina said.

"Let's wait a few minutes, so they don't know we heard them fighting."

We stared at the trees, we stared at the sky, we stared at the stars, we saw everything anyone could possibly see in the middle of the country in the dark. Including Mina's new red shoes.

"Where did you get those?"

"These? I found them."

"Between leaving the house tonight and now?"

"Pretty much. You like them? They're a little tight."

"But where did they come from?"

"Some careless woman sitting next to me at Cirk. She kicks off her shoes to get comfortable, I understand that, but you don't just let nice shoes like these float around. You've got to keep your eye on them."

"Didn't she have a matching purse?"

"I don't know, I . . . Listen, I wouldn't take her purse even if she had one. It's not like I'm a crook."

I stared at the stars some more.

"So, do you like them?"

"I like them, they're great with your dress."

"You're lucky you didn't lose your boots. I almost took them to teach you a lesson. You're too trusting."

"I'll remember that."

A few more minutes passed. Time for an innocent entrance.

"You stay here, Mina. I'll run in, ask about Abra, then we'll take off."

"Good plan."

I ran up the stairs. "Hello, ladies," I said, opening the door. I was going for gaiety, but missed the mark.

Lili was sitting on Margo's lap, her arms thrown around her neck, her head on Margo's shoulders as if she were a small child. Her eyes were red. Her cheeks were red. Margo's arms were around Lili's waist, and she wore the same red eyes as Lili and Angel. Looked like one of those relationship disasters that it takes a while to dig your way out of.

I pardoned myself for intruding, said I'd see Abra later. They told me they'd checked on her a few minutes ago—I knew it must have been longer than a few minutes—they said she was sound asleep, so was Joey, and that Lawless had taken care of Rory. They did not act embarrassed, and they invited me not to come back.

It would have been a five-minute walk down the hill to my house, but the drive home around back-country roads took ten minutes. I was glad to be home, even glad when Mina, wearing a different old T-shirt of mine, padded into the sewing room to go to sleep. The day had been an emotionally tossed lifetime. I skipped brushing my teeth, stepped out of my clothes, and collapsed on my bed beneath a window full of stars. I hugged my pillow to my face. Sleep found me before I remember closing my eyes.

〜

I'm in a small city. Black-and-white tiles in geometric designs cover my floor, centuries of gods stand outside my window. I see one god from my own land. This place is good, it's called by the name Pompeii.

I dress my woman. She's beautiful, and she's ready to leave. I hurry so she doesn't get angry. Her temper is quick. We walk past merchant stalls and public baths, chariot wheel ruts five inches deep slice the narrow roads. The smell is strong—humans, animals, and money—so strong, I put my scarf over my mouth and nose. We walk around a corner, men are drinking at a green marble bar.

We walk this way many times, up the same side street and into a business, a building that's a maze of rooms. Ceramic people chase each other across the walls—mosaics of people making love in ways I've never known, men with men, women together, men with animals, midgets with large women. People can buy complicated coupling here, but most don't. We walk down the center hallway to a small room with a stone pallet under a window. I need air. The pallet is covered with rich tapestry. The moisture of human need is heavy. I am hot.

The two women lie down on one of the pallets, one who works here and the one I belong to. Twice the woman who owns me asked for a man, but usually she asks for the same woman. Women don't come here for amusement,

*just men. But my woman is different, a kind of witch, I can't think of an-
other word, a master of primitive forces. She isn't denied much.*

*The two women love each other's bodies, and I have things to do for
them. I take a bottle of perfumed citrus oil and rub their feet. They are lan-
guid, they kiss. I rub oil on one woman's back when she turns away from
me. The oil smells clean, it's the only thing here that does.*

*I hear people in other rooms and I see them. No doors. Men rummage
women and their laughter is rough. The women stare at the painted ceilings
until the man is finished. Soon another man takes his place. I'm glad I
don't work here.*

*My owner and the small woman are different. They caress each other
slowly, by now they know the interiors of each other, the outsides of each
other. Sometimes one turns and kisses me when I stroke oil on a calf or
thigh. The first time I was surprised, but they are kind, there is affection.
They've finished the deep part of their love, the small woman lies in the
arms of the large woman. They laugh like young girls. This is when we
usually go home. But not today.*

*They ask for more oil, the citrus cools their skin, the one who owns me
asks me to lick the small one's skin. I look somewhere else. I'm on my side,
my owner kisses my breast, just lightly, but she does. I feel bad and good all
at once, but before I understand what's happening a large man, drunk,
walks by our room, pushes us aside, jumps on the pallet. He rapes the small
woman. It is fast and it is horrible.*

*My woman pulls up a loose stepping-stone and hits him over the head
until he's dead. A crowd gathers, they're afraid of the large woman, they
run outside. It's noisy, confusing. The business owner is angry, not with my
woman, but with the dead man. He drags his body into the street, chariots
run over him, it's a warning to other clients—mind your own business. The
owner gives the small woman to us. He doesn't want any more trouble, and
he doesn't want the large woman coming back and pestering him with
whatever gods she may know.*

*The small woman cries as we walk home. She'll live with us. I'm relieved
that we're not going back to the place of rough love that's not love at all.*

*Once I had a partner, a husband. He never rubbed oil on me, we just
loved each other. There were also two small children. I don't know about
those dark-skinned people of my blood, where they are. My mind turns
away from that life, it was taken from me, and I was born again to my present*

life. I don't know love here, but there's no cruelty. I thank my own god for that.

≋

I wake up, it's the middle of the night. I stare at the ceiling. No nymphs running across my textured Sheetrock. My bed is soft and wide, it's a Sealy Posturepedic straight out of the twenty-first century. I am in the United States of America, the Northern California sector. I am relieved. I hear Mina's voice inside my head, and my relief just about goes flying out the window. She's saying that love comes in all kinds of packages, one of her favorite lines.

I understand what Mina's talking about, I always have. I also understand that you rarely get to choose the love-package fate hands you. And that's the hard part.

Twelve

$\mathcal{J}$t wasn't quite dawn, but I was awake. The pounding on my door yanked me out of a solid sleep and a strange dream. My heart bumped, preparing me for tragedy. Good news arrives at a decent hour, bad news doesn't know how to tell time.

I pulled on my robe. My feet were cold on the bare floor, but I didn't bother finding my slippers. I wanted the pounding to stop, the one on my door and the one inside my chest.

I peeked through the peephole of my new door. Lawless. He looked as if death ran over him with a steamroller, then backed up, and ran over him again for good measure.

I opened the door, grabbed him by the arm, and pulled him inside. "Get in here, you look like hell. Is Abra all right?"

"She's fine."

I was on automatic, started to pour him a cup of coffee, of course there wasn't any, I started to brew some, and he stopped me.

"Bring me that bottle of Scotch," he said, pointing to my cabinet.

I looked at the clock.

Five o'clock. If he needed Scotch at 5:00 A.M., so would I. I got out two glasses and sat down with him.

He poured himself a stiff one, downing it in two large gulps.

"Margo's gone."

"Margo is gone?"

Lawless poured another. He'd been weeping, and I did him the favor of not noticing.

Lawless talked, his words a jagged piece of broken pottery that pierced my understanding, but the details didn't come through. I only understood one thing: He was there to tell me that Margo Spanger was dead.

I poured myself a tall glass, I saw no reason to remain sober. We studied our Scotch and looked deep into the amber liquid the way adults do in movies when they can't think of anything to say. I licked my lips, I observed the wavy grains in the table. I regarded the walls—they needed painting. I laid my head down on the table; my right cheek would take on a pine pattern. The world tilted at an angle. I cried. Not a wracking sob, but a stream of tears that ran down my face and formed a small pool beneath my eye. My nose was plugged, I couldn't breathe, and I lifted my head. Lawless sat stiff as a post.

I poured another drink. "How?" I asked.

"She was in the trapeze room late last night."

"No catcher?"

"I don't know what that is."

Lawless wasn't connecting with me. His only contact was with the Scotch at the bottom of his glass.

"Typical Margo behavior," I said, angry with her, although I didn't want to be. "Probably wanted to get something out of her system, and that meant being alone. When you're upset, you're a fall waiting to happen. You need someone—a catcher."

Lawless poured himself more Scotch. "The evidence refutes death due to a fall."

"What evidence?"

"A single .25 millimeter bullet to the back of her head."

Margo's death made no sense, none. The cause of her death made less sense.

"Where was she found?"

"On the floor in front of the net, facedown, the bullet in the back of her head." He took another pull of Scotch. "Something like this was bound to happen. The homeless women, her unstable circus employees."

"Lawless, they're not unstable. They live outside the box."

"I don't understand that kind of life."

"You're going to need me on this."

"The police are on it. I am now a private citizen."

"Right. Lawless, you're going to need me on this."

"Want to shove that bottle in this direction?"

"Not if you're driving anywhere," I said.

"I promise to pass out in your Barcalounger."

I pushed the bottle his way. I went cold. I swirled my drink in my glass, took another sip, and asked what I was afraid to ask.

"Rory?"

Lawless said, "He busted into Margo's last night, before her opening night performance, and acted like a jerk."

"I heard."

"When that happens, Margo and Lili don't press charges. Too many times the wife ends up paying for it. They called me, I'm already on the property, so I follow him. At some point, I'll edge him off the road." Lawless skipped the glass and drank straight from the bottle. "We'll have a chat about his behavior, we may even discuss his possible future.

"But my plans change. He's not heading home, he's driving to a house in the Heights, and I'm curious.

"He pulls into a long driveway that curves around the side of the house. He parks under some trees, probably so the neighbors don't notice, and I park next to the curb. He creeps around to the front, has a key to the door, and lets himself in. Obviously, this isn't a first visit. He's met by a woman in the doorway."

Another tug of Scotch.

"Judging from the shadows through the windows, I'd say he was going through the homeowner's very private portfolio."

"If Rory turns up dead," I said, "I am confessing in advance. I'm warning you because I want you to fix it so it looks like I'm innocent."

"Fine with me. Anyway, I expected to see him emerge all bright and chipper first thing in the morning, but I got the call about Margo and took off."

"You don't think Rory could have killed Margo, do you?"

"Possible. When I left, his car was no longer parked by the side of the house. That driveway either extended out the back of the property onto Alameda Road, or I dozed off for a few minutes and he drove off right under my nose."

"Does the house have a back door?"

"Big fancy house, probably has several back doors."

Something wasn't working. That included my brain, but it was something else, too.

"Back up," I said. "He's about to see some rich chick in the Heights. Why waste time going to Margo's office first and making a scene? It doesn't make sense."

"Makes absolute sense," he said. "Doesn't matter if a guy has ten girlfriends, Abra's still his wife. When it gets around town that she's left, it's ego-crushing. His best shot at appearing sane was to go to Margo's, pound on his chest, and insist they release his wife. They'd refuse, and he'd tell anyone who asked that Abra'd lost it, she was under the influence of *those crazy dykes,* and that she'd probably become one herself. Then he'd pull out the big guns and seek custody of his son."

Unfortunately, that seemed a likely scenario.

"But he *was* on the loose when Margo was killed," I said.

"He may have been." Lawless put his head in his hands. "Look, you and I both know that for every person who loved Margo, there were two people she'd pissed off in a major way. Some of them had enough money to buy her murder. Some were ex-employees and knew her habits."

"Late-night trapeze. She should have listened to Lili."

I told Lawless about the fight between Lili and Margo, told him about Angel running out of the office, told him about seeing the two women when they were all yelled out and cried out. He brushed it aside.

"Those three were like family, I've witnessed a few of their spats myself."

He asked me if I'd ever known a couple that didn't have a blowout once in a while. He reminded me that Lili and Margo were mates, not in the legal sense, but in every other. "Not all fights are disasters," he said. "Some of them just clear the air."

I agreed, told him the women were busy making up the last time I'd seen them, but that I thought I ought to mention the fight. Also, that it was bigger than a spat.

"Annie, what we've got here is an argument that will make Margo's death that much harder on Lili."

I'd already thought the same thing. "How's Lili holding up?"

"I have no idea, I couldn't find her. One of their pals whisked her away, I'm sure. That place is truly a zoo now—you wouldn't believe it."

I decided to switch from Scotch to tea.

"I don't want to sound like I'm obsessing," I said, "but I guess I am, so I might as well sound like it."

"Obsess away."

"I have never seen a rage," I said, "of the kind that made Rory tear this door apart. Never."

"Your vote is for Rory. It's noted, and I don't disagree. Or agree. Too soon. Everyone's a suspect unless they're dead."

"Hey, count me out."

"You know what I mean."

"I know what you mean."

The teapot hummed. I lied, said I was on antibiotics, said I shouldn't drink any more Scotch. I didn't figure Lawless for a tea drinker, and I didn't make coffee because I was afraid he'd join me. I didn't want him to perk up—I was planning a quick escape after he passed out.

"Kiddo," he said, "you and I, we need complete cooperation and trust on this one."

I felt like I was being made an honorary deputy sheriff.

"I *am* going to need you," he said, "and the cops are going to need me. They'll get you filtered through me. That's how we'll play this out. The person who killed Margo won't get away with it."

Complete trust. I could probably do that after I cleared up a few details.

"Anyone find the gun?" I said.

"Nope."

"Fingerprints in the practice room?"

"Not yet. And too soon for time of death."

"Well . . ."

"Well . . . we've got our work cut out for us."

He shambled over to the Barcalounger and passed out.

There's a difference between "passed out" and "asleep." You can shake a person who's passed out, and they rarely twitch or move. They might mumble, but then they're gone again. Drool is often involved. No drool, but Lawless was gone.

It was safe for me to make my move. I took off my robe, threw on a clean sweat suit and a pair of worn-out sneakers. My car keys and purse were next to the front door. I was going to pick up Abra, the detail before the complete trust thing happened.

Abra was not safe without Margo on patrol. And Lili would be in a devastated form of hiding that would barely allow her to take care of herself. None of the other women were safe, either. But my daughter was the only one whose husband knew where she was, the only one whose husband had caused a scene the previous night at the office. And she was the only person who belonged to me.

I woke up Mina. I told her not to crash around when she got up, not to wake up Lawless. She groaned and turned over.

"Are you going to remember this conversation?"

"If you don't leave me alone, I'm really going to be awake, then I'll crash into something and wake Lawless up. Not one more sound."

She rolled toward the wall in my sewing room, snoring before I closed the door.

Thirteen

I drove to Margo's office. No good. Crawling with cops. I backed out and pulled into the circus parking lot, to the far western corner. I eased between two redwoods, then edged in a little farther. It was tight, but my car was practically invisible. I found my flashlight in the glove compartment. My front door opened three inches before it hit a tree. I climbed into the backseat. I held my breath, sucked in my stomach, and squeezed out the rear door.

I walked through the forest, keeping the beam of light to a narrow circle in front of me. A person had been murdered in this place. I wished for the company of a large human, dog, or gun. I shouldn't have walked into this situation unarmed, but my urge to move was big. If I felt antsy when we crossed the state line, I could buy a gun at a truck stop in Nevada. Mine would probably be one of the few real IDs they'd see in a month of Sundays.

Three bunkhouses, and none of them Abra's. A chaotic clutter of women packing up and moving out wound through the moist grove. Turned out that most of those cops had come to rescue and relocate the women under the cover of night. I hoped it was not too late to grab Abra.

I wandered into that little ice-cold burbling creek and fell over Mina's stump. I'd found my daughter.

This time I didn't knock before I barged in. Abra sat on her cot. She looked like a foster kid wondering who her new parents would be. Joey was in her lap, sucking two fingers, asleep on his monkey.

There was one female cop across the room helping the women get organized. They were in disarray, some laughing nervously, some just plain nervous.

"Abra, get that quilt off the bed and pack anything else that's yours. Quick."

"You came!"

"Of course I came. No hugging, we'll hug in the car."

For one moment I thought about looking for Lili, offering our condolences, maybe even getting her out of there. But only for a moment—Lawless was right, one of their friends had rescued her from this nightmare, and with Rory on the loose, I wanted Abra out. Now. I grabbed Abra's purse and realized Angel was nowhere in sight and should have been.

"Where's Angel? I thought he was keeping an eye on you."

"I don't know. Things have gone crazy around here, and no one understands why."

"In the car."

"I've got to leave Angel a note so he knows I'm okay."

I pulled out a pen and wrote on the fitted sheet: *Angel—Left with Mom. Not abducted. Abra.*

I wondered if Angel would know what *abducted* meant. The guy was great-looking, but words larger than two syllables were a strain. Sometimes an uncomplicated man is a terrific relief.

We tramped through the woods, not tripping over one fallen tree or into one icy creek, until we reached the parking lot. I fired up the car, and we filled the gas tank at the last station in town. I hit the ATM, and we headed east.

One hundred miles sped by, and I turned south and changed freeways. I wasn't into talking, just putting miles under the tires. We blazed along, watched the sky turn red, then bright. We bought Joey a kid's breakfast and ourselves breakfast burritos and two black coffees.

More road went by, we were entering windmill and stockyard territory.

"Mom, we finished our coffee and Joey's smeared half his breakfast all over his car seat and you're so quiet. Could you please tell me what's going on?"

The words were stuck in my throat. I thought about all those euphemisms like *passed away, gone, passed over.* All those phrases that sugar-coat a permanent parting.

I said, "Margo's dead."

"Dead? That's not possible."

"She's dead, Abra." I put my hand on her leg.

"Heart attack? Maybe she was getting too old for the trapeze rush."

"She was murdered."

Her face went white. "Is that definite, or are you being dramatic?"

"A bullet hole in the head doesn't need dramatic effect from me."

"A bullet. And Lili?"

"We don't know where Lili is," I said. "I don't like the woman, but I hope she doesn't do something stupid and hurt herself."

"You mean kill herself."

"Yes, I guess that's what I mean."

Abra has a way of caving in that is almost supernatural. She climbs inside herself. Her bones recede, her clothes look too big. Maybe a stranger wouldn't notice these subtle changes. They never appear subtle to me.

"Angel said Lawless caught up with Rory last night," she said.

"Lawless followed Rory. Rory gave him the slip, he's still on the loose. This is why we're getting you out of here. There. I want you safe."

"Mom, we can't go to your house."

I hoped her brain had not also receded. She'd need it.

"Abra," I said, "look where we are. We've been driving five hours, there are cows, pigs, more cows, miles of stockyards. The air is so ripe it's about to split open. Joey keeps checking his pants to see if he needs to be changed."

"I thought maybe you were taking the long way around."

I was right. Her brain had indeed receded along with the rest of her, not that I blamed her, but her gray matter was definitely hiding out. I'd better keep that in mind.

"Sweetheart, if we were headed to my house by way of Bakersfield . . . I don't know, it's kind of like going to Vegas by way of Seattle."

I didn't want to tell her where we were going until we were far enough away from home that I was sure she wouldn't bolt. I wanted to leave bus stations behind us, and I was pretty sure Greyhound was one mode of transportation that hadn't filed Chapter 11.

"You aren't going to tell me where we're going, are you?"

"Not quite yet."

"Jesus, where are you taking me? Us?"

I said, "It's not that bad."

"That's hard to believe." She fumbled around in her purse. "You want a piece of gum?"

"What?"

"Gum, it's Blackjack. It calms my nerves."

"Licorice. A traditional Gypsy calming herb."

She crumpled up the wrapper and stuffed it in the ashtray. "That's kind of strange, isn't it?"

No denying blood or celebrating it. It just is. "Part of me is glad you have your grandma in you," I said. "It means you can do anything. The other part of me is unhappy about it because it means you *might* do anything."

She shrugged, she chewed her gum, and she looked at her reflection in the window. Joey woke up and said, "BOTT!" She gave him a bottle of juice, he was happy, then he was asleep. Abra watched the miles roll by.

"What are you thinking?" I said.

"I'm waiting until you're ready to talk."

"That's it?"

"That's it. I'm not going to jump out of this car onto the freeway."

She shook her head, smiled, unwrapped another piece of gum. The wad was getting larger.

"You're doing what you did when we were kids, looking for some coffee shop to drop a bomb. You knew we wouldn't throw a fit in public."

"Busted," I said. "Why didn't you?"

"Throw a fit? Maybe we felt sorry for you. Those outings were a lot harder on you than they were on us. We got hot fudge sundaes out of them."

I pulled off the highway in the town of Needles. It was not 107 degrees outside, that's the best thing you can say about Needles. I spotted the Li'l Dumplin' Cafe, it looked perfect—funky and clean. I'd already dropped two bombs. I'd told her Margo was dead, and I'd told her that Rory was unaccounted for. Two more to go.

"Come on, sweetie," Abra said to Joey, freeing him from his car seat. "You're the first in the next generation to experience the coffee shop newsflash. Get used to it."

Fourteen

She said, "I'm a fugitive because I married a jerk."

"That about sums it up."

"Before that I was in jail because I married a jerk. The same jerk."

"You were at Margo's. You weren't in jail."

"People in witness protection programs aren't in jail, but I bet they feel like they are."

"Yeah, you're probably right."

A neon clock with an old Chevy whizzing around the numbers was mounted on the cafe wall behind the counter. It tocked time between stacks of miniature boxed breakfast cereals and the orange juice machine. Our booth was near the cash register. The bench seats were aqua vinyl, one was split and repaired with duct tape curling at the edges. Teapots were stenciled above the yellowed pine wainscoting. A collection of waffle irons, stretching back through years of garage sales, was displayed in a spotless glass case. Nothing in the cafe matched, including the dishes.

We ordered Joey the traditional sundae, hold the hot fudge. We were, after all, trapped in the car with him. We didn't need to deal with caffeine on top of the sugar. We ordered iced tea and burgers, Joey ate our fries. We were splurging on American comfort food.

"You called Rory a jerk," I said. "You know he was, or is, a jerk?"

"I've known, but I didn't know what to do about it. I've been, you know, numb. I guess I still am," she said. "I *am* clear about this— I don't want him to find me."

Her brain was back on duty. Phew.

"Abra, this whole thing . . . *I'm* disoriented. I can't imagine how you must feel."

"Worried, scared. I don't know how I'm going to take care of us. I don't have any money, then I remember I have credit cards, then I remember he gets the bills, and he's probably canceled the cards by now."

"You don't have one card in your own name?"

"They all have my name on them."

"I mean an account that's just in your name."

"No."

I took out a credit card and handed it to her. "There's no balance on this. It's yours. I'll change the name when I get home. You've got to have your own money."

"Even if my own money is yours."

"That's temporary. I'm not worried about you taking care of yourself. I know you can do it."

She sipped her iced tea. "I hate the idea of divorce. I didn't want my kid to grow up without a dad."

"Not the same way you did."

"I didn't mean it to sound that way."

"It's okay. I didn't want you to grow up without a dad, either. You're making the choice to leave—you have more faith in yourself than you know. I didn't have a choice. Raising you without a dad just happened."

The waitress leaned in and refilled our glasses. Then she leaned in farther, sat down next to Abra, and lit up a cigarette. "Let me tell you something, honey," she said. "There are worse things than being raised up without a daddy. When I was a kid I wished mine was dead almost every night."

We sipped our tea in semi-stunned silence.

"See that guy wiping up the counter?" the waitress said. "Roy?"

We both looked in his direction. Roy was tall and homely. He wore a tooled-leather belt with a silver buckle large enough to pick up television stations on Mars—stand too close to one of those things, and your metal fillings start talking to you. Looked like it'd take a lot to shake Roy's pleasant grin.

"I married that man as soon as I was big enough," our waitress told us. "He isn't much to look at, but he's nuts about me. You get hooked up again, find one who adores you. It makes up for a lot of shortcomings."

She waved and winked at Roy, his grin broadening to a smile that barely cleared his cheeks.

"You want anything else?"

"Maybe," I said.

"Holler when you're ready for the check."

She wiped tables, Roy came out from behind the counter, whapped her on the behind with his rag, and she gave him a playful shove.

"The waitress is right, Abra. Don't go for another guy unless he adores you. Completely."

She sucked the last of her iced tea from the bottom of the glass, and our waitress came over and poured her a refill.

Abra looked at me through those ballistic black eyelashes that had allowed her to escape half her homework and household chores since the third grade.

"We're about to cross the state line," she said.

"I hope so."

"And you're driving me. How do you know I didn't do it?"

There went her brain again. "What are we talking about?"

"Margo. It could have been me."

"Stop it."

"I'm serious."

"What's your motive?"

"You're kidding, right? My husband gets into a big fight with the woman who rescued me, I try to calm him down, he slams me up against a wall, she gets in the middle and tries to stop him. I get ticked off, defend him, and shoot her when she threatens to call Lawless."

"If you killed Margo, you'd better tell me right now so I can pay this bill and we can get the hell out of here and across that state line."

"I just figured it was my turn to do the coffee shop detonation."

"At least you're acting like yourself again. I mean your old, old self. I'd started to forget who you were, too."

We gathered up Joey, cleaned lunch off him, found the restrooms, and paid the bill. Our waitress got in a few more words of advice. The advice involved RVs, Vegas, sex, nighties, and Astro Turf. We hit the road before I laid any more bad news on Abra. I figured Joey deserved an emotionally clean sundae.

The miles wavered by. Even in the winter, desert roads shimmy between the sand and low salt hills.

Abra punched radio buttons, and we listened to a particularly entertaining newstalk host. He screamed at everyone, and we screamed back at him. We lost him—too bad—we were left with static. Abra flipped the radio off.

I caught her face in the side-view mirror. She looked happy, but suddenly she crashed. "You said Lawless lost Rory while he was following him. What happened? Exactly."

Damn. I'd decided we could avoid this until, I don't know, until much later. I was getting sick of talking about her rotten and hopefully soon-to-be-ex-spouse, but she needed to do it, and I was trapped, in more ways than one, so I needed to do it with her.

"After the big scene at the office," I said, "Lawless wanted to follow Rory, do a little road therapy, talk to him about proper behavior, maybe get a little physical if necessary. But Rory didn't head home. And Lawless followed him."

"Where'd he go?"

"Somewhere in the Heights."

"Where in the Heights?"

"Some place on Piedras Negras, the part that backs onto Alameda."

Abra did not recede. She stared ahead as if her mind was simply one more straight line on this empty road.

"What?" I said. "What's that look?"

"Suzanne's house."

"Do I know Suzanne?"

"The maid of honor at my wedding."

"THAT Suzanne? Suzanne who you've known since kindergarten? Suzanne who slept in the top bunkbed on weekends?" Here was the complete and positive last, the very last, straw. "My God, that's a smack in the face. What a bitch! Hey, did I say that or just think it?"

"You said it."

"I was afraid of that."

This drive was not helping my grip on the difference between my thoughts, my words, the sky, or any other piece of the planet. If this is what being one with the universe is, you can have it—I'd hate to think that some corner of enlightenment involves saying whatever pops into your head. Unless it turns into a bubble, or a bird, and flies away. I turned the radio back on. Static made more sense than I did.

Abra looked over at me. "Don't worry. You didn't say whatever you were running down in your head right then."

"My mind was totally blank," I lied. "How'd Suzanne end up in the Heights? Divorce with a big settlement?"

"Hardly. Her parents are aging trust fund babies."

"What? They were so funky—Birkenstocks, junk all over their yard, windows crooked, and a few cracked. They even had a pot-belly pig wandering in and out."

"And two kids in private school, private art lessons, music lessons, two new Volvos. Didn't you ever wonder how they supported all that with a houseplant business?"

"No. I've always believed there's a secret regarding money that some people know and I don't. I thought they knew the secret."

"The secret, in this case, is being born to money. Anyway, Suzanne's a trust fund grandchild, and Grandma bought her the house. Suzanne has stacks of dough—she probably doesn't even know what she's got—and someday she'll have more."

"Someone will be happy to find her money for her."

"Apparently Rory would."

"Did you have any idea this was going on?"

"I suspected something was going on with someone. I assumed it was something most wives go through."

"God, I raised you with these twisted ideas that arose from a vacuum. Believe me, most wives do not have to worry about it." I didn't know if that was true, but it sounded good and like it ought to be true.

Abra looked at me as if she couldn't believe how naive I was. Well, she'd been married as long as I had. Add both our marital experiences together, and it wasn't much.

"But I had no idea it was Suzanne," she said. "How do you have lunch with a friend while you're sleeping with her husband?"

"I don't know, honey. It stinks."

"Damned right it does." She was working herself into righteous anger—a good sign, and a good opening for what she needed to know.

"Abra, his car was parked outside Suzanne's that evening. But when Lawless got the call about Margo, Rory's car was gone."

I let that sink in. I didn't want to get into the obvious implications unless she went there on her own. Rat or un-rat, he was still the father of her son.

"His style is to blow off steam," she said, "simmer down, turn on the charm and act like nothing happened. I can't imagine him committing murder."

"It might take a while, but Lawless and I are determined to find the person who killed Margo. No matter who it was or why they did it. For your sake I hope it wasn't Rory."

"And for Joey's."

Abra looked down in her lap, up at the sky, looked back at Joey, saw her own face in the passenger window. She laid the seat back.

"You mind if I take a nap? I'm so tired."

"I'm good to go. You sleep."

I wasn't good to go, I was beat, I could have used a break. I pulled into a drive-through, bought a large black coffee, and prepared to keep driving until there was nowhere left to drive.

She sat up, looked at me, and said, "Unless you need a break, wake me up when we get to Jack's house."

"Did I say anything about going to Jack's?"

"How many people do we trust who live in the middle of nowhere? How many people do we *know* in the middle of nowhere?"

I didn't understand why she'd gotten such rotten grades in school. I should have pushed her harder. Maybe she was getting smarter with age. As for me, I felt my brainpower decreasing over time. Occasionally I imagined my poor brain cells leaking out my ears while I slept, blissfully unaware that my IQ was ruining my sheets. In that case, sitting with Roy at the L'il Dumplin' would someday be like dining with Albert Einstein.

Fifteen

*W*hen we hit the epicenter of nowhere, and drove another two miles up a dirt road, I spotted twinkling white lights. Small stars fallen to the earth like fish out of water, the lights ran around the rim of Jack's roof. A five-foot Virgin of Guadalupe stood illuminated by a single light strung to a post and jammed into the dirt. If there were any colors missing from the virgin's robes, I didn't see them. In his side yard were inventions. According to Jack, the three square miles around his home were one of the few places on earth where lifeforms could travel between time and universes. An energy node, a hole in the sky. The inventions were built to ease the transition between worlds. Maybe bringing Abra here wasn't such a good idea.

Two reservation dogs greeted us. The yellow one cowered next to the car and peed in the dirt. A black-and-tan dog jumped up and down as if it were wearing springs.

Joey woke up whining. The black dog jumped into the car and licked him. Then Joey started screaming. Abra woke up bitchy, mumbling something like *I can't believe you've taken us somewhere to be eaten by wild dogs*. I knew she was mostly asleep, but I was not enjoying myself, either. When I reached inside the car to rescue Joey, I stepped in the wet dog spot.

At that moment, Jack opened his front door. The porch light sculpted his face into the mask of a stoned angel. Abra snapped to, jumped out of the car, ran up the steps, and threw her arms around him. My kids weren't crazy about the place he lived—during visits they were bored in two days, then they were hell to be around, which is why our trips to his house had been scarce—but they were crazy about him.

When I saw Jack, my heart ached. The memories of my dad were about the same age as Jack. Blue eyes—no green, no hazel—as blue as the world's deepest lakes. He was tan, his sandy blond hair flecked with gray. White filled the creases of his laugh wrinkles. If it were the era of cowboy movies, Jack would be a star, he'd be Dad all over—the rugged man who ran off the outlaws just when they were about to torch you and the farm and the collie dog.

He said to me, "Sweetheart, I thought you were coming two days ago, I was getting worried."

"I just called you yesterday."

"Yesterday? Are you sure?" He scratched his head. "What's today?"

"Today? I don't . . . Never mind. We're here."

Another reason Jack should have been in the movies. The man needed a full-time scriptwriter—at least part of his dialogue would make sense. Those deep blue eyes could only hide the real Jack for a few minutes. I wasn't sure if there was anyone home, or if, there in the desert, he'd found an inner peace usually reserved for short Buddhist monks who write bestsellers. Whatever the cause, he wore space all over his face like it was a born-again religion, and he was too busy enjoying life to sit down and write a bestseller.

I'd phoned Jack before I'd left California, didn't explain, just said I needed to hide Abra. He didn't ask questions—"Come ahead!"—was all he said. Not much dimmed his hospitality or whetted his curiosity.

We laid Joey on the couch and changed him. He curled up and went to sleep, Jack rubbing his back. We gave Jack the details and he was with us. I almost felt guilty for thinking he was empty inside.

"What do we do about Rory?" Abra asked. "I need to go home sometime."

He patted her. "When I know he's in the clear concerning Margo's death, when he calms down and gets a new life that doesn't involve bothering you or your mom . . ."

"That could be a long time."

"Oh, I don't think so."

"I hope you're right."

"Then you'll go home—and you're keeping your options open—home might be someplace new. If it's Sonoma County, then I escort you and tell Rory to stay away from you." Jack patted her leg. "I'll probably threaten to kill him."

Abra said, "You can't go around threatening to kill people."

"Sure you can, honey," he said. "And if he touches you again, it's not a threat. It's a warning. The outcome is up to him."

There were Buddhas and flowers, photos of rock art and a fountain inside. The house was peaceful, and it smelled like piñon.

"I feel like I'm watching a movie," Abra said, "but it's not a movie. It's my life, and I can't get up and leave."

"Who'd want to leave?" he said. "The movie is LIFE. It's not sanitary and it's not tidy, it is glory, it is chaos. Isn't that great?" He smiled his one-hundred-watt smile.

It was a good time to head for bed, and that's what I did.

When I awoke Abra was asleep in the twin bed next to mine, and I hadn't slept long.

Deep in the desert, even winter light is strong and unfiltered. The sky was a muffled blue that rode above the deep orange-and-red bluffs. The adobe walls were whitewashed and clean, the milky silence was calm and reassuring.

I smelled coffee. Jack.

"You didn't have to wake up," I said. "I could have made coffee."

"I'm always up before dawn. I get two, maybe three hours of sleep. Tops."

"How do you do that?"

"Long ago I realized if sleep was so exciting, you wouldn't be able to sleep through it." He shrugged. "So I cut back."

"Jack, this is the kind of thing that makes me question your sanity. Mine, too, because I understand you."

I sipped my coffee, watched the bluffs glow early orange. A sudden movement caught my eye. My breath was pulled out of my chest, and I soared with a red-tailed hawk to the top of the nearest mesa.

"God, this is incredible. It looks like the place Thelma and Louise decided to take their final dive off the edge of the earth."

Jack beamed. "It is. And isn't this a great place to die? Those women had it together. It's one of the reasons I love this place."

"What the hell difference does it make where you die, and why do you want to live where it's a good place to die, assuming there is such a thing?"

"I don't know." He studied his seven-grain cereal. "I really don't know, maybe the last thing we see is important. New babies imprint on their mothers, maybe the place you die imprints you for what's next. And this is a fine next for me."

"You are a nut."

"That's why I live out here. It takes a lot of room to be me."

In the full light of day, he looked like my dad. But the resemblance was only skin-deep. This kind of talk would have gotten Jack several days of hard chores that would have assured him a solid eight hours of sleep.

I collected my purse and my coat. Abra shuffled into the room. When I hugged her she smelled like piñon smoke, and it was a good smell. I tried to push cash on Jack. He pushed it back.

"This is my family. You're all welcome to what I've got, and I've got plenty."

His idea of plenty might be two days of canned vegetarian chili. I stuffed money in Abra's pocket when Jack wasn't looking, and she had the credit card I'd given her. At least they would eat.

"Abra, call me when you want. Work on remembering how to breathe. Jack will take good care of you and Joey." I said, "In another week Joey will be able to outwit him."

I winked at Jack in case he thought I was serious. I wasn't. It'd be at least a month before Joey could outthink Jack.

I walked down the gravel drive, past the plaster Our Lady of Jack's Yard. I opened the car door and turned to wave good-bye. Abra had crawled under Jack's arm, and he was holding Joey. They waved good-bye from the doorway. For one split second I wanted to leave everything I owned behind, physically and spiritually, and stay right there with my family.

It's not just body chemistry and nucleotides that bind us as related. It's the double helix of shared history and family myths. My family was off-center, but they were good people and I belonged to them. Abra ran to the car and stuck her head in the window.

"Thanks for bringing me here. It was a long haul, and I didn't help."

"Hey, you know I'm an old road warrior. You worry about you."

The warrior was beat all to hell and back, but this part was tidied up. Now on to the less emotionally exhausting part: discovering who had the nerve to kill Margo, a woman who, as far as I was concerned, deserved to be honored in plaster and vibrant colors every bit as much as Ms. Virgin de Guadalupe.

Sixteen

"I can't believe you did something so irresponsible."

"Lawless, are you finished reading me the riot act? Because I stopped paying attention two first downs ago." Another touchdown. The crowd cheered me across the desert.

"Are you listening to sports?"

"See what you've driven me to? I'm listening to eleventh-graders whomp each other on a playing field two states away just so I don't have to hear you."

"What was I saying?"

"I told you I had Abra safely stashed, that I was heading home, and you told me I was irresponsible. Plus a lot of other stuff that I tuned out."

"Everyone around here is disappearing, and I'm nervous. When you and Abra disappeared . . ."

"I left a note."

"Where?"

"On Abra's sheet. It was written to Angel."

"Directly on the sheet?"

"I was in a hurry."

"Gee, I can't believe I didn't find it."

"I said I was in a hurry."

"I thought we agreed to trust each other. That means confide in each other, not wait until one passes out while the other sneaks away."

"Okay, okay. Trust each other."

"Just be here for the funeral. The killer will be at the funeral."

"Do you know who did it?"

"No. But they always show up at the service."

"Lawless, get real. Do you know how large this funeral will be?"

There was silence that crackled through the pass just before Bumble Bee Junction. I held the cell phone connection open.

"Did you hear me?" I said.

"The number of people at Margo's funeral. I hadn't thought of that."

"Is something wrong with you? You sound like you've gone off the deep end. And don't blame it on me."

"I am staying at your house"—he dropped a heavy pause and half an octave—"guarding Mina."

He was bordering on Mina-induced hysteria. That's what was wrong.

"I understand perfectly. I've spent many years in her presence."

"But she wasn't hitting on you."

"You're one up on me there. Lawless, as we speak, I am trundling home at a little less than the speed of light. When I arrive I'll defuse Mina."

"Good, because she's ready to go off."

I thought about the years this tough guy had been in Homicide and about Mina driving him to the brink of lunacy in a very short period of time. It made me feel pretty good about myself. I'd put up with her for ages and hadn't cracked.

"She's hitting on you hard, huh?"

"Both fists, left and right. I actually thought about calling my wife and asking her to rescue me, but you know how women are. First Mina and Ruth start talking, then they get chummy, they're good friends, and then they start laughing about me."

"Get a grip," I said. "Let me know what you've found out. Other than what a stud you are."

"I told you—people are disappearing. That's not quite true. One has never reappeared."

"Lili?"

"Right."

"Angel?"

"He's just shown up, I was hoping he and Lili were together."

"So was I."

"He hasn't seen her. He took to the ocean, sort of buried himself in a sleeping bag for two days."

Here was that question I hated to ask because I didn't want the answer. "What about Rory?"

"We found him."

"Still at the top of your list of suspects in Margo's death?"

"Nope. He has an alibi. He left the house in the Heights around the back, just as we'd discussed, while I was sitting there watching the front."

"That's when he could have gone to Margo's and killed her."

"I would love to pin it on him, real satisfying. But the guy's in the clear."

"Convince me."

"I questioned the young woman in the fancy home, the girlfriend. Seems she was putting an end to the affair, her parents didn't trust the guy. She told me she knew he was married, said her parents didn't, or they really would have had a fit."

"Having a fit doesn't begin to describe it."

I told Lawless about the many weekends sweet Suzanne had spent eating popcorn in my family room, watching MTV until 2:00 A.M., eating refined sugar products and doing other things that weren't allowed in her PC household. I told him about the wedding.

"She was your daughter's maid of honor? Wow."

"Too bad her parents interfered—Suzanne and Rory deserve each other."

"Mommy and Daddy's visit was just before I arrived, the night of the murder. They told her to choose between the guy they'd never met but didn't trust, or Grandma's dough. It wasn't a difficult choice. That night she gave him the heave-ho."

"He left quietly?"

"Hard to believe, but that's what she said. And yeah, he knew I was tailing him. The guy's not stupid, plus he has eyes in the back of his head. Makes me think he's developed them out of necessity."

"I'm sure he has."

"Anyway, that driveway curves to the back and dumps right onto Alameda Road. He didn't head to Margo's and do her in. He was drowning his sorrow in booze and women over at Juanita's."

"Juanita's?"

"You think the place is too seedy for him? You don't get it. The guy may wear three-hundred-dollar shoes, but he is trash."

"Did some other seedy person in expensive clothes spot him there?"

"We placed him there through credit card activity. He charged enough at Juanita's to party hard all night long"—he cleared his throat—"and a couple of witnesses swear he was busy with them."

"He knows how to turn on the charm. Someone at Juanita's could have run up his card to protect him."

"I know, but Juanita remembers him being there, too. She knows him—he's a regular—and she wouldn't lie to me in order to protect him. She's into protecting her business."

This wasn't a lot worse than what I already knew about Rory. What could be worse than the abuse, the affair with the best friend? But it made me feel hard, as if I'd suddenly grown armor.

"He didn't get off at Suzanne's," I said, "so he went to Juanita's and really got off. Like with more than one woman."

"Annie, if Abra were my daughter, I'd gently suggest she get tested for STDs."

"How do I gently suggest that?"

"Got me."

I wanted a three-week vacation from my life. I didn't know how, but I knew if I left, everything would be cleared up by the time I returned. I considered driving to the airport. I was tired of feeling as if the world were going to fall apart if I didn't stand on it. I thought about Jack on the edge of nowhere. For the first time I un-
,derstood his desire to be there. And, for the first time, it seemed absolutely sane, and so did he. Maybe I'd ask Jack to mention the STD thing. He could work it, enthusiastically, into his *life is chaos* spiel.

"Annie, are you there? You're breaking up."

"Breaking up, cracking up, all of it."

"What?"

"Nothing. Damn. I'm being followed."

"You're bringing flowers? Don't bother."

"I can't hear you."

I was, indeed, being followed, by a car with red-and-blue flashing lights.

I looked at my speedometer.

One hundred and seven miles per hour. Approximately.

I pulled over, and I turned off the cell phone. There wasn't one soul I wanted to speak with after I'd finished sweet-talking my way out of a ticket and a whopping fine. Maybe I'd get lucky and they'd throw me in jail for the night. Peace, quiet, and instant mashed potatoes.

Seventeen

When I pulled into my driveway I saw Lawless's Chevy out front. It was a good time to collect the grief he had waiting for me. I was too tired to care. I walked inside. He was waiting on my couch, his arms folded across his chest. I hoped it wouldn't take long.

"You made it home in record time," Lawless said.

"I would have been here sooner if I hadn't been followed."

"What!"

"I told you on the phone that I was being followed."

"I thought you said you were bringing flowers. To the funeral. Who followed you?"

"Some highway patrol guy with blond hair on his arms."

"Why was he following you?"

"He said I was driving too fast."

"How too fast?"

"One hundred and ten miles per hour. Actually my speedometer said 107."

"Your speedometer is off. I hope you're going to fight it."

"You think I should?"

"Why aren't you in jail?"

"Can you talk without yelling?"

"Yes."

"You'll like this," I said to him. "The guy with blond hair on his arms was following me at my exact speed. He pulled me over and told me how fast I was driving. When he leaned in the window, I leaned toward him and stroked his arm and told him that he should watch his speed—driving so fast was dangerous."

"You did not."

"I did. The patrolman laughed. Then he radioed somewhere to make sure the car wasn't stolen, came back and told me that every highway patrolman throughout Nevada had my plate numbers and that he'd let me go, but no more speeding. I kept it down to eighty-five, and here I am. I should have been home two hours ago."

"You would have been a terrific con man."

"I know. Unfortunately, I was raised in the Baptist church, and con men were frowned upon unless they were clearly sponsored by God and highly successful. I never had that much ambition . . . I think listening to seventeen hours of newstalk radio has permanently warped my mind."

"Don't worry. It was bent to begin with."

I looked around the house. All was quiet. "Mina tired of you already?"

"She found new prey."

Lawless stood, opened the back door, and pointed to Mina, her hands on her hips and her head tossed back in careless abandon. Her girlish laugh filled the air. A man scooted out from under her trailer. He wore a T-shirt and jeans. His jeans, when hoisted up, were still halfway down his butt. When he turned to climb the trailer steps, Mina was one step behind him ogling the view.

"Who is that man?"

"I was saved by the plumber."

I patted Lawless on the chest. "Lucky you." Then I remembered we had a funeral to attend, and it was that day, not the next. "What's the plan for this afternoon?"

"I go home and get changed. I come back in three hours with Ruth, and we pick you up."

"It's in three hours?"

"No, but I want to get there early. You're right, there will be loads of people. I don't relish waiting in line to get into a funeral," he said. "You must be tired. Sure you're up to this?"

"Are you kidding? I gooed all over a uniformed guy with hairy arms so I'd make the service." I'd lost a day somewhere. Probably when it turned dark and the few radio personalities I could get told me I was going to hell. Which reminded me—"Any sign of Lili yet?"

"Nope."

"Any thoughts?"

"If she's not at the funeral, we call out the dogs."

"I thought you already did that," I said.

"She hasn't been gone long enough for the big dogs. If she's a no-show this afternoon, we try for attention."

"Any of her belongings missing?"

"We've been concentrating on Margo's murder, not on Lili. Choosing between investigating a murder and a missing person is a no-brainer."

"Unless they're connected. Which is starting to seem likely."

"It's too early to consider that as likely."

"Lili could have shot Margo and split."

"That's not possible."

"Of course it's possible."

"All right, it's possible," Lawless said, but I knew he didn't think it was possible. "I'm more concerned about Lili as a victim than a suspect."

"I know. But we, you, need to keep an open mind."

"You're one to talk. You don't even like Lili."

"What gave you that idea?"

"You called her a short neo-Nazi."

"I admit, that doesn't sound great, but Lili was a little scary."

"*Was* scary?"

"You know what I mean."

"I know you used past tense when speaking about Lili. Don't talk with the cops in terms of past tense when it comes to Lili."

"The cops? Why would I talk to them about Lili at all?"

"You and Margo were close friends, you're a single woman—someone might come to the wrong conclusion about your relationship."

"You're crazy."

"Really? People, including me, have heard you make derogatory remarks about Lili. You're known to own firearms, have been known, on occasion, to use them. You and Margo were close. And you were one of the last people who saw them both alive."

"Did Mina feed you hallucinatory plants?"

"For a smart woman you can be very dense," he said. "I'm telling you to mind what you say about Lili until she turns up. And how you say it."

Lawless was scared and nervous. I didn't like it. "You really think something happened to Lili?"

"I don't know," he said. "If whoever killed Margo was a threat to Lili, she may be hiding out. Lili may have been kidnapped, or she may have harmed herself. She may have been murdered at the scene of Margo's murder and her body removed. There are many scenarios, and every one of them works. At this point, give the police the smallest fragment of evidence, or a phrase wrongly turned, and that's the trail they'll follow."

"I'll try to keep a lid on it."

"Trying isn't good enough. Do it."

"Okay."

I would do as he suggested, speak only when spoken to and be polite. It wouldn't be easy.

Lawless looked at his watch. "I am going to be back here in exactly three hours to pick you up for Margo's service. Wear something conservative. I hope you own something conservative."

He skittered out, cutting a wide swath around Mina.

She looked up and waved to him. "Good-bye, Lawless. Thanks for the great night!"

Lawless fell all over himself getting his engine started and his wheels moving. When he returned, he'd have his wife for protection.

I ambled over to Mina and inspected the man under the trailer. All I saw were Vibram soles.

"Why did you say that to Lawless?" I asked her. "He's already scared to death of you."

"I'm trying to make the plumber jealous."

"I thought you had a business relationship."

"He talks to me about his stress. When the stress deals with

intimate human things like plumbing, it's not unusual for a romantic relationship to develop."

"Is he good-looking? I've only seen his butt."

"Then you've seen his best feature," Mina said, winking at me.
"Frank has a great sense of humor. Look at this."

She held my hand and walked me around to the trailer's front
door. He had tacked a sign on it. The sign read, IF THIS TRAILER'S
ROCKIN', DON'T COME KNOCKIN'.

"Mina, if the man makes you laugh, I'm all for it. He's not moving in, is he?"

"God, I hope not."

So did I, but give a man with tools a project, and sometimes he
starts feeling territorial.

"You coming to the funeral?" I asked her.

"Not a chance. I got pregnant at one funeral, and someone
dropped dead at the last one," she said. "Did I tell you about that?
Pretty convenient, it ended up being two for the price of one. Still,
it was a shock. I'm taking a vacation from funerals."

I turned toward my house, and she called my name.

"Don't go inside yet," Mina said. "I've got something to tell
you."

"What?"

"Come over here so I'm not yelling this all over the place."

I did what I was told.

"Pretty soon," she said, "you're going to have company."

"Lawless and Ruth. They're picking me up."

"Before that."

"Who?"

"Lawless hired Angel to protect you. He's moving here until
they find Margo's killer."

"Oh no, he's not."

"He already has some stuff here, and I couldn't kick him out.
He's too nice to look at."

"What was Lawless thinking?"

"That the dead person was your neighbor, mine, too, and that we
might have seen something we don't know we saw. Or we might
not have seen something that the killer thinks we saw."

"I guess that makes sense."

"Also, Lawless said that, from what he's seen, you and Angel get along okay. That you're not as crabby when Angel's around."

"What did you say?"

"Give me some credit," she said. "I laughed and told him he was mistaken, that you were crabby with everyone."

Eighteen

I showered, but I did not nap. Once my eyes closed, I figured I was in for a solid twenty hours. Maybe someday I would achieve enlightenment, or blankhood, and require only three hours of sleep per day.

I threw on my old terry cloth robe, blow-dried my hair, and put on makeup. I sorted through clothes and tried to choose something for the funeral. Margo wouldn't have cared if I'd worn my robe, but Lawless would care, and he was my ride.

I owned black, but only small sexy black dresses that didn't fit anymore. Red wouldn't work, maybe dark red, but I really wasn't up to wearing any kind of red. I needed something restful. I found a middle blue dress, pretty conservative, except for the plunging neckline. I could wrap a silk scarf around my neck. I never thought I'd be old enough to own scarves, never mind wear them, but they come in handy. I wondered if my mother had thought the same thing about her scarves. The dress was the color of Margo's eyes.

I wore tights to keep my legs warm and pulled my dark green wool cape out of a dry cleaner's bag.

I realized I hadn't called Jack and thought I'd better so they wouldn't worry about me. No answer. He now had an answering machine, a modern leap into technology for Jack, and the recorded message was that of Abra and Jack singing together. Off-key and full of fun, it sounded like they were having a good time. Abra had probably dragged him to Target for some basic necessities, and that would include an answering machine. I hoped she had charged it and that Jack wasn't shelling out money to fulfill his role of indulgent uncle.

I left a perky message, said I was fine and dandy, told them I had charmed a cop out of a speeding ticket. A beep cut me off, and I hung up. I wondered where they were and what they were doing. I started to worry—Jack's car looked like a breakdown waiting to happen, it was held together with baling wire and chewing gum, but he'd had it longer than anything or anyone. It was a powder blue Dodge Dart 1963 wagon that had belonged to our aunt, and it stubbornly refused to die. Our aunt hadn't been nearly as stubborn as her car.

I threw the cape around my shoulders and went outside to wait for Lawless. Mina trundled out of her trailer pink-cheeked, the plumber right behind her. She motioned for him to go back inside the trailer. He did as he was told. Mina had found herself a well-behaved spaniel. This wouldn't last long.

I said, "Are you falling in love?"

"No, but Frank may be. He's clingy, and that I don't need. I'm looking for amusement, not a permanent fixture."

"Seems wise."

"Hard to believe coming from me, isn't it? Maybe I've had enough permanent fixtures in my life," she said. "Hey, how did Abra settle in at Jack's?"

"She was mad when we got there, and she was happy when I left."

"Your brother has the kind of spirit that does not accept darkness of any kind. Does he still have that trick dog of your father's that someone stuffed?"

"Bullet is now an end table next to the couch."

"Wait a minute," Mina said. "I'm trying to picture that."

"Jack saddled him up, poured resin in the curve and, voilà, an end table."

"He's a clever man. How come he never has a permanent woman?"

"Because he has a long string of temporary ones. And somehow he remains friends with all of them."

"The right woman will come along. He attracts manipulative

women who want to tie him up. Then he's not beautiful anymore, and they don't want him. He needs a person like himself, someone who glides on the air so they can fly together. A nice Aquarian woman."

Mina was exactly right.

"Okay, I'm going back into my house," she said. "I've recovered enough to give the plumber his healing session."

I looked at my watch, fifteen minutes until Lawless. I sat on the porch swing and pulled out the mystery I was reading, an old Robert B. Parker. It seemed macabre to read a book about murder on that particular day, but it was my third time through *Rachel Wallace,* and it was like visiting an old friend.

A beige Ford Taurus pulled in. Looked like the kind of family car Lawless would own. Angel stepped out.

As always, he was gorgeous. Part of his charm was that he performed none of the poses handsome men are prone to, no deep looks, no raised eyebrows. No waiting for the swoon or pant.

I patted the seat of the porch swing, he sat next to me. "Did Lawless tell you he asked me to keep an eye on you?"

I laid my book down, its spine pointing straight up. I considered Angel. "Mina told me. At first I was horrified, but Lawless is right," I said, "I need you. How is this for you?"

"Fine. I'll take the couch."

He picked up the book I was reading. "Mystery?"

"I don't like heavy books. Characters who wander aimlessly through chapters that are barren landscapes screwed up by unhappy childhoods. Who needs it? Where do you want to focus? That's the point. Do you read?"

"I'm making you nervous, maybe this won't work."

I picked up my book, fiddled with the cover. "We're both adults and sometimes we have to act mature—unfortunate, but true. Let's not get complicated, and let's remember we like each other."

We had a pretty good rock going on the porch swing.

I said to him, "Lawless will be here any minute. You riding with us?"

"No, I'm going by myself," Angel said. "The funeral doesn't start for more than an hour, and it's just over the hill."

"Lawless wants to get in before the crowd arrives."

"I'd hoped we'd have time to talk, really talk, before he got here."

"He's not here yet. Talk."

He crossed his leg and looked at the sole of his left boot and stuck his finger in a small hole growing between the layered leather.

"That fight you saw in the office, the night of Margo's death."

"I didn't know you'd seen me. You were wiped out."

"I hate fights, any kind of fights."

"Lawless told me it wasn't unusual for the three of you to have it out, that you were like family."

"The fight was brutal. Some things were said . . . I don't know if the words could have been taken back."

"What kind of things?"

"Things that were hard on Margo and Lili's relationship."

"A breakup?"

"That could never happen."

"I'm not so sure."

"They were soulmates, and sometimes soulmates are the hardest people to live with. So many lives together, so many unresolved problems."

I made a mental note to myself: Never sit alone in a room with Angel, Jack, and Mina. If at all possible, keep the three from ever being in the same room at the same time.

"Let's stick to one problem per lifetime," I said. "What was the fight about?"

Just then, like a bad clock, a Lincoln Town Car pulled in. Lawless and Ruth.

"We'll finish this at the funeral," Angel said. "There's someone I want you to meet—he'll be there."

"Okay. I cannot believe Lawless has a Lincoln."

"I'd say it's ten years old," Angel said. "It's not a big deal. You aren't curious?"

"About a Lincoln? Now that I know it's not new, no."

"I mean about the person I want you to meet."

"You're fixing me up with someone at my friend's funeral. This happens to me all the time."

"I wish you'd be serious."

"Angel, serious is not possible right now. I'm holding on, but I'm scared. If I get serious, I won't be able to keep it together."

"This isn't a blind date," he said. "It's someone who may help us figure out what happened to Margo, maybe to Lili." He looked at me with a lot more innocence than was decent considering his age and our past. "I'm scared, too."

"Are you nuts! Don't tell me that, you're supposed to be a guard dog, not a poodle."

Lawless was standing by the back door of the Lincoln, door open, and pointing to his watch.

I said, "God, that man lives by the clock."

"We need Lawless on our side. Stay friends with him."

"He has allowed me no other choice. And would you stop sounding so ominous and looking so frightened. Try to relax."

"Relax? Are you kidding?"

"Look brave," I said. "Fake it."

He kissed me on the cheek. "Okay, we'll fake it together."

"Angel, Lawless is about to have a coronary, but one quick question. Did Margo's women all find homes?"

"Not all. I'm working on it, so are the police."

"Good."

Lawless was standing by the open door of the driver's seat. He leaned in and beeped his horn. He pointed to his watch again. I pointed at my own watch and stuck my tongue out.

"Angel, want to give me a great big kiss and then forget it happened?"

He looked puzzled.

"Don't look puzzled, just do it."

He stood up, I stood up. He gave it all he got, which was plenty. I squeezed his behind and scooted off the porch. Angel was dumbfounded. So was Lawless.

I climbed into the backseat.

Lawless turned around. "What was that all about?"

"That? Nothing." I patted his arm. "Thanks for asking Angel to stay at my place. He's a great guy, and we feel really safe having him around."

"Women!"

Ruth looked over her shoulder at Angel as Lawless put the Lincoln in reverse. "Honey," she said, "if you're ever out of town and I need protection, that's the guy I want."

Lawless revved the engine, and we took off in a cloud of redwood bark and loose soil.

Nineteen

A couple of miles rolled by before Lawless spoke. I thought he was fuming, but he wasn't. He was in mourning, maybe in a mild state of shock and dreading this final farewell to Margo. Because that's what a funeral is—final. It's a gathering of people telling each other, *This is no nightmare, this is real, they are gone.* I'd stop messing with Lawless's head. I felt guilty about using Angel to tease him, although that kiss was pretty terrific. And I really should have called Lawless when I took off with Abra. Well, not before we left, but I could have called him from the road. I should have realized he'd be worried about us. I vowed to be nice, even sensitive. I caught him glance at me in his rearview mirror, then I caught his glance once again.

"You need to play in your own league," he said to me. "You're too old for that guy."

What a remark. This dialogue was not going to help me keep my vow. "I'm not too old for him, he's too young for me."

A fatal mistake—Lawless guffawed.

"How did you get to be this old without your wife killing you?"

Ruth craned her head in my direction, and she draped her arm over the seat. "Believe me, I've considered murder several times. Divorce never, but murder, yes."

Ruth was my kind of person. I understood why Lawless and I got along. He liked spunky women, and he liked to pretend that he didn't. What I got out of him—I wasn't sure about that. I did know the gloves were coming off. If the man could dish out insults, he could withstand retaliation.

"Romance gums up the works," he said to me. And here I thought we'd moved on. "The point in having Angel around is to keep you safe, not to get you hot and bothered."

"Get him hot and bothered."

He sighed. "If thinking that boosts your ego . . ."

"Oh, drop it," I said. "Angel will hang around for free, meaning I can afford him. He needs company, he's lost, he's scared, and I think he might be angry. If I get into a pinch, there's a lot of emotional juice to call on. And he's strong. You noticed his muscle tone, didn't you?"

Ruth said, "How could you *not*? That man is a hunk."

Lawless gave Ruth a withering stare, and she enjoyed every inch of it.

"You inherited a bunch of dough from the last homicide I worked," he said. "How come you can't afford to pay for protection? You run through the money already?"

Throughout the silence, throughout the banter, he and Ruth had played dueling radio stations. She'd punch classical, he'd punch football. She'd punch NPR, he'd punch Rush Limbaugh. I hoped he was keeping his eye on the road.

"Time-out," I said. "Are you paying attention to your driving? I don't want to kiss life good-bye on a curve with Rush Limbaugh's voice violating my ears."

"Fine." The duel ended, Mozart won. "About the dough," he said. "What'd you do with it?"

"Lawless, you ever inherit an indecent sum of money?"

"No."

"Jerry Baumann was my best friend, but I'm starting to feel the same way Mina does about this. You don't leave someone a pile of dough unless you've got it in for them. If I ever see anything after the lawyers and tax people get their bite, I'll probably be able to take a trip to Hawaii for ten days instead of seven."

"You're exaggerating. Again."

"Money is money, but you'd rather not get it from someone's death. I'm told this sort of estate often takes years to sort out. Of course, I'm told this by the same lawyers who would like the process to take decades."

"Lawyers are like catfish. A nibble here, a nibble there . . . before you know it the principal's gone, you've got a pile of bills, and not much else."

I thought about the women in the bunkhouses. Most of them wouldn't have legal bills if they landed in court, they'd have public attorneys. For different reasons, but that breed of attorney sounded as bad as the catfish.

"Lawless," I said, "what happens to women in the legal system when they're broke?"

"They get screwed."

That was an ugly piece of reality he'd tossed into the backseat.

"Angel said most of Margo's women were rescued. Is that true?"

"Those women were screwed by many systems," he said, "but they are extraordinary. They'll make it. As far as where they're living? We're still finding places. One woman's living with us—Ruth would take them all if we had a bigger house."

She beamed him a ray of love, and he beamed it back. I thought how nice it would be to have that, and how rarely it comes along. Even more rare—to know you've got it and to keep it.

I said, "And Cirk is shut down temporarily. No income for the women from that source."

"No, and it's some money maker. If it wasn't supporting entire families, it could make one family very wealthy."

"Maybe Lili will run it."

"If we find Lili, she wouldn't take it on. Margo had the energy of three people. You know that."

"Lili inherits it, though."

"I don't know their legal relationship."

"Something to check out."

"Yes, something to check out."

I'd turned Lawless sour, but discovering who benefited from Margo's death was standard. Just then I remembered Margo blowing her ominous eighty-six-proof question in my face, *How much is my life worth?* Someone must be digging in the direction of wills and life insurance. I was depending on Lawless to get us over the ridge in one piece; it was time to lighten his mood.

"I'm going up the hill this afternoon to help with the animals, Lawless. I thought about those giraffes, and I'm worried about them."

"The performers are feeding them, finding homes at zoos. Like everything else, it's a mess, but it'll work out."

"I'll miss those animals."

I sat in their big Lincoln backseat, all dressed up, and I felt like a kid driving to church with my parents. The Christmas movie *It's a Wonderful Life* came to mind. Jimmy Stewart never knew how many ripples spread from the little pebble in the pond that was him. A frothy wake followed Margo's life force.

"I don't blame Lili for taking off," Ruth turned and said to me. "And I don't think we should jump to any conclusions." Ruth smoothed the top of Lawless's hair, she knew what his mind was turning over. "Her world has collapsed, she knows people will fuss all over her, she'd hate that, and everyone would want a piece of her while pretending they didn't."

Lawless agreed. "Ruth, it'd be just like those catfish. Lili would get nibbled to pieces, bit by bit. She's a very delicate woman."

Oh, brother. I said, "Are adults allowed to just disappear?"

"Happens all the time. She's not a suspect running from a crime, she's running from grief. Maybe she has a family. I don't know a lot about Lili."

"I'll ask Angel when we get home."

He turned right up a road that would lead us east over sloping hills. It was a no-man's-land that felt unaligned with any city, county, or state. A place still uncluttered by grapevines and boutique tasting rooms.

The hillsides were soft, winter grass loved this place. Winter grass is intensely green, Crayola green. It vibrates. The ridges wobbled by in undulating waves. Here there were no mansions. Deer paths crossed the road, the sound of vagrant, tiny creeks cut random routes, and wild boar roamed the peaks. This place was a throwback, a place, mercifully, left out of time's loop.

"Lawless," I said, "you remember what this area was like before the landed gentry arrived?"

"Sure. I've fished around these parts since I was a kid."

"It was all like this."

"I remember."

"I miss it. And it's not just about the houses that have grown up like bunions on our hills."

"It's too damned pretty now," he said. "Too refined."

"Some things should be left alone, should be left raw and wild and untouched. It's being raw and wild that makes things magnificent. Then one day it's gone . . ."

"Raw power scares people," he said. "And people can't resist the urge to tame what's wild."

"And when they tame it, they flatten it."

We both knew we were talking about Margo, and we didn't say anything, just enjoyed, in quiet reverence, the hills slowly rolling past our windows. Soon they might be gone, soon they might be covered with huge houses on small lots, but today they were here and I felt a particular need to notice them.

Twenty

And come he slow, or come he fast,
It is but Death who comes at last.
> —Wordsworth, *The Lay of the Last Minstrel*

This is the craziest funeral I ever saw. It is profane. It is a mockery of everything that is sacred. It's not even a side show, it's the whole damned circus! She would have loved it.
> —Lawless to Annie Szabo

We turned into the cemetery parking lot. There were no clouds in the thin, cold sky, and no sign of rain. Lawless parked, and we walked up the winding road to the burial site. I was amazed that Margo had wanted a traditional ceremony in a traditional cemetery.

We crested the hill and saw a striped circus tent erected over a hole in the ground, presumably Margo's final resting place. A calliope loomed next to the hole, and someone worked the bellows. A temporary high wire was erected over the small side road.

Lawless was flabbergasted. "What the hell is this! Margo's gone for just a few days and the inmates have taken over the asylum!"

Ruth held her husband's hand. "Dear, Pope John Paul I said, 'Circus performers are at peace with their own bodies and also with animals.' That was the good pope, not the one we don't like."

"You're the Catholic, not me, and I don't remember hearing about any pope being buried next to a calliope and a circus tent!"

A solemn-faced little man wearing a black suit appeared next to Lawless, shaking his head. "Sir, this was Margo's request, she arranged her own funeral. Many prefer to save their loved ones pain in their time of need. And, frankly," he said, "some people cannot give up control, even beyond the grave."

"This must be against your rules or laws or something."

"We don't have rules. We do have policy, this is definitely against policy, but we made an exception for Margo."

"In other words, she paid big for the funeral she wanted."

"Money is not really an appropriate topic at this time."

"She paid big," Lawless said. "Well, if this is what she wanted . . ."

Just then a woman wearing a flimsy gown tottered by riding an elephant.

"Well, I did not agree to THAT!" Waving his arms, the man ran after the woman and the elephant.

Lawless said, "God almighty. Any minute someone's going to ask me if they can guess my weight."

We were approached by the first solemn man's clone—this one had a wild streak—his suit was navy blue. He pulled out brochures. He handed one to each of us, but he addressed Lawless. "If you'd like to follow your friend's lead and ease your loved ones' grief after your death . . ."

Lawless took his, Ruth's, and my brochure and flung them into number two's face. "When I'm dead, my loved ones can just cope!"

"Take it easy," I said, "it's not like you're the one who has to clean up the elephant poop."

"Margo told me she was a Methodist."

"She told me she was Catholic," I said. "Apparently her religion was a flavor-of-the-month affair."

"I expected a regular Methodist funeral."

"Lawless, nothing about Margo was regular. Would you have expected her final bow to be?"

Lawless had been right in getting us there early, packs of people were arriving. Ruth, wearing a pale mint green dress, moved to Lawless's side. She put her arm around him, and he nestled into her. His face crumpled up, but not one tear escaped.

He mumbled, "I want her to go out with respect."

"You think there's one person here who didn't respect and love Margo? Lawless, you're wrong," I said, "and since she chose this, let's show some respect and enjoy it."

He shook his head in sorry agreement.

Ruth comforted Lawless. I wandered away.

I wouldn't have admitted it to Lawless, but the event was a mild shock, even for me. Mina had the right idea—after this I was boycotting funerals. During Jerry's funeral, he became welded for all eternity to German auto parts. During my dad's funeral, they rolled out his stuffed horse, Silver. Next came his dog, Bullet. They were solemnly presented to Jack and me. You have never seen anything until you've seen a horse—one who you used to feed apples and ride on long trails—stuffed. That is unless you've seen it tacked to large brown wheels and hauled up a cemetery hill leaving deep green marks in the moist lawn. Silver was sort of like the Trojan horse—everyone half-expected the cavalry and a tribe of Indians to erupt from his midsection and roar across the lawn. Bullet wasn't so bad, but even a stuffed dog still wrecks the grass when it's on wheels. I was drunk for my husband's funeral, thank God, because I don't remember anything. Mina organized it, and only in my wildest nightmares can I begin to imagine what it must have been like.

Capri breezed by, her hand full of peanuts.

"Do they have a bar set up?" I asked, surveying her peanuts. "I could use a drink."

"No, this is the elephant's food. You like my dress?"

It was shaped like a long elegant cigar, rich chocolate brown, dotted with pale copper sequins.

"It's beautiful."

"You know how hard it is to dress for a funeral."

"Of course I know, I dressed you for the last one."

"Big improvement, this time I pulled it off alone. I still don't own black, but brown is dignified, and the sequins add fun."

"The best of both worlds."

"Thinking is easy when you're sober," Capri said. "Who knew? See you later, I just spotted some old friends."

She joined three laughing women, I think they were women. One of them took Capri's peanuts and threw them down the front of her dress.

A hearse pulled up, and there was a dark shape inside, a casket I assumed, I couldn't tell through the smoky glass. Angel stepped out of the hearse and joined me.

"Hi, Angel. I guess somewhere Margo's laughing her head off at us."

"God, I hope so," he said.

The whole thing—funerals, boxes for bodies, fancy clothes—seemed barbaric. I wished for an anonymous parting.

"Angel," I said, "I want to die when I'm eighty-five in a fiery motorcycle crash while exploring the wilds of Borneo. I want natives to find my carcass, pick my pockets, and throw a big bash with the booty—maybe they'd perform semi-obscene ritualistic dances around my mangled body. When they were all danced out, they'd get down on their knees and thank their lucky deities that some old white woman was crazy enough to die in their piece of the jungle."

"You are very odd."

"That's why you're too young for me." I looked him over. "You think I'm odd, and that I need to be fixed, instead of just enjoying the way I am."

Angel was puzzled. He'd figure it out or not. I was betting on *not*. He was a good person, but he wasn't deep enough to even approach odd. He was complicated; that's different, complicated is one-dimensional.

Angel's eyes lit up. He'd spotted a man standing across from us under a large oak. Wow. Zorba-esque, he practically vibrated right along with the tree and the calliope and the green, green grass. He was so full of sparkle he could shine your shoes just by smiling at them.

He approached us, a bear's walk, and wrapped Angel in a hug. They rocked back and forth. Only Texans and Italian men can get away with that kind of same-sex hug without some wise guy snickering behind their backs.

"Annie, this is the man I wanted you to meet. He knows our history, mine, Margo's, and Lili's. I'm sure he can help us make sense out of Margo's death. Her murder. I can hardly say that word."

"Angel," the man said, "you think this death involves history?"

"I know we need help, and you're the one who's always there to give it."

"Angel doesn't do well with introductions," the sparkly man said. "I thought I'd raised him better."

"You're his dad?"

"No, but I'm the man who raised him."

I whacked Angel across the stomach. "Well, other than the manners, he turned out pretty well."

The man turned his head to the sky and laughed. He stuck out his hand. "We'll have to do this on our own. I'm Leo Rosetti. You are?"

"My name is Szabo, Annie Szabo."

"Any relation to the soaring Szabos?"

"Szabo was my husband's name. My maiden name was Wilde. Annie Wilde."

"From Los Angeles?"

"A long time ago."

He stood back and studied me as if I were an old painting in an out-of-business gallery. "Will Wilde's little girl grown up."

"How do you know that?"

"You look like your dad. And I remember you."

"You remember me?"

"I was a stunt man, long time ago. Sometimes trapeze artists fall into that for the money. I didn't stay in it long, I preferred my art, but I saw you at your dad's ranch. You were a kid, a teenager, but those eyes are still the same. You were showing off, jumping that horse, taking too many chances. Your dad was a terrific man."

"Thank you. He's long gone."

"I know."

"That horse is in my daughter's trailer." He tilted his head. "No, no," I said, "the horse is dead." I said. "Stuffed."

"Your dad was one of a kind. He's not stuffed, too, is he?"

I laughed and assured him he was not. Leo had lightened the whole thing up, good thing, because I was falling into an emotional black hole in Borneo with strangers dancing around my body, and he'd caught me. Having gotten tangled up with the Szabos, it wasn't often that I was remembered for my own family history.

"Annie," Leo said, "I'm happy to talk with you about Margo, Angel thinks I can puzzle anything out. It's flattering, but untrue."

"We don't know what may help us."

"Come by my place tomorrow, we'll talk." He checked out my body. "Do you fly?"

"Not for a while."

"Come ready to fly in case the mood strikes you." He gave me his address.

"Detective Lawless is working on this. An ex-cop. Should I bring him?"

"Circus people are like Gypsies in a lot of ways—we carry our money in cash and jewels, and we don't trust the law," he said. "Don't bring him."

"Okay if I tell him where I'm going?"

"As long as he doesn't follow. I'll leave that up to you."

He looked at me, he looked at Angel.

"What?" I said to Leo.

"Angel tells me you're a reporter. I don't trust them, either."

"I write for *The National Eye.*"

That cleared up the trust issue—Leo was a regular reader. Leo said he looked forward to my visit. Excusing himself, he walked away, and people slowly gathered around him.

"Why didn't you tell me you had a family member, or almost family member, who is completely stellar?"

Angel said, "If that means you like him, forget it."

"Are you jealous? I've forgotten about you, almost, and don't look hurt, you've forgotten about me, too."

The calliope's sudden bellows blew us into stunned silence. A man moved front and center and announced that he'd been asked to give the eulogy. Leo.

He prayed Margo's spirit would find peace, something that had eluded her during life. The prayer finished, his voice changed from intonation to revival-style rhythm.

"Margo Spanger was an Amazon of the heart and spirit. She was the high priestess of passion, elemental, a healing force and a destruction. She understood circus style and she saw it hidden everywhere— in politicos, street people, and moms at the supermarket.

"I grew up in the circus," Leo said. "but I didn't know about it, not really, until Margo showed me the papers, posters, and journals she'd gathered. Circus was a religion, a high art, a brilliant escape from a sometimes grim life, a song of this country and its changes.

"I fantasized running away *from* the circus. But the world outside our very close community didn't look welcoming, and it lacked imagination. I stayed."

He turned to the calliope and motioned as if he were conducting an orchestra. The calliope pumped up and played.

Capri lumbered through the crowd riding an elephant. She had changed out of her brown, sequined dress into a flimsy Cleopatra gown that displayed cleavage and skin down to her belly button. Mina had saved herself a heart attack by staying home. Capri stopped the elephant at the edge of the crowd, and the elephant became enamored of one man's silk tie. He fondled the tie with his trunk.

"Margo loved the surreal, and she loved sex," Leo said. "The circus taught us sexuality is a fluid thing, that even the distinction between animals and humans is fluid. One hundred years ago trapeze artists became birds and butterflies. Today we have Cirk."

The crowd was huge, and he held them, a true showman who loved Margo and loved the circus.

"She was taken from us by a horrible act, but her life was joyous. Her crowning achievement was her unrelenting desire to take care of women, to make their lives beautiful. Margo left us too soon," he said. "There's so much work to do.

"She dreamed passion into reality. That's what we'll remember."

Damn. I had tears in my eyes and I do not like to cry in public. I drifted to the nearest solid object, a tree, and leaned against it. I pulled a used Kleenex from the bottom of my purse and dabbed my eyes. I spotted Lawless—one arm around Ruth and the other around a clown. Lawless had to be propped up.

I surveyed the gathered masses and received the full wallop of Margo's life. In attendance were men wearing five-thousand-dollar suits. Women wore dresses of like value, and they didn't seem bothered about ruining their five-hundred-dollar pumps on the moist lawn. The state chair of the Women's Republican Committee and the State Democratic leader of the House chatted amiably. There was a madam from San Francisco talking with Juanita. She had climbed out of bed, all 350 pounds of her, and was wearing her best wool hat with silk flowers sewn on the brim. I thought about Lawless saying how many powerful people Margo had aggravated— some of them were present.

There were clowns, maybe twenty or thirty. A man towered above them wearing stilts and the old favorite, an Uncle Sam outfit. One clown broke through the crowd and slipped on the grass. The clown grabbed the man on stilts for balance, and they both went down. There were some words exchanged, not audible, but urgent and, I would imagine, a little angry. Three people helped the man up and eased him back into the stratosphere. The clumsy clown disappeared into the crowd.

Two midgets, both men, stood next to a man wearing alligator cowboy boots. I recognized him, a wine baron from Texas who had moved west. The midgets held hands, the Texan tried not to notice. One started crying, and the Texan patted him, somewhat uneasily.

Voices, two of them, rose to meet the clouds, angelic voices. I turned in their direction. It was an honest-to-God pair of Siamese twins joined at the head singing "You'll Never Walk Alone." The casket was rolled to the dark, damp hole. Those two had never spent one moment alone. I tried not to look at the twins, I felt a laugh sneaking up, made the mistake of taking another quick peek, and once I started laughing I couldn't stop. Other people joined in. There was a giant hiss, and the bad kids, including me, shut up. Margo was something, all right.

I backed up and tried to blend in with the crowd. There was no one I could blend in with.

A large black woman took the twins' place. The fat lady was going to sing—this was the end of the service. I thought she'd launch into a traditional version of "Amazing Grace," we'd all join in or not, and then we'd shake hands, hug, and straggle off. It was not to be. The woman broke into a Bessie Smith song, one that was the very pulse and raw rhythm of life, music that laughed in the face of death.

I'd have to find out when Margo made these funeral arrangements. It occurred to me that if someone had threatened her, and she wasn't going to cave in, she might have decided to arrange this ceremony. Just in case. It also occurred to me that if someone had gone beyond mere threats, had actually injured her, she would never report it to the police. I'd ask Lawless to check her medical records. She wouldn't report an injury, but she might see a doctor if the injury needed attention. Lawless would probably give me the standard *You have such a wild imagination* response. I wasn't giving up on my imagination, and I didn't want it to give up on me.

Under an old oak, I spotted Capri without the elephant. She hovered over a small fire, another infraction of policy, I was sure.

"What are you doing?" I said to her.

"A Gypsy good-bye. This should be done as soon as the last breath is taken, but . . . better late than never. It eases people into the next world."

Capri said to me, "We throw herbs on the fire in the right order so anyone who's watching knows we mean business. That's especially important in a graveyard. You never know *who* is watching around here. First thyme, then sage, and rosemary . . .

"Annie," she said, "move out of my way. I have to say Margo's name seven times while I'm walking backward."

I left Capri to the duty of easing Margo's transition. If anyone needed easing, it would be Margo. People milled around, speaking in hushed respectful tones. If I shook the hand of one more midget, I would be permanently stooped. As the crowd was breaking up, Louis Armstrong sang "What a Wonderful World" through four large speakers. It was the most beautiful funeral I have ever attended—just the right mix of reverence and respect and the bizarre.

My mom, always a rebel, loved Woody Guthrie. She would have liked one of his Wobblie songs at my dad's funeral, but she was the only one who knew all the words, and you don't hand out song sheets at a funeral. Instead we all sang, "So Long, It's Been Good to Know You."

I walked to Margo's casket and sang one line of that song as a gift from my mom to Margo. Except I changed the words to "Hello, it's so good to see you . . ." I hoped they were somewhere together drinking Scotch and smoking a joint and eating chocolate and telling jokes. And, if I listened real carefully, I could swear I heard their laughter.

Twenty-one

I'd counted on getting a ride back home with Angel, but I didn't see him anywhere. I hate being without my own wheels.

I found Lawless and Ruth. They asked if I wanted to go by Margo's for the postfuneral food and booze. I said I didn't, they didn't either. The wake was a bunkhouse affair, and I didn't want to smile and act nice to strangers. I expected Lawless felt the same way. When I stopped to think about it, I was sure that's where Angel was.

I hated to bring this up—Lawless might make a citizen's arrest right there in his Lincoln—but Ruth was a good buffer.

"Lawless, I didn't see Lili anywhere. You?"

Ruth cut in. "We looked, but not a sign of her. I'd be broken up if my husband died, don't let this go to your head, dear," she said to him, "but I'd still manage to do *something*. I asked the florist—not even a wreath or an arrangement from her."

"Ruth," he said sternly, "everyone handles grief differently. That's enough."

"You have not told me when to talk and when not to talk since I was eighteen and you certainly are not going to start now," Ruth said, "and do *not* use that tone with me."

Lawless said, "How would anyone know if Lili was there? God, those Siamese twins. That used to be one of my favorite songs."

Ruth ignored him. "Lawless, she was not there."

Lawless ignored her in return. "I understand show people live in a different world. But that was a very unusual Methodist minister. Are Methodist ministers allowed to drink?"

Lawless was already suffering, he didn't need to know Leo was not a Methodist minister. "Under special circumstances," I said, "they are allowed to really tie one on."

"How do you know that?"

"Methodists are similar to Baptists. Baptists are allowed to overeat and have sex with their friend's wife, but they are not allowed to dance or drink. I don't know where Methodists stand as far as dancing and adultery, but I'm pretty sure alcohol is fine."

"What has that got to do . . . What were we talking about? Sometimes you drive me up the wall."

"Not while you're driving."

"I really like you," Ruth said to me.

"I was afraid of this," Lawless said.

She smooched her hand and rubbed it on his cheek.

"I remember," he said, "Lili. No one saw her at the funeral and I don't want to talk about it anymore."

Ruth turned around, looked at me in the backseat, and sighed.

"Lawless," I said, "since Ruth's in the car to keep you from jumping down my throat, and as long as you're mad at me anyway, can I ask you a question?"

The muscles in the joint of his jaw did a woggy dance. "Go ahead."

"Why haven't those idiots in uniforms found a weapon? Never mind," I said. "They can't find Lili, how can we expect them to find something as small as a gun?"

He jaw did another woggy dance. "I'm as frustrated as you are. More so. This is my profession. I'd hoped the funeral would point us in the right direction."

"You remember your giant SFPD Book of the Dead? At least five inches thick, all unsolved murder cases? I do not want Margo's death to go down as an unsolved crime."

"Either the killer didn't show, or we didn't notice them, maybe a lone person standing off to the side."

"Right. The fog rolls in, there are twenty people dressed in black, one guy leaning against a tree smoking a cigarette. The lightbulb goes on, and there's your killer," I said. "That's only in the movies, and Margo's life was bigger than a movie."

"You sure you didn't spot anyone who stood out from the rest?"

"Three," I said. "You, me, and Ruth. I'm pretty sure we didn't do it. We're nowhere, aren't we?"

"We're somewhere. It's like driving in the fog. Eventually we'll hit the bot stops or a bright green light. For now, we keep cruising."

I didn't know if Angel was in the same off-limits territory as Lili, but I decided to wander in and find out.

"Lawless, Angel said he was fingerprinted. How'd he take it?"

"Fine. The poor guy is totally broken up."

"So you hired me broken protection. Who's supposed to take care of who? Whom?"

"Exactly how much did you say you were paying this guy?"

"Not a dime."

"You get what you pay for, but if someone's prowling around, a man's presence is important."

"Especially a big man," Ruth said.

"It's okay," I said. "I don't mind babysitting for Angel until he stops being broken."

"That didn't look like a babysitter's kiss on your porch."

Mrs. Lawless said, "We rented an X-rated movie last month where the babysitter and the boy kissed exactly like that."

"Ruth!"

"Forget the stupid kiss," I said. "It was solely for your benefit."

"You are so adolescent."

"I know. And Angel's a trophy bodyguard."

"When push comes to shove," he said, "I have faith that you and Mina can take care of anyone. You would shoot them, and she would poison them or drive them crazy or both. I'm not all that worried about you two."

"Thanks a lot."

"Don't women want to be thought of as resourceful and self-reliant?"

"Of course. It doesn't mean you can't pretend to think we need help, then pretend to offer it and let us decline the offer."

"You amaze me," Ruth said to her husband. "What dance do you think we've been doing for more than three decades?"

The car turned right into my drive. Home sweet home. Safe. I could take off my pantyhose and breathe again.

I stepped out of their car, I turned back and leaned in his window. "Lawless, just intuition, but I think Angel may know what happened to Lili."

"You find out anything, let me know."

"Of course I'll let you know."

He didn't believe me. I was beginning to think Lawless had real trust issues.

Twenty-two

J squirmed out of my conservative dress and my grisly pantyhose. They both worked ten years and ten pounds ago, but no more. I tossed the dress in my Goodwill box. As glorious as Margo's send-off was, I wanted no permanent reminder hanging in my closet.

I slipped on an old sweatsuit and decided it was far past cocktail time. I had no idea what time it was, but that's what my body told me.

I poured myself a glass of wine and sat at the kitchen table. There were the photocopied memoirs, the photos of Hannah and Jonathan, the articles about the freaks who staged the freak rebellion. I could write a book—it would have to be science fiction—using the materials she had given me.

This was Margo's strange legacy to me. I wished I hadn't returned the route book she'd offered, I wished I'd accepted her gift graciously, that I'd accepted the entire treasure trove of originals she'd offered. She was impulsive. If she intended to lighten her load, she could have done exactly that right after she staggered up the hill.

I understand the impulse to get rid of accumulated clutter. It is righteous, and it usually arrives after too much coffee or too much wine. You stuff garbage bags until they're ready to burst—the process is merciless—and there's no looking back. Those route books could be sitting in Hefty Lawn & Leaf bags in the corner of Margo's office! Lili would have a fit if Margo wanted to get rid of one iota of memorabilia.

But Lili wasn't around to have a fit about anything, and Margo wouldn't want the assorted strangers who now marched through her domain breaking up her collection.

I was going to Margo's office. If it was locked, I was breaking in. I was gathering things she wanted me to have, no more, no less. The longer I thought about it, the more sensible it seemed, illustrating just how sloshed I was. I poured another glass of wine. I'd need to get in and out of there fast. If necessary, I could climb in through a window. Several months ago I'd gotten stuck in a window while breaking into my own home. It's not very dignified to have your behind on one side of a window and the rest of you on another. Dignity is such a nuisance. I was going up to Margo's.

I pulled down a bottle of Jack Daniel's, brand-new since Margo had polished off the last one. In her honor, I poured myself a shot. Then I thought about Angel. He was staying at my place, he would recognize Margo's things when I brought them home. Would he rat me out to Lawless? I wanted the option of telling Lawless myself that I had broken into Margo's.

On the other hand, if Angel knew where Lili was hiding, he'd rat me out to *her,* and she'd come flying out of the woodwork—straight for my neck—like a banshee. Her reappearance would answer some questions. If she didn't reappear, that would tell us something, too. It was a good plan, a very good plan. I was sure Lawless would approve. I toasted Margo, we drank to my brainstorm. I placed my empty whiskey glass on the table.

I barely knew Leo, but I called him. I told him what I was up to. He didn't sound alarmed or surprised. He sounded asleep. He invited me, again, to come over tomorrow, and for tonight, if I pulled this off, to hide everything under my bed. He hung up. I took a last pull of bourbon, this one from the bottle. I wanted sneakers, but I could only find my boots and I slipped them on with no socks. I was out of the door.

I walked to Mina's trailer and stopped midknock. The trailer swayed rhythmically, and sounds of delight poured out the single-pane windows. I'd already been warned—the trailer was rockin', so I wasn't knockin'.

I turned and walked a few feet from the trailer in the direction of Margo's, but I was losing my nerve. Maybe a trip to her place was stupid. I kicked a little dirt and wondered what I was doing.

The trailer door opened. Mina stood in the doorway, tossing a robe around her shoulders. She stopped at the bottom step and shielded her eyes as if blinded by a summer sun instead of a winter moon.

She said, "What?"

"What do you mean 'what'?"

"I could feel you out here. On the Marla Trent Show they call that multi-tasking."

"One task at a time, Mina. I didn't mean to bother you."

"If the plumber was all that great, my mind wouldn't be outside roaming around. What do you want?"

"I'm going to break into Margo's office."

"The woman is dead. What's the problem? It's not like her spirit can call the cops, and it's not like she would call the cops if she were alive. Good night."

She turned and climbed step one.

"I'm going to steal some things," I said to her back. "If I get arrested, I want to call you for bail money. Do you have cash around?"

Cash and theft and possible arrest. I had her attention. She turned, walked toward me, and stopped about one foot in front of me.

"Of course I have cash around. What are you planning to steal?"

I told her.

"Papers and books?" she said. "Is there an actual law against stealing these worthless things?"

"They're not worthless, they're very old. But before Margo died she said she wanted me to have them."

"The universe knows this. You're in the clear."

"Just answer the phone if it rings, okay?"

Mina held me by the arm and looked at my face. She put my left earlobe between her fingers and rubbed. Right earlobe, same routine.

A man hollered to her from inside. Mina cupped her hand around her mouth. "Take care of yourself for a minute or two, would you?"

"Are you shivering from the cold or from your nerves?" she said to me.

"I don't know."

She said, "Come inside with me."

I did.

"Doll"—this from the plumber in the back room—"you left me all dressed up with no place to go."

"Don't say anything naughty, and keep your pants on, would you? I mean, put them back on, I have work to do."

"At this time of night?" He groaned. "We were busy."

She leaned into the hall. "Don't whine. I hate men who whine," she said to him, "it's family business. You're a number of steps below family, Frank."

"What work?" I said to her.

"We're going to make you invisible. You drink this tea I've got brewing while I get organized."

"Mina, I'm drunk. I almost thought you said I was going to become invisible, and you were going to make it happen."

"Can you be quiet and cooperate? You don't get to direct the help you receive after you ask for it."

She rummaged through drawers, went back into her bedroom, went into the empty bedroom, made another sharp remark to Frank, padded into the living room where I sat huddled.

"Listen up, Annie. I am only going to do this once. Mess this up, and you could die."

"I'm all ears." I wasn't kidding. My earlobes were the only part of my body that felt . . . anything.

"Heliotrope," she said. "I don't have very much, and I don't give it to just anybody. Papers and old books? Phoo! People will rob you blind for heliotrope. The reason you've got to pay attention to me is that it's poison. But this is an emergency. I'm hoping you're sober enough for it to work."

She poured some heliotrope into a small bone horn. It was attached to a thong necklace.

"You wear this. In your pocket it brings money, but you and I have enough money problems. Around your neck, it makes you invisible."

All I'd wanted to know was did she have cash around and would she answer the phone, and now we were making me invisible. "Do invisible people wear clothes?"

Mina didn't laugh. "Heliotrope causes your actions and your movements to go unnoticed. You're not going to become Casper the ghost."

"I guess it can't hurt."

"Not unless you eat it. Also, wear it when you go to sleep. Heliotrope brings prophetic dreams. I feel big dreams are out there waiting for you, it's like they're waiting to be born. The heliotrope will put you in a dream labor that will birth them," she said, slipping the thong around my neck. "Maybe they're waiting to tell you what happened to Margo."

I fingered the horn and wondered what I'd gotten into.

"I made you invisible," Mina said, "I gave you big-deal dreams, I've got cash for bail money, and I gave your ears enough circulation to be able to hear a pin drop in the next county—not bad for ten minutes' work. Okay if I go back to bed?"

"Yeah, go back to bed. Sorry I interrupted."

"No problem. Say hello to Margo for me."

"What?"

"She's not gone yet. Spirits who've been yanked from one world to the next have a hard time letting go. Don't ask questions, just do this as a favor—say hello."

She bent down over me—I was sealed with a kiss. I got out of there before the trailer started rocking again.

I made my way to Margo's. First I fell into the rusty swing set that hasn't known action for ten years. Next I stumbled into the chicken coop, waking up every fowl inside. No wonder I rarely got eggs—those lazy dames slept all the time. A few more steps, and I tumbled over my oldest daughter's contribution to the world of psychotic art. Mina should have conferred night vision upon me. Farther from my own home, closer to the open space between Margo's place and mine, there were few obstacles. I spotted her office, a dim glow from a yellow porchlight, and no lights were on inside.

I crept closer, no police present. They'd already done their search-and-seizure damage. There was a bolt on the door. No big deal if you have a bolt cutter. I didn't.

I crept around to a side window and tried easing it open. It was glued shut with layers of oil-based paint. I tapped, I shook gently, I jiggled, it started to give. I opened the window. Four inches up, it came to a halt.

I tapped and jiggled at an angle, it flew up fast and banged. I hunkered down and waited. No one. Through the far bushes I saw lights blazing in one bunkhouse. Music blew through the trees like an ill wind, some brand of MTV heavy metal head-banging skult.

I tottered up to my tiptoes, and eased myself into the window. I was inside. It was dark.

I remembered where the route book was, where the entire collection was. They were stacked in the bookshelf next to the *Siamese Twins Marry Midget Twins!* poster. Maybe I'd also swipe that.

I felt around, found Lili's desk, and oriented myself. I didn't remember any gewgaws around the perimeter of the room, but you can't be too careful. I moved like a cat. I smacked into the coffee table—why do people own these stupid pieces of furniture—and I cussed at the top of my lungs. To hell with it. There was no way I could get what I wanted in the dark. I peered out the window. More party noises, same music, no one around. No Nazis, no barking German shepherds. I took off my scarf, draped it over the shade of the floor lamp next to the couch, and turned on the light.

There was the bookshelf, there were the books. I stuffed books and journals in my backpack. Forget the poster, too big for a hasty getaway. I tossed the backpack on the couch.

The file cabinet next to the bookshelf, I had a little time. Maybe something would lead me in the right direction. Someone Margo was blackmailing, someone blackmailing her. Receipts. People who'd given her money. Anything. I started with the middle drawer. File folders with women's names, alphabetized and organized by year.

I flipped through the letters of the alphabet until I got to the S's. There was Abra, Abra Slade. My grandson would wear that name forever. Taking the file seemed like a good idea, no one needed to know about our lives, about her life. Jack was listed as next of kin.

No one needed to know about him, either. I lifted my backpack off the couch, unzipped it, stashed her file inside.

The room was too close, I could almost hear the walls breathe. Hearing walls breathe—an obvious sign of heightened senses. I didn't feel so great. The walls pulsed with plans, with layers of paint, with hungry years. I turned in a slow circle, studied the room.

On the coffee table, two iron banks, a music box, a carved erotic marble statue, and an umbrella stand in the corner of the room. On the couch, my backpack. The desktop was protected by a scrolled leather blotter. And there was a gun lying on the blotter, a .25 mm. I was pretty sure it was the kind of thing the police would have noticed.

The horrible and the fantastic—I was mesmerized. I picked up the gun and studied it. For a small gun it had nice weight, good balance.

There was a harsh mind-splitting noise, worse than the head-banger stuff coming from the bungalow. An air raid on amphetamines.

The smoke alarm. Damn. I tossed the gun on the coffee table, I pulled my smoldering scarf off the lamp and jammed it in my pocket. I grabbed the umbrella by the door and climbed on Lili's desk. I beat the alarm into oblivion. It hung by two wires. A red blinking light gave up the ghost and went dark.

The slam of a door, maybe a car door, I didn't know, outside. I heard fast steps, they raced to the office, there was pounding on the door. Repeated pounding that ran straight to my stomach. I grabbed the gun and pointed it at the door. I squeezed the trigger and then let up in case someone official was on the other side. A fireman, a policeman, an Indian chief, Rory, Margo's killer. I turned out the light and ran to the window.

I tossed the backpack out, tossed myself out, and ran. Felt like there was nothing but air beneath my feet. I bumped into a tree, fell flat on my behind. Not a tree, Angel.

He gave me his hand. I extended my right hand, the one that held the gun.

"What are you doing?" he said.

"Falling over you."

"With the gun."

"I didn't know I had a gun." I was telling the truth. I'd run off with the stupid gun and now I was running home with it.

"Where are you going?" I said to him. I thought I'd turn the tables. I needed time to think and to collect oxygen.

"To your house. This is Maria Tomi," he said, looking at Maria Tomi with pity, "the last woman without a place to go. I told her she could stay with us."

"With us. Sure, why not? See you at home."

I stood and waited for them to take off. Maria was a round, dark, little woman. Hard to see her at night, but something about Maria— I didn't think sunlight would improve her appearance.

"We'll walk with you," Angel said.

"No, I need a little air." I lied. I needed a lot of air. "I may take a drive."

"Annie, you're not thinking right." He handed the gun to me. "Put this back inside your house and go to bed. You're acting crazy, and you certainly shouldn't be driving."

Why did he have to choose that particular time to turn on the lights inside his head? I decided to tell him the partial truth. "Mina gave me something. An herb. I think it made me goofy."

"Exactly why you need to go home."

He said something to Maria, cowering next to him like a whipped dog.

"She's frightened," he said, "her husband was a brute. I told her you grew up with guns, you're good with them, and you were doing target practice."

"At night?"

"She's Italian, she thinks Americans are crazy. I'm not going home without you."

"Angel. This is me. Start telling me what to do and . . ."

"Yes, I know how you get." He faced me. "You won't let yourself be helped."

I looked at Maria. She was still cowering but was starting to resemble a woman down on her luck rather than a whipped dog.

"Angel, did you hear pounding on the office door, a rush of it, just a few minutes before I bumped into you?"

"No. I was at the party. I left, started walking to your place, and I ran into Maria wandering around. She doesn't have a home yet, she was scared by all the police, and she's been hiding out here."

"Maria doesn't understand English?" I asked.

"No."

"This means she can't speak English?"

"Of course that's what it means."

"She'll be a relief to have around. I'll see you in a little bit."

He looked doubtful.

"You have enough women to babysit for without worrying about me," I said. "I didn't imagine someone knocking on Margo's door, it was an angry knock, and that person may be headed to our house. Go."

Angel was activated. He turned to soothe Maria and lead her down the hill. No Maria. "Where did she go?" he said, anxiety icing his words.

"Some babysitter. You've already lost one of your charges. Find her and check on Mina. I do not need help."

"At least you're armed," he said, "but don't shoot someone by mistake. Like me."

"I'd only shoot you on purpose."

Angel wandered off. I waited and watched his slow, searching shadow recede. I ran up the hill, scooted back through the office window, and put the gun back on the desk. No need for a possible murder weapon to live at my house.

I flopped out the window again, backpack still attached to my back, ran toward the gate, and saw Maria squatting in the bushes. If she was staying with me, she'd better get used to indoor plumbing.

"Where's Angel?" I said.

She spoke to me in a wave of Italian, and I shrugged. She shrugged back.

He was probably wandering around looking for her, and she'd been looking for a private moment. I had other fish to fry. A matter of fingerprints on a maybe—murder weapon and letting the cops know about the weapon without getting into hot water.

I climbed into my car, pulled the keys out from under the seat. I removed my backpack—you can't drive wearing one of those things—hunchbacks must have custom seats or take the bus. I tossed the pack into the rear seat. What a stupid idea. My fingerprints were smeared high and low inside Margo's office, and I'd almost shot a lunatic pounding on the door. Perhaps the lunatic had even seen me.

I should have left Margo's books alone. I didn't need them. I'd never write a book of any sort—too hard to sit still that long—and I would certainly not write a science fiction book. This planet was weird enough. I fingered the horn of heliotrope around my neck. Plenty weird.

I hightailed it to the safety of the next county.

Twenty-three

I drove south to Marin County, used the phone booth in front of a Stop'N Rob, and called the local sheriff's department. I stuck on an English accent, the only accent I do that sounds real. I gave them Margo's address, told them there was a gun on her desk, and they ought to check it out. After I told them which Margo I was talking about, they got interested. They wondered who I was, how I knew, and why I was calling them. I said I'd been given the information and not to be fussy about it. Using the word *fussy* reinforced the English accent.

What did these guys expect, the truth? "Hey, guys, I'm not calling from home, not even my own county, and I'm making this fast before you can trace the call." I was doing my duty, informing them about a possible murder weapon. And I was stalling—there was the issue of fingerprints, and I wanted to give Lawless time to rescue me from myself.

I got into my car, drove at the speed limit, and called Lawless on my cell phone.

"Lawless, here's the deal."

"Is this Annie?"

"Yes, it's Annie.

"I thought it was someone with a phony English accent. Must have been the tailend of a dream."

"I haven't changed gears yet."

"What?"

"Just listen. We've got to make this fast."

"I'm listening." Giant sigh. Wait until he found out what he was going to hear.

"I broke into Margo's office and there's a gun on the desk, a .25 that wasn't there before, it couldn't have been, or the police would have found it. I heard noises, I freaked out, I picked up the gun and almost blasted someone standing on the other side of the door. I went out the window . . ."

"You went out the window?"

"Same window I climbed in. The place was bolted up tight." I could almost hear him wonder if he had any Maalox in the house. "I picked up the gun and headed home, then I decided that was a bad idea, so I ran up the hill and put it back on the desk."

"Tell me this is a bad dream."

"I'd like to, but I'd be lying."

"Breaking and entering is fine, handling a possible murder weapon is fine, but no fibs from Annie. It's good to have boundaries."

"Do you want to know the rest?"

"No."

"Then I drove down to Marin County and called the Sheriff's Office from a phone booth to buy myself some time until you could figure out what we need to do, and now I'm driving home. What is that noise?"

"The toilet. I've been getting dressed since the beginning of this conversation. You on your own cell phone? Not one that's stolen?"

"It's my own phone."

"Hang up and I'll call you back when I hit the road."

Three or four minutes, no call, I checked to see if my phone was on, it was. It rang. I answered. I heard the soft purr of an engine, Lawless driving his Lincoln.

He said, "I'm driving to the scene of your crime. Continue."

"When I called the Sheriff's Office—this is where the English accent came in—"

"Clever."

". . . and suggested they check it out, I remembered that I'd left the window open and that my fingerprints are all over the place."

"Oh, for God sakes . . ." I heard someone honk, I heard Lawless swear. "Okay, okay, let me think."

There was silence.

"What are you doing?" I said.

"I'm still thinking." I could hear his wheels turn, and not just the ones on the road.

"I can get you out of this," he said. "You were sitting around the house, thinking about Margo. The day of her funeral, that's natural. You wanted something of hers. Something that reminded you of her. Can we make this work?"

"Sure, she'd offered me a few books of hers. Old ones, valuable. She said she wanted me to have them. They were in the office."

"Her things, not Lili's?"

"Right."

"Very good. You only took what belonged to you, typical grief pattern after a sudden death. Sort of."

"And I grabbed Abra's file, then the smoke alarm went off. There's private information in there."

"I don't want to know why the smoke alarm went off."

"I didn't burn anything down."

"You not only went there to collect your memories, you also wanted your daughter's file. You were desperate, distraught."

"I never knew there *was* a file on her until I'd broken into the office, I rummaged through their cabinet, and found it. By mistake."

"No. You *saw* Margo put your daughter's file into that cabinet the night your daughter arrived. Her husband is violent, I have photos of the damage he inflicted upon her. You wanted that file to protect her, it had information about her current whereabouts."

"Okay." This was starting to sound pretty good.

"You took her file and saw the gun on the desk and heard noises and panicked and picked up the gun, you thought her husband might have followed you, then you put it back on the desk and ran as fast as you could. And you called a friend in Marin—do you have a friend in Marin who could back this up?—and that friend called the police for you."

"I like it."

"So there'll be your fingerprints and the killer's fingerprints on the gun. And we'll finally have the murder weapon."

"Also Angel's prints and some Italian woman who moved into my house."

"What?"

"I ran into them, literally, on my way home before I put the gun back. Wait a minute. Only Angel's prints and mine. The Italian woman was scared, she never touched the gun. She thinks Americans are crazy."

"If she's spent her recent time around circus people, an abusive husband, and you, I understand where she got that impression."

"I just met her." Silence. "Lawless," I said, "are you still there?"

"I'm thinking again. Sometimes people do that."

He was grouchy—definitely not a night person.

"Okay," he said. "Angel lives up there, and he was rescuing the Italian woman. He rushed to the office when he heard the smoke alarm. I assume there is evidence that the alarm was dismantled."

"It's pretty hard to miss."

"He rushed to the office when he heard the smoke alarm, you'd already dismantled it. You were scared and needed help. You were wearing the pack of books, you handed Angel the gun out the window, told him to check out the area, find out who'd been beating on the door. He said you were nuts, he handed it to you, and insisted that you put it back and leave. Angel helped you out the window. You wanted your daughter's file, he waited while you got it, and you ran like hell."

"If I'd known her name at that time, I would have grabbed the Italian woman's file, too."

"What's her name?"

"Maria Tomi."

"We've got the story straight. Tell Angel, so that if anyone asks, he'll know what he did this evening."

"What about the Marin cops?

"I'm almost at Margo's office. I'll tell them you're an old friend, you called me worried sick about your daughter and about your actions. I'll meet them over there. There's a reason for you to be there, we don't have to worry about your prints. I will even, God help us, vouch for your character if necessary."

"Are you sure you don't want me just to head up there and wipe my fingerprints off the windowsill and the gun?"

A small blast. I thought it was early for roadwork, it was. It was Lawless blowing up. Mina was right. The man needed to get his blood pressure checked.

"I am absolutely sure! And don't say one word of this to anyone other than Angel."

"Okay, calm down," I said. "It'll be just like it never happened."

"They already have Angel's prints," he said. "They'll want to print you so they can eliminate your prints from that of the suspect's on the weapon."

"My prints are on record. Several places. You know that."

He didn't say anything. I didn't say anything. "Annie. You there?"

"I'm here."

"It scares me when you're quiet."

"I don't want to get nailed for Margo's murder."

"If I let you live long enough to get through this, you won't get nailed for her murder. Good-bye."

That was a nice thing to say.

I was trying to remember our story. I thought it made sense—I was feeling sentimental, went up to Margo's to get something she'd given me, saw the file cabinet, and wanted Abra's private business out of there. Angel was rescuing Maria, heard the smoke alarm. I handed him the gun and asked him to check out the place. He had a fit and told me to put it back. We went home, I called a friend in Marin, and she called the cops. It was so real, so plausible! I would definitely have broken in and stolen Abra's records if I'd known any existed.

Twenty-four

By the time I got home from Marin County, I was feeling pretty mellow. Lawless would handle everything. He was hooked into watching my backside, I didn't know why, but I'd decided he was one of the best, and most surprising, things that had happened to me in a long time.

My daughter was out of a lousy marriage, and she was in the middle of nowhere learning who she was. She did have input from Jack, I wondered about that, but I knew she was safe. Jack would treat Joey like a gift from God and drag him everywhere. I hoped this would not include peyote ceremonies and overnight visits with women, but there would be no violence. That was huge.

I walked into my house, and there was Angel, plus the strange woman he'd rescued from Margo's ghost town.

I hadn't gotten a good look at her in the woods. I knew she was round and short. She was. But the round bordered on dumpy, the worst stereotype of a homely Italian woman complete with one continuous eyebrow and a discernible moustache. She could use Jenny Craig, electrolysis, and a hot wax job.

Angel said, "Where have you been?" He looked worried.

"Don't you have my cell phone number?"

"You never wanted me to have it."

"Oh." I'd forgotten that. "I was airing out, I told you I'd be home in a little while, and here I am. Mina okay?"

"Mina appears to be fine. She has company."

"The plumber."

"From the sound of it, I'd say yes."

I looked at Maria again, trying to get used to her.

"Let me do the introductions," he said to me, "you've already gotten me once about my manners today. Annie Szabo, this is Maria Tomi. Maria, Annie."

She smiled and repeated her name and bowed her head a couple of times. Then she did it again.

"I know she doesn't speak English, but is she okay? I mean, mentally?"

"Just nervous."

I could understand that.

"Angel, I have to tell you something, and you have to pay attention. Really pay attention."

He was patting Maria's leg. Was she a new love interest? Was Angel why her husband had lost it? The heart is a strange and mysterious place.

"Wait. First I need to talk with you about Maria," he said.

"No, you need to listen to me." My voice was sharp. I didn't expect them, but in case the cops showed up I wanted Angel up to speed. "This story isn't true," I said, "but you're going to remember it, and you're going to pretend it's real."

He looked puzzled and a little scared. "Okay."

I ran down the deal, he repeated it, and he screwed up a couple of times. I made him say it until he got it right.

"Now it's your turn," I said. "What's the story with Maria? And by the way, you need to teach her the wonders of indoor plumbing."

"Maria is an animal caretaker, her husband was an aerialist, they worked for Margo. He got rough with her, Margo fired him. Immediately. Then Margo moved Maria into one of the bunkhouses."

"Margo must have been fit to be tied when one of her employees got out of line."

"Furious. Her employees knew what she expected, and there were no second chances."

"Do we know where Mr. Tomi is?"

Angel spoke to Maria in Italian, she shrugged, said something in reply.

"He could be working in the city, or sleeping under a bridge waiting for an opportunity to grab Maria. He could have moved to a circus casino in Reno."

"Was his temper tantrum unusual, or was it standard behavior?"

"Terrible temper. Margo put up with him because he was incredible, and in the past he'd taken his tantrums out on coffee mugs and furniture. He was also nervy. She caught him opening night, after he'd been fired, trying to sneak into the Cirk performance." The flame-tossing look I'd seen Margo send toward the stage opening night . . . "Tomi hoped that with a stupendous showing he could weasel his way back into Margo's good graces."

"Fat chance."

"No chance. She went backstage, found him, and asked me to drive him to Highway 101. He was wearing a perfectly good costume, kind of a waste. I decided making him hitchhike dressed as a bird was worth losing the costume."

"He could have walked back to the property from the highway."

"It would have taken a few hours, but sure, he could have."

"Maybe he's our killer."

"He was mad enough to kill."

"You have a thing with his wife?"

He acted stunned, too stunned. "Absolutely not."

"Just checking."

"About Maria," he said. "At some point he'll want to grab her, maybe head home to Italy. You sure you don't mind her staying here?"

I looked at Maria.

"She has no family," he said, "no anybody. She can't speak English. She's in a bind."

"Tell her I'll buy a ticket to Italy. She can work off the money by doing chores around here."

They spoke a few words, words edged with disagreement. I thought my offer was pretty generous, but she slumped and looked pouty.

"What's with her?"

"She likes the States, she doesn't want to go home."

"Great. If she can find someplace in the US where they only

speak Italian, where her husband won't find her, and where there are lots of large animals to train, I'll buy her a ticket there tonight."

He passed it on. She shrugged a teenage-girl kind of shrug. Not very endearing.

I'd start looking for a ticket to Italy before she'd done many chores. I could figure her work at a high rate per hour.

I tossed Angel enough blankets and pillows for two, told him to tuck Maria into the sewing room.

I pulled on flannel pajamas and brushed my teeth. The face looking back at me in the mirror was amused and curious. Curious if Angel would share the extra room with Maria. I had no idea what my face found so amusing. I told myself Angel was none of my business. For a brief moment I wondered if, before morning, I'd be hauled off for breaking and entering. I didn't look amused any longer.

The telephone rang. Lawless.

"Okay, I got there before the cops arrived," he said. "The woman with Angel was named Maria Tomi? I checked through the files, thought I'd grab hers in case her husband was the nut on the loose. No file," he said. "You sure about her?"

"Sure she exists? She's in my house."

"Who brought her to Margo's?"

"Margo did. Maria was an animal trainer whose husband, an aerialist, got rough with her. Margo showed him the door in no uncertain terms. As a matter of fact, it was just before Margo died. Angel said he has a bad temper."

"Angel knows him."

"Both of them. I believe he may be comforting the wife as we speak."

"Known whereabouts for Mr. Tomi?"

I told him the last time he'd been seen he was standing on the shoulder of Highway 101 wearing a Cirk bird costume and sticking out his thumb.

Lawless laughed, then stopped. "Not that far to walk back to Margo's. Especially if he was pumped up."

"Not far, and what are the chances that someone's going to pick up a hitchhiker dressed as a bird?"

"I'll follow up on the Tomis with the few employees left at Margos. I guess you're stuck—there's no need for Maria up there, the animals have been cleared out."

"Except for two giraffes. No one wants them."

"Annie, you know what? Forget being stuck," he said. "I don't like this. You're harboring a woman whose husband may be more dangerous than Rory."

"Maria's not going to be here long."

I heard the click of a lighter, an inhalation of breath. "Do me a favor, will you?"

"Sure."

"Get Mina in the house with you. And the plumber."

"How did you know the plumber was here?"

"Lucky guess."

"Lawless, about the gun—you'll tell me if I'm in trouble."

"You're not."

"You sure?"

"There was no gun, and no gun means no prints."

"I saw the gun, I held it, I put it back on Lili's desk."

"I don't know what to tell you."

"You believe me?"

"I believe you've been under a lot of stress. Your daughter shows up battered—I've been there—I know the emotional damage that causes a parent. A close friend and neighbor was killed. You drive your daughter seventeen hours, each way, to save her from her insane husband, get home, and go directly to a funeral. You had, what, maybe two or three hours' sleep? Total. That's what I told the cops, and you are a non-factor. Because stress and death and lack of sleep make our imagination run wild. It turns our fears into real form."

"You don't believe me."

"You need a good night's sleep, and you should be concerned about Mr. Tomi. That's what I believe."

"Lawless? Thanks."

"No problem. Except for the ones caused by other people. I'm going to take care of that."

"We're going to."

"Get some sleep. Take a pill if you need to."

I called Jack. He said they were all doing great, I said how dare they when I wasn't around to enjoy it, and he mentioned that Abra was sitting on the porch with a nice young man. Jack's words.

"He understands Abra's situation. They're just looking at the stars and talking. But I know men," Jack said, "he's good, but none of us are *that* good, and she's not going anywhere with him."

"Thanks, Jack."

"No problem. You okay?"

"Fine, just tired."

He ordered me to get some sleep. Compared to me, Jack sounded stable—I was in real trouble.

I fingered the horn of heliotrope and drifted off thinking about Jack and Abra, the lost-in-space family members. According to Lawless, I was joining them in the ozone. It didn't seem out of the question, and God knows what was in that tea Mina gave me before I was gifted with the invisible and prophetic herbal necklace.

~~~

A mob chases me, I need to hide. There's a cave. The opening is small, but I squeeze inside. Neon-colored algae throbs against the walls as if kids went wild with Day-Glo paint. I stay still until my eyes get used to the dark. Drawings are chipped into the rock, fresh drawings, they mar the algae. I hear footsteps outside, running past the cave.

In the corner of the cave are thirty, forty skulls. They feel blessed, not frightening.

Suddenly there's a man sitting next to me. He says, "Do you like our bone boxes?"

Bone boxes. "What are they?" I ask him. "Should I be afraid of you?"

"You're safe. Bone boxes are the skulls of people who were our dreamers, the skulls of people who could read our lives. We keep the bone boxes to hold our dreams and the secrets of our future. Sitting with them is like visiting old relations—generous and kind. We call them the talking heads."

He pulls out a lighter, lights up a cigarette. In the frail light I see Margo sitting behind the pile of skulls. She's tremendously peaceful.

"We've been waiting for you," he says to me. "She knew you'd come."

Margo says about the man, "You can trust him, I want you to understand that, to know it." She smiles, and like the Cheshire cat she disappears until the last thing left is her smile. Then that's gone, too.

I lean into the man, he puts his arm around me. I wish he were a cave I could climb inside.

Margo reappears. "I forgot to introduce you."

"No need," I say to her, "we've known each other a very long time." Margo's gone again.

Siamese twins dance across the cave wall for us.

We sit, just sit, with each other and speak our silent words to the ancient skulls. I feel like I've entered the door of my own home after a long absence. The skulls laugh, the man laughs. I wake up.

≋

I'll still visit Leo, but I won't tell him about the dream. I won't tell him that I saw him and Margo sitting inside an ancient cave filled with skulls crowned by grace and illuminated algae.

Twenty-five

You can't fall from grace, you can only fall into it. And grace arrives with trust.

—Leo Rosetti, from *The Book of Fallen Flyers*

The only grace I really know about is my old neighbor, Grace Chu. I *do* know if you're not falling flat on your face, something's wrong. Get up and fall. Get up and fail. This is all part of something called life. And maybe Life is another word for Grace.

—Madame Mina to Leo Rosetti

O woke up after a deep sleep filled with vivid dreaming. I padded into the kitchen and opted for Lipton tea instead of coffee. A little caffeine, but not a jolt. On the floor I spotted a note that had been pushed under the door. It read: *No more battered women at Margo's, Maria was the last. Thanks for giving her a home, but stay alert. I'm working on finding her husband—Lawless.*

Home? Not for long.

Angel was asleep on the living room floor, curled up in a blanket by the woodstove. Mina and the plumber were asleep on the pull-out couch. I assumed Maria was zonked out in the sewing room. Almost 8:00 A.M., all sleeping late. Skip the tea—I'd treat myself to a diner breakfast, then drive to Leo Rosetti's.

I found the street address he'd given me and drove under the arches of the Cadillac RV Park, searching for his numbered parking space.

There were old RVs that hadn't seen the road for years parked next to shiny RVs belonging to tourists who'd wandered in for a few nights. Two giant stainless-steel toaster-trailers, beautiful Airstreams, were parked side by side, laundry hanging between them. On Leo's lane, scattered single-wides perched on cinder-block piers.

I would have found Leo's home without knowing his street number.

A trapeze rig hovered between his trailer and an empty parking space. The rig was a kinesthetic sculpture built with odds and ends from a hardware store and the dump—soldered pipe and clamps and wires and ropes. No net, the bar wasn't very high off the ground, and several old mattresses were tossed beneath it. The trapeze itself hung from a straight tree branch halfway across the rig. About twenty feet across from the flyer's pedestal was a piece of equipment that looked as if it came from an abandoned playground. It was forged of hard steel pipes, and the catcher's cradle hung suspended from it.

Leo's platform was wide, five or six feet. A plaid couch and a trash bin were perched on the platform. An empty beer can rolled on its side next to the trash bin. The whole contraption could have been named *Rube Goldberg Has an Affair with John Ringling.*

Music poured out of the trailer, an old show tune. I knocked on the trailer door, the music died. I was drawn back to the rig, a kid's wildest fantasy given life.

The door opened. Leo smiled at me "You like it?"

"I love it. It should be in MOMA."

"Come on in. I've just baked brownies, you can help me eat them."

"I'm trying to watch my weight."

Why did I say that? I'm always watching my weight. Watching in horror as I see it enter uncharted territory.

"You're perfect," he said, "and I hate cooking when there's no one to enjoy my food."

"You sound like a Jewish mama."

"I'm an Italian mama. No difference."

I followed him into the kitchen. The smell of real cocoa, not the kind that's buried in a Betty Crocker brownie mix, was enough to make anyone throw Dr. Atkins out the window. We sat at his table, a rippled gray-and-white Formica rimmed with stainless steel, eating warm brownies from the baking dish.

When you don't know what to say it's always best to dive right in and say it. At least it's out of the way.

I said, "Tell me why Angel thinks we should talk."

I watched him think how to phrase his response. Forget his response. I watched him just for the pleasure of it.

You usually don't notice or feel attraction at a funeral, but I'd noticed it yesterday. Shameless and bizarre, but true. Leo was stocky, a true bear man, a beautiful man. Protective. He had chunky white-and-black hair, thick and gorgeous. Walnut brown eyes. I was falling into a warm deep pool; I didn't want to go there, but I was already on the slide. Sometimes you suck water up your nose, sometimes you're in for a delicious swim. But you *never* avoid the slide.

He said, "Angel wants me to tell you about the quarrel you heard the night of Margo's death."

Sex and death—the eternal roommates.

"Okay," I said.

"The police can look for angry politicos or husbands regarding Margo's death, and they might find her killer among them. But this is a lead they won't follow because they can't."

"Maybe I need another brownie."

"It involves a family secret that should never have been a secret."

"No matter how deep you bury them," I said, "sometime or other they'll be exhumed."

"Exactly," he said. He shifted his head—one side, then the other. "I know you."

What was this about?

"Right, the funeral yesterday, and from seeing me show off on my dad's horse several light-years ago."

"No, it seems like something . . . I don't know, forget it."

The bone box dream yanked at me, I pushed it away. "The family secret?" I said. "I don't like to waste calories unless there's stress or celebration involved."

His revelation would fall into the stress category. Leo was a composed man, but it was obvious that he wasn't looking forward to this conversation.

"I've known Margo and Lili for years," Leo said. "We were kids together. Margo was a little older than me, she was older still than Lili."

"Yow. You know Margo's childhood?"

"All of it. Our folks worked the circuit together. My family was close, loving. Her family was . . . It was the opposite," he said, pinching the hard corner crust off a brownie, dusting the crumbs off the table. "Margo's mom was quiet and pleasant, but she was beaten down. There's nothing pleasant about that.

"Margo's dad was the circus bookkeeper. He was so tight, you'd have thought it was his own money. Every Friday, same song and dance, people pounding on the Spanger door hollering to get paid.

"There was always a row coming from the Spangers', we were used to it, but one day it all ended. Margo's mother was dead."

"What did Margo's mother die of?"

"More like *who* did she die of. No investigations—bad press— we closed ranks. With movies getting grander, the circus was on its way out. We were already viewed as a bunch of outcasts. We were, but we didn't want to be thought of as murderers."

"You think Margo's dad killed her mom?"

Leo must have played this out many times in his head. "Yes," he said. "That fight wasn't the usual shouting and screaming followed by words dropping one by one at the end of a rainstorm. It was a tyranny of noise, then utter silence when the fight ended."

"Where was Margo?"

"In the tent with them," Leo said. "He'd slapped Margo around more than once. She was tough, but her mother, she was such a tiny woman . . . Margo took off."

It was a terrible pain to imagine Margo's childhood, terrible because I could feel the truth in it. I could see the way she'd carried the wounds and turned them into scars, pushing her into battle.

"I missed her when she left," he said. "I had a terrible crush on her."

"You and half the other men and women she knew."

"She had a huge appetite, that was her great appeal. I never knew what became of her until she hit it big."

"You said Lili was there, too? I thought she was from Eastern Europe, the accent, the attitude."

"Lili was born in Baraboo, Wisconsin. Margo used to babysit for her. Lili's family didn't speak much English, only enough to ask for their paycheck."

"Leo," I said, "do you know where Lili is?"

His eyes drilled me flat against my chair, then he relaxed. "I cannot imagine Lili living without Margo. She was Lili's life force."

"Margo was mythic."

"Margo put on a good show," he said, moving on. "Lili, when she was fifteen, fell in love with a very good-looking man in our troupe. He was twenty-eight."

"Are you sure we're talking about a man?"

"The person Lili was in love with? I'm sure."

"But she and Margo."

"Oh, that was later, and they fell in love with each other, not their bodies. That was just a tough break."

"Not very politically correct."

"Life is hard enough without falling in love with someone of the same sex. I doubt it's something most people would choose, but I'm wrong about a lot of things. I only know Lili and the man were in love, and Lili and Margo were in love."

"Love is tricky."

"At best."

"Is this the family secret? That Lili had once been in love with an older man and that Margo had an abusive childhood? It would explain the women's shelter."

He took a sip of tea, offered me another brownie, pulling his into unappetizing shreds.

"This trailer's too small for more big stories, and my behind is stiff from this chair," he said. "You want to see my rig?"

"If that's a come-on line, the answer is no. If you mean your trapeze rig, sure."

Leo's eyes twinkled. Of course it was a come-on line, and a highly original one at that. We'd let it pass for now.

"I used to fly at Margo's," I said. "My passion for it is a lot greater than my skill."

"You're built for it. Compact"—he touched my shoulders, ran his hand down my back—"with good upper body strength. About five feet five, five-six?"

"Boy, do you have an eye."

"It used to be my life," he said. "Now I don't know what it is."

One look, I knew what it was. "It's your spark."

He laughed. "Okay, let's talk on the platform, then we fly."

Twenty-six

We climbed a steep ladder, and we both swung up to the pedestal. The trapeze hung beneath branches that were bare of leaves. I imagined the trapeze in the spring, and flying beneath a rain forest canopy. The platform couch was gold-and-brown plaid, the fabric felt like a combination of polyester and string cheese—it was a lot more comfortable than it looked.

Lili was in love with an older guy, Margo was running from a brutal childhood, and I didn't see what any of this had to do with Margo's murder. Leo was settling into the plaid, and it looked like I was trapped in the web of other people's lives, not where I wanted to be. My spirit was climbing that tree, wandering through the branches, scooting out to the very edge. Leo talked, and I'd tune in and out . . . Now Lili was giving up her contortion act, learning to clown, and telling Leo she was in trouble. Trouble?

I left the tree and zoomed in on Leo. Seems the older guy had gotten Lili pregnant, she didn't want to tell him, or her family. When the baby was about to pop, she asked Leo to drive her to Canada. He had no idea what they were going to do there, but Lili said she had a plan. He said he'd give her a ride. They checked into a motel in Toronto and waited for the blessed event.

This was getting pretty interesting, considering the cast of characters. Leo, all heart from head to toe, and Lili, who, if she'd ever had a heart, lost it or kept it well hidden.

"What happened in Toronto?"

"We're there one week, we celebrated her birthday in that motel room playing gin rummy. She goes into labor, we go to the hospital, she has a beautiful boy. I figure she's putting the baby up for adoption, but no, we leave the hospital with the baby, and she won't talk to me about her so-called plan."

"Teenage girls can almost, *almost,* plan what pair of shoes they're going to wear that evening," I said. "That's about it."

"So I learned. I fall asleep wondering what we're going to do with this kid. I'm getting a sinking feeling—the ship's going down, and there aren't any life vests."

Leo stared into the barren branches, a jumble of skewed patterns and human-shaped limbs. I studied his face while he was lost in the branches. Leo was time-traveling, and the trip angered him.

"I wake up, I scan the motel walls covered with scruffy dawnlight. The baby's squalling, and I'm waiting for Lili—she's in the other bed—to get up and feed him. He keeps crying, I look around the room, no Lili in the other bed."

"What?"

"No bag, and not one trace of Mama. I'm mad, but I'm mostly scared. I don't know anything about babies. What if I kill it by mistake? I bundle him up in the motel blanket and take him to the store. I buy those paper diapers," Leo said, "and some formula, a couple of baby outfits that were too big. Then I really panic. What am I going to tell everyone back home? I've lost Lili and gained a baby."

"Tough to explain," I said. "You consider taking the baby to an orphanage?"

"Never crossed my mind. Doesn't fit the way I live my life, in here." He rubbed his chest. "I piled the baby and me into my old Ford Galaxie. The winter is the only time the damn thing didn't overheat, and I think, *If Lili had to leave me with a baby, at least she picked the right time of year.*"

Leo told me that he drove all night, and by the time he hit the circus grounds, he was a ticking time bomb. The first person Leo saw was Lili's father—he was fit to be tied—Leo had no use for him. He grabbed Leo by the collar. Leo, carrying the baby wrapped like a little mummy, pushed him aside. Leo had a destination, and nothing was getting in his way.

"Why didn't you give the baby to Lili's father, the grandfather?"

Leo's hand, the one closest to me, was closed in a tight fist—pumping open then closed—a mollusk adrift. Leo's right hand worked the armrest of the couch. He found a thread, pulled it, tried to stuff it back in place.

"Because the baby's father was the one responsible for that child being in the world," Leo said. "I walked to my brother's tent, and Al's in there with the fortuneteller. She sees the look on my face, jumps out of bed, and starts pulling on her clothes. I snarl at her, *See anything unusual in his cards?* She stops dressing and says, *Money will come his way,* and she zips out of the tent half-dressed.

"I hand the bundle to my brother Al, and I say, 'Here's your son. What do you intend to do about him?'"

"The baby was your nephew."

"That's why no orphanage," he said. "Al took the baby, smiled at him, and fainted dead on the floor. I caught the baby before it hit the floor, too."

"Leo, Lili never told Al about the baby-to-be. He didn't have a chance to step up to the plate."

"I know, it wasn't rational, but I was furious with both of them. I got over it—I had to, or it would have eaten me alive—and for a while Al and I raised the baby together, he even stopped chasing skirts. He quit the family business, said he'd come back when he made some real money and had a decent home, but he never did." Leo said, "Al changed his name and started over."

A foam Nerf ball landed on the platform. Leo tossed the ball back to a neighbor kid. Leo was angry, he hadn't gotten over it, and if that ball hadn't been foam rubber it would have landed in another county. The kid waved and thanked him, Leo gave him a distracted wave, told him to come back later for brownies. The kid ran off.

"You raised Al's son for him?"

"That baby had a father and mother who deserted him. I didn't know one damned thing about kids, but I understood love. So I decided, considering his parental options, he was better off with me," Leo said. "The boy always felt like my son, still does. My anger wasn't about feeling burdened, it was about feeling used. Raising that kid was a gift, I can't imagine life without him."

"You were like me, Leo. Both the mom and the dad."

He lightened up, and, stroking my cheek, said, "How does a man learn to bake brownies from scratch unless he's been a mom?"

A lightbulb appeared over my head. This was the man introduced to me at the funeral as the person who raised Angel.

"Where is your son now?"

He looked puzzled. "He said he was staying at your house."

"Angel."

"Angel Verona—the Flying Verona Brothers were magic. I gave him their last name."

Then the lightbulb flashed, and the light knocked me on my behind. "Wait a minute. Angel is Lili's son!"

"He is."

"Jesus God," I said. "Does, did, Margo know Angel was Lili's son?"

"Eventually," he said. "You a good friend of Margo's?"

"I thought so, but it turns out I knew about one-tenth of her life. If that much."

"That's more than she showed most people. When Lili resurfaced with Margo here in Sonoma, I visited them, and Angel was with me. Lili wanted Angel to know she was his mother, but she insisted we not tell Margo. Lili could be the stupidest person."

Leo said he and Angel visited the two women regularly, and Leo worked with him on the trapeze. Here was this kid visiting every week, and Margo didn't have one clue in the world that he was Lili's kid. Finally, Lili couldn't stand it, and she told Margo the truth. Margo was outraged, she felt like a fool, she felt betrayed, then she turned her love light on Angel hard and strong.

"Lili's life must have been a rough ride when she came out with the truth."

"And Al's. Margo bombarded him with calls—he was a coward, he should have given Angel money, no college tuition, no cars, none of the things a rich dad usually provides."

"The fortuneteller was right? What's Al's job in Wisconsin, Cheese King?"

"He lives in Sonoma County. You probably know him," Leo said. "Everyone around here does."

"Al Rosetti, I don't think so."

"Al Rose. I told you, he changed his name."

"Not Al Rose as in owner of the second largest food franchise?"

"My brother, the Clowny Drive-Thru king."

"Angel's father and Lili's ex-lover."

"Yep."

There was Al, right over the hill, with enough dough to buy and sell twenty women's shelters and a circus besides. His son was working for Margo. He was Lili's ex-lover, and for some reason he'd changed his name and left every inch of his old life behind. I couldn't wait to tell Mina.

I said, "You and your brother ever speak to each other?"

Leo smiled, and his smile was right next door to a miracle. "Al?" he said, "of course. He's the idiot prince, but he's still my brother."

"You know what? If I were Lili, I might have gone to Al after Margo died. A shared history, they have a kid, they both knew Margo . . ."

"She could have come to me. She did the last time she was in a jam."

"Nope. Al owed Lili, you didn't."

"Not a chance Lili'd run to Al," Leo said.

I didn't say anything more. Of course there was a chance. Especially if she thought she could throw a monkey wrench into Al's life.

"Where'd you say your brother lives?"

"I didn't," Leo said. "He lives in the Heights."

"Did he change his name so Lili couldn't find him?"

"No, no. He's passing. When he left the circus he was determined to make something of himself, his words. *Italian businessmen aren't respected unless they work for the mob,* he said. Al changed his name to Rose, started going to temple, and bought a nice bench in the front. Even had his kid bar mitzvahed."

"Al's married."

"Sylvia." The way he said her name let me know exactly the way Leo felt about his sister-in-law, Sylvia Rose.

GADS. Was I slow or what? Of course Al was married to Sylvia, and it was Sylvia that everyone in the Valley knew, not Al. She was rich, she knew it, and she made sure you knew it. She's one of the few short women who can look down their noses at anyone.

"Sylvia is a world-class snob," I said. "I thought her husband must have invented nuclear power. I had no idea he was the head Bozo of Clowny Drive-Thrus."

Then I thought what being connected to Margo and her crowd would do to Sylvia's standing in the community, Sylvia's standing inside her own head, and I said, "Leo, does Sylvia know about Angel? About Al's past? About you?"

"Before Margo died there was a lot of grief about that."

"Let me guess—Margo wanted to out the truth."

"Exactly. Al kept tabs on Angel, but he'd made a new life and decided just to let go of the old one. That meant letting go of Angel. Okay with Lili. She didn't want to push him."

"Where the hell does Angel think he came from? He's a little old for cabbage patches and the stork."

"Angel thought Lili was his mother and that I raised him because her health was poor. He thought his father ran out on them, and she never heard from him again. It's pretty close to the truth."

"*Angel thought* as in past tense," I said. "Margo spilled the beans?"

"Of course she did. One night Margo got drunk and opened the can of family worms for Angel's consumption. She thought he had a right to know his dad."

"This relates to the grief just before Margo died."

"Margo wanted us to trot over to Al's and confront him and Sylvia about Angel. I wasn't crazy about the idea, but I said I'd go with them if it happened. Margo thanked me for the moral support. I wasn't offering moral support. I figured they'd need a referee."

"What happened?"

"A lot of brouhaha between Lili and Margo about it, then Margo was dead, and I don't know if the whole mess happened. If they saw Al, no one ever told me."

"Call me crazy, but it's possible that the revelation, or the threat of it, and Margo's death may be connected."

"Only a possibility, but that's why you and I are having this talk."

"Leo, I'm going to visit the Roses."

"What reason could you possibly have to show up at some strangers' house?"

"I can always think of an excuse to drop in on someone's life."

Leo squirmed, pulled at his socks, then pushed the skin around on his forehead. "I don't like it," he said. "Rich people can be dangerous. Angel wanted you in on this, but it's really not right."

"Smart people are dangerous, too. I'll be okay."

I stood on the platform and thought how pleasant it would be to feel a gentle breeze blowing from one ear right through to the other. I imagined the serene joy of an empty head.

"You want to play on the trapeze?" I asked.

"Absolutely. Now even this big blue sky is filled with old stories that no small house could hold. Let's give the sky a reason to smile."

Twenty-seven

*T*otal abandon.
 Total.
I wanted it.

Leo checked the bar, made sure it was wrapped tight. He gave me leather strips to protect my hands. I still had calluses, but they weren't much. He asked if I wanted to make a couple of practice swings. I did.

My form was off, I hadn't moved yet, but I could feel it. I was too much in my head.

"Point your toes and smile," Leo said, and Angel had said that to me, too. He'd learned it from Leo who'd learned it from . . .

"Stop thinking," Leo said. "Shake your fingers. Breathe. Now get out there and make some beauty!"

Beauty is exactly where the calm center place exists, and its part-ner is Grace. If you're graceful, it has to work. If you're not, it won't. Simple as that. I shut my eyes, I waited to feel the wind ruf-fle my hair across my face. I waited until it whispered my name.

I took a couple of test swings, did a shoot over the bar, and I blew it royally. I was grateful for the mattresses. I climbed back to the pedestal. I was getting pumped up, I was feeling the adrenaline rush.

Leo spotted it. He clapped his hands together one time. "Now you're ready, you're there. You can't feel anything but the soft space you're in, pretty soon you won't hear my voice."

I lost his voice and I was scared to death and I lost time completely, the most amazing thing, like losing time under a chair cushion, fretting about it, and finally forgetting about it, then finding it again one day. But once you lose time, you never want to wear a watch again. And once you lose gravity, you never want to feel its tug again. I was sure I had not made beauty, but it was as close to eternity as I'd ever get.

Leo caught me from the catcher's cradle. He didn't have to get into an awkward position—shift too high or too low—we were in perfect sync. I did a half turn and returned to the bar.

It was Leo's turn. I'd only been a catcher a few times, but he trusted me. He said he was able to fall on the mattress without hurting himself, told me not to worry about him. He eased my mind and made my job easier.

He did a few practice swings to me, I had to adjust myself a bit higher to prepare for his arc as he went down. That's where I would catch him.

"I can't do what I used to do," he said, "this thing's too low, but we'll make something happen."

I sat in the catcher's seat waiting. I could hardly breathe. He forced out gracefully, I swear he could have traversed the entire twenty-foot length with one jump. It was one of the most incredible things I've ever seen, as wild as the ocean, but as straight and focused as a Zen master's arrow. He flew back to the pedestal looking for more momentum and found it. Leo was in the middle of timelessness—it's as breathless to see it as to be there. He flew into his set, one hard break, and sailed into a single layout. With the right equipment it would have been a double, maybe even a triple.

We stretched our hands toward each other, and we touched lightly. We were smack in the middle of that painting of God touching Adam's finger and giving him the permanent zap. I caught him.

Leo played with architecture and nature. When he needed spring, he was the steel reinforcement in a skyscraper, a river reed when he needed to bend. He experimented with sweet, fine, delicate, strong. I was aware of being in the presence of someone extraordinary.

We fooled around for another hour. We both knew when we were finished, as easily as we'd known when it was time to begin. Our timing was impeccable.

Leo was more than sparkle and dash. A grown man in the middle of his power, he knew himself, and he trusted himself.

"You like beer?" he said.

Beer sort of bursts the bubble of magnificence.

"It makes me fat," I said.

"That's not what I asked you."

"I like beer."

He pulled two beers from the cooler next to the couch on the plywood pedestal. We sipped and looked at our feet. I looked at the rig, fuzzed my focus, and did my best to relive that feeling of loose and eternal grace and beauty.

I hoisted my beer and pointed to the rig. "Leo, thank you. That was fantastic."

"I practice pretty often, but it's much better with someone else."

"I'm poor company."

"Your skill level? Who cares? What matters is your spirit. I've been doing this since I was a kid, and I come back over and over to find myself and lose myself. I'm not sure what the kick is, but it's like a drug."

"The drug is danger," I said, "and dancing with it feels like an aphrodisiac the gods brewed up in an inky iron kettle."

Leo nodded his head in slow agreement. "Exactly."

He draped his arm over the back of the couch. "If you want to stay for dinner, we can order something in and watch that old Burt Lancaster movie, *Trapeze*."

We quoted the best line in the movie—*When circus was real, flying was a religion*—together. We laughed, I nestled into his chest, his arm around me on the ratty plaid couch by the trapeze.

We woke up the next morning. I smiled into Leo, he smiled into me.

He said, "I would say we make beauty together."

"I dreamed about you the night before last."

"You sure it was me? We only saw each other a few minutes at the funeral."

"I'm sure, and Margo was there. She said I could trust you." I stroked his head, resting on my chest. "Absolutely sure it was you. You're distinctly and beautifully full, another part of my own self."

He lifted my chin and grinned. "Point your toes and smile . . ."

I did, and he did, and another two hours fell down the rabbit hole before I took a shower, ate some Wheat Chex, and drove home.

Twenty-eight

$\mathcal{I}$ said, "If you're going to yell at me, then I'm not hanging around."

"You sound like a teenager who's mad at her parents because they caught her sneaking into the house."

Mina was already dressed, it was early for her to be in full regalia. Probably had a client coming. Mina and a client in the trailer—I didn't know where she'd stash the plumber while she did her reading.

"I guess I should have called."

"I know what kind of person you are. If you spend the night with a man, is that such a big surprise? No. But when I've got death and disappearance and a good-looking guy I don't know PLUS a fat Italian girl who is totally uninteresting—I can't talk to her at all—then I worry about you." Her voice tapered off.

I said, "Are you starting to like me?"

"What the hell happened to you? Wow, that's the second time I've used a swear word. If I'm going to take up swearing, I'd better come up with some new words."

"You have enough hobbies."

"True. Where were you?"

I didn't answer. I walked to my room, Mina following. Enter the plumber, hot on her heels.

"Could you excuse me," I said to him, "I'm going to get changed."

The plumber looked clueless, as if the English language had run away from the unfurnished apartment between his ears.

Mina turned to him. "Frank. Go back to the trailer and wait until I tell you what to do. Annie and I are going to talk. Alone."

"Oh," Frank said. "Okay."

Frank was a walking zombie.

"What did you do to that guy?"

"Same thing I been doing to men the better part of my life, except I'm not so sure it *is* the better part." She hiked up her skirt, dark purple velveteen with gold satin trim, and scooched it over a few inches so the seam was on the left side. "Between me and the healing I laid on him, Frank doesn't know the floor from the ceiling."

"He's not moving in, is he?"

"Didn't you already ask me that?"

"I did. But now he looks like a stray dog you fed on the porch who has decided that you're home sweet home. So I thought I'd better ask again."

"I've had it up to here with men."

"Since when?"

"I didn't even know I was going to say that until it popped out of my mouth," she said. "Abra called last night."

"Why didn't you tell me as soon as I walked in the door?"

"Calm down. She's fine, the baby's fine. She and Jack are thinking of ways for her to make a living. I had some ideas, too."

"She needs to figure out how to make a living where she actually lives."

"Jack says until he hears that Rory didn't off Margo, and until he's sure that Rory won't bother Abra, she's staying put."

I imagined hearing that line until Joey's wedding day. I groaned and leaned against the wall. "She may be stuck there forever."

"You want the truth? I don't think she feels stuck at all. That might be her place."

"It's too far."

"It's a car ride."

"A seventeen-hour car ride."

"Her voice sounds good. She tells you she wants to stay in that part of the world, you support her and don't think about yourself. I had to be without my grandkids because you were too stubborn to see me. At least you could see Joey whenever you wanted."

"I wasn't too stubborn. You hated me."

"I only hated you a little. You should have tried to change my mind."

Change Mina's mind. That would be equivalent to changing a weather pattern.

"Let's forget it," I said. "You see your grandkids now."

"Yes. Life moves on, it's all a matter of rhythm. Don't get in the way of your daughter's rhythm, you understand me?"

I did understand, but it wasn't easy.

"This is the thing about being a parent," she said. "Do a good job, and your kids feel like they can take on the entire world, and sometimes that involves a world that's not anywhere near you. Do a lousy job, and they cling to your skirt and suck their thumbs—which is not so attractive in an adult person—but you do get to see them. Like all the time. You've got to let go, Annie."

"I've been letting go my whole life."

"Look at it this way—You've got to let go in order to pick up something new."

While we were talking I'd pulled out a dark red pantsuit that was kind of sassy, but not too much. I had to wear something stylish enough to make Sylvia think I was worth talking to, and sexy enough to make Al feel like staying in the room while we were talking. There's a fine line between slut and strut, and this outfit could walk it.

"That's a good shade of red"—Mina turned me around and faced me toward the mirror—"kind of like the color in your cheeks." Now she turned me to the side. "Even your stomach looks flatter. All the signs of a fiery night."

"Mina, I flew on the trapeze and it was breathtaking, it was ecstasy, it was wearing wings, it was breathing underwater."

"Right."

"It was."

"I believe you. I also believe you spent the night tumbling with the same fire that's in your cheeks. You walked in here with the same dumb look Frank the plumber's wearing."

"It's that obvious?"

"Not anymore. I've been working to pull you into your center so you can maintain in the world. I left you enough to spark any man who sees you, at least until this afternoon," she said. "It's got to end sometime."

"Why are you acting so nice?"

"I was wondering the same thing. Maybe I have a terminal disease, Frank told me some people are allergic to the Formica in the paneling of new trailers. I better go see what he's up to. If he's not in bed, he's poking the pipes or he's eating. I don't know which is worse."

Mina left, I looked in the mirror again. She was right, I looked pretty good.

I was heading out the door to the Roses' place, and I wasn't sure if I should tell Angel. After I decided not to find him, there he was sitting knee to knee with Maria on the porch swing. The inseparable dynamic duo.

I was going to give this dreary woman another chance at gratitude. "Maria," I said, "I'm buying you a ticket to Italy so you can get together with your family. Isn't that nice?"

Angel translated, she responded, patting his leg. Angel's face went sheepish.

"What?"

"She wonders if you're slow. She already said she didn't want to go back to Italy, that her family is right here."

"You better find a rental for your new family, Angel. You've got two weeks. Maximum."

"Speaking of family," he said, "Lawless called you twice last night and once this morning. You'd better call him. He was mad at me because I'd let you go out."

"*Let* me go out?"

"Hey, I'm just passing along the message. Call him before you leave again, or he'll bite my head off."

I walked back into the kitchen, set my purse on the counter, and dialed his number. Ruth answered. "Ruth, please tell me your husband is busy."

"He's in the garage changing the oil, but I'm sure he'll want to talk with you."

"That's okay. I'd rather talk to you."

"So he can yell at me instead of you? Forget it."

I heard her call him, I heard an army of clanking sounds, then I heard a door slam, water running, and steps across the floor. I was in trouble, and we hadn't even connected yet.

He said, "Do you know how much hot water my butt is in because of you?"

"How much?"

"I am practically stew meat."

"Because I wasn't home last night?"

"No, that was mere aggravation. I'm talking real trouble. I'd conned the first cop into buying the story about you climbing into the window to get Abra's file. After he got home, he got worried—chain of command and all that. He passed me to Officer Strunk, your old buddy."

I had never known a policeman in my entire life until the last few months. Now they either wanted to save my ass, or they wanted to fry it. How had this happened? I wanted my behind to go unnoticed.

I said, "You're kidding."

"You remember Strunk can't stand me, thinks I've got a Big City Ego? He believes I may have tampered with evidence, or helped you destroy evidence, that's related to Margo's murder."

"Ridiculous."

"He's threatening to pull my license, and I'm so mad at you my blood is boiling."

"You're not mad at me. You're mad at Strunk."

"I don't like being mad at a cop."

"Welcome to the human race."

He groaned. "It's not just the license thing, I don't want them chasing down a wrong path. And you are the wrong path."

"Now what?"

"I don't know," he said. "There are too many paths, and I am beyond worried about Lili. I keep waiting for the police to call and say they've found her body."

"Lawless, I've got the same feeling. I don't even know where to begin to look for her."

"You shouldn't begin anywhere."

Mina had told me Lawless was my father in a past life. If I hadn't been currently iffy on reincarnation, I'd believe her. "I'm going out for a while. I called because I had a grown-up night and Angel said you were mad at him. But I didn't report my grown-up night to him, either."

"Where are you going now?"

"Grocery shopping. This and that. You know."

"Just make sure someone knows where you are."

He hung up on me, and he who hangs up first has the last word.

Mina washed her cups in the sink. My sink. Another ploy to avoid Frank.

"Hey," she said, "I was so busy grounding you, I almost forgot to ask—you find out anything last night about Margo? And skip the 'How did you know?' part."

I told her about Leo, about him raising Angel. I told her about Al and Lili.

She sat down. "Lili is a mother?"

"Unbelievable, but true."

"And that's what those three were arguing about after the performance," she said, with too much enthusiasm, meaning volume, "the rat who ran out on Lili."

I shushed her.

"What am I shushing about? Angel"—she leaned her head out the back door—"come in here."

"Why are you dragging him into this?"

"Because it's his own life! And we don't have to worry about Maria listening in. She's stupid."

"Maria is not stupid," Angel said, walking inside. "She's in a state of shock. She's lost her home, her husband, and she's been battered. She lost her animals, and she's very attached to them."

"That figures," Mina said.

Twenty-nine

*A*ngel's friends and lovers do not need your stamp of approval."

"Of course not," Mina said to me, "but I'm a Libra, and I have a hard time being around ugly people and thoughts."

"Angel looks good enough for three people—you can handle one funny-looking person."

Why was I defending Maria? I wanted her out of my house. Moustache or no—it was her personality that was ugly—not her person.

Angel put his hands on his hips. "I didn't grow up with a mom. Listening to the two of you makes me feel like I didn't miss much."

Mina pounced on me. "See what you made him do? Now he hates mothers."

"I didn't say that," Angel said, coming to my rescue. "And, yes, that's what we argued about the night you two were standing outside the office listening to us yell and wishing you weren't. Mothers and fathers."

Angel told us about the fight, and it matched Leo's version with one added zinger.

Angel looked at the pattern on my floor, his voice one notch above a whisper. "Lili said Al had been the love of her life, and that he'd let her down when she needed him."

"The love of her life? That must have stung Margo."

"Did it ever. Margo flared, calmed down and said she was

working on letting it all go, but it was hard. That she had lots of loose ends to tie up, and so did Lili, and she hated unfinished business."

"You were the loose end?"

"One of them. Margo got revenge for the *He was the love of my life* remark. She told Lili she was ashamed of her, that she'd always admired her courage and wondered where it had gone now that they both needed it."

"You were just standing there like a floor lamp while they verbally duked it out?"

"Pretty much. I'd heard them fight, but this was a knock-down, drag-out. I'm leaving the worst parts out."

"We heard some of the worst parts."

"I just wanted them to stop."

His eyes were filling up. Maria stood passively by the door, then she turned her back on us and walked outside to pet one of the cats. Emotional material without understanding the words—who wouldn't leave? You get the vibes but none of the details.

"I was confused, I didn't know how to make them both happy." Angel put his head in his hands, he ran his fingers through his hair, and he scratched his scalp with anxious enthusiasm. "He's my father, of course I'd like to know him as a person," he said. "But I'm a grown man, and I understand him not wanting his present life and his old life getting mixed up.

"I saw him at Leo's when I was a kid, he was Leo's nice brother, a guy who hung out with us and brought me model airplanes. That's it. I've tried to peel back time and see if there were any hidden words or messages—any secret signals he sent that he was my dad—there weren't any."

"I'd feel as if I'd been lied to every day of my life," I said.

"There's some of that, but mostly I feel sad about what this did to Lili and Margo. And Al? Al got into something when he was young, the wheels started rolling, and he couldn't stop the train long enough for me to jump on."

That was very understanding of Angel, and I didn't buy it for a minute. It had to hurt. A few stray tears hung around the corners of his eyes. "I had Leo when I needed a dad"—here he laughed—"and Margo became dad number two. She took me to my first whorehouse, I didn't let her know a bareback rider had taken care of that when I was thirteen. Margo took me right down the road to Juanita's."

Was there one life in the valley that Juanita had not touched?

"I hated Margo the night of that fight," he said. "How do I live with my last thoughts of her being hateful? But she was so loud, so much bigger than Lili—Lili was frail, Margo was indestructible."

We'd all thought that; it turned out she wasn't indestructible. Far from it.

Angel, wiping those stray tears away, said, "I loved Margo. When Lili and Margo began organizing Cirk, Leo spoke with them about me. Margo welcomed me into their circle." Distant memories made him smile, probably jokes Margo played on Angel to initiate him into their family of performers. "Leo worked for Cirk when it opened, he met his wife there. Did he tell you that?"

"I didn't know about a wife."

Angel's smeared expression said he'd just walked inside a barn and stepped in a warm cow pie. "I shouldn't have gotten into this, it's none of my business."

"It is now."

He took a deep breath, hoping for a hole in the earth to swallow him.

No hole in sight, Angel said, "Leo met Celeste at Margo's, Celeste was a flyer from Spain. To watch them together . . . totally unreal, as if you'd pulled back the draperies of heaven and were allowed to watch two angels. Intimate, you know? There's always risk involved in flying, one of the highs about it. Practice was going well, then disaster. Celeste went onto the arena floor."

Angel didn't say anything. He gave me time to process the reality—and the horror—of the event.

"Leo blamed himself," Angel said. "He said Celeste's arc was higher than usual, and he should have adjusted. But none of us blamed him, we all understood—a simple miscalculation on her part, on Leo's part. A vagrant worry about bills, a dog left untied. Anything," Angel said. "That finished circus arts for Leo."

I understood Leo's trailer, his near isolation, his warm and tattered heart. I understood the gift of Leo's invitation to me, and I understood the trust it must have taken to welcome me inside his well-lit and eccentric den.

"Nine months after he quit Cirk," Angel said, "Leo climbed out of his cave and built that rig, but he hasn't caught anyone since Celeste. He flies solo. It's lonely, but it's safe."

"He caught me," I said.

Angel stopped watching the linoleum, his eyes jumped up to meet mine. He was stunned. Angel held my hand and squeezed. "He's healing," Angel said, and that was all he said.

It was disgusting to tell Angel, a perfectly kind human being, that Sylvia and Al might not want him in their life because he didn't measure up. I would omit the emotional juice, but I decided to tell Angel where I was going. Just in case.

I saw Maria outside my window, probably looking for one of the cats. I vowed once more to try and be kind. Sending warm thoughts her way, I watched as she rounded the barn and walked toward Margo's. It was difficult to miss Maria's probable destination—the animals. New ones.

"Angel, are those two giraffes on my property or Margo's?"

"Oh, that."

"Yes, that. Those."

"They're on your property. No one wants giraffes," he said. "Zoos have enough, they're pretty common."

"They are not common on a regular piece of land that is someone's yard. My yard."

"We had to get them out of Margo's so they could be cared for, and it was easier to take down a patch of your fence and guide them here than it was to find a new home."

"You didn't."

"It's okay. We put the fence back up, they're not going to get loose. Lawless said he'd arrange for your wildlife license to be processed right away."

"When did he say that?"

"Last night, the second or third time he called looking for you. He's the one who suggested we bring the animals over here. For a policeman, he's a pretty good guy."

"Ex-policeman. Yes, he's very thoughtful."

I stood for a moment trying to figure out how I could get two giraffes into the back of a pickup truck, drive them to the Russian River, and send them to live with Lawless and Ruth. The only thing I could imagine was tranquilizing them, lashing them together, tying them down to the bed, and strapping a red flag on their feet indicating a long load. What I couldn't imagine was the logistics of hauling their bulk into the truck. Lawless was lucky I didn't have a friend who was a crane operator.

First Lawless had tried to convince me there was no gun— there definitely was. Now he was into animal pranks. I'd resolve issue number one first, and a way to avenge animal pranks would come to me.

I said to Angel, "When I bumped into you the other night . . ."

"When you were running from Margo's."

"Right. Did I have a gun?"

He put a hand on my forehead.

"What are you doing?"

"I'm checking to see if you're all right," Angel said. "Of course you had a gun, we had an argument about it. I told you to lock it in your drawer, didn't you do that? I wish you'd get rid of those things."

"Yeah, yeah, I'll check my drawer. I was looking in the cabinet."

He exhaled his relief. So who the hell had snagged that .25 off Lili's desk?

"Angel, Lawless insists I did not have a gun. If you talk with him before I do, will you please tell him you saw the gun, that you even held it?"

"Sure."

"I have another favor. Mina, this involves you, too."

She scooted her chair closer. A favor means a debt, and debts come in handy.

"Angel," I said, "you're younger than I am."

"You've mentioned that before. Actually, you said I acted like I was ten years old."

"I was mad about something. Anyway, you're going to live longer than me," I looked at Mina—"and you probably will, too—I think

you'll live to be older than God. You both have to promise me
something."

Angel was solemn, Mina was pleased that I'd come to the real-
ization she was an aging minor deity with no expiration date in
sight.

"What are their names?" I asked Angel.

"Whose names?"

"The giraffes."

"Frog and Toad."

Mina laughed herself into a snort.

"You stop," I said. "You are in the middle of a solemn promise."

She saluted me. "Make the promise short," she said, "I've got
things to do."

"When I drop dead, those two animals will not be stuffed and
hauled to my funeral service," I told them. "I do not want giraffes
on wooden wheels screwing up perfectly nice grass, and I don't
want my daughters fighting over who has to take them. Especially
when there are three daughters and two giraffes. One will get off
scot-free."

"I promise," Mina said.

Angel promised, too. He said if worse came to worst, he would
take both of them so there'd be no fighting.

Once again I wondered how I'd gotten stuck with dad's stuffed
horse while Jack enjoyed the convenient dog turned into an end
table. "I'm leaving. Angel, you tell Lawless I love the giraffes. That
I'm surprised he didn't want them—he could have gone fishing
with two pets named Frog and Toad."

"Do I tell him you've gone to Al and Sylvia's?"

I thought it over. "If it gets dark and I'm not back, call and tell
him where I went. I don't want him barging in, guns blazing, just
when I'm getting close to something. Unless I need help."

"You sure you want to go there?"

"No. But when Margo died she was set on clearing the air about
your past, your connections, every detail. Could be some people,
let's take a wild guess, Al and Sylvia, wouldn't want the same thing."

"But it *is* the past, it's over."

"Is it? You and I are assuming all ties between Lili and Al were cut. We don't know that for a fact."

"I guess not." Misery wrapped him like a heavy fisherman's net.

I laid my hands on his curls. "You really are beautiful, your name suits you."

I turned from him, and he pulled me back by the hand. "Annie," he said, "you spent the night with Leo."

"It was . . ."

"You're a good pair. Did you love the flying?"

"Fantastic."

"You trusted him, and he trusted himself."

Angel kissed me on the forehead. I felt like I was the ten-year-old, and he was the dad. Things do just go around like that.

"Okay," I said, pulling myself out of gooey-sweet emotional reverie, "everyone out. I have a phone call to make. It's hard for me to spin a good whopper when I have an audience."

Mina said, "Don't sell yourself short. And remember, be bold about your lies, or people won't believe them."

Sound advice from the queen of prevarication. She waited until Angel left the room.

"Annie, you're walking into the past. It's not yours, so it's not supposed to catch up with you. It's supposed to catch up with the people who belong to it. Be careful—this past might have everything to do with Margo's death."

Thirty

 he voice that answered the phone was Latina.

"May I speak to Sylvia Rose, please?" I said to the voice.

"Un momento, por favor."

Spanish flew back and forth, evidently Sylvia had learned kitchen Spanish to work with her help over the years.

The click of an earring being pulled off. "This is Mrs. Rose."

"Sylvia! Great to hear your voice. This is Annie Szabo."

I could almost hear the pages of her internal Rolodex flipping down to the 's' in the alphabet. I'd let her flip for a little while. Time up.

"Annie Szabo, *Valley Sentinel,* special features?" I wrote for them until the editor and I had a brief falling-out that become permanent due to his insistence upon . . . I don't actually remember why we got cranky with each other, why I quit, or why he fired me. But we'd come to an understanding. I still fed him stories, and he pretended they weren't from me.

"We've met at several fund-raisers, Sylvia," I said. "Your generosity is legend."

I heard her heart go pitter-pat inside her Carrera blouse. "Wonderful of you to say, why has it been so long!" She put her hand over the mouthpiece, and I heard her muffled voice. No words, but the tone was exasperation. The maid was in temporary disfavor with the Red Queen. "How can I help you, Annie?"

I lowered my voice to convey respect and awe and admiration—

those can only be imparted in a sonorous tone. "Sylvia, you have been grossly overlooked as a prime benefactress and moving force in this community. I assumed we'd done several articles on you, but checking our archives, I found none. Can this possibly be true?"

"It is. I'm not in it for the glory, but a little appreciation is always welcome. Most of all, I'd like an opportunity to inform readers about important issues within our county. You never know when someone will feel moved to open their wallet."

"Absolutely true. I was afraid you might be a private person, hence the lack of notoriety."

"Just lack of attention from the press!"

"Let's get this article set up."

"Next Wednesday would be great for me."

"Sylvia, let me cut to the chase," I said, using my confidential tone. "I was handed the assignment to interview a mover and shaker just this morning. The regular reporter flaked, and I've got a deadline breathing down my neck. If it's not this afternoon, I'll have to find someone else."

"This afternoon."

"It's short notice. I could include you in the holiday special features section about people who serve our community. Next year."

"My hair's a wreck."

"I've never seen you look anything but fabulous."

"And I need a facial."

"I'll use a soft-focus lens."

"Oh, what the hey! Let's go for it. How about lunch?" She glittered, she gleamed, I was in. "Al's always home for lunch, I know he'd enjoy meeting you, too. Isabel can fix something, and we'll eat in the sunroom. It's light and cheery regardless of the season."

She meant the sunroom lighting was good and golden. What the hey! Sylvia was even trying to get her husband good press. I wondered how convivial she'd be if Al or Margo had dropped the shady-past-life bomb, and the resultant fallout had ended in a death. In most relationships, it would be batten-down-the-hatches-and-bolt-the-door time. But Sylvia was society, she was bred to put on a good face, particularly if the good face was going to wind up in the newspaper. *The show must go on* was a term invented by the rich and borrowed by the theater.

If I played my cards right, I could pull it off. I'd be a combination of the sweet naïveté that was Angel and the manipulation masked as goodwill that was Sylvia. It was my best shot at learning the Roses' status quo without ruffling feathers. I also knew Sylvia's good cheer was the sort that turns on a dime.

Thirty-one

It was a picture-postcard drive to Al and Sylvia's, the kind Lawless and I had bemoaned on our way to the funeral—too pretty, all the wildness stomped right out of the earth. Some nutty widow with enough money to buy truckloads of tulip bulbs had done just that. She hired help, Mexican guys who hang out on the corner of Old Redwood Highway and Fulton, but she'd been on her hands and knees with them planting the damned things, blighting the landscape with their inappropriate presence. She'd received permission to fill public land with as many bulbs as her heart desired.

The varieties were staggered so that one-quarter of them were in bloom any time of the year. The winter blossoms were a frilly deep purple headed to black, straight from Morticia Addams's garden.

Farther up the road, California oaks spread their curving branches, dignified and soft. Furniture hung from the branches, red iron beds, porch swings, even an old tractor. When they say the rich are different, they're not kidding. No trailer court would allow their residents to hang beds from trees. Do it in a million-dollar neighborhood, and you're delightfully eccentric.

There I was, driving through a surreal landscape of black flowers and hanging beds, when it all came to a screeching halt. The nutty widow had run out of bulbs, and whoever hung that furniture had recovered from their love affair with Goodwill.

At this climax point, the wild hills interfered and crept into some of the bulbs and under the trees. Soon there'd be an all-out war between the wild and the nurtured—I was rooting for the wild.

The streets wound left and switched back to the right for no apparent reason other than curves are prestigious. Now and then a lawn popped up, pristine as a putting green. In front of one wall stood a black iron jockey with a ring in his hand. I thought those had been banned.

Privacy increased as the hill, and the land values, grew steeper. Scattered rooflines of shake shingles and Mexican tiles were barely visible, houses hid behind stone walls. A few imported palm trees grew, things of an awkward beauty far from home.

Almost noon, the sun sliced the sky and peeked through the gash. A balmy seventy winter degrees was forecast. I was spunky and loose.

If I closed my eyes—which I didn't because I was driving—I could still feel Leo next to me. What I remembered most about the night was how he wrapped me in his arms while we slept. I don't like that, I never have. I don't want anyone, ever, close enough to get inside my dreams. I spent the first hour wondering how many angles I could mentally reconfigure the wall in order to entertain myself for seven hours. Then I listened to his easy breathing, he'd gone out like a light. I didn't expect sleep, I was happy listening to him and feeling his arms around me. Then it was morning and when I awoke we were facing each other, breathing each other's exhalations. His eyes popped open. We didn't hide our morning breath beneath the sheet, and I didn't wonder where to put this in my life. It just was.

Twenty-two four-eighty Citrus Lane whizzed by, the numbers embedded in a white terra-cotta wall. I turned around in the middle of the road and took another spin to the Roses' home. I pulled into the front drive and found the metal gate locked. I wondered if Al ever felt as if he were living in the gorilla cage. I rolled down my window, stuck out my hand, and hit the buzzer.

The Latina voice again, Isabel. I told Isabel, in perfect Spanish, that I'd come to see Sylvia and Al Rose, then I asked her to wash my hair with soup and sell me a fish. She laughed, translated my request, and buzzed the gate open.

I'd learned Spanish last year so that when I traveled in Mexico I could shop and bargain and find a bathroom. I was determined to make this work. The double oak door opened, and I shook Isabel's hand. I asked her if she was married to an onion. She laughed. Sylvia stood next to her, said something to Isabel, who by that time had tears running from her eyes. With only the slightest accent, Isabel said that our lunches were on the sunroom table.

Sylvia extended her hand, and said, "Annie, it's very nice to see you again."

I carried my Brenda Starr girl reporter camera and my matching notebook. I felt as if I'd won first prize in a 1960 box-top contest. All I needed was knee-high socks, horn-rimmed glasses, and a plaid skirt.

I was ushered into the sunroom, no Al, but Isabel served our lunch. It was a delicious salad, fresh Sonoma greens, big chunks of goat cheese, and caramelized walnuts. They sell the whole deal, premixed, at the Big Three. Isabel probably had a pretty good gig here.

Sylvia flapped her linen napkin with the proper amount of flourish. It was a creamy winter white bordered with sage-colored geometric designs. The dishes matched the linen. A far cry from the Li'l Dumplin', and I had to admit, I liked it. I wouldn't want to live with such order, but it was a pleasant little holiday from chaos.

"Tell me something about yourself," I said, pulling out my notebook and taking my pencil from behind my ear, I actually did have it behind my ear. "I've heard worlds about you, but I don't trust gossip." Again I lowered my voice. "In your circle there are too many people with axes to grind."

"Isn't that the truth! I hate to say it, but most axes are ground on the stone of jealousy."

"Good quote! I'll use it."

She was pleased, she was mine.

Sylvia tapped her chin while trying to remember her life. "Let's see. I went to Cal Berkeley, studied political science, thought I'd become a lawyer and work in my father's law firm. I was an intern in his office. I hated it. Obviously, I'd need an advanced degree, but I didn't have a clue where I was going.

"I spent two years in the Peace Corps, Ghana, quite a wonderful experience. When I returned home I knew where I was going.

"I worked at a homeless shelter in Marin City, and it was a real eye-opener. It was real, period. Soon I founded RealPeopleAid. I used my father's connections and my social passion to hit rich people up for money."

Jeez! Sylvia was one hell of a woman. I'd sold her short because of her alpha position on the food chain. She'd used the circumstances of a fortunate birth as a means to help other humans. A rare thing.

"That's a little blunt," she said. "I've surprised you."

"Honesty makes a better article."

I studied her. Talking about her work, she'd become vibrant. A woman who knew what she wanted, who'd be relentless about getting it. A woman who had a lot more at stake if something went lopsided in her world than I had imagined.

"Annie, are you still with me?"

"You're an extraordinary woman, Sylvia."

She blushed, actually blushed. How was this possible?

"The board has offered me a hefty salary three times, and I've never taken it," she said. "I have plenty of money, someday I'll inherit more. I can't see taking a paycheck when I have a nice house, nice clothes . . . an embarrassment of riches."

Something went click inside my head. I believed Sylvia worked for free and that she did good work. Whatever Sylvia got out of a job, it would never be about money. It was about respect and admiration. It didn't lessen the good she did; but it told me something about who she was—an American princess aiming for sainthood.

"I was a terrific workaholic, that is until I met Al," she said. "We met at a fund-raiser for the ACLU. He was a huge contributor to many causes, but he was so busy growing his business, we'd never run into each other. I'd say it was love at first sight, but that isn't exactly right, is it Al?"

She reached up her hand and wiggled her fingers behind her. Al moved forward and kissed the fingers. Al was a big guy, but I hadn't noticed when he entered the room. Sylvia's energy was a whirlpool that sucked nearby creatures into its vortex.

Al bent over, shook my hand, and introduced himself to me before sitting next to his wife. I looked at Al. Not much resemblance to Angel, but his bear shape was similar to Leo's. If Al had ever possessed Leo's spark, it had been extinguished by a life of good deeds and cheap burger drive-ins.

"Love at first sight?" he said. "Not hardly. I was clowning around, had a few too many drinks under my belt. I'd brought one woman, and I ditched her, she was a bore. Then I spotted Sylvia. So did every other guy in the room. I wanted to impress her, I wanted to stand out from the pack.

"I had a backseat full of novelty items, a polite euphemism for plastic dog-doo and whoopee cushions—I'd go to a new franchise, the kids loved that stuff. I even had whoopee cushions with our company logo imprinted on them. A cute saying, too: 'When you eat at Clowny's you'll say Whoopee!' The guys in marketing pulled it. They said talking about food and gas at the same time wasn't polite. It was for kids! Of course it wasn't polite!"

Sylvia patted his hand. I had the impression he was her Raggedy Andy, and she was his blankie.

"Let me guess," I said. "You were being yourself the night you two met, and Sylvia wasn't impressed."

"How did you know?"

"Most love stories start that way."

"Would a guy who slipped plastic dog-doo in your silk purse impress you?"

"Definitely. Not in a good way."

Sylvia laughed. With Al present her laughter sounded like a wind chime. Time to test the love fest.

"Sylvia, in retrospect, you couldn't be surprised. Your husband started out in the circus, he's bound to be a funny guy. Only a few clowns make us cry, and they're not very popular!"

Boy, was I chipper and friendly while hurling hand grenades.

Sylvia's face froze, but she managed to keep the smile. She was as well-bred as a Bichon Frise.

She said, "Al's a self-made man, one of the things I admire about him. He had loads of jobs while he worked his way through college. Right dear?"

Al pushed his lettuce around. "Loads, nothing was going to hold Al Rose back." But he didn't look up from his lettuce when he said it.

Sylvia had bought the Clowny Drive-Thru public relations about its beloved founder. I loved it.

I let the ball sit on the table, decided to see which one of them picked it up while I munched on a large bite of salad with a perfect walnut hiding in the cheese. I'd have to blow some bucks and buy this sometime.

It was Sylvia who picked up the ball. "But Al, you never told me about your time with the circus. That must have been fascinating!"

She turned to me. "Summer in New York can be so miserable, I'm sure it was nice for a young man to hit the road and earn money along the way. "And"—here she had a sparkle in her eye— "when you're an only child, sometimes parents enjoy their private time."

Sylvia had saved his butt, whether she'd intended to or not. My gut feeling was that she'd intended to, but I wasn't sure. I always wish I could be somewhere after I leave to see if anything hits the fan—I'd love to be a witness to fallout.

"Yes, it was healthy to get into the fresh air," he said, "although you can hardly call elephant dung fresh! But learning juggling! What a time."

"Is that where you learned?" She shook her head and smiled as if Al were a naughty boy. That was an understatement. "Annie," she said, "you learn something new about your husband no matter how long you've been married. He taught our son to juggle. I thought they'd learned together."

"Tell me about your son."

I hadn't meant for this to be a loaded question, but if the chandelier had crashed onto the center of the table, the pleasantries could not have been more shattered.

I was on the verge of losing Sylvia. That was the last thing I wanted.

"This article's about you," I said. "We don't have to go into kids at all."

Maybe there'd been a horrible accident, he was in jail, on drugs.

"That's very kind of you," she answered, and her subdued voice was real. "All I can say is that he's not the same boy we raised and loved. At the age of nineteen he was diagnosed with paranoid schizophrenia—he's institutionalized. I tried keeping him at home, it was impossible."

"No way we could get him to take his meds on time or even take them at all," Al added in defense.

"I'm so sorry." I really was. You love your kid with all your heart, and they become a stranger who's living inside your kid's body. Sheer and total devastation.

"This will not be in the article," I assured them. "This is private, nothing at all to do with your public personas."

Sylvia tried on a small smile. "It did give me one more charity to become involved with. The women's shelter in Santa Rosa and schizophrenia are my two passions."

"The women's shelter in Santa Rosa . . . Do you know about Margo?" I said.

"One of the few who knew her work. Margo's death is a tremendous loss, a shock to everyone."

"Were you involved in funding her women's project?"

"Margo had plenty of money, and how much can weekend re-treats cost? I helped out with food and clothing donations, but I felt her financial needs were met. The city shelter, those are the women who need us."

I'd learned quite a lot. Sylvia didn't know squat about Margo's real work. Al had grown up in New York City, not Wisconsin. Al was an only child, Leo would be surprised to learn that. Al had never come clean about his past, or Sylvia was keeping his myth alive, and I learned they lived a tragedy with their only child. If that related to the present situation, I didn't see it.

The atmosphere wasn't good. I got my pencil moving, I nudged us back into the friendly relationship of an interview. In a flat voice, Sylvia gave me a rehearsed version of her childhood. Her dad was THE attorney in San Francisco. Her uncle had been the attorney general of the United States. Sylvia had her ticket stamped from here to kingdom come.

I managed small talk, even pulled a few laughs out of the Roses.

Our lunch was recovering. I snapped photos in the sunroom of Al and Sylvia together. They faked being a jolly couple, they cheered up. I suggested we adjourn to the living room, where I could take photos of Sylvia on the red Chinese silk couch. I assured Sylvia I would make her look beautiful. No biggie. She *was* beautiful.

Sylvia wrapped herself on the couch with her arms outstretched on either side of her. I didn't know what her idea of a wreck was, but her hair was perfect, and her nails were perfect. A few blue veins rose along the back of her hands, but her fingers were fine and delicate. So were her porcelain skin and patrician nose.

Maybe on my drive home some thought or image would flit by and set off my alarm system. Right then I didn't hear anything that couldn't be explained. I did have an article I could sell to the *Sentinel,* but that wasn't why I'd come.

I thanked them both, said they'd been terrific, and made my farewells. I asked them to pass my compliments to Isabel for a fabulous lunch.

Al and Sylvia walked me to the front double doors.

Al turned to Sylvia. "Syl, what do you think about showing Annie the community service awards Clowny Drive-Thrus have received?"

"I should have thought of that," she said. Her skin was growing pale beneath her foundation makeup. "It's a good idea, but you'll have to excuse me. I'm on the verge of a terrible headache."

She reached up, gave me a weak and stiff hug. Al called Isabel. Sylvia retired to her room, Isabel following her, carrying a chilled bowl of wet cloths.

"Migraines," Al said to me. "They really get her down. Come on in my office. There might be a good photo or two in there you could use."

A covered slate walkway led to the side of the house. Al's office was approximately the size of my entire house, and the paneled office wore leather floorcovering. "Al," I said, "it looks as if the leather fell off your furniture onto the floor."

He laughed a big hearty laugh. "That's exactly what I told Sylvia. She had the place redecorated. Isn't it the strangest damn thing?"

"It does look nice."

"Yeah, if you don't own pets, and you don't put a drink on the floor next to you while you're on the couch, you could almost live with it."

I studied the room. The file cabinets matched the rosewood paneling. A dark green leather blotter covered most of his desk. His office supplies were lined up in a tidy row. Not one speck of dust. There was plenty of quiet for international phone calls, negotiating property deals, and for a mess to hit the fan without even one soul hearing the whir of the blades.

"Al, can we talk candidly?"

"Sure," Al said, but he looked kind of nervous.

I would have been, too. A candid talk, with anyone, sounds as if it could be the first step on the way to big trouble.

Thirty-two

 A l directed me to his award wall, extending his arm with a flourish, a game show host displaying a thirty-cubic-foot Amana refrigerator.

"You want candid? No problem," Al said. "I did not buy these awards."

"That never occurred to me."

"Listen, don't worry about it," he said. "People see this kind of stuff, they think, *He must have given them one hell of a lot of money.* They're right," he said, "I donate money out the wazoo."

And there, right on the wall behind his desk, was a painting of Lili.

"Al, I don't . . ."

"Listen, we can't all donate, and I give enough money for you, too," he said, wiping his forehead with his handkerchief, stuffing it into his jacket pocket, "but the most important thing I give is my time. That's why all the awards," Al said. "Money's cheap—any schmo can pull out a checkbook—but time is priceless."

He was waiting for me to write down that line. I obliged him.

I pointed to the painting above his deak, pretending it had caught my fancy. I raised my eyes in a question mark.

"My mother," Al said. "Beautiful, wasn't she?"

"Extraordinary to have a mother who's younger than you are," I said, letting that settle in. "Al, have you gotten yourself into a hole, or what?"

"Pardon me?"

"The portrait of your mother. AKA Lili Öoberlund."

I watched as Al turned bright red, then he turned scarlet, then he got up and slammed his fist in the wall. The paneling didn't budge an inch, but it sure must have hurt his knuckles. Al turned to face me. I was a little frightened, but not much. I've seen angry people before—take, for example, the nut who recently kicked in my door. I really did need a vacation.

Al screamed at me. "Who the hell are you!"

"I'm Annie Szabo, Sylvia introduced us, remember?"

"Jesus H. Christ, how dare you come into this house and . . ." Old Al had a sudden thought and his bright red skin went a little green. He was beginning to look fairly festive. "How long were you alone with Sylvia? Did you talk to her about Lili?"

"God, no, Al. I don't want to cause any trouble."

Whoops. Back to red. The guy was a regular neon light hanging over the door of a neighborhood tavern.

Al picked up his desk phone. "I'm calling neighborhood security," he said to me. "You entered my home under false pretenses, you took advantage of our hospitality. You could be some kind of terrorist lunatic!"

I waited until he called the Heights Security Agency, Sam and Justin. Sam Williams had dated my oldest daughter in high school, his younger brother Justin drooling in their wake, hoping she'd toss him a scrap of attention.

Al yelled into the phone, grumbled, talked, grumbled some more. He hung up.

"Apparently security knows you. Williams said you are, indeed, a lunatic but that you are not dangerous. I am to call him again in five minutes if you have not left the premises."

"Al, aren't you curious about why I'm here and how I know Lili?"

In the middle of his mad-on, Al's curiosity didn't have a fighting chance. His face morphed into something else, someone who was keeping his distance but *was* beginning to wonder why I'd dropped into his world.

"You have five minutes," he said, "tops. And it had better be good. If it's not, I call the real cops."

"More than fair, Al," I said, "this may be a tremendous relief. I know all about your life."

I folded my hands in my lap and waited for the light to dawn. I saw a pale glimmer of pink, but apparently it was a mighty foggy dawn because he said, "How much?"

He walked to his desk drawer and pulled out a three-ring binder checkbook.

"Money? I don't have any diseases that require a charitable contribution."

"Very funny. How much do you want to keep quiet?"

Leo was right. Al was the idiot prince.

"Al. I don't want your stupid money, and close that drawer unless you've got an all-expense-paid trip to Hawaii in there."

What did I want? And what the hell was I doing there? I was a woman who'd lost a friend, and Al was connected to her, and I was likely on a wild-goose chase trying to clear up her murder.

"Al, let's both relax. Margo was my neighbor, a good friend. Which meant I had to be around Lili—the price for being around Margo—that's why I recognize the woman in that painting."

Al lost five pounds of air in his gut and put five years on his face.

"Margo and Lili . . . Lili was lovable, sweet, the most beautiful young girl you've ever seen."

More Lili magic that had eluded me. "So beautiful that after you knocked her up you left your brother holding the bag, rather the baby, and you never bothered trying to find her."

"Jesus, how do you know all this stuff?"

"Al, I know your family. I know Angel. I know Leo. I know you've spent your entire adult life inventing yourself. How do you live with that?" I asked. I really did wonder. "There's got to be some body part screaming at you."

"Physically, emotionally, it's taken its toll."

Al looked past me, lost in a distant dream.

"And Sylvia doesn't notice?" I asked.

"Of course she notices. She has her migraines, I have my colitis. We're at a standoff."

"She really knows nothing about your past, I mean the real one, or was she faking it in there?"

"She doesn't know one thing. We live well, we enjoy the same things—golf, cruises, camera safaris. We like the same people. What else do you need?"

"Honesty?"

He stood up. I had a feeling we were heading back into the red range of the rainbow. "None of this is your business," he said, "and I can't believe I said the word *colitis* to a total stranger."

"Al, you can still back into the truth. You've helped lots of strangers, maybe it's time to work on your family."

He plopped down in his leather recliner. Its green leather matched the blotter. Sylvia's decorator had a real fascination with leather. He tilted back, way back; I thought he was a goner, but the man knew the limits of his chair. He stared at Lili's painting. His voice was faint. "I'm not brave enough."

"Al, you started with zip, possibly selling plastic dog-doo is lower than zip, and you built an empire." I pointed to the award wall. "And you've done a lot of good. All that takes courage."

"I abandoned people along the way," he said. "That didn't take any courage."

"Time to make amends and move on."

"That's what Leo says. But Sylvia."

"Sylvia might surprise you. I'm sure her father didn't consider you decent marriage material, but she married you anyway."

"Please. I was the last thing he had in mind. Other than going to temple regularly."

"Your one stamp of approval, and even it was based on a lie."

"You're spooky."

"You don't know the half of it," I said, "and wipe that scared expression off your face. I'm not a witch come to send you a plague of ills. Your body's already on the case."

He pulled at his hair, he paced. His hair was a lot thinner than Leo's, probably caused by a regular regimen of hair-pulling. I'd have to warn Angel about that. You never know which idiosyncrasies are genetic.

He blurted out, "Sometimes I feel like jumping off a cliff!"

"Way to go, Al. Let's really abandon everyone."

"I don't know what to do."

"For starters, face the people in your life, all of them," I said. "They need you. And help us figure out what happened to Margo."

Al sat. His hands were folded. He laced his fingers in and out, a loom of raw skin and bones. He wanted to tell me something, and he didn't want to tell me something.

I said, "You're driving me nuts. Would you just say it?"

"I didn't exactly turn my back on everyone."

He looked up at me, looked back into his hands, a sly grin spreading across his face.

"How not exactly?" I said. Al felt good about something, and he wanted to share it. "Al, whatever you tell me stays in this room." It was the truth, and Al believed me.

"I own that land of Margo's," he said. "It's titled under a non-profit corporation impossible to trace, well not impossible, but who'd bother. I am, or I was, Margo's major benefactor. Totally anonymous, that includes anonymous to Sylvia, too. And, I've been bringing Margo and Lili a sack of cash every month—cash that cannot be traced. This has been going on for years."

"And Angel?"

"For all practical purposes, Angel is my only child. Problem is, he's not Sylvia's."

"Maybe Sylvia would accept another son. Angel's grown, someday he'll get married and have kids," I said. "You may be denying her grandchildren."

"Maybe you have more faith in the Roses than I do."

"I have faith that people are basically good. It's a problem, but at least it doesn't cause colitis. Can I ask something about your brother?"

"Please. I'm tired of me."

"Any chance he's hiding Lili out?"

"I seriously doubt it. He was burned by her once."

"How about you?"

Al brushed that notion aside as totally nuts. He studied me. He leaned back in his recliner again, put his feet smack up in the middle of his blotter. "I got rich because I can read people, it's my biggest asset," Al said. "I don't think Leo's helping Lili out, but I don't know. I do think your interest in Leo may be more than casual."

"I'm in deep admiration and possibly slight infatuation."

He hooted. "Is that cautious or what?" Al said, softening. "I love my brother, it's hard not having him in my life. You know the times I'm happiest?"

"When you're playing golf?"

He waved that away. "It's when I'm at Leo's and we're sitting on that crappy couch on the big plywood pedestal. We're drinking beer and watching the sunrise, and I mean rise, not set. We're talking about our folks and about friends who are long gone. And I think, *God let me die right now. I'm totally at peace, totally happy . . . Totally myself.*"

"It's a hell of a thing when you have to sneak to your brother's and sit on a ratty couch ten feet off the ground to feel like yourself."

"Tell me about it." Al ran his hand over his head, and looked at the paneled ceiling. "I'm the one with the dough, and he's the one with the soul—that was some service he performed for Margo, wasn't it?"

"You were there?"

"Sure. Margo drove me crazy, she was like you, a terrible noodge. But we had a long history, we even loved the same woman."

"There weren't many regular-looking people at her service. I'm surprised I didn't notice you."

"Did you see Uncle Sam?"

"The guy on stilts who was tripped by the clown?"

"That was me."

"Al, you're good. You could sneak in and out of any circus funeral."

He smiled at me, proud.

". . . or Margo's place," I said. "Who would notice one more character up there? You'd have less money going out every month, no Margo rattling your cage and threatening to shake your life upside down."

He leaned forward and shook his finger back and forth, shook it right in my face.

"I never sneaked into Margo's, and I didn't kill her. Don't start thinking that way," Al said. "As long as Sylvia wasn't at the funeral, I figured I'd give Margo one last laugh at my expense."

"Probably been a long time since you and Margo shared a laugh."

"Yeah, and things were really rough between us at the end. Margo said she was giving me one more day, then she was tromping over here with Lili and Angel and we'd all sit down and have a nice chat. She said she wanted to make sure Angel was taken care of. Financially, you know, in case I did them the favor of dropping dead."

"What'd you say?"

"I told her to cool it for a day or two, and I'd lay this all out for Sylvia. That it'd go a lot smoother if she didn't come marching in here like she was storming Normandy."

"Then what?"

"Then nothing. Margo died before Sylvia learned the truth about me." Al thought for a minute. "Unless Margo made one of her rabid calls to Sylvia, and Sylvia's been waiting for just the right time to go for the jugular or take off."

That was a possibility. Margo talks to Sylvia, Al doesn't know. Sylvia takes a solo vacation, Al gets slammed with divorce papers. It was also possible Margo had respected Al's request for a short reprieve.

I said, "Only one thing seems obvious—Margo's exit was convenient, Al, and Lili doesn't appear to be a problem anymore."

His face went white. "Lili? What are you talking about?"

"No one's seen Lili since before Margo's funeral. That's why I asked if you or Leo were hiding her out."

"Why haven't I read about that in the paper? Why wasn't I notified? What the hell was going on with those women?"

Al paced his leather floor—that's something you don't see every day. He stopped just short of wearing a trail in the dead cow's hide. He hit the palm of his hand with his fist.

He said, "That's the last straw. The more I think about Leo and Angel . . . I want my son. I want my family. Sylvia will just have to understand."

"Al, before you get Angel involved, tell Sylvia, and let her do the hysterical number in the privacy of your bedroom," I said. "Angel's pretty shaky."

"Done," Al said, his resolve growing stronger. "Where's Angel living now that the bunkhouses aren't occupied?"

"Temporarily stationed at my house. A well-meaning ex-cop asked him to protect me."

Al laughed. He stopped himself. "Sorry, that caught me off guard."

"Believe me, I feel the same way. Also, Angel rescued some ugly little Italian woman, and he's stashed her at my house. I want to buy her a ticket home, she wants to move in. I think she and Angel might have a thing going on," I said. "Hard to say, she doesn't speak English."

"How do you know she doesn't want to go to Italy?"

"Angel's been interpreting."

"That kid can order in an Italian restaurant, not much more."

"I heard him speaking with her, it sounded like Italian."

"Maybe he's gotten better. When Sylvia and I come to your place, I'll translate," he said. "The poor woman probably hasn't got a clue about what's going to happen to her."

"When you and Sylvia come to my place? Did I black out while extending an invitation?"

"I want to talk with Angel, and I want Sylvia with me. Angel's living with you—it makes perfect sense."

"Leo's house makes perfect sense."

"I've got to introduce my brother and Angel to Sylvia while we're sitting around Leo's trailer? Sylvia may bolt the second we drive under the arches of the Cadillac RV Park."

I didn't want to see his point, but I did.

"When is this going to occur?" I asked. "I want to know, so that I'm not home."

"Let's get it over with. Tomorrow, dinner." He squared his shoulders. "And invite my brother, would you? I will bet that if he's there, you'll be home," he said. "I'm nervy, but I'm not going to your house unless you're home."

"Maybe after you guys get the truth on the table, we can figure out who wanted Margo dead."

I had several ideas, but my five minutes were more than up.

Thirty-three

Attraction Magic: First you sew a pink pouch and embroider your name on it. Every morning, before you eat or drink, go outside, find an acorn, and slip it into this fancy pouch. Sleep with it under your pillow every night. It's decent to stop at seven acorns, that's the number of people who'll love you, but you could have more or less.

Some people, they get an urge, hand someone money, and for one hour that person pretends they're in love with them. I'm old-fashioned. I like the kind of love that takes work, even if it involves embroidery, which is a major headache.

—Madame Mina to Juanita the madam

Honey, I couldn't agree with you more.

—Juanita the madam to Madame Mina

As long as I was in the Heights, I thought I'd drive by Sweet Suzanne's and have a chat with her. Maybe tell her if I were still her Brownie leader, I'd make her earn a wheelbarrow full of good conduct badges.

I drove into the lower Heights, still million-dollar houses, but they were poor relations compared to Sylvia and Al's place. The houses didn't hide behind stone walls, and they were identical to each other with slight variations—flipped at a different angle or a mirror image of a model two houses down. A very ritzy tract, the homes were pale salmon or pale beige or pale gray, all with white trim, all pale. I turned onto Piedras Negras, big lots, plenty of trees. There was her house number, and there, if I was not mistaken, was Rory's car.

The mean and spiteful part of me, probably the rational part, wished I had not returned the gun to Lili's desk. Wished I had tossed it on the seat of Rory's car, called the cops, and waited out front until I saw Rory hauled away.

Unfortunately, the opportunity, just like the gun, had disappeared.

I wanted to talk to Suzanne, but I didn't want to see Rory. I had some time, was only ten minutes from Juanita's, so I decided to drop in on her. We had shared more than one beer while discussing the general state of mankind, emphasis on man. I thought Juanita might offer me another view of the truth concerning my dear son-in-law's movements the night of Margo's death than she had given Lawless.

It was midafternoon, a good time to visit. Juanita's would start heating up around dinnertime. It would come to a full boil well past midnight.

Juanita's establishment was in a large, rambly house built in the 1920s. It had been owned, abandoned, owned, abandoned for years, then completely taken over by Juanita. It was the third building in town that had housed her enterprise. When it came to Juanita, the law looked the other way—she'd call if she needed them. Juanita's could only happen in a small town where people make allowances for each other.

The interior walls were painted bright green, and the trim was sunflower yellow, both low-gloss. In one corner of the front parlor stood a parrot's tall stand. I walked past Mike, a stunning Brazilian parrot with long tail feathers.

He squawked, "Bloody hell! What big knockers!"

I stroked the top of his head. "Mike, you flirt, you say that to every chick who walks by."

Juanita claimed she didn't know who'd taught him that greeting. My guess was Juanita.

The front room held two pool tables. One was used for playing pool, the other as a banquet table. Juanita not only offered illegal entertainment that shouldn't be illegal, she also served food—and it was her food that should have been illegal. Many laws do not make sense. Her clientele included scroungy locals, just plain folks, and the slumming rich. Everyone in the Valley, at one time or another, for one reason or another, patronized Juanita's.

Upstairs were seven bedrooms, each opening onto a long hall. Downstairs, just past the kitchen, was Juanita's combination bedroom and office. Juanita weighed 350 pounds, more or less. She held court from her bed, a giant four-poster covered with a satin spread. On each bed poster hung three or four frilly hats decorated with ribbons and bows. Juanita's desk was against one wall. From this one room, she successfully ran a small empire.

I passed the billiard room, the room closest to Juanita's private domain. A small monkey with a white bottom lunged at me. I shook him off, and another flew at me from the drapery rod. He landed on my shoulder and stuck his tongue in my mouth. I hated those monkeys. They were like a bad boyfriend—the more you tried to shake them, they more persistent they became. My giraffes were far superior. God, I already thought of them as *my giraffes*.

Juanita reclined in a peach bed jacket and matching housecoat reading *Ladies' Home Journal*.

I poked my head in. "Are you accepting company?"

"Annie! Company, yes, suitors, no. Come on in. Want something to drink?"

"That's okay, it's early."

"I meant tea."

"Oh, sure."

An antique Limoges tea set stood on her bedside table. She sat a little straighter, pouring us each a cup of Earl Grey. She offered me tea cakes, and I declined. She helped herself, then helped herself to more.

"It's too early for anything but private time with the Old Gal. What's up, kid?"

"I saw you at Margo's funeral."

"Yeah, I saw you, too. We were some of the only people there who weren't freaks."

"You and Margo were pals."

"Good pals."

"You wouldn't want to give her possible killer an alibi."

"Of course not. Besides being Margo's friend, I'm also a good citizen."

"I want to talk with you about Rory Slade."

Her face went blank.

"I'm not a cop, and I know you're acquainted with Rory."

"How," she said, "do you know him?"

"He's married to my daughter."

She shook her head. "Bad husband material. Very bad."

"Understatement," I said. "Lawless said you gave Rory an alibi for the time of Margo's death. You said Rory was here the night of her death—all night."

"I know Lawless isn't a cop anymore, but he used to be."

"So you're careful with him."

"You bet. I went through my records and found Rory's charge receipt. I thought it was strange, Rory usually pays cash, but that night he used his MasterCard. Doesn't matter to me," she said, "money is money." She put her teacup down, hoisted herself up a bit more, and rested her chin on the palm of her hand. "Lawless asked me how much time that amount of money would cover, I told him."

"But I thought you told him Rory was here all evening."

"Do you honestly think I keep my eye on everyone at every minute, or that I'd *want* to? If Lawless got that impression, he was jumping to conclusions."

Juanita was growing restless, huffy, and defensive. I had to give her space. She was too big to get up and run out of the room, but she could order me out. I chatted aimlessly, talking about Mina and the plumber, and about Lawless sneaking the giraffes onto my place. She got a kick out of that. Juanita said if I didn't want the giraffes, she'd take them. This was my chance to dump the long-necked creatures.

"I'll have to think about it. Mina likes their faces, and my kids might want them after I kick the bucket."

What was going on? Apparently, I'd decided to keep the beasts, and I hadn't so much as discussed it with myself.

Juanita set her teacup down and asked me to fluff her pillows. She had relaxed. I forged ahead. "Juanita, I believe Rory was with someone, and that you didn't mention the someone to Lawless."

She went blank again. You can't beat years of practice—she knew how to go right there.

"Juanita, it's me. I did a great article on you that provided more protection than any cop or rich executive ever did. Several senators discussed making you a historical landmark after it went into print," I reminded her, "a designation generally reserved for buildings."

"Sheer coincidence. The senators were both old friends."

"I also know there was no antique ruby necklace in the last two houses that burned to the ground, and each time the insurance money you received for it allowed you to expand. You ready to talk?"

"You're playing hardball. Not like you."

"Not like me unless I'm pushed. My friend is dead, so is yours, I might add, and my daughter's husband might have done it. I had to hide Abra from him because he beat her. I don't want to twist the facts to make him appear guilty of murder just because he hurt my daughter. On the other hand, I don't want to shield him from it just because he's my grandson's father."

"You're in a mess."

"You're very astute."

"Of course I am. How many madams you know who get to be this old?"

Easy answer, she was the only madam I knew.

"Look," she said, "if I'd known he was married to your daughter, I would have barred the door to him years ago."

"If he hadn't been here, he would have been someplace else."

"I just want you to know I'm sorry. I had six lousy husbands myself. Six! Worked myself silly flat on my back for every one of them—gave it to them for free—and all I got was heartache. It's a wonder I didn't turn the same way as Margo did."

"Back to Rory."

"He was a regular, he behaved himself and tipped well. Then one time he got rough with one of my girls. Wild is one thing," Juanita said, "but I won't stand for rough, and he was put on probation with me for six months. When his six months were over, I made him buy a nice piece of jewelry for the woman he'd hurt. I made him buy jewelry for me, too. He behaved after that.

"You're right about him bringing a companion the night Margo died. A nice-looking young woman—I noticed because he never brought a date before."

I described Suzanne, and the description fit the woman on Rory's arm. I told Juanita who she was, and Juanita knew of her. Juanita had serviced Suzanne's grandfather, a wealthy San Francisco businessman, when she was in her prime.

"He was a good egg, never anything but sweet, and he gave me nice presents. I could have fallen hard for him, " she said, "if he wasn't married and I wasn't married."

"Juanita, from what you've told me, you couldn't possibly know if Rory was here all night. Suzanne might be the only one who'd know that."

"I guess so, but I told Lawless as much as I needed to. I saw Rory arrive, and I saw him leave real early in the morning. Guys don't leave in the middle of night—they're either busy or all wore-out. I have to protect my customers a little, or I'd be out of business."

"Lawless said you have to cooperate with the law, or you're out of business."

"It's a delicate line. Given another chance, I'd go into some other line of work. Maybe be a dental hygienist, I'm fascinated with people's mouths," Juanita said, "and you leave work behind you at 5:00 P.M. Anyway, the cops and the customers think I'm on their side. They're both right."

"What's the word on Suzanne?"

"She's a spoiled mixed-up kid, and she's getting too old to keep pushing her family's buttons with her stunts. Suzanne did a stint as a stripper at a cheap joint on Columbus down in the city. Imagine that! There's more, talk gets around, but that tells you plenty."

"She never worked . . ."

"Here? You've got to be kidding. This isn't stripping for the cheap thrill of taking your clothes off for a bunch of drooling goons. This place is hard work, she'd never make it. That's the trouble with rich kids—no work ethic."

"Let me ask you something about Margo."

"Shoot. I don't mind answering questions about dead people. Especially a dead friend with a killer who needs to be taken out."

If we found the killer, they'd better hope they were behind bars when Juanita learned their name. She had the connections and the money and the guts to make that threat a reality.

"When Margo used to come here, did she bring Lili?"

"Regular? God no. She brought Lili once for dinner. Lili couldn't handle the food—you'd have thought she'd been poisoned—and she hated the confusion. I enjoy chaos. Lili likes order." The Nazi thing again. "Margo talked Lili into playing pool, she'd never done that before. Don't those krauts have pool tables?"

"I don't know, Juanita," I answered truthfully. "When Margo came by herself, did she ask for a man or a woman?"

"Mostly me."

I looked amazed, I could feel it all over my face. I could even feel it in my shoulders.

Juanita hooted and laughed and coughed, then she pulled herself together. "Had you going, didn't I?"

"I love you," I said, "but you are impossible."

"Part of my charm. Margo and me, we were talking buddies. Look at this place! If this isn't like running a circus, I don't know what is. Also, I'm training and rehabilitating abused women, I'm giving them a home. We were practically in the same line of work, and it's not easy. I handle the stress by eating, Margo didn't know what to do with it. She had horrible headaches and back pain."

"I never knew that."

"Everyone treated Margo like she was some old workhorse that could just keep going 'round and 'round the track, but she was lots more delicate and sensitive than Lili. You could set fire to that woman, and she'd coolly reckon how to put herself out. Between you and me, I didn't like her."

"Me either. Lawless thinks she's a saint."

"Lesbian or no, she's got that girly little body and those pale blue eyes make men think she's a weak creature who needs to be taken care of. But I know women, and there's nothing helpless about Lili. How's she holding up, anyway?"

"She disappeared."

"Aha," she said, with an all-knowing aha, "anybody but me think she could have been the one killed Margo, then took off?"

"You know how they felt about each other."

"And what has that got to do with the price of beans?"

Juanita and I both knew that often only a couple in love is intimate enough to consider a dance with death.

I said, "Did Margo ever have other women, sexually, while she was here?"

"Women, no. Every once in a while she had a man. I always keep one good-looking straight guy on staff. I'm going to have to hire another one."

"He quitting?"

"Nah, the guy is overworked. There's only so long a bull can stand up in that pasture without falling over, you know? I need to get me another bull."

"Margo liked being with men?"

"Margo liked pushing boundaries, especially her own. And maybe she wanted to make sure she wasn't missing out on something she wanted."

"Was she?"

"I thought one time she was having a fling behind Lili's back with a good-looking young guy. Boy, I'd hire him in a minute!"

Juanita described him. I swear I could hear her heart race, and I knew exactly who she was talking about.

I said, "Angel."

"Didn't hear his name, but he looked like one. They didn't spend the night. He was here another time with Margo, and that was it. Far as I know."

"And if you'd seen them every night, you wouldn't tell."

She lifted her bulk off the mattress and poured herself another cup. She smiled, toasting me with her cool cup of tea. "Here's all you've got to know about Margo's love life—she liked men plenty. Problem was she loved Lili, and no matter what body that woman would have come in, those two were set up to love each other."

"Thanks, Juanita."

I bent down and kissed her forehead. I'd always considered Juanita to be timeless, ageless, but that wasn't true. Someday she'd be gone. Just like the hills, she'd be one more beautiful and wild thing gone.

"You see any hunks looking for hard work, send them my way. And Annie," she said, "say hi to Lawless for me. I'd appreciate it if you don't tell him that I play both sides of the fence."

"Not a word."

Thirty-four

I thought I'd cruise by Suzanne's house again. It was on my way home if I drove a back road, doubled back, turned left, and followed the road east for one mile. I was sick of playing cat and mouse with Rory. I wanted to face him, scare him into thinking that I'd found something out from one of the girls at Juanita's. Maybe discovered his time of departure and a predawn return. He'd break down, admit he killed Margo, he'd go to jail forever, Margo's death would be avenged, and my daughter could come home.

It was not that simple.

I pulled in front of Suzanne's house, and Rory's car was gone. What the hell, I was already there. I'd pump Suzanne, that little backstabbing creep, and get the goods on Rory. Then Margo's death would be avenged, and my daughter could come home.

I rang the bell, no one answered. I knocked, no one answered. I jiggled the doorknob. The house was unlocked. Suzanne had breezed in and out of my house plenty of times when she was a kid, I was going to do the same thing.

I opened the door. What a place, a fabric and floorcovering nightmare. The living room looked like it belonged to someone who'd died thirty years ago. *Decorated by Grandma* was stamped on every piece of antique furniture, taupe damask fabic, and swatch of cream wallpaper. No funky little wooden steps painted lilac and mint green with hearts and the word *LOVE* stenciled on every other step . . . Grandma had made *that* mistake with Suzanne's folks, and it wasn't going to happen again. This place was class, pure old cold class.

And there sat Suzanne on an ancient settee, the loneliest orphan in the Western world. She looked at me, didn't register surprise, didn't register anything. I sat across from her in a matching chair. Her cheek was swollen, and her eye was joining it. Unless she'd had a motorcycle accident, Rory had struck again. I walked into the kitchen and found a large pack of frozen peas.

I knelt in front of her and held the pack to her face. "Suzanne," I whispered, "what happened to you?" I stroked her hair with my free hand.

"I told him that I didn't know where Abra was, and he didn't believe me."

Rory, yes indeed.

Suzanne's voice had retreated to the age of seven, a safe time. "He said to me, *You're best friends, of course you know where Abra is.* I told him we'd stopped being best friends when he and I happened, that he'd put a damper on our relationship. He considered that talking back. I told him my folks didn't want him around, and now, neither did I. I didn't even see it coming. He slapped me across the cheek with the back of his hand—so hard—it knocked me off my feet.

"Then he told me that Abra and I weren't friends anymore because I was a slut, and I wasn't good enough for her."

Suzanne cried softly. I held her against my chest and rubbed her back. "Suzanne," I said, "I'd call the guy a monster, but that would give Frankenstein a bad name. Not to mention many others in the firmament of monsters who have more redeeming qualities than Rory."

She leaned out of my chest and looked at me, her doe brown eyes the same as they were when she was little. "I forgot you're funny. I forgot you guys were like family. I don't know how this happened."

How many times had I heard that lately? Do we all wander about blindly until we fall into a hole, and wonder how the hell we got down there? Easy. It happens when we walk around at night without a flashlight.

"Suzanne," I said, "you need to file a police report. Your folks and your grandmother are rich enough to protect you."

"He'll kill me. Then he'll find Abra and kill her."

"He'll never find Abra, and if he does, we'll all be glad. He would not survive the hunt."

"My folks told me to get rid of him. They were right."

"You're going to have to swallow your pride and tell them they were right, tell them you need help. Other than not letting you eat Snickers bars or chocolate ice cream, your parents were perfectly nice people," I said. "I'm sure they still are."

I handed her Lawless's card. "Give them this card, or call this man yourself. Right now. He's an ex-cop, don't worry, 'ex' is the operative word, and saving women at risk has become his mission."

As long as she was in this state, maybe she'd head somewhere near the truth with me. "Suzanne, tell me about the time you and Rory went to Juanita's together."

"A few nights ago, three, four, I don't remember."

"Right. Did you spend the entire night together?"

"Alone together?"

"I mean, do you absolutely know he was there all night?"

She sounded confused. "We went together, we left together . . ."

"Suzanne, I understand you're in a state of shock. You're being dense because of that, or you're being dense to protect yourself, or Rory, which is hard to believe."

"Do you mean did I keep my eyes on him every minute?"

"How about every hour? That would be close enough."

"Time was kind of funky."

"Time was funky. I'm not following you."

"I took Ecstasy. That's why we ended up spending the night."

"Did Rory take it with you?"

"No, he got it for me from someone at Juanita's. He knows I like it. He doesn't do drugs."

No drugs, no guns. Rory was on his way to becoming a poster boy for clean living.

"Did Rory give an employee a big wad of cash before you left, and ask them to tell anyone who wondered, including Juanita, that you'd both been there and busy all night? Or did he charge a really big tip to make his credit card bill larger?"

"I have no idea."

"But you don't know."

"Have you ever taken E?"

"That's one chemical wonder that wasn't invented when I was young."

"Old people take it, too." Thanks, Suzanne. She was moving back down on my list. "You pretty much don't know what time it is, and if it's bad E, you spend a lot of time grinding your teeth and your jaw gets sore. My jaw wasn't sore at all the next morning, I'm sure I had a really good time. That's all I'm sure of."

She was not a teenager; she was too old to be such a mess.

"Suzanne, get it together! All this money"—I motioned to her house, her clothes, her everything—"has screwed you up royally."

"My parents think so, too. They're watching me like a hawk, and they're threatening to send me to Europe for six months if I don't clean up my act."

"You have friends over there?" Like friends who run a rehab center or a farm where they work your buns off.

"I have friends in Paris right now," she said. "They're moving to Amsterdam in another month. They're visiting museums, that's what my folks said. Lots of good art in Europe."

Mom and Dad were considering the safety of sending her to Europe with other kids like her, kids with endless credit cards. I hadn't heard the word *job* mentioned, so I assumed she'd be free to hang out in Amsterdam with her buddies and run up the plastic at a hash bar. What planet had Suzanne's parents moved to, anyway?

"Suzanne, you know my phone number. If you want to have a genuine talk about your life, give me a call, would you? Including from Europe. Including a collect call."

"You don't hate me?"

There she sat in that big stupid house all by herself. "I'd like to hate you, but I can't get into it. I'm pretty busy right now."

"Thank you." She leaned into my chest again. Genuine gratitude. It was a good start.

I picked up the phone. I called her parents. No, I couldn't wait until they arrived, yes, they had a key, and I'd lock the door behind me. They'd hop in their Volvo wagon and be over faster than the speed of sound. And they'd call the police.

I lifted her hand to the frozen peas and asked her to keep it pressed against her cheek.

"Suzanne, use your money for something good, for taking care of Suzanne."

"You know what? He said that Abra had found another guy. I actually felt sorry for Rory, that's why I got involved with him."

Thirty-five

As soon as I climbed into my car, I picked up my cell phone.

"Lawless. Trouble. I'm headed home, Rory's on the loose, and his alibi may not be as airtight as we thought."

I gave him the rundown on Suzanne, her situation, and what I'd learned from Juanita. He said he'd follow up on Suzanne and meet me at my house.

I was home in fifteen minutes. Rory's car wasn't out front, neither was Lawless's.

Angel and Maria were cozy on the porch swing. Sitting next to Angel didn't improve her appearance. Very few people could sit next to Angel and look gorgeous. I could look okay. Maria—forget it.

"Angel," I said, "prepare to guard our bodies. We may have company."

Angel rose and stood by the door, wearing a serious and puzzled expression. He resembled a family dentist who'd been called up from the reserves for combat duty and didn't have a clue what his duties were.

"Here's your job description. If a guy you don't know walks in," I said, "just slug him."

He relaxed. He understood.

A car pulled in. Angel's muscles tensed, a nice sight. It was Lawless. I told Angel to take a break, but to stay on the alert. And to keep an eye on Maria, now standing right next to him—he had a lot more tolerance for spaniel relationships than Mina did. I smelled

Maria for a snoop, the kind who rifles through your closet. Next thing you know your blouse walks out on the snoop's torso.

"I talked to the sheriff," Lawless said, "and gave him the low-down. Rory was on his way over here, they snagged him just a couple of blocks away."

"Can they keep him until his testosterone level drops? I hear after the age of forty men start to mellow out."

"That's only what, ten years?"

"About. Lawless, when neither Suzanne or Juanita can really account for Rory's time the night of Margo's murder, I don't know, it's got to mean something."

"It's some help, not much. You did right by calling Suzanne's parents," Lawless said. "They're with her, so are the police, and she's filing a formal complaint."

"Then we should be able to hold him for a little while."

"He'll just get someone to bail him out."

"The guy is like lice. Just when you think you've gotten rid of him, your scalp starts itching again."

"Rory may bother you for some time. You can get a restraining order against him, he can violate it, but it'll slow him down a little."

"Then the cycle begins anew, and he's lice again?"

"We can hope for a miracle." Lawless looked at me, and he looked up at the cloudless sky. He sat down on my porch swing. "Come sit with me," he said. "Porches are good places to wait for miracles."

Sometimes he's astonishing.

We sat on the porch swing, and no miracles were forthcoming, just hot dinner smells wafting from inside my house. Maria. She was cooking dinner. I cranked my head as far as it would go, peering through my kitchen window. Angel handing her things, Angel solicitous, Angel opening jars for her. Love. Go figure.

I gave Lawless Margo and Lili as seen through the eyes of Juanita, but I omitted our speculation that Lili might have killed Margo in the midst of a big fight and fled. I knew where that road would lead.

Lawless said, "Juanita let me down."

"What?"

"She didn't tell me the truth."

"As far as she knew, Rory was there all night—he'd paid enough to be. You know where her office is. You expect her to keep an eye on everything?"

"I know, I know."

"Don't come down on Juanita too hard."

"I wouldn't come down on her at all. I like her," he said. "She's part of this place, part of the past that's not so glitzy and glamorous."

I rocked a little on the swing. "Margo and Juanita were pals," I said. "Margo used her as a shrink. No judgment, just talk."

"Not surprising."

I was headed into territory that Lawless would either take with a grain of salt, or it would shock him to the end of his toes. But it was something he might need to know.

"Juanita said Margo liked to try out a man once in a while to remember what equipment she was missing."

Without missing a beat he said, "I wish I'd known that. Ruth probably would have loaned me to her."

I slugged him on his arm. "Cut it out. Anyway, I'm wondering if during one of her visits, Margo might have seen someone who didn't want to be seen. Some family-values politico running around wearing a black leather thong at one o'clock in the morning."

"She could have."

"And she could have threatened to go public with the high jinks. Maybe we should talk to Juanita again."

"It doesn't wash. There's a sanctity about those places, Juanita's in particular. People leave their ideologies at the front door, they cast off their false superegos and away they go. It's fantasy time, and *We're all in this together* is a mutual agreement."

"How come you know so much about this?"

"I told you. Stint in Vice. I never understood why we arrested those people. The whips-and-chains types who inflict damage upon seriously damaged people? That makes complete sense. But regular adults minding their own business? I sure felt like it was none of mine. We came up against bigwigs of every political ilk in those places. If one wanted to tell on the other, the whole shooting match would be over in a matter of minutes."

"We're all brothers and sisters under our kinky skins?"

"I think so."

We sat in comfortable silence and rocked. We watched a harvest moon come up deep orange, floating across the felt blue sky.

"By the way," I said, "I ordered the giraffes food from Pete's Hardware and charged it to your account. I was sure you wouldn't mind, Pete was sure, too."

Lawless tried to look grim but he couldn't carry it off.

"Also," I said, "I'm sorry your ass is stew meat on my account."

"Ah, I've been stew before. A lot of people owe me favors. It'll work itself out."

"People trust you."

"But I can't pull any more tricks like last night and get away with it for some time. I used my big get-out-of-jail-free card."

"Sorry, Lawless."

"You already said you were sorry. Knock it off."

"Nothing new on any front or you would have told me," I said.

"Nothing new, and there should be. By now I'm pretty sure Lili is gone forever. We have APBs on her all over the place. We have notified every agency possible, including Interpol. They'll be checking for her passport, or someone using her passport."

"You still don't think she did it and ran."

"My gut says no. I trust myself in this area."

I didn't say anything. And then I didn't say anything a little longer.

Lawless rubbed his chin. "But I don't listen to my gut without some backup," he said. "I personally have checked trains, airlines, buses, even ships out of San Francisco. Not one damned thing. It's not easy to fake a name for travel these days, especially if you have to use a passport."

"Unless you buy a really good one with legs."

"Which takes planning and foresight. Gut feeling number two: I don't think anything premeditated occured in the trapeze arena room where we found Margo."

I ignored him, our guts spoke different languages. "Lili either planned her departure in advance, so long forever, Lili, or she witnessed a crime, and she's waiting for the killer to be caught."

"And maybe she flew into that lonely ocean," he said.

"Lawless, we're back to square one. Again."

"Maybe, but killers trip up, they return to the scene. Of course, other than the cops, you're the only one who's been back to Margo's place."

"Ha-ha. By the way, Angel will confirm that I was holding a gun when we ran into each other on the hillside. He won't confirm that I put it back on Lili's desk, he thought it belonged to me. But I don't own a .25, you know that."

"Someone placed it on the desk, an obvious spot, because we weren't smart enough to find it at the crime scene. And you found it."

"And someone else didn't want us to have it, so they retrieved it. Maybe the person I heard pounding on that door."

He stopped the swing midrock. "Annie, you're wrong. We're not back to square one. Someone knows you had the murder weapon," Lawless said. "I want you to forget about going to the Roses'."

"I already went. I was hoping to find out just how inconvenient Margo was."

"Dammit! You have a death wish or something?"

I was starting to worry about me, too, but really, for a cop Lawless was very given to hysterics, and what I was about to lay on him wouldn't help his mental health—I told him about my visit with Al and Sylvia and their family tree, rotting at the roots. I told him about Angel and Al, about their long history with Lili and Margo. He was dismayed, and his dismay turned him glum. His blue quiet scared me. Lawless stood and poked his head into the house. He reminded Angel to remain on the alert.

Lawless gave Maria the once-over, and I walked him to his car.

He leaned against his Lincoln. Its deep green paint shone flecks of metallic glow and spun them off into the soft evening light. He put his arms around me, hugging me. If I hadn't been scared before, that would have done it.

"What are you going to do with Maria?" he said. "She gives me the willies."

"It only gets better," I said. "She thinks she's moving in with me."

He brushed some dust off the back of his pants. "How do you get yourself into these things?"

"How did I get myself into two giraffes? With help."

He remembered that he'd caused me trouble, and it perked him right up.

"Don't be so happy, Lawless. I like the giraffes, they're a lot more pleasant than Maria. Someone's coming over to translate for her tomorrow. I'm sure she'll be out of here as soon as the language problem gets cleared up."

"Good. Some friend of Mina's?"

"No, Al Rose, Angel's long-lost daddy. The family is convening at my house for dinner."

He told me I was sponsoring no such event, and hadn't I heard him say the Roses were dangerous, and that their whole dumb little world could go flushing down the toilet if Angel and the phony life got out, and then I thought: Maybe that's just what Al wants—for his whole dumb world to go down the toilet so he can get back the world he lost. Which might include Lili and their son.

What I said was, "Al's brother Leo will also be here."

"Leo from the funeral who said all that nice stuff about Margo but isn't a real Methodist minister?"

"The same Leo."

He cocked his head and he shook his head. "I thought you were nuts when I met you. My opinion hasn't changed. Why do I even bother?"

"You're kidding, right? You sane people need us nuts to make you feel alive, you know that."

Once again, he said he was glad that his wife and I didn't know each other better. And he smiled, not big, but he did.

Thirty-six

I watched Maria cook and peel and slice and grind and crush at least four pounds of garlic. We would have no evil spirits in the house for the next ten years. Nor would we have any friends. At least she was still wearing her own clothes.

My cupboards held PopTarts, Campbell's soup, and dried cereals. Two containers of low-fat yogurt, expired, sat in the refrigerator door. There was also cold pizza and salad-in-a-bag. If it doesn't contain the three basic food groups—sugar, fat, and salt—I'm not all that interested. I didn't know where Maria was purchasing her food items, but I was sure I was paying for them.

"Making sure Maria doesn't steal anything?" Mina said, over my shoulder.

"You scared me."

"Are you done being scared? Because I want to tell you something—you're staring at her so hard, she couldn't steal anything if she wanted to. You want to catch her stealing, you got to pretend you're not looking."

We sat at the kitchen table, and we acted like there wasn't another human in the room, except that there was, and ignoring her was kind of an effort.

"Mina, you look pooped. Plumber wearing you out?"

"I like being on my own."

"Since when did you start sounding like Greta Garbo?"

"Since I had plumbing installed, and I ended up installing the plumber, too."

"You want me to kick him out?"

"No, I'll do it. I was sure I could be mean enough to give him the boot, but his dopey grin makes it hard."

"What about your stick for warding off love and all your other defenses against unwanted affection?"

"It's like a doctor treating herself. It doesn't work so hot."

Maria stirred the pot, then walked past Mina, saying something like "Linguini Cannelloni Roma Sorrento Alto" in a deep scruffy voice.

"What are we going to do about that?"

I said, "Some guy's coming over to tell her, in decent Italian, that I'll pay for her to go anywhere she wants, that I'll drive her anywhere she wants. But that she needs to adopt another family."

"You don't even know her, and you're paying money you don't hardly have to get rid of her?"

"You're letting a homeless girl and her cats live in your building rent-free."

"Okay, okay, we're both suckers. Don't tell anyone, you understand? I'll be doing free readings left and right."

"Your secret is safe," I said. "Hey, did your cats ever show up?"

"Yes, thank God. They're my best hope for gently getting rid of Frank the Plumber. He's allergic to cats. I came over here to borrow one of yours."

"Mine are outdoor cats."

"Until Frank gets asthma and decides breathing is better than having me, your cats can live inside." Mina glanced at Maria slumped over her marinara sauce. "Just looking at her gives me a headache."

"The headache's not from Maria, you're worn-out. You want some aspirin?"

"Okay," she said. "I've got a pile of willow bark I laid in for Margo's headaches, but it's in the trailer, and part of getting rid of this headache is taking a break from Frank."

"Aspirin's as strong as willow bark?"

"They're the same thing. Most drugstore magic starts in the

forests or deserts or oceans, and then big factories turn the plants into pills. Aspirin? Even young bucks, when their furry little horns grow in, rub them on a willow tree because the bark eases pain. You watch animals, and you learn how to take care of yourself. Except for dogs. What's with eating out of kitty litter boxes? That one I've never understood."

I handed her three aspirin.

She said, "This is one of the things I prefer about aspirin—other than it's ninety-nine cents for a bottle of generic—no soaking the bark, no steaming, and you know exactly how much you're taking."

"Did the bark relieve Margo's headaches?"

"Some. She was a tall woman, big-boned, so I gave her a large dose. Still, I never gave anybody an infusion that was so strong with so little effect. She said it made her better, but the colors around her, her aura, weren't good. After a session with the bark, she'd turn a healing green, but the healing didn't last long.

"I told her to see a regular doctor. I don't have much faith in them, but I thought maybe they'd recommend a shrink, someone who'd listen and understand. I know when I'm in over my head, and with Margo I was practically drowning. So much pain."

"I never spotted the trouble."

"Margo was a performer. You know my family was in theater forever. We performed through death, birth, toothaches, heartaches— you name it—and always two steps ahead of the law," she said, "so you learn to fake it."

"Too many needy people tugging at her," I said. "It was enough to make anyone sick. She pretended life was one big party, and we bought it."

"Lawless find out anything?"

"Lots of pieces that don't fit together."

"He'll discover the truth, he has a good heart. Too bad he's married."

"He is, forget it."

"He let me know that in capital letters."

Mina leaned forward and smoothed down her skirt, she looked in either direction as if she were about to shoplift a pair of rhinestone sunglasses.

"Are we alone," she said, "I mean other than the foreign house-mouse?"

"All clear."

"Once Margo told me she tried men at Juanita's. You think Lili ever knew about that? Because I think she would have been mad."

"That's putting it mildly. And Juanita gave me the same story about Margo—headaches and men."

"Those two go together a lot, don't they? At least Margo knew she wasn't pregnant, not by Lili, anyway."

I studied Mina as if she'd just landed on earth from a planet where the highest form of life is blue-green mold.

"Miracles happen," Mina said. "You want to argue with me about that?"

"No. But you can say the dumbest things."

"Once again, we're even," Mina said. "Did Juanita tell you that Margo thought she was going to die? That she even dreamed about it?"

"No, but Margo was theater, you said so yourself."

I flashed on her abusive childhood, how she'd pulled herself out of that, how much juice it must have taken to keep putting one foot in front of the other. Mina was right, a shrink might have helped.

I poked Mina in the ribs. "Watch this," I said to Mina. "Hey, Maria, what's for dinner?"

She answered me, "Maria Callas Mama Mia Rigatoni Palermo." She posed it as a question, and when I didn't answer, she shrugged. Her voice sounded as if she'd been smoking a carton a day for ten years.

"What's with her voice?" Mina said.

"Angel said her husband knocked her on the floor, put his soft-soled shoe on her throat, and she's still recovering from the damage."

"This is a terrible thing to say, and I may pay for it someday, but I'll throw in money to get her a one-way ticket anywhere."

"At least we'll be paying for our terrible thoughts together."

"Who's the stud that's going to translate for you?" she said.

"He's not a stud."

Mina said, "An Italian who isn't a stud? Maybe he's related to Maria."

"He walked around Margo's funeral on stilts dressed up like Uncle Sam. Get this—he's Angel's long-lost dad."

"The rat-father of our Angel in the other room?"

"The very rat. And he's coming here."

Maria dropped a spoon, picked it up, and blopped sauce into a pan of noodles and cheese. A pretty good-sized blop fell onto the oven and dribbled onto the floor. Another dip into the kettle, and this time a giant glop of sauce landed on the linoleum. It was on its way to making a permanent red stain, threatening to eat through my floorcovering. The sauce was practically nuclear.

Mina and I both bent to our knees, a can of Comet between us, and each with a rag. We scrubbed.

She said, "You got to get her out of here—ugly is one thing, gruff is one thing—but clumsy is dangerous to your house."

Maria gazed down upon us, cleaning up her mess, and sent us a look that could have sharpened scissors.

Mina pretended she didn't notice, and said, "Did the guy on stilts say when he was coming over?"

I lied and told her I didn't have a clue, but it'd be sometime in the next week or two. Mina and I looked at each other, and our thoughts joined hands. This woman might know English and didn't want us, or Angel, to know.

I helped Mina up off her knees; she grabbed a sleeping cat from the porch, stuffing him under her arm.

"We can find another cat if that one's not enough ammunition."

"This one has long fur, very bad for allergies," Mina said, petting the cat and rubbing him against her face. "He's worth two or three cats."

The cat hung under her arm like a wet piece of orange laundry or a long bathroom rug, the shag variety.

"I hate to leave you with the Italian bombshell, but I've got work to do." Mina lowered her voice. "Don't say anything . . ."

". . . that I don't want Maria to know? I'm with you."

Thirty-seven

*D*inner was ready. I buzzed Mina on the trailer intercom she'd insisted upon—family unity in case of tragedy or good news. I hoped the intercom was the end of her electrical desires. Once we dumped Frank, I didn't want an electrician moving in.

Mina pulled down plates and set the table. "I'm hoping between the cats and Capri, Frank will hit the road. I told him that my daughter's moving in, and I don't want her to get jealous of him and me."

"Did he buy it?"

"He bought the part about Capri moving in."

"But she's not, right?"

"Where is she going to go? She said she's moving back to the city. It's not a good idea."

"Remember you told me to leave Abra alone?" I said. "Leave Capri alone."

"I told you that Capri's impossible since she got sober. She says she could only stay one night, maybe two, before I'd drive her crazy. She just wants to stay long enough to work through issues and to process. What are we, Velveeta cheese or something? I don't want to process."

"Just be quiet and let her talk."

"I guess I can do that."

"I mean really be quiet and let her talk."

"She wants to see you, too."

"Hey, I don't want to process, I never messed around with her head."

"She just wants to talk with you about"—here Mina looked at Maria—"miscellaneous details about her life."

"Miscellaneous details? What does that mean?"

Mina rolled her eyes in Maria's direction. We weren't saying anything important in case Maria understood English. No problem. I understand English, and half the time I don't understand Mina.

Whatever Capri wanted, it sounded heavy, but I could deal with it, it would be fine. The doorbell rang. I hoped it wasn't her.

Maria slunk to the door, actually slunk, answering it as if she were working her way into my employ as maid, cook, *and* butler. My credit card was itching to remove her.

It was Leo. Maria lowered her head, waving him in with her little hand as if she were a whipped servant. I tried to remember she was a beaten-down wife. It wasn't easy.

Leo. He stood like the picture of an old-fashioned suitor. He held a bouquet of blue wildflowers, here in the dead of winter, a box of chocolates, and a plastic bag filled with rental videos.

"Did we have plans?" I asked him.

Just when I think I've fulfilled my quotient of stupid remarks, I begin to believe my mouth is attached to a bottomless well of them.

"If we have plans, and you forget them," he said, "please pretend you didn't."

Good save. I needed someone with a sense of humor and a strong ego.

Maria took the flowers and slunk into the other room in search of a vase. I was beginning to think of her as Lurch.

Mina stood speechless. She turned to me, pointing to Leo as if he were a virtual man who'd landed in my living room straight from her fantasy mail-order catalogue.

"That," she said, "is possibly, except for my sons, the most magnificent man I have ever seen."

I studied him, and he let himself be studied. So comfortable with himself. He was magnificent, and it had nothing to do with his looks. He was a lion uncaged, untamed, wild and affectionate, huge. And he had style—I was sure he'd never wear black socks with sandals. He grinned at me, opened his mouth, and showed me the space where a molar used to be.

"Far from magnificent, and too old to be anything but myself."

Drooling in Leo's direction, Mina said to me, "Because of the Italian spy, I never got to tell you my Capri story and why she wants to talk with you, but she doesn't want you for processing."

"Out with the Capri story," I said, "then out with you."

"She wants to talk with you about Margo dead in the practice room. I said to her, *Leave Annie out, leave me out, and leave yourself out.* If she wants to talk about Margo's heart and mind, fine. About Margo's empty shell? We don't need death's clutter floating around our inner lives."

"If Capri has real information, she ought to talk with Lawless, not me. I'll see what I can do." I edged Mina toward the door.

"I don't think she knows anything," Mina said. "I think it's an excuse to come down here and get into a fight, and if she doesn't become a drunk right after our fight, I'll probably start drinking. I wish you'd talk to her."

"Mina, I'll see what I can do."

Speaking of clutter, I looked around for Maria, and I didn't see her. Angel walked in, he and Leo hugged each other.

"Where's Maria?" I said to Angel.

"All that cooking and cleaning, I'm sure she's asleep in your sewing room." Angel caught the whiff of a romantic evening in the works, and said, "It's a nice night, I'm going outside to enjoy the hammock under the stars."

Leo said, "Are you sure?"

"He's sure," Mina and I said with one voice. "I'll leave you alone now, too," she said. "With any luck, the plumber will die in his sleep and I won't have to dump him."

Angel grabbed his sleeping bag near the woodstove. Angel looked at me, and he said to Leo, "I think you're big enough for her."

Leo gave him a playful smack.

Angel said, "I don't mean that way." And he walked outside to sleep under the bright cold sky and the moon's pale light.

I held Leo by the shoulders. "He's right. I think you might be big enough for me."

We folded each other in a jumble of heat and spirit that pulsed into something big right there on the living room couch. Anyone could have walked in, but no one did, and I wouldn't have cared.

We threw our clothes back on, wound ourselves around each other, and watched a few old movies. They were sappy, and so was Leo. When King Kong was dive-bombed, he got teary. When it was obvious that Kong's number was up, I asked Leo if he'd ever seen Margo's circus memorabilia. He'd seen some, not much, but he'd heard she had an incredible collection.

"She did. I swiped it."

He didn't act surprised, he was tickled. "That night you called? Good for you. I figured you'd passed out before you completed the raid."

I shuffled items around under my bed. My grandmother's tea set rattled like a set of false teeth. Someday I'd have to clean under there. I hauled the circus stuff out and dragged it into the living room.

We flipped through pages of route books and articles together.

There was a clipped section from Carl Hagenbeck's autobiography written in the 1880s, *Of Beasts and Men*. It was about animal trainers, the methods they employed, and the latest thought pattern of the day—which was that human animals should treat other animals with kindness. Mabel Stark, Frank Bostock, all the biggies of their time, believed in kind animal treatment. Someday we'd get an inkling that humans should treat other human animals kindly, too.

I asked Leo if he knew Maria. He didn't, but Leo didn't go up to Cirk that often. He did think he'd heard of an aerialist by the name of Tomi, had also heard rumors about his temper. "But," he said, "it's not such an unusual name and Italians stagger under the weight of the temper bias."

It appeared, upon further reading, that training animals was considered to be part of the white man's burden. We skimmed through *The Circus Age,* and learned that trainers wore military uniforms and likened animals from tropical zones to people of color from nonindustrial societies over which we white folks were king of the planetary jungle.

"Those old trainers were fascists, racists, really," he said. "The best trainers slip inside the animal's mind and work with their animal, become the animal. There's complete trust, a solid bond of love. It's rare, and the outcome is obvious," Leo said. "Maria, I'm certain, misses her animals. The psychic tie is intense."

We gently closed the pages of a world long gone and a card fell out. An appointment card for Margo with dates scheduled once a week through the end of this month. The card didn't tell us much—Gravenstein Holistic Health Center.

"What is this place?" Leo asked.

"Doctors, chiropractors, shrinks, aromatherapists, and a dentist who uses no mercury in his fillings—a little of everything."

"But once a week?"

"Some people see a chiropractor or masseuse every week."

"We need to find out what she was doing there."

"I'll pass this to Lawless. He can track it down," I said, imagining Lawless in a feng shui office with some amount of sadistic delight. "Juanita and Mina both said Margo was suffering from stress, maybe she decided to hash out her childhood with a therapist."

"She could have used some shrinking, that's a fact."

We were making the move from the couch to the bed when we spotted Mina by the living room door. "Are we still watching movies? I could make popcorn."

"What are you doing in here? It's two A.M.," I said.

She plopped down on the couch. "The plumber snores."

"The plumber snores?"

"You don't believe me? Go listen for yourself."

"I don't believe you're hiding out in my house because the plumber snores. We're going to bed."

She looked us up and down, our clothes were disheveled, but Mina appeared to be setting up camp for the night.

"Look. One night on the couch," she said, "then tomorrow you can kick the plumber out."

"I can kick the plumber out."

"This is your place, you're the one who has that right. You even offered to do it."

I didn't want to explode, not in front of Leo. He put his arm around me, patting Mina on the knee. He said, "Mina, your daughter-in-law and I want privacy. We can drive to my place, it's not that far."

"Drive you out of your own house?" she said to me. "I wouldn't think of it. I'll jab the plumber in the ribs—I don't have to be hit over the head to get the message."

She walked out the door, disappearing into the dark. We watched until she was safely inside with Frank. We locked the front door and went to bed.

≋

I was born in the year of the dragon. They'd like it if I tore him apart, instead I rip the air with my claws and toss my huge head side to side. I lion roar, the crowd roars back. A graceless imitation of a roar. The man smiles with his eyes. I narrow mine to slits, this is how I see him best. He trusts me, and everyone thinks he shouldn't. This makes it more delicious. He was born in the year of the tiger.

My paws flex, they dig into the clay. Flex again, I feel my muscles quiver up both front legs. He narrows his eyes to slits, they're a mirror of my eyes, and he walks toward me, cooing soft noises. Cooing until the throb of a thousand human voices turns to fuzz. Now purring his noise, he comes closer.

I lick my lips, toss my head back. He rubs my chin across the grain of my fur. I open my mouth, I take his head inside my mouth. I feel his soft hair on the roof of my mouth. I want to bite down. Just a little. I never do. He holds my mouth open, brushes against my tongue with one of his hands. I close my eyes, I wait. There it is—the huge full sound, the deep music that fills my body when he is inside me, and I am perfectly still. He withdraws. I lower my head, he puts his forehead against mine, we are brain to brain. He rubs his face in my mane, tonight he'll brush my fur.

The crowd goes crazy—they'd prefer devastation to love—still they're impressed with his courage. We have spun this dance of danger and dark and wet for so long, his breath blowing down my throat, his breath filling my lungs. His body inside mine, we've become the same animal. He chose me because I bring him luck—I was born in the year of the dragon, he was born in the year of the tiger—and only a tiger can tame a dragon.

≋

Thirty-eight

It may be the goal of the soul to recover its wings . . .

—Sam Keen from *Learning to Fly*

Listen . . . Our wings are there, humming our name in one ear
so we never forget who we are.

—Leo Rosetti from *The Book of Fallen Flyers*

Flying is no big deal. Hindus carry mustard seed in red cloth
bags to travel through the air. When the Gypsies left India, they
remembered this.

—Madame Mina to Leo Rosetti

*L*eo and I watched the sunrise, drinking strong coffee, a winter
brew. There must have been sleep, tumbled images of warm
and gold wrapped me, but I didn't remember dreaming. And when
I awoke, I half expected to see Mina propped up dozing in a
kitchen chair. She wasn't.

"Leo, once I asked Angel if he ever craved attention. It's so quiet
in that catcher's seat, no glory."

"And?"

"He said if he wanted attention, he'd drop the flyer."

Leo's eyes went bright and vexed. The fire died to a dark glow,
but the heat was still visible.

"That's too real to be funny," he said.

"I never used him for my catcher again."

"Of course you didn't. You don't fool around when it comes to
someone's life."

"No, you don't."

Leo hadn't told me about his wife. I assumed he would when he
was ready, and maybe he'd never be ready. But I knew how unfunny
this had to be for him, and it should have been for Angel, too.

Leo stared into his coffee as if tea leaves were floating in the bottom instead of a few scarce grounds. I'd taken the zip out of him, but Angel's comment . . . Something was nagging at me, and it couldn't be left unsaid or unexplored.

"Leo"—I put my hand on his wrist, bringing him back to me—"do you think Angel could hurt someone?"

He didn't respond in the negative, not immediately. He sat with the idea and batted it between his ears. "No. But throughout my life, there have been occasions when people have surprised me, when they acted in ways that were unbelievable to me."

"Violence isn't out of the question."

Leo leaned back, put both hands behind his head, and laced his fingers.

"Annie, violence is not out of the question for anyone. Neither is love or hurt or pain or beauty. They're part of the human palette. Some of us use a range of colors, some people dip their brush into black paint once, just once, and it shades the rest of their life." Leo sighed, and his skin fell loose around his jawline, as if it was tired of fighting gravity. "I don't," he said, "know what else to tell you."

"I want to know if we're worried about Angel."

"Am I worried about how he will face Al and Sylvia? Yes. Am I worried that Angel killed Margo because Lili, not a great mother, but still his mother, was being bullied by Margo into disclosing a hidden past? No."

"That's enough for me."

He leaned forward and kissed my cheek, just lightly, and held both my hands.

I phoned Lawless, told him about the medical appointment card we'd found in Margo's belongings, the address, the dates.

"At last," he said. "Something."

"She could have been having regular skin peels," I said.

"Skin peels?"

"As we've agreed, she was vain."

"I'm driving over there, I'm sure they won't give me information on the phone." He groaned. "I hate that place. Ruth went there so she could sniff steamed herbs. Why she wanted to do that,

I don't know. The whole place smells like a head shop from 1968. I know. I used to make regular busts in those places."

"Lawless, it's early, nobody's going to be there, and nobody's going to make you sniff patchouli oil."

"At 9:01 I'll be at their door," he said. "I should let the cops do this. Maybe I will."

I knew he'd do it himself.

"Are a patient's records confidential after they die?" I said.

"Technically, yes. In the case of murder, everything's open for subpoena. Most doctors give them up without one. I don't know about the people over there, I only know real doctors. What was Margo thinking?"

I hung up the phone.

"Lawless will be at Gravenstein Center at 9:01," I said, "and he will be wearing a gas mask."

I pulled on a sweater, bent down, and gave Leo a light kiss. A familiar kiss that in some ways felt more passionate than the deep kind of kiss. Then he pulled me into his lap and wanted the deep whooshy kind of kiss. Just when you think a guy is being sensitive.

I said, "Are you trying to keep me from going out?"

"Absolutely. I'd like to get you back into bed."

At least Leo was honest about having only one thing on his mind.

"Aren't you at some watershed age where this activity is supposed to slow down?"

"Who spreads these rumors?" Around this topic he was animated, the king of spunk. "I've spent my entire adult life saying 'Down Boy!'—people think the brain's the most important sex organ? HAH! That's the guy who puts the brakes on!"

"Leo," I said, "I cannot tell you how lucky you are that Mina was not in the kitchen to hear what you just said."

He had loads of pizzazz, more than most men of any age. I was climbing out of his lap, escape was not easy, I didn't really want to escape, and he asked me, "Where are you headed so early?"

"Capri wants to come down here. I'd like to head her off at the pass."

"Capri Baumann? The trapeze artist? She's glorious. Why would you want to stop her from visiting?"

"You know Capri?"

"She's practically an institution. I've never known anyone who could toss down the sauce like she does and still fly as light as a bird. It's surreal."

"She dried out."

"Probably saved her own life."

"And she is Mina's daughter and my sister-in-law."

"You're kidding."

"Sobering up has been great for Capri's soul and body, but it's been hard on Mina, and now Capri wants to come down the hill and talk with her mother with a Capital 'T.'" I said, "You could say I am intervening upon a truth-a-thon."

"They'll work it out."

"But not around here," I said. "Mina said Capri wants to tell me something she saw at the practice room. Mina's convinced it's an excuse for Capri to torture her with memories of childhood woes. I'd like to get back to using this house as an office—you know, income, bills, groceries."

"Annie," he said, still not letting me off his lap, and me still not wanting to go, "you work for your family around the edges while holding their center together. Your own center, too."

I wanted to cry.

Instead, I gave him a snappy, "Thanks for noticing. And thanks for saying it."

"Remember, when you see Capri, she's out of a job. Be kind."

"I am not pulling *her* center together. We've already done that."

"Just be patient."

"Patience isn't one of my virtues," I said, "and you ought to be damned glad or that couch would not be such a mess and neither would my room or yours."

"Who's complaining? Passion wins out over patience every time in my book," he said. "Now get up that hill and grab Capri."

I found a house key inside a dusty coffee cup and shoved it inside my pocket. "Seen the quiet Italian?"

"No, don't worry about her. Go."

And just like a cold war drop-drill blare, the telephone rang. I didn't want to answer it, but I couldn't stand the tension, and I picked it up.

"Well, that sounds great," I said to the family member so full of enthusiasm on the other end of the line.

I shifted my weight from foot to foot.

I said, "No kidding! Isn't that terrific luck?"

More news assaulted me from the other end.

"Well, I'm behind you a hundred percent. Go for it! Bye!"

I hung up.

Leo said, "Your face doesn't match your enthusiasm."

"Dissonance, a shrink would call it."

"Dissonance."

"Right. Abra has decided to remain in the epicenter of scorching nowhere. She has found a place to live in the town near Jack's house. A booming metropolis of three hundred people."

"What's wrong with that?"

"Nothing. She's picking up things from Goodwill, and she'll move in the next couple of days."

"Seems like it'd be hard to support yourself in a town that size." Now he was getting the picture. "Is that what you're upset about?"

"No problem! She and my brother came up with a business for her."

"Uh-oh."

"See, you don't even know Jack, and you're saying *uh-oh*. He's installing two extra phone lines in her new house and she's working on a Web site. Abra is opening a psychic hotline."

"You have got to wake up Mina and tell her. Right now."

"Stop laughing."

Why was he laughing? This wasn't funny. Abra settling in the middle of nowhere, setting up her own business, a business that was definitely too far away, and a grandson who'd only know me from the cash stuffed into his birthday card.

"You wake Mina up. I'm going to miss the proud grandmother routine."

Thirty-nine

Many circus performers, just like Gypsies, did not keep money in the bank. Instead they bought loose diamonds and kept them around their necks in chamois pouches called grouch bags. One hotel clerk commented, 'There's enough diamonds worn by that gang to set up a jewelry store.'

—Zora, *Sawdust and Solitude*

I trudged up the hill to Margo's, the place would always be Margo's. I said hello to Frog and Toad, I stopped and rubbed their necks. I could tell them apart. Frog had a white blaze down his muzzle, Toad's was tan. They bent their heads. This was a mildly scary event—these animals are huge—but I took a breath and scratched them behind their ears. I'd treat them like a couple of stray dogs, and keep ordering feed from Pete's until Lawless cut me off.

Frog licked me across the face—one swipe of a giraffe's tongue and your entire face is covered in a substance resembling library paste. Kissed by a giraffe, that was something I'd never expected. Well, I've done worse. At least these guys were cute.

I jiggled the gate, unlatched it, and walked through. Walked through just as if it were any other day that I'd traipsed up the hill to visit my buddy. I missed her. I stood still and felt the air. It's thinner during the winter. Margo hated winter. I'd thought it was because she'd grown up in the South. It was because she'd wintered in Wisconsin in a harsh childhood that ice storms would have made harsher still.

Before Mina asked me to speak with Capri, I'd known I was going to walk this hill. Capri was a good excuse to do what I'd already intended to do. I had a key to the women's house, they had a key to mine, and *this* was not a crime. This was my final gift to Margo. Lawless would never find out. He had a near coronary because

I'd taken some stupid books and magazines that sort of belonged to me. If he found out about this escapade, he'd soon be joining Margo.

Margo told me many stories, including several versions of her childhood. Not one version included an abusive family and a father who'd possibly killed her mother in Baraboo, Wisconsin. Every version included a Southern accent. Now I assumed she picked up the accent because it was warm and liquid and because she liked Southern bourbon. Margo's lies made her truths more important.

One of her biggest truths was her devotion to Lili. I didn't like the woman, and I didn't know what had become of her. That didn't matter. There was something close to Margo's heart, a gift Lili bought her on one of their trips to Italy. I was going to the house and taking it. If Lili resurfaced, I'd return it. Until then, I wouldn't have it auctioned off or stolen by a kid on the prowl. I didn't have to climb through windows, just use my key and claim a piece of Margo that she loved.

I opened the front door. Dust had settled on furniture, usually waxed to a dull gleam.

There it was—old, ugly, and on the mantel—a vase that looked as if it had come off the discount table at Pier 1 Imports.

But *old* was wrong, the vase was ancient, a museum-quality piece of crockery. It was decorated with the black-and-white geometric patterns I'd dreamed about the other night. Maybe Margo had spoken to me, had asked me to take this and keep it for her.

I didn't touch the vase, not yet. I'd explore, see if the police had missed anything, particularly anything pertaining to Lili. And if I saw a gun, I wasn't going to touch it.

I wandered around Lili and Margo's life, taking my time. So much different than one of their parties, when the house was a ca-cophony of jouncing energy. Walking through their home I felt the peace, I felt the spirit, and I felt two full lives. Both of them were gone. One vanished, the other dead.

One of Margo's paintings hung on a bedroom wall. It was bril-liant, probably painted when she was very young. Bright turquoise parrot poppies decorated the body of a rust-colored horse. The flowers climbed down his back as if it were a trellis, his mane and the blossoms became a jungled cape flowing behind him in the wind.

The walls in another bedroom were covered with grass wallpaper. It was shredded from the brief time they'd owned a cat. The cat had packed up and moved to my house, he never used my walls as a scratching post. Even the toughest tom isn't big on tackling plaster.

I was easing myself into possibilities, into the unknown. Into looking for something I didn't want to find. Lili's body. In the movies, on television, when the cops or neighbors break into a house, they reel backward gagging from the smell of an overripe body. But what if someone's wrapped in plastic, what if someone's beginning eternity in the freezer next to a Stouffer's dinner? I could think of many reasons a body might not smell. None of them were pretty.

Behind the curtains, it was the least likely place for Lili, a good place to begin. Turned out to be very good, because I didn't find anything.

I went from Pollyanna to gruesome and headed straight for the freezer. A butchered buffalo, according to the white paper wrap on the roasts and steaks. I supposed it could have been Lili—how would I know—but it was doubtful someone would take the time to wrap, label, and date body parts. Several gallons of Rocky Road and a box of Reese's Peanut Butter Cups. Odds and ends, none of them human.

Now, the very last place I wanted to investigate, their bedroom. On top of their bureau sat an old photograph of my three daughters. I held it to my chest, it made my heart ache to know my family lived on Margo's dresser. It was someone's birthday, there were balloons. In the top drawer was Lili's passport, and there was Margo's. Margo hadn't needed a passport when she departed. Apparently Lili hadn't either.

Beneath the double-hung window, a girlish purse with plastic froufrous on the handles, was casually tossed on a chaise lounge. I checked the driver's license. Margo's purse with a wallet full of cash and credit cards. Lili's backpack was tossed on an identical lounge. It also held a healthy wallet filled with cash and cards.

Under the bed, a perfect place for a body, if the body was small. Several metal lockboxes, long and thin, were under the bed. I crawled beneath the box springs and slid my way across the slick hardwood floor, my breath ragged with dust bunnies—their maid had been into surface cleaning. I reached for one box, grabbed it, then grabbed the other. I eased out backward, sneezed four times in a row, dusted myself off, and spit the fluff from my mouth.

I opened the first box. A stack of cash—maybe Old Al and his monthly paper bag routine. He either gave them an extreme amount every month, or they were saving it against a rainy day. There was another green metal box with a thin handle. These boxes have locks, but you can pry them open with a plastic butter knife. Nobody had bothered with the lock, and there were passports inside, lots of them, from an amazing array of countries. Only a guess, but I'd say Lili and Margo held their employees' passports hostage to keep anyone from running out on a debt or an advance, a fight, theft—any number of things. I flipped through them, and there was Maria's. I couldn't have shipped that woman to Italy if I'd wanted to. I stuffed her passport in my back pocket. I looked for Mr. Tomi's and couldn't find it. Another guess . . . Margo returned it when she fired him, hoping he'd scoot back home. Maybe she'd given him enough cash to disappear and bought him an airplane ticket. I understood exactly how she felt.

I'd tell Lawless about the passports and that, yes, my fingerprints were all over everything, and no, I wasn't stealing or tampering with evidence. But they'd better get busy on Lili because loads of money and her passport were in that room, along with a closet stuffed with clothing. All signs of a person who had no intention of going anywhere. Meaning she had taken a long leap into the big ocean or she'd been nabbed by the person who picked Margo off.

I was done rousting the bedroom. No dead bodies. Boy, was that a relief.

I brushed myself off once again, sneezed twice, picked up the cruddy vase, and cradled it in my arms.

Forty

One last look, and I'd blow Margo a good-bye kiss. She'd built this house with big plate-glass windows. Elegant and ecologically insane. Baby oaks grew at every corner of the house; some fine day they'd lift the edge of the foundation and crack it like a nutcracker going at a walnut shell. At night deer appear, a few foxes peek in the windows, and of course there were opossums and skunks and racoons. Margo used to feed the raccoons jelly doughnuts. On the refrigerator was a photo magnet of us at Russian River Vineyards, Sunday brunch on a sunny morning, the light through the climbing grapevines speckling our faces. A happy picture.

I looked up and saw Lili outside the long, louvered window by the refrigerator. The real breathing Lili, I was sure of it.

I struggled to open the window, one of those crank jobs held together by dust and mildew.

"Lili, Lili!" The person didn't slow down and didn't run.

I tried again. No sign of recognition. I followed her trail to another window in another part of the house, cracked it open, and jammed as much of my mouth as possible through a slit. The mildew and dust tasted gross, I'd use Listerine later.

"LILI!" I yelled to the back of a receding blond head. No difference in speed. She was casual, she was some taller than Lili, I thought, and her hair flashed red highlights, no spikes. But there was something about that Germanic bearing. Posture is like a voice.

Difficult to change, difficult to disguise, as unique as a fingerprint. Maybe it was Lili's ghost, and she'd visited the heavenly makeover counter.

I was losing it, and I was getting out of there before I lost it all over Margo's house. I locked up tight, held the precious vase to my chest, and ran like hell to bunkhouse number seven. The vase jiggled in my arms; it wasn't heavy but it was large enough to be awkward. I didn't want to drop it and smash it to smithereens. Was I nuts or something? I couldn't be trusted with a priceless vase. I include breakage as part of my monthly expenses.

If I *was* losing it, Capri was a good destination. We'd seen each other in every possible form of cosmetic and psychic disrepair.

I knocked on the door of number seven. This bunkhouse was different than Abra's. Four separate apartments for stars who wouldn't accept less, who had earned a good place to live. And according to Leo, Capri was an institution. Who knew?

She opened the door. "Jesus, Annie, what are you doing here, and why are you carrying that crummy old thing for holding ashes? Get rid of it."

"This is called a vase."

"I know what it is," she said. "It's that disgusting thing from Lili and Margo's that's even older than my mother. It's one of those things you keep burned-up dead people in."

"Are you sure?"

"Really sure. I was at their place after one of their trips to Italy, the house is so nice, new linoleum in the kitchen, sparkling wood floors—although who wants to mess around with cleaning wood floors?—and I see this cruddy thing on their table.

"I say to Margo, *Why have you got this ugly thing when you've got enough money to have pretty things? Let's go to Pier 1. You can trade this back in.*

"She tells me it's some kind of urn from Italy, before the place was called Italy, and they stuck dead people in it. Well, it saves room on the planet, but who'd want it around your house? You could be harboring the ashes of a total nut."

I placed it on her bed.

"For God's sake," she said, "stick that thing on the floor, not right where I sleep. Who knows what kind of dreams I'll have with dead cooties sitting on my mattress."

"What the hell am I going to do with it?"

"Why did you take it?"

"Because I know Margo loved it, and Lili gave it to her, and I was afraid the cops would break it by mistake while they were snooping around, and if Lili shows up, I thought it'd be a nice gesture to hand it to her in one piece."

"You're sentimental, you know that? No wonder you ended up with those giraffes."

"You know about them?"

"We all know. I'm the only one who didn't help move them. Everyone got a good laugh out of it, and to be honest, I laughed, too. But I still didn't help move them."

"They had no place else to go."

"Phooey. They're trained to act calm around humans, you can get them to sit, and they'll even kiss you."

"Then why are they at my house instead of a petting zoo in Cincinnati?"

"Lawless. He has a strange sense of revenge. He's trying to reach you the night before last, he gets ticked off, and he pays a couple of guys to take down the fence and they rope the giraffes, what do they think they are, cattle? and before you know it they're munching your trees."

"I don't know how to take care of them."

"They're probably better off at your place then being petted by kids who are covered with viruses and who feed them cotton candy."

Lawless was really in for it.

"I could kill that guy."

"The last time you said that, someone turned up dead. Do me a favor," she said, "and don't ever say that about me."

"My giraffes, Frog and Toad. Your mother says they have nice faces."

"My mother."

"You know, the one who's living in my house with a trailer that's soon to become purple."

"No matter how crazy she drives me," Capri said, "I've got to admit she has good taste."

"It's never boring."

Capri said, "How is she with life in general?"

"She's sad because you won't make contact. She doesn't want you to start drinking again, but she can't figure out why you can't see her without turning to the bottle after a visit."

Capri gave me a look.

"I said *she* doesn't understand. I understand perfectly."

"She's completely impossible. You ignore her, and she's more determined than ever to drive you insane. Or at least to hand you the car keys so you can drive yourself there."

"I tune her out. I pretend she's a radio, I'm driving between two mountain ranges, her voice breaks up and sometimes—if I'm lucky—it disappears."

"That's dangerous."

"There's a plumber living in her trailer, two giraffes roaming free, an ugly Italian woman who hates me, and Angel are all living at my house. It happened because I wasn't paying attention."

"When did this catastrophe begin?"

"I know exactly when life began unraveling. It was when Rory smacked Abra, he ran to my house looking for her, and he kicked the door in."

"Rory did what?"

"He gave Abra a swollen cheek, a black eye, bruises around the neck . . ."

"I've got to get back in touch with the family. This is my niece! Has my mother killed him yet?"

"No."

"No? We're going to your place. Now. If she hasn't killed him, it's because she's about to die and hasn't wanted to bother us about it."

"Capri, take your jacket off and think. If your mother was about to die, do you think she'd keep it to herself or that she'd moan and groan and guilt us into waiting on her hand and foot?"

Capri sat. She thought, and not for long. "What was I thinking of?"

"You forgot who your mother is. That's probably good."

"It can't be bad," she said. "Where's Abra now? Please don't tell me she went back to the horrible husband with her beautiful boy."

"She's hiding out in the desert with my brother Jack. Nobody knows about it. Well, that's not true. I know it, Mina knows it, Leo knows it . . ."

Way to keep a secret, Annie.

"Leo Rosetti?" she said. "How do you know Leo?"

"Angel introduced us."

"You've had a smorgasbord of the best men I know."

"Angel was only brief. Well, not that brief," I said. "Sporadic."

"Nomadic? He's always lived around here," Capri said, puzzled. "He's Jell-O, sweet and not very solid. Leo is something else. Who knew a man in his midsixties could fly like that? It's amazing for a man of any age."

Something cockeyed must have crossed my face.

She said, "You didn't know his age."

"His age, I don't know, it didn't seem relevant. When you say it out loud . . ."

"His age doesn't matter," she said. "That's not true. It matters, but in a good way."

Capri was right.

"Why is it," I said, "that when a terrific man shows interest in me, you and Mina act like it's practically supernatural?"

"I don't know, but there must be some reason."

They were my family, but they sure weren't a support group. Which reminded me. "No issues or processing or regressing at my house," I said. "Do that somewhere else. Coffee shops are good."

" 'Issues' was an excuse to talk with you about something puzzling. I figured Mom and I would get into it, we always do, so issues would be a good cover."

"What did you want to tell me?"

"I'm seeing ghosts," Capri said, "I'm very sure Lili is dead."

I'd gone on a ghost fantasy trip myself, but Mina and Capri made me look as if I were the Rock of Gibraltar. You don't often get to say this to adults, but I said to her, "Tell me about the ghosts."

"The night Margo died? There was a woman up here, and I know she killed Lili."

"Start at the beginning."

She settled herself on the bunk and knocked over Margo's vase with her foot. A small amount of ash spilled out. I should have let a bum make off with the thing. It wasn't too late.

"There's a woman leaving the practice room the night Margo died. I'd never seen her before. I thought Angel was giving her a late-night lesson because she couldn't sleep. Sometimes he does that."

"I'll bet he does."

"What you're thinking is right. There are lessons, and then there are *lessons*." She raised her eyebrows. I was sure Capri had several of Angel's lessons under her own belt. The woman was a Szabo—she'd stopped drinking, but she hadn't stopped breathing.

"Next morning," she said, "I see the woman walk into one of the bunkhouses for abused women, Angel's walking with her, and I figured I'd been right about them. Of course, I didn't know yet that Margo was dead. None of us did. By the way," she said in a rush almost too fast to keep up with, "I was boiling mad the cops didn't tell us about Margo as soon as they found her. What do we have loudspeakers for, anyway?"

"Capri. I've got the picture. A new woman was admitted to the program. You saw her at the practice room, and you figured Angel was being therapeutic. Next morning you see them together at the bunkhouse."

"Right."

"What has this got to do with ghosts and the identity of Margo's killer?" The entire clan of Szabos, they could exasperate the socks right off a marble statue.

"You *are* being dense. A new woman shows up the same night Margo dies? Then she disappears. Is that a coincidence?"

"Abra showed up that night, too," I said.

"Do not tell the police that."

A woman shows up, Margo's dead, then the mystery woman's gone . . . Maybe Capri was onto something. The marble statue could pull his socks back up.

"Was Margo angry with any of the women around here?"

"Of course, men, too."

"She fired Mr. Tomi," I said. "You think it could have been a man you saw with Angel?"

Capri kneaded this thought like a warm loaf of bread dough.

"I don't know Mr. Tomi," she said, "but sometimes Italian women look like men, and sometimes the men look like women, and we've got lots of Italians around here, but Angel's friends are usually women, not men. Maybe," Capri said, "the Italian woman was one of Margo's lovers."

It must be a pain to be omni-sexual—anyone is a possible love interest. It's a lot easier if you can forget at least part of the menu.

"Capri, I'm assuming the person with Angel was real. Are we going to forget talking about the ghost? Because that would be my preference."

"No, no. That's where I wanted to begin."

There was a perfectly nice man at my house. Why hadn't I just stayed in bed?

"I'm taking out the trash this morning," she said, "and I think I see Lili rooting around the trash bin. I'm glad she's okay—she's always been very kind to me—she understood my trouble with drinking and never held it against me. I call to her, she doesn't turn her head, I run to her, and she's gone," she said. "Sure signs of a ghost."

"I thought I saw Lili, too."

"Her ghost also appeared to you?"

"Yes, but her ghost was taller and didn't have a very good dye job. And you usually need a death to conclude there's a ghost. As far as we know, Lili's alive."

"We'd better talk to my mother about this, this is her line of work."

"Or we could call Abra. She's opened a psychic hotline."

"Isn't that wonderful! She'll do very well. At last," Capri said, "someone with business sense in this family."

Forty-one

"*I* had a key," I said to Lawless.

"To?"

"Margo and Lili's."

Groan. "You had regular access to the house?"

"Yes, I fed their cat until their cat moved closer to the food source. Here."

"The house was not a crime scene, you're a concerned neighbor, you did nothing illegal."

"See, I told you it's okay."

Because of the passports and the cash, I couldn't make off with that damned ugly vase without phoning Lawless and filling him in on the details.

He said, "Fingerprints are okay, too."

"That's good because they're all over the place."

Silence.

"Maybe you'd better tell me why you went there to start with. And then tell me why you can't stay away, because it looks like you're returning to the edges of the crime scene. As a matter of fact, it looks as if you're *obsessed* with doing so."

"There was an old vase, really ugly, and it used to hold dead people's ashes. Margo liked it. I took it. You can forget you know that. But the thing is probably worth a healthy chunk of change."

"Great. Felony one."

"No problem, right? I had a key."

"You're not allowed to loot just because you have a key."

"Anyway, as long as I was up there I thought I'd search for Lili's body."

"Lili's body? Annie! You have got to get Mina out of your house. She has driven you completely over the edge."

"I was over the edge a long time ago. Speaking of the edge, thanks again for the giraffes. They kissed me, I love them."

"It wasn't my . . ."

"Can it. I'll get even," I said. "Listen up. No clothes are missing. Their two purses are stashed with cash and credit cards, and the top drawer holds both their passports."

"You're telling me the only item stolen is the museum-quality vase you walked out with."

"Could we move on? Under their bed are passports for the foreign citizens in their employ. Someone might have come in and swiped their own passport—Mr. Tomi's was missing—if they killed Lili and Margo and needed to split in a hurry. Someone should check the employee records against the remaining passports."

I had his attention. It was about time.

"Also," I said, "there was a pile of dough under their bed."

"Tell me you didn't take it."

"I'm not a common criminal."

"No you're not. You'd probably beat any rap with an insanity plea."

"And here's a newsflash—while I was investigating, I thought I saw Lili out the window."

"Are you sure?"

"Am I sure I thought I saw her? Yes. Am I sure it was her? Absolutely not."

"We'd better get started on that house. I'll push hard. They're leaving it alone because Lili's body hasn't turned up, and Margo's body wasn't found in the house."

"Sure, might as well wait until the place gets cleaned out."

"You're a fine one to talk."

"Capri is still living in a performer's bunkhouse," I said to him. "You remember Capri?"

"She's a drunk and a trapeze artist and very good-looking."

"She dried out. She saw a strange woman leave the practice room the night of Margo's death, the woman was with Angel. Probably. And Capri thinks she's seen Lili up there. Maybe a couple of times, the last time being this morning."

"What was Lili doing?"

"She was going through the trash bin."

"We'll check out the trash bin. How about Capri? Was she certain it was Lili she saw?"

"She was sure it was Lili's ghost."

I waited for a long "AAAARRRRGGGGHHHH!" response, but that's not what I got. I received a long lecture given in conversational silence. Then Lawless translated that lecture into English.

"You know what?" he said. "What with the ghost stories, a strange woman showing up when Margo dies, cash that should have been missing but isn't, and the passports . . . Add that to someone who looks like Lili rooting around in the garbage and the real Lili's disappearance? Annie," he said, "the cauldron is beginning to boil. I want you out of your house."

"I can't leave. I'm having company for dinner."

"Not the Roses. I told you to cancel."

"I love other people's family reunions."

I got the "AAAARRRRGGGGHHHH!" response I'd expected earlier. "Margo's death was too convenient for Sylvia and Al Rose, I don't want you around them, and we already went over this. Twice."

"Angel's here to protect me."

"I believe you remarked to me that *you* are babysitting for *him*."

The Roses were liars and cowards and phonies, but other than that, they were perfectly nice. I said, "They're using this as neutral territory to talk about their family, the true story, then decide what to do with the truth. I want to be in on it."

"Do me a favor. Have Mina with you at all times."

"This is the second time you've wanted her to cover my back."

"She's a better bodyguard than Angel, and at least we know she's on your side."

"Things are desperate when I'm depending on her to pull me out of a jam."

"That's where you stand," he said. "I'd come over, but it's Ruth's birthday, the kids have planned a big party for her, it's a surprise party. She hates surprises. Are you listening to me?"

"I am."

"When we hang up, I want you to use your cell phone and call my pager number. Don't use your cell again, understand?"

"Yes."

"I'll wear my pager very minute," he said. "You get into a situation that feels uncomfortable, press the redial button on your phone. Paint it with red nail polish so you can find it immediately. I'll be there."

"Thank you."

"That's not all," Lawless said, using his comforting in-charge voice, "at exactly ten o'clock I want you to check into the Timber Cove Inn. I'll make a reservation for you. No one is to know where you're going," he said, "and I mean no one. You will call me when you arrive at Timber Cove. If you don't, I'll send one cop car to your house and one to Timber Cove. Got it?"

"You're really worried."

"Damn straight. A mom always knows the day before her kid comes down with a cold. I know when trouble's about to hit. That time is now."

He hung up. No good-bye. I was sure he called Timber Cove the moment we disconnected. I behaved and dialed his pager from my cell phone, then disconnected.

Capri sat at my table. She tapped her fingers on the tabletop, a staccato of nerves.

She said, "What did Lawless say?"

"He thinks we're both crazy and that we're in danger, at least I am."

Maria shambled toward my oven. She was starting to take on the appearance of an old appliance.

Capri motioned for me, big urgent gestures. She whispered to me, the loud sort of whisper that flings spit into your ear. "That's the woman I saw at the women's bunkhouse, the one who was in the practice room with Angel."

"Look really hard," I said. "Are you sure?"

The woman turned to face us, as if she understood, then turned and sorted through the spices, a look of dissatisfaction on her face. I was sure she'd ask Angel to drive her to the market pretty soon.

Capri craned her neck, she turned to the left, then to the right. She walked to the spice shelf and studied the anise. Standing by the spices, Capri looked directly in the woman's face. She brought me the anise. I don't even know what anise is for.

"The face is very similar, but before I made such an accusation—*That's the person who walked from the House of Death*—I'd want to be certain," Capri said. "I do know bodies. This one is rounder than the person who was with Angel."

Maria shuffled into the sewing room, mumbling something in Italian. I don't understand Italian, but I do understand the language of naps.

Leo wandered in with Mina. He'd spent part of the day deflecting the plumber's advances on her behalf, and I wasn't letting him go anywhere. I wanted him present when his crew showed up.

Leo sat next to me, Mina on his other side. She put her hand over Capri's tap-dancing fingers. "You're going to get boils on your back if you don't cut that out." Capri tapped the table using her other hand.

With Maria taking a nap, I was allowed to cook in my own kitchen. I wanted something that was not tomato sauce and basil infested. We waited for the Roses' arrival. We didn't have long to wait.

Forty-two

They were driving a Cadillac Seville. Cadillacs look like Toyotas now. If I had a Cadillac, I'd want a big honking pimpmobile. I don't understand these pale imitations of Japanese imports. Understated elegance, who needs it? Mina would have to stop buying new cars and stick to reconditioned models. They were the ones that sliced asphalt clean and clear.

The Roses walked to my door arm in arm, an elegant pair.

They'd brought a nice bottle of Cabernet, and I asked Al to open it. He looked at me, he looked at Sylvia. I hadn't known this was a difficult request.

"The wine will not have time to breathe," Sylvia said. "It's a gift."

The Roses wouldn't be staying. Not for dinner and not for drinks. And Mrs. Rose understood that I understood.

"Tonight's not doable, dear," Sylvia said to me. "We'll have to take a rain check." She surveyed my house as if she'd stepped inside a college dorm. They'd be leaving soon. She wouldn't risk my bathroom, and she hadn't even seen it yet.

"Al thought it would be nice to get together," I said. "Maybe discuss your projects a bit more."

"That was sweet of him, but we're airing ourselves out at the ocean with a stroll, then meeting friends for drinks and dinner at the harbor." She patted Al's cheek. "My husband's heart was in the right place, but I do the social calendar, and he just tags along!"

Meaning we weren't friends, could never be friends, and this was a pity social visit to maintain good relations with the press. I also understood something else. Al hadn't leveled with Sylvia, that small shimmer of perspiration on his upper lip was a dead give-away. It was the cold sweat of fear that I'd blow his cover.

Then Al's sweat really went for a ride. I turned around and saw why. Angel and Maria had walked into the kitchen through the back door. Angel took one look at Al and stopped dead in his tracks. He composed himself, pretending he'd never seen the guy before. If he were my dad, I'd pretend the same thing.

Maria intercepted my intention to cook. She pulled a giant pot of sauce from the refrigerator. She slumped over her ever-ready floor-eating sauce and stirred with a vengeance. She had imposed herself upon my household in such a major way that I barely knew where anything was. Even Mr. Coffee had moved to a new neighborhood.

I caught Maria glancing at Al under her lashes, and I thought, *Oh great, she's flirting with Al.* Sylvia leaned against one wall, arms folded across her chest, one knee bent, an ankle crossed over the other ankle in an oh-so-bored stance that bordered between Grace Kelly and rude. Sylvia was fascinated with her nails, I half expected her to pull out an emery board and go to it. She was oblivious of Angel and Leo. She wouldn't have been so remote if she knew she was related to them, at least by marriage.

I couldn't think of one word to break a silence that was thicker than Maria's marinara sauce. I joined Sylvia in the fine art of nail studying and feigned boredom.

I caught another whiff of Maria checking out Al, and what I saw was not flirtation. It was a drop-dead-and-rot-in-hell expression. Leo sat at the table, now playing solitaire, Angel by his side. The silence got worse, it strained at the seams. As long as they'd announced they wouldn't be staying, I wished the Roses would air themselves out with the upper class so the rest of us could enjoy ourselves.

But Leo had a different idea. He slapped his losing hand on the table, looked up at Al, and said, "You look like a handy guy."

This amused Sylvia.

"Not really," Al said.

"Ah, I don't believe it. My nephew here's an artist," he said, pointing to Angel, "totally useless when it comes to practical things. But you're a man's man," he said taking Al's elbow, "I've got an air-lock somewhere that I can't make heads or tails out of."

The two of them were heading out the door toward the source of plumbing problems, Mina's trailer, probably the only place on my property *without* plumbing problems.

Sylvia said, "His clothes . . ."

I said to Angel, "Offer Mrs. Rose some tea or wine. Something. I'm going to stick with these guys and make sure they don't break my house."

Another drop-dead look from Maria, this one aimed at me. The army ought to hire that woman. But not for homeland defense; we needed her elsewhere. Anywhere elsewhere. I thought Sylvia wouldn't mind delaying her exit a few minutes if she were able to sip tea and look at Angel. I glanced over my shoulder. I wasn't wrong. She was enjoying herself.

We walked into the yard, and stood for, possibly, three seconds before I grabbed Al by the front of his shirt.

"You chickened out, you rotten little coward. You haven't said one word to Sylvia about Angel. I cannot imagine why Margo thought you should be part of Angel's life. Other than your money," I said, "you are totally worthless."

Al's lips were trembling. I don't think it's wonderful when men blubber all over themselves during a Hallmark commercial or a rough spot in the road. But Al had probably done as much as he was capable of doing—he'd given the women money every month. He hadn't given them himself, and he hadn't given himself to his son. That was what Margo wanted, but it would never happen. Lili knew that. But for now, Al was at my house, and I was angry with him.

"Were you the squirreliest kid at the circus or what?" I said to Al. "Leo, what was he like as a kid?" Al looked toward the house. I said, "Would you stop waiting for Sylvia to rescue you?"

"Al was a nice kid," Leo said, "but as a brother, he stunk. Never a week went by without him ratting me out to the folks about one thing or another."

"That's not true," Al said.

Leo stood back, his hands on his hips. He started at Al's hairline and worked his way down, shaking his head as memories flitted by.

"As far as I can see, you've been a coward most of your life," Leo said to him. "This time I figured you already had it all, maybe you'd come through. I thought you might realize that you had more to gain than lose, including your self-respect."

"I'm protecting someone."

"Al, you're protecting Al."

"Oh, come on. Give me a little credit."

"Who is it? Sylvia? Margo's memory? Lili? Angel? No protection necessary," Leo said to him. "Al, I repeat, you're a coward."

"Not in the big world out there. I can talk to anyone. I can pick up the phone and talk to the governor!"

"That's probably because you're a major contributor. That's not about family, and it's not about friends. It's your money that allows you the phone call, Al. Big deal."

"What the hell is wrong with money?"

"It's a giant prop, and you think it's real. You may be able to speak with the governor, but when it comes to women and grown children, wives and lovers and brothers, you can't face them. Us."

"Where do you come off calling me a coward?" Al snarled. "When you finally decided to get married, you dropped your family in the biggest way. Right now you're some bum who lives in a trailer."

"Al," I said, "let's call it quits right here."

He didn't hear me. "You dropped your wife and you killed her, Leo," Al said, "and how do you live with that? You hide in your trailer, the absolute king of cowards."

Leo belted Al, and he flew against the trailer. Al melted down the siding. There was a slight indentation, and it slowly popped back out to its original shape.

I half expected them to do what brothers do in movies and on television, shed a few tears, help each other up, smile and say, "Boy, you haven't lost your punch!" Then they'd slap each other on the back and pop open a couple of beers.

But Al decided one whap against the trailer deserved retaliation.

The two men tussled, a few flying fists, sometimes it was hard to tell which animal was which. The one with the long legs and the suede shoes was Al, I was pretty sure of that. I didn't see any real damage being done, then one face turned up, a little blood in the corner of the mouth. Al. Not much, but if blood was flowing, it was time for it to end.

I yelled at them. It didn't make a dent in their determination to knock each other's teeth out. Time for the last resort. They were acting like dogs, I'd treat them like dogs. I turned on the hose and let them both have it full blast.

The yelling and the trailer-denting, the water hitting the windows and Al calling me a crazy bitch—all that unglued Sylvia from the seat of her chair and moved her perfect Sole Solé loafers, pronto, to my back door. And there were Angel and Maria standing right behind her. Capri and Mina opened Mina's trailer door in mystified amusement. They both love a good fight. I wondered what the dent had sounded like from inside. Maybe a Jamaican drum.

Angel was in near shock. It didn't begin to match Sylvia's.

"Al!" she said, clutching her bosom. "We are meeting the Artellos in one hour. Look at you! We barely have time to get you home and cleaned up. And," she said, really sticking in the knife, "there goes our walk on the beach!"

"Sylvia," Al said, "cool it! I've just had more exercise than I would have had taking a stroll on the damned beach. Getting sand in my shoes and sitting there in that damned sterile restaurant—I hate the waiters at that place, they act like they make more money than I do—and having a drink and pretending my feet weren't wet and frozen solid when they were. Are. Who needs it?" His face was into the red neon zone he'd worn in his office. Al changed colors faster than many reptiles.

"Fine! You don't have to take it out on me! I am not the one who's been rolling around like a crazy person!"

Then Sylvia said to me, "Annie, I am so sorry this happened at your home." I'm sure she was. "I've known Al most of my adult life," she said, "and I have never seen him behave this way. To top it off, he begins his career in brawling with a total stranger! I hope you won't mention this in the article. It's very unlike Al."

Career in street brawling . . . I could already hear her turning this into a quirky story about her husband of the plastic dog-doo origins.

"It's not part of the article," I told her. She was grateful, but she didn't quite believe me.

"Annie, thanks for being a good sport." Then Sylvia turned to Al. "Dear, let's go. If we hurry, we'll only miss our walk."

Al said, some amount of annoyance etching his words, "Give me a minute, will you?"

The guy was plenty wet, but he picked up the hose and rinsed dirt off his face and spit the grass from his mouth. He slicked back his hair. Leo watched Al. Now they'd do the brotherly hug routine. Nope.

Sylvia moved away from Al, and she watched him as if she were watching a movie. I saw disgust rise on her face like a new day.

She told Al she'd meet him in the car, that she'd had quite enough, and maybe they'd better rethink their plans about dinner and drinks. She walked right up to him, straight into his comfort zone, and I expected a quick dramatic slap across his face. She ruffled his wet hair and kissed his cheek.

At that moment, there was something about Sylvia I liked. She had her own money, she knew she was a hundred percent fine in the world with or without a man, and that included Al. She could leave any moment, comfortably start a new life, and within a short period of time, with the support of friends, be certain she'd done the right thing.

I believed Sylvia could leave any moment, and that she never would. I believed she loved Al, that sometimes she wondered why, but that she loved him.

Forty-three

Mina stood on her front porch, waiting until Sylvia was out of sight.

She shook her head back and forth, resting her hands on her hips.

"What's with two brothers fighting all over the exact spot I'm going to plant flowers next spring?"

"How did you know we were brothers?" Al said.

"Number one, you've got to be family to fight that hard," Mina said, smiling. I noticed she was missing a couple of teeth. She must wear a bridge. "Also there's a family resemblance. Not in your looks, but in the way you carry yourselves through the world, your energy patterns.

"Both of you, come inside my trailer, I know your wife is waiting," she said to Al, "I saw her walk to the drive, but she'll keep. Let's get you warm, it's too cold to be soaked with hose water. You, too, Leo."

She ushered them inside and said to me over her shoulder, "You definitely got the best of the brothers. Annie, you come inside, too. Maybe you'll learn something."

The guys were cleaning up and drying off. Now was the quiet and embarrassed awareness. Still no apologies, but their silence was anguish, not anger.

"I'm going to throw something together to heal a family rift." Mina looked at them, considering their ages. "I don't suppose your mother is still alive?"

This got a quick shake of the head from one, a smile and a simple "no" from the other.

"Too bad. Nothing heals a family like a piece of the mother's hair used in a charm."

She ordered them to bend over the sink. They did, each in turn, and she cut a small chunk of hair from the back of each brother's head. She told us she'd be right back, returned within minutes, carrying a dried oak leaf in her hand. Mina snipped some of her own hair from the nape of her neck. She placed their hair inside the leaf, and she rolled the leaf. She tied the bundle together with her own hair.

"After you're gone," she told the brothers, "I'll bury this under the same tree the leaf fell from—I can bring the mother medicine to this. Now, you must do like we force little kids to do. Put your fingertips together. Al you go first, touch fingers with Leo." Al was embarrassed. "Don't laugh," she said, "just do it."

Al stuck out his pointer finger, Leo did the same.

Mina whapped Al and Leo upside the backs of their heads as if they were silly boys. I was pretty impressed with her ability to nail them simultaneously.

"Would it kill you to spread out *each* finger and really make contact? How do you boys expect healing energy to flow through just one finger?" She said, "It's asking too much."

They tried again. It looked like they were doing "the itsy-bitsy spider" together, they couldn't do it without laughing, and the laughter finally carried them into a hug. It was real.

Leo and Al cleared out of Mina's trailer. I heard the plumber rustling around in the back.

Mina dusted off her hands as if it had been a bad dirty business. "At least we don't have a bunch of family skeletons rattling in our own closet. We've mostly never *owned* a closet, but what do you do at storytelling time if you don't tell stories about your family? It's a good thing—everyone ends up knowing everything."

"You really going to bury that thing?"

"Nah." She dumped the hair wad in the trash. "It doesn't do any good without the mother's hair. They made up, it's already done its job."

I remembered something, something very important. Running out of the trailer, I saw Sylvia and Al settled into their faux-Japanese car, the engine was running, and Sylvia was behind the wheel. Al leaned his head on her shoulder like a drunk leaning against a solid wall. She smoothed his hair. I motioned to them, but they were already in gear and rolling. I was too late.

I walked into the kitchen, Leo was a muddy mess, and he was talking with Angel.

"My money was on Leo," Angel said to me. "I saw those two fighting when I was a kid. Good thing you got out the hose, probably saved Al's nose from being broken again."

Maria sat across from them, her head in her arms, forlorn and frightened. I'd told Angel to relay the message that Al was going to translate. But Al was gone, and Maria had witnessed the opportunity to understand her life drive off with a silk-bloused woman in a ritzy American car. I wasn't all that happy, either. I told Leo we'd lost Al, that I was still stuck with Maria, and that my hospitality was at the end of its rope.

"Look," Leo said, "my Italian's not as good as Al's, but it's sure better than Angel's. I'm going home to clean up, and I'll take Maria with me."

I'll take Maria . . . Had words ever sounded sweeter?

"I've got that extra room," he said, "and I'll keep her, and you, safe from whatever stray husband's roaming around until we buy her a ticket out. There must be people who miss her."

I wasn't sure about that, but I was grateful to excess. I sent Leo to my bedroom to reclaim her passport. I'd shoved it somewhere, I'd searched high and low, and now, God help me, I couldn't find it. I hoped it had not gone through the washer and dryer.

I helped Maria with her coat, not easy when a person won't lift her head enough to make real eye contact. I stuck on a cheerful voice. She didn't understand me. Angel spoke with her. Ooops! Now she understood. Maria shook her head violently. She didn't want to go, perhaps she didn't want to be separated from Angel.

I had a thing or two to say to this woman, and a simple language barrier was not going to stop me.

"Maria, it's been swell," I said, "but you can't hang around here in permanent limbo waiting for life to get back on track. It won't."

Capri walked in and grabbed an apple from the fruit bowl. She looked at Maria and stopped mid-bite.

"What?" I said.

"I don't know. I recognize her."

"Think. Where have you seen her?"

Another bite of apple, a crunch and a chew. She pointed to Maria with her apple core. "Gorillas. She worked the gorillas. They're very stubborn animals," Capri said. "She's wearing a coat. That looks like a good sign."

"If Leo finds her passport and jams her into his car, it is."

"Is Leo coming back tonight?"

"No, I need downtime. I'm going to the Timber Cove Inn."

"I don't understand. How could you need a break from a beautiful man?"

"You're starting to sound like your mother."

"God help us."

"It's the healthy part of your mother."

Relieved, Capri stood with one arm around her waist and used her free hand to eat the apple core.

Leo strolled in, breaking into a cheer. Waving Maria's passport above his head, he did a jig around my kitchen, he whirled me around, then he grabbed Maria and danced with her. He said something in Italian to her. Maria went through the roof.

"What the hell did you say to her! We've got to drag Al back here."

"I told her we'd find her family."

"Tell her we *won't* find her family."

Leo took a long look at Maria pouting by the door. He narrowed his eyes. I didn't know he could produce that brand of energy— stern, unyielding. Leo spoke to her in Italian. Sharp. She shrugged, walked outside to his car, and climbed inside it. She didn't give me so much as a "thanks it's been swell" or a simple good-bye. I wouldn't have understood the words, but I would have understood the gesture.

Leo turned and faced me. Holding my shoulders, he stared into my eyes the way someone will when they're handing you the secret of the universe on a silver platter. Unfortunately, cosmic secrets are just that, secrets.

Leo said, "Listen to me." His eyes were no longer stern, but they were still unyielding. "You have been at the circus in the biggest way," he told me. "And at the circus nothing and no one is what they appear to be."

"Why are you telling me this?"

"The point of a circus is to play with your head, to stretch your limits, and the people you've been dealing with are professionals. That includes Al."

"Does it also include you?" I panicked. My heart always runs a month or two in front of my head, sometimes I pay for that, but I hoped this was not one of those times.

"Take care of yourself and pay attention," he said.

This is why I'd gotten involved with Angel. He was sweet, uncomplicated, and kind. I would never fall hard for him in a million years, I would never have my heart broken, and he would never give me the creeps.

I looked at Maria waiting in Leo's car, slumped and miserable. She dragged that misery around like an old purse and tossed it wherever she landed.

"Leo," I said, "when the Maria matter is cleared up, you can explain to me what you're talking about. And maybe we better do it on the phone." If my heart was going to be broken, I didn't want it to happen eyeball-to-eyeball.

He was aggravated, maybe agitated. We'd clear this up or we wouldn't. I missed him already.

I watched him leaving me from my doorway. Maria tugged at her seat belt, Leo walked to the passenger side, gave it one hard yank, and buckled her up. He walked to the driver's side, looked my way, and had a second thought. He came back to me, holding me without a word, my head under his chin.

"Come over tonight," he said in my ear.

"I need a break from the circus, Leo. I need a real ocean where every drop of water is exactly what it appears to be."

Capri appeared next to me, and said, "That means she'll be at the

Timber Cove Inn if you still want her tonight. Midnight, maybe later—passion doesn't wear a watch!"

I jabbed Capri in the ribs.

He walked to the car, his slow step replaced by an almost jaunty sprint.

"What is wrong with your brain?"

"If he was looking at me like that, I'd have given him a room key."

Forty-four

*C*apri and I decided it was time to rescue Mina from the plumber. She wasn't indestructible, and there are only so many men you can dump without it taking a toll.

"Capri, Annie," she said, "thank you for coming inside this trailer that no longer feels like mine. I think Frank's leaving, but who knows? He is the original Home Shopping Network AmazinGlue. Help."

Cabinets slamming, water running, a few soft curse words— Frank in the bathroom.

"What is he doing in there?"

"He's fixing his toupee," Mina said.

"It's hard to imagine that a man who lets the world see his butt is worried about his scalp."

"I didn't say it made sense. I'm just telling you."

The plumber appeared, black duffel bag flung over his shoulder. The three of us sat on a cheer. Frank shook Capri's hand and he shook my hand. He whisked Mina backward in a tango of a kiss that she withstood with a high degree of charm.

He left. Mina opened the door and blew him a kiss.

"Worried about needing plumbing again, aren't you?" I said to her back.

Smiling and waving to him, she said between her teeth, "No point in burning bridges."

Frank's pickup truck roared. Mina exhaled a sigh of relief that was almost as large as his 1989 GMC 3500 engine turning over.

She touched Capri's knee, and said, "Honey, could we skip the blending process? I'm not up to it. Tomorrow," she said, "you get my full attention."

"Mom, of course."

"Such a good daughter. Annie, you don't want to get into issues with me, do you?"

"God, no."

"I knew I could count on you to stick your head in the sand. Thanks." Mina said, "Capri, you sleep out here in the trailer. We three could have a slumber party and watch television. We don't talk about anything deeper than if we like Brad Pitt better in *Thelma & Louise* or in that movie where he plays the devil. We'll eat popcorn and look at Brad's butt on the video. Then we'll say Susan Sarandon is so beautiful, she must have Gypsy blood."

"Okay," Capri said.

"Fine with me," I said. "I like all of Brad's parts, but I can't spend the night. I need time alone."

"You know, I've never understood your need to be alone," Mina said, "but after the plumber, I understand it from every angle."

Capri opened herself a can of diet soda. "Mom, you may have driven me nuts, but at least I've always known what's on your mind."

"I'm sorry about that."

"It's not bad."

"Oh. Good thing, because I don't really want to change, and how come you're acting so nice with me and we're just talking and you're not tearing me apart tissue by tissue?"

"Issue. Because up at Margo's, for one minute, I thought you might be dying."

"Dying? Did you have a dream?"

"No, when Annie told me what happened to Abra, then told me that you didn't kill her husband, I was sure you must be dying."

"I appreciate the faith you have in me. Some people think I'm not as threatening as I used to be, but I made a solemn promise to this person"—she pointed to me—"so I must stick around. It has to do with Frog and Toad."

"The giraffes?" Capri said.

"Annie's dying wish, and I'd never go back on that for as long as I live, so while she's around you can count on me being around." Then she added, "Capri, can I say what's on my mind without you getting drunk?"

"I'm an adult, and I'm responsible for my own actions, Mother."

"I can't keep track of how I messed up, and what I did that was right."

"You always did right because you were always yourself."

Mina held Capri's chin. "No kidding?"

"No kidding. It's just that I needed a heavy screen between you and me, it's as if you were a sky full of flies or a raging dust storm."

"I'm not feeling so warm and fuzzy anymore."

"I'm telling you the truth."

"I wish I knew what was so great about the truth."

"You're the one who practically invented it," Capri said. "You tell me."

Forty-five

*A*fter we had our share of Brad Pitt's body, we decided to go down the road to Juanita's and celebrate the end of the plumber's attentions.

We drove separate cars because I'd be leaving early—going to the Timber Cove Inn to hide from the Roses—but that seemed pretty ridiculous now. I was really going because I'd given Lawless enough grief. I was trying, basically, to do what he asked me to do for a change.

The moon was turning slim. It felt good to be in my car alone. I drove onto a shoulder soft with redwood bark. I stood up through the sunroof and waved hello to the moon, I honked my horn. I whooped and I howled. My idea of camping is staying at a Motel 6 instead of a real place; but this night, I'd like to sleep outside and feel the pebbles beneath my back and smell the wild earth under my head. Juanita's place was full of wild things, but not the kind of wild I wanted.

I pulled into Juanita's a few minutes before Capri and Mina arrived. We walked inside and sent a note to Juanita's room.

A mere ten minutes later Juanita appeared, fully dressed, an impressive sight. She joined us, talking about the Roses, Rory, his arrest, and his one day in jail. Juanita verified Lawless's grim prediction—she said Rory was sentenced to an anger management course and probation, end of story. He would be taught to evolve nonviolently. I think the men who make it to the meetings are the men who need it least.

I had a cold beer and whipped Capri at a game of pool. I checked out the wall clock. A monkey perched on its carved top, and I waited for the monkey to lunge. It didn't happen—my hormones must have been on the blink. Thirty minutes, then I'd drive to Timber Cove. I left Capri at the pool table with two handsome men.

Juanita worked the crowd with rowdy jokes and a display of pink flesh. Mina, now alone, motioned me over. "I've been studying on this," she said, "and I've almost got it, but not quite. I'll tell you what I've come up with."

"First tell me what you're talking about."

"About your dream."

"What dream?"

She tapped my head. "Knock, knock, anyone home?"

"No."

"I'll talk slow. The dream you told me about in Pompeii? That is not a regular dream. You spoke to me about it like it's happening right now. When there are bad smells, you cover your nose, where there is death, you see familiar gods. Annie," Mina said, "this is a past life dream."

"Is it related to my current life? Because this life is more than enough."

"I know it's you and Margo and Lili."

"You know this."

"For a fact."

I bubbled the dream back up to the surface of my mind. I could imagine Margo, the tall slave owner, picking up a stone and bashing someone on the head because they'd hurt Lili.

"But this dream isn't what you think." Mina sounded like Leo, cryptic. I wasn't going to like this. "The tall woman is not Margo— too obvious. We don't come back the same, tall woman, tall woman, tall woman . . . There's nothing to learn in that. The tall woman may be you, it may be Lili. Here's what I think—I think you were the slave, and Lili was Margo's owner," she said, "the person who killed the rough man. Lili was the tall one."

"Margo was the small timid prostitute, my close friend?"

"That's what I think."

I tried to imagine why this mattered. Even if it were true.

"So?" I said.

"It's your dream, I'm just giving you the cast of characters. There are things you don't understand, not yet, but understanding will come."

"That would be a first."

"You can be so negative. Listen, a bowl and the green marble bar represent deep secrets, and you survived plunging into the secrets. Drunkenness means seeing without clarity, the courtyard gods mean there are large unseen forces at work."

"I had a past life as a black slave who worked for two lesbians."

"I don't live inside your spiritual life. You've got to figure this stuff out for yourself! Just keep your eye on Lili—if you can find her—I still feel her life force. I'd tell you to keep your eye on Margo, but she's not around, so you don't have to do that." Mina laughed, then stopped herself. "Wait a minute," she said, "I'm pretty sure she's not around. Wouldn't it be just like Margo to die and change her mind about it?"

"Leo told me that life is a circus, and no one and nothing is as it seems. Then he told me to be careful."

"Hmmm. He may have second sight, that would explain his personal magnetism. Some part of him that's connected to you may have felt Rory's presence and may know that Rory was the rapist in that past life. Leo knew you needed protection and chose this time to come into your field."

"Rory?" I said.

"The rapist's energy is the same. I was supposed to let you figure this out on your own."

"I've had more than one lifetime with Rory?"

"It's possible."

"You know how I've been iffy about reincarnation? I've decided that I don't believe in it. Period."

"Good for you."

"Good for me?"

"It's good to know what you believe. But let me tell you something: It doesn't matter to reincarnation whether you believe in it or not, it doesn't matter to God whether you believe in Her or not. You don't believe in me? Who cares? I'm still here drinking a nice cold beer and visiting my friend Juanita, and your belief doesn't make me real or imaginary."

Forty-six

I had been cooped up for a couple of days, and it didn't suit me. I'd figure Leo out later. Zipping around curves on the way to Timber Cove, I hummed, and I was untamed. I was me. I roared over a damp country road, moist eucalyptus filling the air with a pungent urge for mischief. Boy, did I love my car.

I was running early, and ten minutes down the road I was pricked by curiosity, the very part of me that drove Lawless into hypertensive hell. He could take an extra pill. I was taking a quick spin by the Roses' to check for fallout, if any. I did not for one minute believe that Sylvia and Al were going ahead with their plans to dine at a swanky joint when he was covered head to toe with my front yard.

I buzzed up the winding and chic Citrus Lane. There was one light on in the Rose home. If I was not mistaken, it was in the room where I'd taken Sylvia's photo under a portrait of herself on a red silk couch, looking exquisite and smart.

I rang the buzzer at the gate, no Isabel. Sylvia answered.

"Could I see you and Al? For just one moment?"

"Al's not home," she said, "I'm sure you can guess where he is."

She buzzed me in. I pulled up to the house, and she stood waiting in her doorway.

"Sylvia," I said. "Al's at Leo's house?"

"Yes. Come in."

"You never made it for cocktails."

"Hardly."

"I'm sorry things got out of hand," I said. "I could feel it coming, but I didn't know how to stop it."

She raised her hand and put an end to my apology. We sat together on the lush red Chinese silk.

"Al came unglued on the drive home," Sylvia said. "He started weeping." She lit a cigarette. "He said he wanted to tell me about his life, his real life. I told him to save it until we got home so I could sit on the couch and have a drink and look in his eyes instead of staring at the asphalt and the speedometer."

"Why isn't he here?"

"Were you actually hoping to see Al?"

"No. I hoped you'd be alone so we could talk."

"That's what I thought."

"I wondered if he'd come clean with you, then I wondered what he'd tell you about the present situation."

"He came clean."

"You know everything?"

"I've always known about Al."

She fell into a thick silence made thicker by the smoke from her cigarette. She inhaled, lifted her chin, and blew a puff of smoke out her nostrils.

"Sylvia?"

"Who did Al think he was marrying?" Her voice was that of a queen scorned, the voice of a bright woman stupefied by her own stupidity.

She said, "He was marrying Sylvia Roth. My father was Robert Roth. My family is related to European royalty, and yes, there is Jewish royalty."

I wished Al were home to deflect Sylvia, now that I'd started this I didn't know how to get myself out. Sylvia looked ready to kill, Al in particular. When I stopped to think about it, I was pretty glad Al wasn't around.

"There was no way Robert Roth was going to let his daughter marry someone without hiring a private detective to check out very inch of that man's life."

"You knew about Al from day one?"

"I knew things about Al *he* didn't know. I knew the where-abouts of his son, the mother. I knew Al's childhood."

"It didn't stop you from marrying him."

"I had several choices, but Al was the only choice I was in love with. Dad did the background check, thinking that would put an end to the romance. It only made Al more exciting. If I'd wanted a guy in an expensive suit, I would have married one. Al could leave the circus, but not completely—Al is a circus. He laughs, and it's real. Do you know how rare that is?"

"I do know."

"I loved him for who he was."

"Why didn't you tell him?"

"I wanted him to trust me, to tell me the story himself. He never did. He thought I'd leave. Maybe If I were in his shoes," she said, "I'd have thought the same thing. After several years of marriage it felt awkward and ridiculous to bring it up. What would I have said?"

"Sylvia, dumping the mythology could have been a birthday present."

"You have children, you must have been married."

"My husband died before we got past the problems of raising little kids and paying the mortgage. We didn't have time for heavy personal issues—that would have come later."

"Well, sometimes a marriage works because of what you don't say." And Sylvia sat there, saying nothing.

The house didn't feel so warm and cozy, and it wasn't just the lost, gold glow of the sunroom. Her silence felt pretty solid, and I wondered if this experience had created a permanent faultline. And then I wondered something else.

"Why is Al at Leo's now instead of here with you?"

"He's seeing that woman."

"What woman?"

"The Italian. I promised I wouldn't say anything about her."

"How the hell does she fit into this?" I said, completely amazed. "Maria has been a bad vapor floating around the bottom of my house for a couple of days."

"I'll bet she has. Al's helping Leo get her out—Leo will make the arrangements, Al will pay the expenses. She won't float around your house any longer."

"Is she a long-lost sister? Because if she is, Leo and Al sure got the best end of the gene pool."

"I'm not supposed to say anything, I'm to wait here until Al gets home, then Al and I will talk."

"I hate TALKS in capital letters," I said.

"Who doesn't? I already know all I want to know."

Sylvia rose, poured herself another drink. She'd skipped from a regular martini to straight gin. She offered me some. Gin is a summer drink, and then it's only for rare occasions when one feels like drinking perfume. I politely refused.

I was getting that itch, the one that tells me a truth is about to escape. Therapists know it, reporters know it, and probably most detectives. It's an itch that must be scratched carefully. I enjoy the game, I love herding someone into the corral. They never notice I'm a border collie nudging them in the right direction.

"Sylvia, Maria's not moving in with you until Al and Leo make arrangements for her, is she? You'll never get rid of her."

Sylvia worked herself up to a twinkle. "She's not moving in with me, or with Al."

"Put your foot down about her, you can't have her around, she's . . ."

Sylvia cut me off. "You know what? Forget my promise to Al, it doesn't deserved to be honored. Let me tell you why she can't move in with us, and why you and I are both sitting ducks."

"I don't want her moving back in with me."

"You most assuredly do not," she said.

Forty-seven

$\mathcal{I}$ was ensconced in my room at the Timber Cove Inn, 9:53 P.M., and I didn't wait for his call. I called him.

Lawless said to me, "Maybe you're better off at home."

"I wish you'd make up your mind. Sylvia said Al and Leo are taking care of the situation. I believe her." Soon Al and Leo would have escorted the maniac out; maybe they already had.

"What situation, exactly, and why the hell do you always have to stick your nose where it doesn't belong?"

"Because it's my job?"

"No. Because it's you," he said, "and your job has brought out the worst in you."

"For God sakes, I came here because you told me to, I didn't really want to, and now you're telling me to leave. I've already paid for the room, and I love this place. I'm reading a trashy book, then I'm going to sleep, and you have to stop worrying because I'm not worried, but I will be if you don't relax."

"This is crazy. Tell me everything Sylvia told you."

"Let me ask you something first. Any luck with Gravenstein Holistic Health Center?"

"Margo was seeing a homeopathic doctor, and he's uncooperative. He's one of Margo's minions, a supporter. He insists on a subpoena before opening her medical records."

I didn't want to be the one to tell him what I'd learned, I knew I would be, but I didn't want to tell him over the phone.

"Lawless, we need to talk, but the conversation needs to happen in person."

"I'm on my way over."

"No, you're not. Ruth will start hating me if you run in my direction every time drama rears its head," I said. "It can wait until tomorrow. I'll come to your house."

I wanted Ruth to take care of Lawless when he heard what I had to tell him.

"No good. I'm on my way."

"You are the most exasperating man. I'll tell you the big part now, the rest tomorrow, and you will promise me that you'll stay home."

I couldn't hear his flooring squeak, but I knew he was pacing, cutting a deal in his head.

"Fine. Talk."

"I know what you'll find in Margo's medical records."

There was no way to soft pedal this. I should have refused to tell him, driven over to his place, given him something other than two disconnected voices walking together through a dark garden.

"Lawless," I said, "Margo had cancer."

Silence, then, "That can't be."

"It began several years ago in her breast, it spread to her liver, and was raging through her body."

"You heard this from Sylvia Rose?"

"Yes."

"And she got it from . . ."

"Al."

"How would those people . . . ? I don't understand. And I don't believe it, either."

"Believe me when I tell you this is something Margo didn't want us to know, or she would have told us herself. I'll clear up the details tomorrow, Lawless. But not on the phone."

"I hate this."

"I know. Do you trust me?"

"I trust that you think you're doing the right thing. I don't trust that you are."

"That's as close as we're going to get," I said.

There was another silence—a long one. I thought I'd lost him. He said, "Margo didn't act like she had cancer."

"Can you imagine Margo losing her hair, acting brave, going through it?"

"Absolutely."

"You're wrong. She nurtured others' weaknesses, she couldn't tolerate weakness in herself," I said. "She couldn't have coped with people waiting on her, and she couldn't have coped with the pain."

"I disagree about how she'd handle the challenge. Besides," he said, "what does cancer have to do with being shot in the back of the head? She certainly didn't commit suicide."

Here's where I was giving the whole picture a lot of room. I wanted Maria to get away, it wasn't legal, and I was afraid Lawless would be obligated by his sense of duty. He'd bent the law plenty as of late, and he needed a vacation from the vagaries of justice as opposed to the reality of law.

A final question, this one he voiced from a place that squeezed his voice to tin. He said, "And Lili?"

"I don't really know. I *am* sure that she went around the bend."

"You think she killed herself?"

"You're the one who told me Margo was the glue who kept Lili together," I said.

"And you told me that Lili was paranoid and needy and jealous. That's not very together."

"No, it's not," I said, "Lawless, I'm beat. I'm going to read, then get a good night's sleep."

"This time have your cell set to dial my home if you punch re-dial. Call immediately if there's an emergency. Even one that's just in your imagination."

"I don't want to wake you up in the middle of the night."

"I won't be asleep."

"Okay," I said, "don't sleep. I'll sleep for both of us."

~

I walk to my window because I smell orange blossoms. I look outside. The small woman lies crumpled on the paving stones. The scent of citrus fills my head, it fills my heart, I don't want to smell it, and I don't want my life without her. We were friends.

*The small woman was fragile, it took only one blow to bring her down.
I should run away. If the large woman can do that to her, a person she
loved, she can do that to me. I'm just a slave, not someone she loves.*

*Large black men, very black, from the same part of the world as me,
crowd the courtyard, wrapping the woman in wet bark. They're building a
bower woven of dried grapevines and olive branches, a platform on top. I
know what's going to happen.*

*It's finally dusk, I see her body on the platform. The fire is small and
slow, the smell is horrendous. In the morning I will wake up and this will
be a bad dream.*

*But morning arrives, and it isn't a dream. Peacocks roam the courtyard,
dogs run back and forth sniffing the ground, the peacocks jump onto a bench
and screech at the dogs. A priest wearing deep red robes, robes the color of
blood and bad dreams, has spent the night tossing incense onto the fire. He's
cleaning up his work. He dusts the remains of the small woman from her
wrap and pours it into a vase covered with black-and-white rectangles and
triangles. Crude, rough clay, with crude designs.*

*I wonder how long I'll live here with the large woman gone insane. In-
sane with grief for what she's done to the small woman, and angry that the
small woman caused her own death by her actions. "If only she had listened to me," I hear the large woman telling the man in deep red robes.*

≈

"Lawless?"

"It's 2 A.M."

"You told me to call, I'm calling."

Panic in his voice. "You okay?"

"I think I'd better tell you what's going on."

"The truth?"

"I did tell you the truth. But I'd better fill in the holes."

Forty-eight

*M*argo needed Al's help."

"Okay."

"Margo had cancer."

His voice was soft, comforting. "We went over this. Go back to sleep, Annie."

"Please, don't interrupt. Margo asked Lili to do the impossible. She asked Lili to kill her."

"What?"

"You think Margo was a big brave lion, so did I. Turned out death was the biggest test in her life, and she couldn't face it. Margo was convinced Lili could do anything. She asked Lili to give her an overdose of pills if the pain became unbearable. The doctor wouldn't give pills to Lili, he knew what they were for. He told Lili when the pain became severe, they'd bring a morphine drip to the house, and Margo could live out the rest of her life in a morphine haze.

"As long as no one was around to witness her decline, Margo was willing to embrace that option. Lili wouldn't consider it.

"No morphine haze in sight, Margo asked Lili to kill her. The method was irrelevant. She depended upon Lili's courage, insanity, and love to pull it off. They bought a gun, a small gun. Lili wasn't sure she could do it, but she agreed, and Margo insisted upon one thing—that she'd never see it coming. Margo arranged for Lili's safety in advance."

"Oh my God," he moaned, collapsing under Lili's burden. "Poor Lili. We've got to find her."

He asked me if I felt ashamed of the way I'd talked about Lili. I told him I didn't feel ashamed. I thought he might hang up on me.

I said, "They bought Mrs. Tomi a passport."

"You just lost me. Annie, you're right, we'll get together in the morning when you're coherent," he said. "I'm sorry I came down on you. Abra, Rory, Margo's death . . . I should have realized the toll this past week has taken."

"After they had Mrs. Tomi's passport in hand," I said, "Lili was fitted as a Cirk performer, an Italian Mama bodysuit. Leo told me that years ago they'd all done the clown gig, and that Lili was a natural. Cirk creates hundreds of costumes each year, and each performer's responsible for the care of their own costume."

He started to say something, but I wouldn't let him.

"Lawless, stay with me."

I should have waited until morning to tell him. He thought I'd lost it, but that dream shook me—I was already in it up to my hips, and I couldn't turn back.

I said, "Margo told the costume department it would be fun if Lili had another turn at clowning. Margo gave them the costume specifications, telling them Italian Mamas, blown into gross stereotypes, were staple acts in the last century.

"Lili, already losing her toehold on planet normal, tried to weasel her way into Cirk's opening night performance. Margo was livid. It was imperative that Lili not blow her cover. But Lili never expected to use her cover," I said. "She hoped that one morning Margo simply would not wake up. Meanwhile, Margo began planning her own funeral with all the fervor of a bride planning her wedding.

"That final night in the practice room, Margo was losing her nerve and losing her strength—she wanted out of everything. She infuriated Lili, and she lied to her," I said. "Margo manufactured years of indiscretions and love affairs, she threw them in Lili's face. She played on her jealous nature, and it worked. Margo turned her back, and Lili shot her. Lili handed the gun to Angel."

I was exhausted. I'd just done a lot of heavy lifting, then I'd handed the load to Lawless. I waited. Finally, he said, "I feel as if you're talking about people I never knew. Why didn't they tell me? I would have thought of something, I would have helped."

"Lawless, I understand. It feels like a betrayal, but they were dealing with death. They were walking through a landscape we know nothing about. Nothing."

Lawless sighed. He blew his nose. I heard Ruth mumble in the background, a question. He said he'd tell her everything when he got off the phone. At least he had someone to share this with. Someone who would hold him. I had the ocean and I had my pillow for comfort. One lover was wet and overwhelming, the other was polyester foam.

"How does Al fit into this? Did Lili ask him to take over and help, you know, with Margo's request?"

"Lili met Al at Margo's funeral," I said, "the clown who tripped the guy on stilts. Lili told him it was time to put the plan for her escape in motion."

"And Al's part was to do what he does best—he gave her money."

"Right. Angel and Lili, mother and son, were in possession of two passports, good ones, identifying them as Mr. and Mrs. Tomi. Al had bought them."

Lawless asked, "Why drag Angel into this?"

"Because Lili and Angel would need each other after Margo's death. Al felt that Lili was already unstable, and he encouraged Angel to leave the country with his mother. A gutsy move on Al's part—he had an actual opinion based on a family connection, and he expressed it."

"This is more gruesome than a story you'd invent for *The National Eye*. I am having a very difficult time taking this in."

"But you believe it."

"God help me, I do. Only the truth smells this strange. But," he said, "why did Margo go along with this?"

"Lawless, Margo was handed a death sentence. You think that makes for rational decisions? Her major concern was that she die fast and Lili get out of the States without ever facing murder charges. She also insisted that Al shell out the dough whenever it was needed."

"Holy God," Lawless said.

"That's an understatement," I said.

"You know what? This was insane," he said, "but it was genius."

"Lawless, you've finally got the picture."

Lawless laughed, a big out-front belly laugh. I really should have waited until morning to lay this on him.

"So, Lili's been living at your house," he said, pulling himself together, "dressed as a homely Italian woman, and not one of us recognized her."

"I think she may be crazier than even I thought. Possibly multiple personality disorder."

"Now, now. Don't get nasty because you were duped. We all were," he said. "Margo negotiated the terms of her own death, I have to appreciate that." Quiet, and then that duty thing popped up on his screen. I'd been waiting for this. "Annie," he said, "what do we do about this mess?"

"You're the ex-law, you tell me."

"You think Lili's out of the country yet?"

"I think she and Angel are in the air. It's been five hours since I talked with Sylvia."

"Tomorrow, maybe the next day, I'll go through the movements and look for Mrs. Tomi."

"No evidence against her."

"None."

"Officially speaking, why are you looking for her?" I said.

"Because she was one of the last people to be seen with Margo."

No reason to search for Mrs. Tomi, but if it eased his legal conscience, why not? My stomach had twisted itself into a knot while we were talking. We were missing something, I knew it, I felt as if we were walking through a dark field on a moonless night and, somewhere on the path just ahead of us, was a giant sinkhole.

"This is pretty irrelevant," Lawless said, "but I'm curious. Where did Lili learn Italian?"

"If I had to make a guess, I'd say from her first lover."

Lawless heard me, but he wasn't listening. No words from him, just the sound of steady breathing. Then his voice sliced his breath, and, if I wasn't mistaken, he'd spotted the sinkhole. Good, maybe we could avoid it.

He said, "Did Sylvia tell you what happened to the gun?"

The gun. The sinkhole. "It's got to be in the US of A. It can't follow them through customs."

"Let's hope it never turns up."

I held the phone, Lawless held the phone. We were quiet companions in fear and disbelief.

"Lawless? It's against the law to kill someone who's dying, even when they want to die. I don't know how I feel about that."

"It's against the law, and Lili's in very serious trouble. In reality? Christ, it's against the law to kill *yourself*," he said, "and in that case you're only in trouble if you're unsuccessful at breaking the law. Pull it off, and you're home free. Figure that one out."

"I want to go home."

He said, "I don't like the idea of you driving around in the middle of the night. The only people on the roads are drunks."

"I know."

"What's the lock on your door like?"

"It's locked."

"Bolted?"

"It's the kind of lock that has a button inside the knob. No bolt."

If I sounded half as forlorn as I felt, I sounded pretty bad—one of those cartoon cats turned inside out.

"You know what?" he said. "Check out of the inn. Drive slow, watch both lanes for swerving drivers. You need to be with someone. Call first and tell Mina you're on the way so you don't scare her."

I didn't say anything.

"You okay?" he said.

"Of course I'm not okay. Lili's been living at my house, and she shot Margo, and I don't know if that was a heroic act or an act of brutality."

He said, "And we only have Sylvia's word about the cancer."

I hadn't run that one through properly. Sylvia looking so serene, Sylvia tanked up on Bombay gin, reclining on her delicious sofa.

I said, "Lawless, get the doctor's records."

"First thing in the morning. I'll break in if I have to."

"Good."

We hung up.

I rolled on my side and pulled open the drapes. They were limp and loosely woven and the hem was crooked. It was nearing 3:00 A.M. It was cold outside. The deck was cantilevered above the sea, this was my favorite room, black rocks tumbling down the cliff straight to the bottom of the ocean.

I opened the sliding glass window so I could lie in bed, just for a tiny time, and listen to the ocean roar. When its voice made me feel safe and real, I'd leave. I wrapped myself in soft thermal blankets, a thick cocoon. It was drizzling rain and damp ocean mist. The sheets were cold on the other side of the bed.

I checked my cell phone. It was plugged into the wall, it was charging. I checked again to make sure Lawless's number was on my redial. I phoned Mina from the room phone. She told me she'd been dreaming about a handsome man and that things were just heating up when the phone rang and I'd spoiled her fun. I told her I'd be home soon.

I thought about my feet hitting the cold floor. The bed was nice and warm, nice and warm. I heard the rain hitting glass in pellets that sounded more like hail than rain . . . How cold my car would be. I was drifting on a soft marshmallow pillow, the smell of lemon furniture polish rocking me. And that was about it until I woke up looking into Lili's ice-blue eyes twelve inches above mine.

Forty-nine

I brought the ice-blue eyes into focus. It was Lili, all right, and she wasn't on a plane winging her way to a foreign land with Angel. This definitely wasn't a dream—she was crushing my chest, and she'd pinned my arms and hands on either side of my head.

"Lili, what the hell are you doing here? Get off my chest!"

"You and Margo putting your heads together"—her voice sounded somewhere between a purr and dark water running down a gutter—"always with your heads together."

"Margo is dead."

"All because of you. Margo told me about your affair, every bit of it."

"Lili, I can't breathe, and I'm about to lose my temper."

"You destroyed our family."

"Margo loved you deeply. No one else."

"She told you everything about us, she inflamed you with the details of our passion."

I was in deep trouble here.

"I knew less about Margo than I did about my hairdresser. Get the hell off me!"

Lili started crying; I would never have guessed she owned a set of tear ducts. Then she started screaming while she was crying. When she began pounding my chest with her head, I snapped.

"I don't know why the hell Margo loved you, but she did," I

screamed, "and if I happened to like women, I would have given you one hell of a run for your money."

I tried to roll out from under her, but she was straddling me—my arms were useless, and my legs were tangled in the blankets. For a small woman she was strong, very strong. I succeeded in nudging myself over a few inches and I hit the area where my sheets were ice-cold.

Lili's eyes held a rant most often reserved for those who stand on street corners and yell at signal lights.

"I could have forgotten that Al left me," Lili's voice, now steady and calm, scarier than the screaming voice, "I could almost have forgotten that I deserted my own son. But you and Margo put Angel right in the center of my life—all the while I'm mothering Angel, you two were fooling around behind my back."

We'd left psycholand behind several miles ago. I had to get her off me and free my hands. I'd try a purr, but mine would be soft and sweet.

"Lili. Margo had cancer, I know that. She asked you to do the impossible, you couldn't do it, and she blew her own brains out."

This was totally impossible, but Lili was in a crazy quilt place that might buy a delusion.

"It's not possible to blow your own brains out from the back of your head," she said. "I wasn't brave enough to kill her, but then she told me terrible things, things that made our life a lie. She told me about the two of you, other women and men, too."

I had almost eased my knees together. One good kick with both knees, and something would give.

"Even though she'd cheated on me," Lili said, "I couldn't look into her eyes and kill her. But that last night, Margo said something sick about you and Angel and her. She turned her back on me and started to walk away," Lili said, "and it was easy to shoot her."

Lili had calmly fallen over the precipice of humanity. A dangerous place. For me.

"I'm sorry Angel was there, Lili." I was sorry, but I'd invoked his name hoping to warm her with notions of mothering.

"Leo, the perfect father, couldn't protect Angel from that night. Who asked Leo to be the perfect father? I didn't want to see him or

Al again, but Leo took the baby, and he wouldn't let me forget he was my son."

Boy, that Leo. What a rat.

"And," she said, registering high on the anger scale again, "you got involved with Leo! He is rotten to the inside. Why am I the only one who sees it?"

That made me colder than the sheets. I stopped struggling. "Lili. Where is Leo?"

"He's taken care of."

I should have listened to my heart. I should have trusted Leo.

Lili was nuts, but she read me. "Don't be alarmed. I didn't want Angel, but I owe Leo something for his care. Leo is all right, just detained."

Detained. I had to move, I had to think my way out of this before I was "detained" on a permanent basis in the holding tank of heaven.

"Lili," I said, talking smooth and low, "you didn't kill Margo, you hurried the inevitable. No blame, no blame."

She narrowed her eyes, not a nice sight. "Who told you she had cancer?"

A quick fake. "She left me a note."

"Margo was wild, no one could control her mouth or her pen. By the way," she said, "you treat servants miserably."

"I'll try harder with my next maid."

She shook both my arms. Did she see a rattle when she looked at me? She'd done a supreme job of working herself into a frenzy, and I wasn't going to talk her down. I had to get it into overdrive and fast.

I jammed my knees up hard and quick, my kick was buffered by the covers. She fell on her side. I yanked one arm loose from the grip of her wrists and reached for my cell phone—not close enough. She tried to grab both my wrists again, I jammed the heel of my hand under the bottom of her chin. She was off me. She went for the table lamp and was back on top of me while I battled the covers for freedom.

Lili brandished the lamp with its solid resin base over my head.

"Lili, put that down. Now!"

"You destroyed me. You forced me to shoot Margo, and Angel must now protect his terrible mother."

I suddenly understood Angel's part in this, seeing it like a yellowing piece of 16mm film running through my fingers.

"Angel couldn't live with what you'd done, could he? He put the gun on your desk, hoping the fingerprints would lead us to you. While he wandered in the woods trying to find you, you climbed through the office window and took the gun off your desk."

"Of course I took it. Angel can be such an idiot."

She hoisted the lamp higher—this was probably the only hotel left in America where the lamps weren't screwed to the tables. Lili was about to bring it crashing down on my tiny brain, but she stopped midcrash. Her face was a black hole, water spinning down its center. She was filled with lust for the act she was about to commit.

"Thank you for giving Mrs. Tomi's passport to Leo," she said, the smile of a person long dead crawling across her face. "I couldn't get into my house for it, too many spies."

Lili made the mistake of reflection, something that for one moment diminished her desire to kill me. I climbed inside that moment, kicked hard, and pushed with both arms. We fell onto the floor, and we rolled. Sweating as if we were twin mad women, I landed on top of the bundle that was us. I didn't know who was winning or losing, the fight was a dance, one leads the other follows, we were in it together. I wanted a director to stand up and say, "Cut!"

Lili was as attached to me as if we were wearing Velcro clothing; wherever I rolled, Lili was there. She'd dropped the table lamp, or I'd grabbed it and thrown it across the room. Our arms and legs were tangled, she actually bit me—mentally, I scheduled a rabies shot. I looked up, and rain was falling on my cheeks, I was disoriented . . . a leaky roof?

We'd tumbled onto the balcony, and for the first time I realized I might not get out of this in one piece. I wanted to live. She was crazy and wanted me to die. Crazy beats the hell out of sane-but-scared any day. If I shifted my leg just a little, I could squeeze her around the neck. The waves crashed below us, and the rain poured down, a hard rain. I didn't notice being cold or wet. I was a tiring animal. She pulled me toward the railing, I couldn't move my legs against her neck.

"Annie! Let go, don't hold her."

Don't hold her? I thought she was holding me, I couldn't tell my body from hers, I didn't know how to let go, and who was talking to me? My guardian angel, my subconscious, my good sense? I didn't know I had any, I tried to let go.

Lili kicked out three slats of the balcony railing, and tattered redwood tumbled to the sea. She curled around me, a tight little ball, a cat holding its mouse. We were hugging the hole in the balcony, gateway to the big, cold Pacific. Suddenly, she pushed one of her legs through the gateway to eternity, her leg dangling into a void I couldn't see, but I felt its weight tugging me.

"Lili," I screamed, "I don't want to die, and neither do you!"

But I looked in her face and I knew she did want to die and I knew she didn't care if I went along for the ride.

Strong arms pulled me from behind, unwinding the human cat-ball. Lili's back was lit by the light reflected off the morning ocean rising around the eastern point, her chest was level with the horizon—Lili was holding my wrists with her hands as if she were a trapeze flyer, and I was the catcher. She rolled toward the gateway, both legs now dangling above the rocks. I told her to hang on to me. She smiled. She intended to.

The voice. This time firm, frightened. "Annie. Let her go!"

Then arms around my back, freeing one of my wrists, prying Lili's fingernails out of my skin, freeing the other wrist. He held me from behind. Leo.

I saw Lili, tumbling, tumbing away from me, and we heard the crash. Lili hit the rocks, the sound barely distinguishable from the winter waves hitting the rocks, or the rain pounding the shore's jagged edges. In the first light I saw a small, rumpled body that was shattered and broken, that was squeezing and oozing between the rocks and the moss and water and fish, swaying with the seaweed and the tide.

★   ★   ★

Lili's bag was by the door, a sensible plaid travel bag. She wouldn't need it. Her clothes were folded, on top of the stack were her foam bodysuit and a gun. I picked up the gun by the trigger safety. I held it up, only a few prints on the handle. There was one print that no lab would need to run tests upon—a lipstick print on the barrel. Lili was angry, but she had kissed Margo good-bye.

My legs were rubberized Gumby legs. Leo helped me out of the room and into his car.

Fifty

*L*eo, Capri, and I sat on the floor drinking eggnog and playing Monopoly. Mina sat on the couch, asking us to roll the dice for her, and Capri moved her piece around the board for her. Madame Mina was winning.

Lawless and Ruth had stopped by earlier on their Christmas rounds. They brought their daughter so I could see her, so I'd know she was doing all right. I told Lawless that Abra was pulling herself together, that her psychic hotline was up and running and doing great. Ruth and their daughter considered this wonderful news. Lawless smacked himself on the forehead and shook his head. Ruth had baked us a plate of cookies, delivering it with a warm cookie hug. Mina took an interest in Ruth and looked at the lines in her palm. I tuned them out.

Lawless pulled me aside, asking me if I was okay. He meant after seeing a woman whose intention was to murder me break on the jagged rocks below me.

I said I was as okay as I could be. Lawless told me a shrink friend said Lili hadn't gone after me with the gun because, in Lili's upside-down heart, Margo's murder had consecrated that gun, and the holy object could not be used again. It was one of the few times I'd been spared by madness.

The night Lili died, Lawless had arrived shortly after Leo. Lawless called the cops, and they cleaned Lili off the rocks below. Leo and I gave them a statement and left. I didn't wait to see Lili scraped out of a tide pool. I didn't like Lili, but she'd been wacky from the get-go. Losing Margo, and having been the one to take her out, pulled the last screw out of her loosely dangling hinge. She wouldn't have lasted in jail.

Leo had recognized Lili when he danced her around my kitchen, and he didn't like what he saw. He'd taken her out of my house, knowing that I was a ready target for whatever she needed to unleash. One look, two, trapped in the car together, he knew she'd come unbound by all laws that apply to man and beast, that she'd been undone by a mountain of guilt and remorse and regret and a hard family.

At Leo's trailer that night, Lili cried after Al left. She said she needed air. Leo waited for her to come back inside the house. And waited. He walked outside, no Lili, and no neighbor's car.

Capri had saved my butt by telling Leo where I'd be that night. I owed her for that. I considered letting her beat me at Monopoly, but I hate to lose. I'd think of something.

Abra phoned, full of yuletide 'cheer—she'd earned a thousand bucks that week. She said she had mailed me a check for the things she'd charged. I told her I'd tear the check up, and to consider it a Christmas gift. I wasn't going to tell her about Lili, but she'd read about her in the newspaper.

Happy talk all around, we passed the phone once more when Jack got on. And then they were gone, tumbling, tumbling away from me.

"Abra's something, isn't she?" Mina said. "A successful businesswoman, and she doesn't even have to deal with men falling in love with her all over the place."

"Jack said there's someone who stops by to see her. No big deal. He comes by for dinner and brings videos."

Mina said, "This sounds like good medicine."

"It's too early. I thought she could avoid men by being in the middle of nowhere."

"Sometimes I wonder where you come up with this silly stuff," she said. "Does Jack like him?"

"He does."

"What's his name?"

"Ryfred Manygoats."

"I didn't hear you."

"You did. It's Ryfred Manygoats."

"What kind of name is this? How in the middle of nowhere is Abra, is the name human, Martian . . . ? "

"It's Navajo."

Mina didn't have one clue if Navajo was a small planet somewhere between Earth and Mars or anywhere else.

"I guess that's not as bad as a regular white guy, but it's still *gaje*. I think. I'll have to check that out."

"With who?"

"I don't know," she said. "You worry too much about details."

Capri rolled the dice for Mina. Boardwalk. Mina didn't want to buy it. She said she preferred being a slum landlord and that Baltic Avenue was the best buy on the board. We couldn't argue, she was winning.

Capri rolled for herself. "I guess I'm out of a job for good, but at least I'm not seeing ghosts. I couldn't see much point in being sober if you still see those things outside your window."

"Ghosts are everywhere. You stay sober so you *can* see them," Mina said.

"And you've got a job when you want one," Leo said, rolling a double. "Al sold Cirk in a ten-minute phone call to a casino in Reno. Everything Lili and Margo had goes to Angel. He's not into performance, but he wants to reopen the women's shelter."

"What does he know about running that place?" Mina said.

"Nothing," Leo said. "He'll hire social workers, therapists . . . Angel will do what he does best with the women."

"Mina," I said, warning her, "not one word."

"Have I opened my mouth?"

"I know what you were thinking."

"Maybe *you* should open a psychic hotline," she said to me.

Leo smiled, he knew what Mina was thinking, too, what all three women were thinking. "Angel will give trapeze lessons and hope the women learn to risk, and fly, and trust. He'll teach them the lesson of gravity and give them the gift of flight—all important for making a new life."

Mina landed on Illinois, my property with three houses, but I was in jail and couldn't collect rent. She got a kick out of that. Sipping her eggnog, she said, "This is another one of those American things I like. Eggnog."

"I think it's English," Leo said.

"Oh. *Those* people," she said.

I wondered, not for the first time, if there were any groups of people Mina liked other than Gypsies. She liked Americans in general, but the only Americans she specifically liked were movie stars and Gypsies.

Mina took another turn and landed on Leo's property, a hotel on Pennsylvania. The rent was steep.

"Good investment," she said. "I may have to rethink my slum landlord strategy."

She shelled out the rent money. Looking at me and pointing to Leo, she said, "Don't kill this one. He's too good to be dead for a while yet."

Leo looked ready to run, and I could hardly blame him.

"Mina, I haven't killed anyone."

"My oldest son died in a motorcycle accident while he was married to you—he was whispering your name when his body kissed the sky—a mother knows these things. My second son disappeared right after you had a fling."

"Jozef said no commitments, no cages, no traps. That was fine with me."

"My Hummingbird said that? What is wrong with you and him? We are tribal, all of us," she said. "We're not floating in this soup called life alone."

A knock on the door, it was Christmas Eve, and everyone was welcome. I wasn't doing the rounds this year, but I usually did. Probably another neighbor with another plate of cookies—I'd have to weigh myself on a truck scale by the time the holidays were over.

I got up to answer the knock, laughing as Leo took another trip around Mina's property without landing on her slums. Nat King Cole warbled on a CD behind me.

I opened the door. Rory. With a Bible.

Leo took one look at our guest and rose to his feet, standing in the doorway next to me. I was speechless, a rare event.

Rory extended his hand, introducing himself to Leo as if he were an old family friend. Rory thanked me for getting the cops involved with Suzanne. I was hoping he wouldn't know I'd done that. He was relaxed and polite. Seeing Rory in control was scarier than seeing him out of control.

I said, "You joined a men's group?"

"No. God's group," he blurted.

Uh-oh.

"I only had to spend one night in jail before I raised bail, but that night changed my life," he said. "I owe it all to you."

"Rory, you don't owe me anything."

"I want to thank you, and to apologize."

"Rory, I've got to be honest—Margo said violent men don't change. I believe that."

"Margo didn't deal with the larger powers." He surveyed the room, peeking into the house.

"I don't want you inside my home."

"I understand," Rory said. "I assumed since it was Christmas, Abra and Joey would be here."

"Wrong."

"Wrong is right," Mina hollered from the other room. "As a matter of fact, she is now dating a goat. Or at least seeing one."

"She's seeing goats?" Rory said, his eyes wide. "The Devil . . . I knew something was very wrong. I pray for her every day. I pray for Joey, too, of course."

"That's nice, Rory," I said. "Happy holidays. Bye."

I started to close the door. Rory put his hand up, stopping the door from closing.

"Annie, I think I'd better start praying for you, too."

"Please. Don't. I don't want God to know that we know each other."

It was the holiday season, a vacation from bad thoughts and wishes. I shut the door on bad thoughts, and I shut the door on Rory.

Leo hugged me in that wraparound sweater way. We made a

private pact to slip each other Monopoly money. If we pooled our resources, we might have a chance of stopping Mina from whipping the pants off us.

The most beautiful journey is taken through the window.
—*The King of Hearts,* 1976

Acknowledgments

Family Matters: For my beautiful daughter, Allegra. Always brave and nutty enough to jump right in and try something new. And to her husband, Mark Lynch, a good Irish man who loves his family with a passion. Thank you both for giving us Caleb. For my son, Sam, my treasure. You make me laugh out loud, you remind me that sometimes life is scary, but it is never serious. Thanks for being my kids. For the family I inherited—Pam, Adam, Ethan, Eric, Ruth, Aletha—thank you for loving me and letting me love you right back. My Mom, ninety-two-year-old Barbara, life or death, you've always called your own shots, you always will. I am one lucky woman—not one family member is beige.

Matters of the Heart: To Catherine De Prima who's tiptoed with me through the spirit world, and who supported me when I built a new life. To Ann Lasko, dear friend since we both wore Clearasil— a solid and wise woman, a flying wild-art woman, the center of a wonderful family. Living the edge, Liv Needham MacKay, who has launched her life over and over again, always ready to risk and live in bright red colors—thanks for walking the road first. Eric Stone, international man of mystery, my oldest pal, often in trouble, always courting adventure. To Judy Lunde for loving my kids from day one, and for the best line in this book. Peter Morin, always and ever, for the music, for the music . . . To Jean Treece and the Foushees for warming the Blevinses' new nest with straight talk and good food. To the Yoder cheering section—you're the best. And, to the astonishing women I've met over the past year, so many stories, so much courage . . . Thank you for writing me, for letting me into your lives.

Matters of the World: First to Susan Gleason, my agent, a free-spirited woman with both feet on the ground—not an easy balancing act. To Bob Gleason, my editor, who encourages me to keep it coming from the heart. To the support system at Tor/Forge—Tom Doherty, publisher, for his good sense and laughing eyes; Linda Quinton, strong and kind; Jodi Rosoff and Eric Raab and Kathleen Fogarty—thank you for patience and good humor. Big gratitude to the circus artists who shared their tales and expertise and beer. Finally, to Twin Rocks Trading Post for a porch to brainstorm on, and to southeast Utah for giving me a swimming hole and beautiful red rocks to birth my stories.